I0658425

Praise for Lexi Blake and Masters and Mercenaries...

"I can always trust Lexi Blake's Dominants to leave me breathless...and in love. If you want sensual, exciting BDSM wrapped in an awesome love story, then look for a Lexi Blake book."

~Cherise Sinclair USA Today Bestselling author

"Lexi Blake's MASTERS AND MERCENARIES series is beautifully written and deliciously hot. She's got a real way with both action and sex. I also love the way Blake writes her gorgeous Dom heroes--they make me want to do bad, bad things. Her heroines are intelligent and gutsy ladies whose taste for submission definitely does not make them dish rags. Can't wait for the next book!"

~Angela Knight, New York Times Bestselling author

"A Dom is Forever is action packed, both in the bedroom and out. Expect agents, spies, guns, killing and lots of kink as Liam goes after the mysterious Mr. Black and finds his past and his future... The action and espionage keep this story moving along quickly while the sex and kink provides a totally different type of interest. Everything is very well balanced and flows together wonderfully."

~A Night Owl "Top Pick", Terri, Night Owl Erotica

"A Dom Is Forever is everything that is good in erotic romance. The story was fast-paced and suspenseful, the characters were flawed but made me root for them every step of the way, and the hotness factor was off the charts mostly due to a bad boy Dom with a penchant for dirty talk."

~Rho, The Romance Reviews

"A good read that kept me on my toes, guessing until the big reveal, and thinking survival skills should be a must for all men."

~Chris, Night Owl Reviews

"I can't get enough of the Masters and Mercenaries Series! Love and Let Die is Lexi Blake at her best! She writes erotic romantic suspense like no other, and I am always extremely excited when she has something new for us! Intense, heart pounding, and erotically fulfilling, I could not put this book down."

~ Shayna Renee, Shayna Renee's Spicy Reads

"Certain authors and series are on my auto-buy list. Lexi Blake and her Masters & Mercenaries series is at the top of that list... this book offered everything I love about a Masters & Mercenaries book – alpha men, hot sex and sweet loving... As long as Ms. Blake continues to offer such high quality books, I'll be right there, ready to read."

~ Robin, Sizzling Hot Books

"I have absolutely fallen in love with this series. Spies, espionage, and intrigue all packaged up in a hot dominant male package. All the men at McKay-Taggart are smoking hot and the women are amazingly strong sexy submissives."

~Kelley, Smut Book Junkie Book Reviews

Love Another Day

Other Books by Lexi Blake

ROMANTIC SUSPENSE

Masters and Mercenaries
The Dom Who Loved Me
The Men With The Golden Cuffs
A Dom is Forever
On Her Master's Secret Service
Sanctum: A Masters and Mercenaries Novella
Love and Let Die
Unconditional: A Masters and Mercenaries Novella
Dungeon Royale
Dungeon Games: A Masters and Mercenaries Novella
A View to a Thrill
Cherished: A Masters and Mercenaries Novella
You Only Love Twice
Luscious: Masters and Mercenaries~Topped
Adored: A Masters and Mercenaries Novella
Master No
Just One Taste: Masters and Mercenaries~Topped 2
From Sanctum with Love
Devoted: A Masters and Mercenaries Novella
Dominance Never Dies
Submission is Not Enough
Master Bits and Mercenary Bites~The Secret Recipes of Topped
Perfectly Paired: Masters and Mercenaries~Topped 3
For His Eyes Only
Arranged: A Masters and Mercenaries Novella
Love Another Day
At Your Service: Masters and Mercenaries~Topped 4
Master Bits and Mercenary Bites~Girls Night
Nobody Does It Better
Close Cover
Protected: A Masters and Mercenaries Novella
Enchanted: A Masters and Mercenaries Novella
Charmed: A Masters and Mercenaries Novella
Treasured: A Masters and Mercenaries Novella, Coming June 29, 2021

Smoke and Sin
At the Pleasure of the President

URBAN FANTASY

Thieves
Steal the Light
Steal the Day
Steal the Moon
Steal the Sun
Steal the Night
Ripper
Addict
Sleeper
Outcast
Stealing Summer

LEXI BLAKE WRITING AS SOPHIE OAK

Texas Sirens
Small Town Siren
Siren in the City
Siren Enslaved
Siren Beloved
Siren in Waiting
Siren in Bloom
Siren Unleashed
Siren Reborn

Nights in Bliss, Colorado
Three to Ride
Two to Love
One to Keep
Lost in Bliss
Found in Bliss
Pure Bliss
Chasing Bliss
Once Upon a Time in Bliss
Back in Bliss

Sirens in Bliss
Happily Ever After in Bliss
Far From Bliss, Coming 2021

A Faery Story
Bound
Beast
Beauty

Standalone
Away From Me
Snowed In

Love Another Day

Masters and Mercenaries, Book 14

Lexi Blake

Love Another Day
Masters and Mercenaries, Book 14

Published by DLZ Entertainment LLC

Copyright 2017DLZ Entertainment LLC
Edited by Chloe Vale
ISBN: 978-1-937608-62-0

McKay-Taggart logo design by Charity Hendry

All rights reserved. No part of this book may be reproduced, scanned, or distributed in any printed or electronic form without permission. Please do not participate in or encourage piracy of copyrighted materials in violation of the author's rights.

This is a work of fiction. Names, places, characters and incidents are the product of the author's imagination and are fictitious. Any resemblance to actual persons, living or dead, events or establishments is solely coincidental.

Acknowledgments

Thanks to the usual suspects: Kim Guidroz, Liz Berry, Fedora Chen, Stormy Pate, Riane Holt and Kori Smith. Thanks to my amazing husband and son who helped produce this book. Thanks to Danielle Sanchez at Inkslinger. I couldn't do it without you!

Thanks so much to my Aussie girls – Rhian Cahill and Khloe Wren. Anything that sounds right with Brody is thanks to them.

This book is dedicated to Tiffany. I wish you happily ever after, my friend.

Sign up for Lexi Blake's newsletter
and be entered to win a $25 gift certificate
to the bookseller of your choice.

Join us for news, fun, and exclusive content
including free short stories.

There's a new contest every month!

Go to www.LexiBlake.net to subscribe.

Prologue

Sierra Leone, Africa

Stephanie Gibson stared at herself in the mirror, trying to decide if this was the worst idea she'd ever had or the best.

It was probably the worst, but then she was trying to be optimistic.

The good news was her boobs looked pretty damn good. The white silky gown she'd bought for the occasion skimmed her curves and the ivory tone made her skin look warm. Thank god it fit. She'd bought it off the Internet a month before but she'd been too afraid to use it. Now her time was up and she needed to look her best. She'd managed to borrow conditioner from Charlotte Taggart. For once her hair was soft and relatively tame. It was weird not to have it in a ponytail or a practical bun. When had it gotten so long?

The bad news? She was fairly certain Brody Carter would still take one look at her and laugh. Oh, he wouldn't do it in a mean way. He would be kind about it. He would chuckle, that deep voice of his sending a shiver of desire through her right before he explained that despite the roles they'd played for the last few months, he thought of her as a kid sister.

Come on, Steph. Go chuck on some proper clothes, and we'll grab a beer before I stroll out of your life forever.

She could hear him saying the words in his sexy Aussie accent.

Steph took a deep breath and thought about running herself. If she was careful, she could get back to her cabin without anyone seeing her. Maybe Brody wouldn't even come back to the cabin he'd been staying in for the last six months. He'd been attending something called a debrief with Ian Taggart for hours. He would likely take a room at the hotel in the city where the McKay-Taggart team was set up and she might not see him again.

Well, except he'd left his big duffel bag behind. He might come back for that.

She sank down onto the bed he'd been sleeping on and remembered the first day he'd shown up at her clinic here outside of Freetown. She hadn't been sure what to expect when she'd agreed to help McKay-Taggart with a long-term mission. They'd explained that their own operative would run most of the mission and her clinic would give him cover. She hadn't expected for her long dormant sex drive to come alive the minute said operative walked off the plane.

Steph lay down briefly, touching the quilt she'd had made especially for him. At first she'd given him a regular cot, but after she'd realized what that had to be doing to his massive frame, she'd paid a local worker to build this beautiful monstrosity. Brody had argued that he didn't need it, but she'd held firm.

When he was gone, she would move it into her cabin. It would be ridiculous and far too much bed for her, but she wanted some kind of memory of him.

It was over. The mission was over and in a couple of days Brody Carter would be gone. There was no more need for him to stick around because they'd done their duty. That very afternoon the op they'd been prepping for six months had played out. Guns had been fired, men had died, and Theo Taggart was going home.

For six months she'd had a gorgeous, brawny, sexy Australian bodyguard who pretended to be her right-hand man. Together they had navigated the underworld of criminal activity on the continent, all in a crazy attempt to draw out the woman who had kidnapped Theo Taggart. Dr. Hope McDonald hadn't stopped with Theo. She'd kidnapped several other men and ruined their lives, health, and destroyed their memories.

She was going to hold on to the memory of her glorious Aussie never-quite-a-lover.

The door opened suddenly and a massive presence filled the space. Six foot seven. Two hundred seventy pounds of pure muscle. Brody Carter. He stopped as though allowing for his eyes to adjust. It was inky midnight outside, and her camp was far from town. He would have walked in the darkness from his Jeep to the cabin.

"Steph? Luv, what are you doing here?" He stepped inside. "Is something wrong? Something happen at the clinic?"

Oh, god, he was here. What the hell was she doing? He was stunningly gorgeous and she was the shy girl who always sat at the back of the room and hoped no one noticed her.

Except she hadn't always been that girl. Once she'd been the girl who answered all the questions, the girl most likely to succeed.

And then she'd taken her eyes off the road, and in a flash of blinding light and crushed metal, that girl had died.

She stood up. There was a reason she didn't get dressed in lace and silk and try to seduce men. She wasn't that girl and she never would be again. Now she was the girl who repented, the girl who tried to save the world because once she'd destroyed it utterly.

Did she have to stop the rest of her damn life forever because she'd made a mistake? Could she not have one night of respite? One night where she got the guy?

Deep down she knew she wasn't thinking about just one night. Deep down she knew she was crazy about Brody Carter and this was her play.

"Steph, why the hell are you dressed like that?" The question came out of his mouth on a breathless huff, as though he'd just figured out she was half naked in his bedroom. "You shouldn't be here."

But the words were said softly, not with any force of will and not with the abject horror she'd been worried about. He hadn't moved away. He'd walked into the room, his big body taking up so much space she could practically feel the heat rolling off him. He'd closed the door and now it was just the two of them.

"I want to be here." There was no place on earth she would rather be. She'd dreamed about being right here since the moment Liam O'Donnell had introduced her to him. He'd brought Brody with him and they'd sat in a café in Freetown, discussing the mission ahead. She'd known it would be dangerous, but all she'd been able to think about was how amazing the man across the table was.

Over the months he'd become her friend, her protector, her pretend lover, but every single time she thought he would make their ruse into reality, he would turn away.

She couldn't let him turn away tonight. It was her last chance. She could let it slip away or she could reach out for it and have at least one sweet memory.

A shuddering sigh left his chest and she saw the way his hand fisted at his side, as though he didn't trust himself not to reach out and touch her. His jaw tightened and she watched him win the war. "No. I'm not good enough for you, luv. I've known it for a long time. Why do you think I haven't tried to climb into your bed?"

"Because you don't want me." She didn't think so, but she needed to hear it from him. If he told her he didn't, she would be able to walk away. She would be humiliated, but she would have tried.

He was worth trying for. Somewhere along the way he'd decided he was a grunt soldier, pure cannon fodder, but she'd seen another side of the man.

The side she'd fallen in love with. The side that might make all the pain she'd been through worth it. The side that might bring her back to life.

"It ain't that, and you know it." He couldn't seem to look at her. His eyes went to the floor. "I'm not the man for you. You need someone better. Someone more on your level."

She wasn't sure what level he was talking about. She ran a

rough-and-tumble clinic in a place that mostly made the news for its outbreaks of hemorrhagic fever. If she had more than a hundred dollars in her bank account, she counted it as a win. "Shouldn't I be the one to make that decision?"

"Not if you're not smart enough to make the right decision," he replied. "Someone's got to look out for you. You won't listen to your nurses and your head of security is a washed-up drunk. I'm going to hire someone else before I leave."

She couldn't argue with anything he'd said. "If you're leaving then it doesn't matter if we spend the night together."

"It does because you're not doing this for sex. You're doing it because you think it might change my mind about staying here or about taking you with me when I leave, but I won't. I won't do that to you. Stephanie, you're brilliant. You need to be back in the States, learning new techniques and charging a fortune for your expertise. You're going to die out here."

She might, but it would be okay. She'd always known that. Now that her mother was gone, she didn't have any reason to go back to the States. It was better that she stay here where she was needed, where she could do the good work she'd promised to do.

Where she could eternally punish herself.

He took a step back and she thought he would leave. He would pick up his pack and she wouldn't see him again.

One last desperate plea. That was all she had left. She happened to know that he spoke another language, a private one that eased him and softened his soul.

Stephanie dropped to her knees, hoping that weeks of practice had perfected her form. Knees wide, spine straight, head down, and palms up on her thighs. The offering of a submissive to her chosen Dom.

Or at least that was how the books of Serena Dean-Miles explained it. Avery had sent them to her along with a few books by Serena's friends. She'd looked at the salacious covers and rolled her eyes. She'd wanted fiction, not porn.

But then Brody had joined her and one night she'd found herself picking up *The Mercenary I Loved* and falling into the story of

Shane and Gabriella, and she'd found a whole new world.

Brody cursed under his breath, but his boots came back into view. She could feel him looming over her. "You don't know what you're offering."

"I know exactly what I'm offering." She didn't lift her head. "I've never had a Dom. I won't have another one. Not out here. I want the experience, Sir. Or do you have a submissive at home in London?"

His hand touched her head, fingers sinking into her hair. They slid along her scalp, lighting up the skin he touched. "You know I don't."

"Then I don't see the problem, Sir." She had to hope the word *Sir* worked the same kind of magic on Brody that it did on Serena's heroes.

The hand on her head lifted. "The problem is that you're going to want more from me than one night in the sack, Stephanie, and I can't give you more than that. I'm not the kind of guy who settles down. I'm not the one for you."

Yes, she'd heard a whole lot of that. What he really meant was she wasn't the one for him. It wasn't his fault he wasn't attracted to her. She'd misread the situation and it was time to retreat.

She stood up, swearing she wasn't going to cry. Nope. She'd been through way worse shit and one guy rejecting her advances wasn't going to break her. Her inner tough chick made an appearance and she found herself straightening her shoulders and lifting her chin. She rose to her feet. When she thought about it, she was horny. That was all this was about. He was gorgeous and close to her and the adrenaline of the day had affected her.

Yeah, inner tough chick was good at deflection.

"Sorry about that. I didn't understand. I get it now." She held out a hand. "It was nice to meet you, Brody Carter. Have a good life."

He looked down at her hand and sighed. "Steph, let's sit down and talk. I don't think you do understand what I'm saying to you. I'm not trying to hurt you, luv."

He didn't even want to shake her hand? She eased around him.

Inner tough chick had started biting at the bit Steph kept in her mouth. Irrational anger poured through her, but she had to keep a lid on it. It wasn't Brody's fault that she'd gotten her hopes up. "Not necessary, man. It's all cool. I'll see you sometime."

She started for the door.

"Please, Steph, I don't want to say good-bye like this. I don't want you angry with me."

But she was. It wasn't fair, but he was one more disappointment in a lifetime of them. She might deserve it, but it hurt. This one particular snub cut deep. She'd known deep down that she would be alone, but she'd thought there might be moments of respite. These weeks with Brody had refined her need.

Never let them see you hurt. It was far better to look like she didn't care than to sit down like an obedient little girl and let him explain all the ways she wasn't good enough for him. She was certain he would tell her it was the other way around, but what she would hear was that she wasn't sexy enough, her boobs weren't big enough, she was on the thin side, and he was a man who needed curves on his lovers.

"I'm not angry," she said as flippantly as she could. "I'm trying to catch the CIA dude before he turns in. He's bunking down in the clinic. I thought he might want an upgrade."

She wasn't going to look for Ezra Fain. The last thing she needed was a casual hookup. God knew she'd had more than enough of those in her life. Except those hadn't been casual. Those nights hadn't even been about sex. They'd been about obliterating herself.

No, she would go to her cabin and cry and sleep, and in the morning, she would work and begin to forget him.

She started out the door but then felt a hand at her wrist, dragging her back.

Brody's eyes had narrowed, his face turning hard when it was always soft around her. It didn't make him any less beautiful. If anything, that hard edge sent a thrill through her. "What did you say?"

Her first instinct was to drop to her knees and beg his forgiveness, but he didn't want that. He'd rejected that part of her.

So he got the inner tough chick, the part of her that kept on surviving. "I said, I'm going to check and see if Ezra needs some company since you don't want any."

The door slammed and she suddenly found herself with her back against it. Brody crowded in, taking up all the space and staring down at her. His body brushed hers and she found both her wrists captured in one of his. He dragged them over her head, forcing her chest to come out, breasts skimming along his body. "I shouldn't do this."

Tough chick was winning. Steph let her take over. It was surely better than the desperate girl who lived inside her. She kept asking for love and affection and getting swatted away. This was the next best thing, possibly the only thing she would ever get. "Then don't. Let me go and I won't bother you again."

"No, you'll go find Ezra Fain and bother him," Brody said on a growl.

"Somehow, I don't think he'll find me a bother." She'd barely spoken two words to the man, but she wasn't going to admit it. It was better to let Brody think she wasn't a love-starved girl.

"He won't fucking find you anything at all. If you're determined to not sleep alone tonight, you can damn well do it with me." His mouth came down on hers and every inch of her skin came alive. His kiss was overwhelming, hungry. There was no slow meshing of mouths. He took her, his tongue surging inside and dominating her own. He let go of her hands and started to explore her body. His hands were on her hips when he came up for air. "I'm leaving in the morning. I'm going back to London and I can't come back."

She'd known that would probably be his answer. She'd known he wouldn't want to stay and she couldn't leave.

"One night. That's all I want." It was all she could have. It had been foolish to think it could be any different.

His mouth came down on hers again and she let herself get swept away. One night and her life would go back to normal. One night and then she would be alone again. His hands started to roam over her and she tried to forget all the reasons why this was a bad idea.

He stepped back, his entire body set in hard lines. He strode over to the bed and sat down. "Take off the gown. It's pretty, but I want to see you."

She hesitated, all her insecurities coming to the forefront. Somehow, she'd thought he would simply take her. "Let me get the lights."

He was back in her space again, his hand wrapping around her wrist. "I didn't say turn off the lights. I said take off the gown. How am I going to see you if you turn off the lights?"

"Brody," she began.

He was having none of it. "You got on your knees in front of me and you said you knew what you were offering me. The first thing you were offering me was obedience. The second was your body. You're giving me neither right now."

His voice had gone midnight dark and something about the tone made her soften. He was right. She did know what she'd offered him and now she was trying to have it all her way.

There was nothing wrong with her body. It was feminine and she was healthy. What was she afraid of? "All right."

He let go of her wrist and sat back down, looking like a damn king waiting on his concubine's performance. For all his "I'm nothing but a grunt" talk, the man could be incredibly arrogant, and damn if she didn't find it sexy as hell.

Something about that voice let her know that everything was going to be fine. He was past the point of rejection. He was in and that meant he would play her Dom for the night. He would take care of her. She was as safe with him in the bedroom as she'd been in the field.

At least she was safe for the night. In the morning she would be in a world of hurt, but she wasn't thinking past tonight.

Steph eased the strap on her right shoulder down, exposing more skin and the top of her breasts. Brody sat and watched, his eyes latched onto the scene in front of him. He wasn't going anywhere and that meant she needed to make the most of this because he would leave in the morning.

Unless she gave him a reason to stay. Deep down, that was what she truly wanted.

She eased the other strap off and let the gown fall to the floor. Cool air caressed her skin, and she could feel her nipples tighten.

He was silent for a moment, staring at her, but she could feel the heat coming off him. The khakis he wore had tented, so she let go of any silly notion that he didn't want sex. He wanted it bad, and it was there in the hot glare of his eyes, the rigid erection that threatened to split his pants.

Her heart was beating, sounding out a rhythm she hadn't heard or felt in forever.

"Come here." He shifted, spreading his legs and gesturing for her to come closer.

She moved, her feet shuffling across the wooden floor of the cabin. In the soft glow of the lamp, she could almost believe they were somewhere else, in some grand hotel room getting ready to celebrate their…what would they ever celebrate? She let the thought go. There was only the here and the now.

Even seated, his gaze almost lined up with hers. She only had to look down slightly. He was such a big man and she'd always longed to get her hands on all that muscled strength, to feel his skin under hers. But it would have to wait because she was going to be a good sub. It might be her only chance at experiencing this kind of kink, and she wasn't going to ruin it by going too fast for him. She stood there, allowing him to look his fill.

After a long moment, one hand came up. He covered her breast, the heat making her swell against that big palm of his.

"You're every bit as beautiful as I thought you'd be." His voice was a harsh whisper, as though he was trying to be soft with her but simply couldn't manage it. "I knew you'd be delicate and feminine."

"I'm not delicate, Brody." She knew far too well how much damage her body could take. "I don't need you to treat me like I'm made of glass. I need you to remind me that I'm a woman. I sometimes forget. I can be out in the field for weeks at a time and I don't even touch myself. I want you to touch me, to let me feel like I'm more than just a doctor."

It was the one thing she would get out of the night, the memory that once a man as strong and fierce as Brody Carter had wanted her, had needed her.

He leaned over and she felt his lips on her skin, soft kisses that moved from one breast to the other. His hands circled her waist, holding her in place as he nuzzled her. He seemed to breathe her in. She was sure he would take her nipple into his mouth, but then he sat back.

"Turn around."

Like she was moving in a decadent dream, she found herself responding without real thought. She let all rational thinking go. This was about feeling. This was physical, and her body was oftentimes far smarter than her brain. Steph turned, the air soft around her.

"Yes, you're as lovely from the back as you are the front."

She felt him move behind her, shifting her forward as he stood. His heavy boots thudded against the floor as he circled her.

"I can be rough, Steph," he said. He finished his circle and stood behind her, one big finger tracing her spine. "I like things that might scare you."

Like spankings and floggings and kinky sex. "I think I'm weirder than you give me credit for."

He chuckled at that. "All right, let's see how much you can take. Undress me."

She could totally do that. She'd dreamed of that every night for the last six months. Sometimes he would walk around without his shirt on and the sight of his cut chest was enough to make her drool. She wanted to see every inch of his masculine body.

She turned and realized why it was incredibly intimidating. She was already naked and he was standing there staring at her, fully dressed. It was odd to undress another human being.

He reached out and his hand went for her breast. He took her nipple between his thumb and forefinger. She went still, giving over to the sensation of having him touch her.

And then he twisted her nipple, the pain sparking suddenly and making her gasp.

"I said undress me. Did you not understand the command?"

Her eyes had watered at the pain, but it had also shot straight to her pussy. She'd felt that hard twist of his fingers in her womb.

Steph bit her bottom lip before sliding her tongue along it. Her mouth had gone dry. Likely because all the moisture in her body had pooled in her pussy. She could feel how wet she was getting and he'd barely touched her. She found the buttons on his shirt and started undoing them, peeling back the cotton to uncover all that soft skin. Every inch was a revelation. She eased the shirt back and let her palms rest on his chest. He had a light dusting of hair that made him all the more manly. It was neat, forming a triangle that led down to a thin line of hair disappearing into his khakis.

"Get down on your knees and undo my belt," he commanded. He quickly leaned over and hauled his boots off his feet, tossing them along with his socks into the corner.

Steph dropped down in front of him, his height so much more imposing from here. She looked up the length of his body and realized how small she was compared to him. It did something for her.

Her hand went to the buckle of his belt and she undid it. What would it feel like if he used it on her? A vision of her leaning over and taking his discipline assaulted her brain, making her heart race.

She'd read way too many books.

Then she didn't care because all she could think about was the monster in front of her. Brody's cock was built on the same lines as the man himself, and it wasn't waiting for her to politely help him out of his boxers. His cock was poking out of the top as though desperate to get to her.

He stared down at her, his eyes dark as she eased him out of the boxers and khakis.

She folded them and placed them aside and sat back on her heels, waiting for his next command.

If she only had one night with him, she intended to do it right.

She knew in that instant that she might be able to fool Brody Carter, but she couldn't fool herself. She was in love with this man and she might always be.

She placed her hands palms up on her thighs, her body throbbing in anticipation of what came next.

* * * *

Brody looked down at her. She was the perfect picture of submission, but he knew he'd been had. She'd set him up because she wanted this night, probably more.

He couldn't do it. He couldn't do it to her. He wasn't good enough. She had the whole world in front of her and she would grow bored with an Army grunt. At some point, she would stop punishing herself for the sins of her past and get on with her life. He wasn't going to be one more way she hurt herself.

But he couldn't turn away from her. He'd tried. He'd done his best, but now that she was naked and kneeling, he realized this had been inevitable from the start.

If he thought about it, why the hell hadn't he packed up and been ready to go this afternoon? He'd known one way or another the job would be over today, but when he'd gotten ready to go to the hangar where they were supposed to meet McDonald, he'd left his duffel behind. Even as he'd allowed O'Donnell to drive her back to the clinic, he'd known he would spend one last night here. Taggart had offered him a hotel room and he'd given Brody a long look when he'd turned it down.

They'd all known what he was coming back for.

"Touch me." He wanted to feel her hands on him. How many nights had he sat up and wanked his own dick, wishing it had been her small hands on him? Her exceedingly competent hands. He was fascinated with them. They weren't painted and taken care of the way other ladies' were. Steph used her hands every day. She washed them a hundred times after she sewed a cut closed or took out an appendix. He'd seen women with sexy nails and baby-soft skin, but it was Steph's hands he wanted on his body.

She looked at him like she was ready to eat him up, her tongue darting across her lower lip and making his body tighten with pure lust. Her hand reached up and gripped his cock and he had to force himself to breathe.

Oh, all the nasty things he could teach her. She'd only learned about D/s from books. She'd never bottomed for a man before. If he stayed here with her, he could train her. He could take her mouth, shoving his cock deep. He would hold on to the nape of her neck and force his way to the soft, sweet space at the back of her throat. He would watch over her all day, be the good bodyguard, but when night fell, she would be his sub.

Hell, who said he had to wait for night? She pumped his cock in her hand, watching the way the foreskin moved back and up his stalk.

She was surprisingly innocent when it came to relationships. If he wanted to, he could bring her fully into D/s. He'd never given any thought to taking a full-time submissive, but if he wanted to keep her it might be the best way. He could bring her in, convince her that obeying him was best.

He had no right to think those thoughts. No right to take control of her life, but the impulse was there.

"Stop." If he let her continue he was going to come in her hand, and that was the last thing he wanted. He would only allow himself to have this one night with her. He intended to make every second count.

She sat back on her heels, but he reached down and lifted her up. This first time was going to be fast. He couldn't help himself. He needed to get her off because he was worried the minute his dick plunged inside her he would come like a rocket.

He carried her over to the bed, her weight nothing compared to his strength. He laid her out, a feast for his eyes. He'd meant what he told her. She was stunning, so much more in person than in his dreams. He'd known she would have lovely breasts, but had never imagined how perfect and round they would be, how the nipples would be tight pink-and-brown buds. He'd known her body was slender, but not how sleek and sexy she would be without her clothes. Her scrubs hid the graceful curves of her hips and ass. And as often as he'd thought of her pussy, he'd never dreamed it would be perfectly pouty and wet for him.

He lay down beside her, the bed creaking under his weight. He turned on his side and found her mouth with his. She accepted his kiss like a flower opening to full bloom under the sunshine. Her arms came up, wrapping around his neck, and she held back nothing. Her tongue played against his, sliding over and around.

He let his hand cup one breast, loving the silky feel of her skin and how the bud of her nipple pressed into his palm.

His whole body hummed with an energy he hadn't felt in a long time. His blood pounded through his system, all his instincts telling him to take this woman and mark her as his.

He smoothed his hand down her body, skimming over her belly until he could feel the swell of her pussy. Soft and ripe. A single swipe of his hand let him know how wet and ready she was for him.

So ready and yet he wasn't going to take his until she'd screamed for him. That was what truly kept him awake at night, the idea that he might be the one man who could loosen her up, who could remind her there was a world outside of medicine and self-sacrifice. For all that he believed she deserved someone educated and successful, he was also certain that man probably wouldn't dedicate his whole being to bringing her pleasure.

She shivered beneath him as he fingered her clitoris. That ripe bud was practically pulsing with excitement. He kissed her while he ran his finger over and around and pressed down. He shifted so he could work one long finger into her pussy while letting his thumb work her clit over and over again.

His dick throbbed against her hip, every squirm of her body bringing him closer to the point of no return. It didn't matter. She was already squeezing around his finger, coating him in her essence. He pressed down while his finger curled inside her and he felt her nails dig into the flesh of his back. Her head dropped away from his and she screamed out his name.

He gave her another moment as she came down, but it tried his every bit of patience. He couldn't wait another second longer. He rolled her over and made a place for himself between her legs and thrust in. She was incredibly slick, so wet he didn't have to force himself in. It was like she'd been made for him. He fucked her hard, looking down at her body. She was gorgeous, flush with her recent orgasm.

"Please, Brody," she said. "It feels amazing. Like nothing I've had before."

He pulled out and thrust back in, the sensation heavenly.

Because he'd made a big mistake.

"Shit." He forced himself to pull out. What the hell was he doing? "I need a condom."

"On the nightstand." She reached over to the small wooden nightstand by the bed and sure enough, there was a stack of condoms.

She'd come prepared. Before he could calm down and let his mind take over, he grabbed the foil packet, opened it, and rolled the rubber over his cock. He wasn't stopping. There were three condoms there. He intended to use every single one of them.

She'd given herself to him for the night. He wasn't giving her back 'til morning.

Brody gripped her hips and drove in again. He ground down on her, making sure his pelvis hit that sweet clit with every pounding thrust.

She clenched around him, her eyes widening as she came.

And then it was his turn. Pure pleasure coursed through him, making his whole body shake. He drove into her again and again until he had nothing left to give her.

He fell on top of her, not holding off a bit of his weight because she'd agreed to take all of him. He nuzzled her neck and breathed in her scent. "I'm not done with you."

She lifted her head and brought their lips together. Brody started all over again.

Hours later, he stared at her as she slept. She was small in the big bed. Delicate and fragile, and she didn't have any care for herself at all.

She needed someone who would take care of her, but it couldn't be him.

If he stayed with her, he would try to dominate her, try to control her life, and it would wreck them. He would do it because the truth was she scared him in a way no other woman ever had. He would lose her and it was better to walk away now than it was to feel that pain because there was no way he was staying around and becoming one more way she punished herself.

He had many reasons to leave and the only reasons he had to stay were selfish.

God, she was beautiful, and he wished he'd been something more than a soldier. Perhaps if he'd had the patience to go to university...

She was something magnificent and it would take a better man than he to bring her to the place she needed to be.

He turned and promised himself this was all for the best.

He left the cabin quietly and got into his Jeep. At least he'd remembered the damn condom. One problem they wouldn't have.

He told himself it had been one night. But he would remember it for the rest of his life. As for Steph, what could go wrong for her? She would move on, and that was a good thing. Before long she would forget she'd ever met him and get on with her life unencumbered by anything that happened that night.

* * * *

Seven weeks later

Steph stared down at the pregnancy test. "Well, fuck."

Chapter One

Dallas, TX
9 months later

Stephanie stood on the threshold of the big Mediterranean house the O'Donnell family called home and wondered for the thousandth time if she was doing the right thing. She'd already upset Liam and she was going to cause problems with his friends.

Mostly because Liam had gotten a look at the baby in the car seat at her feet and reached the proper conclusions. There had been no questions, no casual wonder about how she'd come to be in Texas with a baby she hadn't mentioned before. She'd hoped someone would ask the question. Who's the dad? She would have mentioned she wasn't sure and moved on.

Nope. Li was far smarter than that. He'd taken one look at her baby boy and vowed to kick his father's arse, as he put it. And he'd known exactly who that was.

"It's going to be okay," Avery said, tugging on her hand as Liam hauled the car seat up.

"How old is this kid?" Li complained. "He feels like a toddler."

"Two months." It was hard to believe two months had already past. She'd dreaded having him and now she wanted time to slow down because he was growing far too fast. It was odd how her world had shifted in two months and three days, how the center had changed and she was better for it. "He weighs fifteen pounds already."

"Bloody Aussie." Liam smiled down at her son. "Hey, boy, I'm your Uncle Li and I'm going to kick yer daddy's arse."

Liam walked inside and Avery closed the door behind them.

She clearly hadn't thought this plan of hers through long enough. But then she'd been far too terrified to be worried that someone might find out how foolish she'd been. "Please. Brody can't know. He doesn't want to know. He doesn't…he doesn't want me. I chose to have Nate. Nate's mine and no one else's."

Avery laughed, the sound musical to Steph's ears. "Oh, dear, I'm afraid that boy belongs to all of us now. Come on. Let's figure this out. I'll make sure Li doesn't get on a plane tomorrow. Now, what kind of trouble are we in?"

So much trouble. "Like I said, someone's trying to kill me and I'm not sure why. I didn't know where else to go. I probably should have called, but I left my cell behind and didn't want to spend the money on another one."

Running a clinic in Africa didn't pay well. She'd pretty much put everything she had into that place. Outside funding was rare and always spent on upgrading her tools. She was constantly begging for old equipment because a twenty-year-old CT scan was better than no CT scan.

"You shouldn't have gone anywhere else," Li replied. "You did the right thing. You came home. We told you after your mum died and you were alone that we were your family now. You always were family to us. Did you think we didn't mean it?"

Tears pierced her eyes. Where was inner tough chick when she needed her? She seemed to have gone dormant in the months since Steph had felt that first kick to her stomach—from the inside. She'd gone all gooey and emotional, unable to hide those parts of herself that had been shoved down before. "I think I hate bringing trouble to your doorstep."

Liam lifted Nate out of his carrier, hefting him up to his chest. "This boy here ain't a bit of trouble, are you? What a handsome young man. And you're strong, aren't you? Look at that. Two months old and he's holding his head up like a champ."

She was grateful for the chance to smile about something. "Yes, he's strong for his age. And big. I had to scramble to find clothes for him. I'd only bought newborn onesies. I didn't realize how big he was going to be."

"And you had him in the field?" Liam asked the question with a soft tone that didn't fool Steph one bit. At some point, Liam O'Donnell had decided she was the little sister he'd never had, and he could bring the hammer down.

"I have my own clinic, Li. I have a surgery and everything. I've done C-sections in the clinic." She backtracked as she saw Li's eyes flare. "Not that I had a C-section. Somehow my vagina was able to spit him out. I didn't even need an episiotomy. Turns out I'm super stretchy down there."

Li frowned, looking over at his wife. "Do I want to know what she's talking about?"

"Absolutely not." Avery led her to a comfy chair in front of the fireplace. "Sit and rest for a bit. We've got a guest room and I'll pull Aidan's travel crib out of the closet."

Stephanie shook her head, grateful to have diverted Liam from his cause. She could give him another one to worry about. "I don't think that's a good idea. Like I said, I'm in trouble and I'm worried about staying in one place for too long. I heard that sometimes McKay-Taggart will stash a client in a safe house. I thought I could stay in a motel tonight if you could get me a meeting in the morning. I know the group has to decide whether or not to take a case. Uhm, they'll also have to decide if they work on a payment plan because I'm going to need one."

Liam held her baby in his big arms and the sight pierced her with longing. Nate had never been held by a man. Her nurses were all women and Alfi Dauterre, her recently hired security expert, had zero interest in babies. The Aussie soldier of fortune sometimes showed up at her clinic, offering her help in exchange for a room, a meal, and free medical care. He needed a lot of antibiotics. Liam picking up her baby was the first time he'd been held in manly arms, and Nathan seemed utterly fascinated with him.

"We'll take the case and there won't be any talk of payment," Liam replied. "And you'll stay right here."

He didn't understand. "I can't thank you enough, but I know you have protocols."

"Not for family, we don't." Li's big hand patted Nathan's back, easing him down until he settled his head against Li's shoulder. "Trust me. We'll meet tomorrow but the only question is going to be what we do to help you. There won't be a question of whether we take the job or not. You do understand that Big Tag owes you? He'll do anything you need. Do you need him to kill Brody Carter? Because he'll do that, too. See, there's a question we *will* have to decide. I say it should be me who murders the big bastard, but Tag might want to play, too."

She couldn't help but laugh a little. "You can't kill Brody."

"Are you trying to tell me this boy ain't his?"

So old-fashioned. "I'm trying to tell you that boy is mine. I chose to have him."

"You didn't conceive him on your own and you know it."

"I think what Stephanie is trying to say is that Brody didn't want a child," Avery explained quietly. "She made the decision to have him. What's his name again?"

"Nathan." She looked up at Avery. "Nathan Avery Gibson."

Avery's eyes were shining as she looked down at her. "That is a lovely name. I can't tell you how much that means to me." She frowned suddenly. "Of course if you thought enough of me to give your son my name, you probably should have called and mentioned that you were pregnant. Steph, I called you not two months ago to tell you that I was pregnant again. You didn't think to mention you'd had one of your own?"

"I wasn't sure how to tell you," she offered lamely. The truth was she'd frozen when she'd gotten the call from Avery. It had been three days after Nate's birth and all she'd been able to think about was the fact that Avery was having baby number two and Nate would be an only child of a single mother who could barely afford the necessities.

"I think what Stephanie's saying is she was ashamed. Which is the bloody stupidest thing I've ever heard." Liam's voice raised and that had Nate's head coming up. She worried he might start crying, but he simply looked at Liam and then turned his head her way as though he totally agreed with the lecture his uncle was delivering. "What exactly did you think would happen, Stephanie? Did you plan on never seeing us again?"

Damn, that was one judgmental Irishman. "No. Not at all. I just didn't know how to tell you."

"I was planning on checking in on you in a month or two. I've got corporate clients who take me into West Africa and I was going to show up on your doorstep. Would I have even been welcome?"

She'd stepped in it. "Of course. I would have been thrilled to see you. And I was going to call. I promise. It didn't go through my head once that I wouldn't see you again. I was going to call and tell you about Nate after I figured out how to make sure you didn't kill his father."

Nate leaned forward and placed a fat baby hand on Liam's nose, touching and patting it like it was a new toy.

"I won't kill him. I'll only make him wish he was dead, and after I'm done with him he won't ever be able to do this to another woman. He won't have the proper parts because I'll cut them off. Then I'll ensure he does his damn duty to you and the boy."

It was hard to take him seriously when he had a baby tugging on his nose, but Liam was a patient man. Probably because he'd had his own son and now had another kid on the way.

"I don't want Nate growing up with a father who resents him, so I've left Brody out of my pregnancy."

Liam's eyes narrowed. "Are you telling me he doesn't know?"

"Of course he knows." She stood up, giving him a frown of her own. "I called him. I called him about ten times, Li. He wouldn't answer the phone. I left him a detailed voice mail about how his seed was growing in my womb. I went into clinical detail. I was pissed at the time."

"And he didn't reply?"

She sighed, her anger fleeing in a moment, replaced with the sadness that invaded any time she thought about that Aussie. "He told me before we slept together that he didn't intend to see me again. He left me a note asking me not to call or try to contact him. I was supposed to contact Damon Knight if I needed anything, but I think he was talking about security concerns. Li, please drop this. He knows. He doesn't care and I'm finally okay with it."

Li's jaw tightened but Avery stepped in.

"Don't make this harder on her. Let me hold that baby and you go and pull out the crib." Avery took Nate, cuddling him close. "And then call Ian and let him know we need a family meeting in the morning."

Liam kissed his wife and stepped back with a shake of his head. "Do you know the name of the person who's coming after you?"

Weariness set in. It had been a hideous few days. She'd had to make her way to Guinea and then to Frankfurt and Dallas, all the while worried there was an army behind her. "He was a mercenary. I'll be honest, Li. I didn't get his name. They all called him boss and that was all. The boss."

"You say he's a merc? Not a warlord?" Li asked.

Liam had spent plenty of time in that part of the world. She rather thought one of his reasons for taking assignments in West Africa had been so he could check up on her, but it also put him in a position to understand the geopolitical forces at work in the region. "He's European. German, or maybe Dutch. I'm crappy with languages. I know they weren't speaking English or Krio. It was a European language he spoke with his men."

"What exactly happened?"

Avery held out a hand. "Li, it's almost midnight and she's been traveling for days. She needs sleep. She can go over all of this in the morning meeting."

"You're sure he's coming after you?" Liam pressed.

"He promised to kill me, but I'm hoping it takes him some time to find me. My friend Alfi found a private plane that took us to Conakry in Guinea. I managed to get a flight to Frankfurt, and from there I made my way to Dallas. I hope he's still looking for me to have flown out of Freetown or to have gone on by car."

Li nodded. "Smart girl. We've got a bit of time. All right, then.

I'll make sure everything is set up and I'll call out for a few additional eyes for the night, just in case."

"He means we'll have a couple of beefy bodyguards here in about an hour or so." Avery sat down in the chair across from her and started to rock back and forth, as though having a few armed guards come to her house wasn't a big deal. "Ian recently hired a bunch of new bodyguards and they are heavenly looking men. My Li is the handsomest of all, of course, but Serena and I are trying to convince a couple of them to be cover models for Serena's new project."

"I'm done with hot bodyguards." She'd totally learned her lesson. Alfi was incredibly handsome and had made it plain he hadn't cared that she was pregnant. He would be happy to sleep with her when he came by. She'd turned him down with a laugh.

Avery studied her for a moment. "I don't know. They are pretty nice to look at and a couple aren't even manwhores. You never know. Unless you're still stuck on Brody."

She wasn't. She'd written him off when he hadn't bothered to call her back to even ask about his son. It had been a kick to the gut as the days had gone by with no return call. She'd tried again when she was four months along and she'd been seized with the morning sickness that should have come in her first tri. She'd called and told him exactly what she thought of him. Explicitly, and with lots of words her child shouldn't have heard even in utero.

He hadn't answered her then, either.

Still, as she'd gone into labor, she'd called one last time, begging him to come to her. She'd left a message pleading with him to come hold her hand.

Never again.

"I'm not even thinking about hooking up, Avery. I'm barely cleared for sex. It will probably be another six months before I even think about it, and then I'm pretty sure I'm going to find myself a nice Hitachi wand and settle down. I'm going to name it and everything."

Avery sighed. "Oh, dear. He did some damage."

Steph shook her head. "He told me what he wanted and I

pushed him. I don't blame him. I simply want to move on without him. I'm good. Well, except for the psychopath chasing after me. And the fact that I need to make up a batch of formula for Nate. One more thing I couldn't manage. I got mastitis a few days after he was born and I had a high fever for days before the antibiotics worked. I don't know if it was all the surgeries after…well, anyway, I can't produce enough milk for him."

There it was, that moment in her life that all roads seemed to lead back to. That one moment when she'd been weak and it had cost the woman in front of her more than most people could imagine.

"It's all right," Avery promised. "He'll be fine on formula. He's a big, healthy boy and you're doing a great job with him."

Maybe it was how tired she was or simply the fact that being around Avery stripped her bare, but the tears started up and she asked the question she'd been thinking about since the moment she'd held her baby. It was a question she'd asked Avery before, but now it meant more. Now she knew what Avery had lost. Now she'd held her own child.

"How can you even look at me?"

Sometimes the accident felt like it had happened to another person, another Stephanie.

Sometimes she could still feel that moment of impact, hear the crash, louder than thunder, like it was happening to her all over again.

She'd been a teen coming home from a party. Her whole world had been laid out in front of her. She would be class valedictorian, get accepted to medical school, make her parents proud.

One single mistake. One moment where she'd taken her eyes off the road and she'd killed Avery Charles's infant daughter and young husband. Avery had been in a coma for months and Stephanie's future died.

Until that day when she'd stood in front of Avery. She'd expected anything from a lecture on how her carelessness had cost Avery everything to Avery telling her to do what her darkest self wanted to do—to die like she should have on that country road.

She'd expected anything but what Avery had given her. Forgiveness.

You owe me a life, Stephanie. You owe me two lives. You don't get to be a coward and take the easy way out. You pay me back by being good. By doing good.

Avery Charles O'Donnell was the single most extraordinary human being Stephanie had ever met. Avery was the reason she was alive and working.

Avery cuddled Nate close and reached for Steph's hand. "I look at you with ease and joy in my heart because you're my friend. Stephanie, there are events that happen in our lives that can devastate us, and we can't control them. The only thing we can control is how we react to them. Something terrible happened and I could have lain in that bed and allowed that one moment to make me bitter and hateful. I could have looked at you and damned you to hell, but that wouldn't have solved anything at all. Forgiveness is a gift we give to ourselves. Who knows what could have happened if we hadn't both been on that road that night. I could be married to Brandon and Maddie might be in high school. Or we could have divorced. Or they could have died some other way because I was always meant to go down *this* path. I can't question why they were taken when they were, but I believe one day I'll have to answer for how I handled it. I chose to live and that meant finding meaning. Hell, maybe it meant making meaning where there was none, but I don't regret forgiving you. Not for a second."

Tears poured from her eyes because she should have done this long ago. Avery was a blessing in her life. "I'm sorry I didn't call."

"I understand and you're here now. So I get to ask you to do something else for me."

"What's that?"

Avery reached out, placing a hand over hers. "Forgive yourself. Come home and raise this baby. Forgive yourself. Forgive Brody. Move on with your life with an open heart. You can't be this child's mother and hate yourself. It's time to come home."

"I thought about putting him up for adoption." She admitted the plan that had come to her in her dark moments.

"Because you don't think you're worthy of him," Avery said. "But you are. While you're here, I want you to see a friend of mine."

She could guess. "Kai Ferguson?"

Avery sat back, Nate settling down against her. "Yes. I know your mom sent you to a therapist, but that was a long time ago and you've done a good job of hiding away from the world. I thought it was good for you at first, but now I wonder. You can do charity work here and raise your baby around family. You can find someone who makes you happy, and I worry you won't even try if you stay out there."

She would do anything for Avery. "I'll see Kai. I'll try."

Avery stood up. "Is his formula in the diaper bag?"

Steph followed her, every bone weary. "Yes. I'll get it if you don't mind me using your kitchen."

Avery pointed her way. "You see, you're acting like you're a burden. That's what we're going to work on."

Liam stepped back out of the hall and picked up her sad suitcase. "Avery knows how to make a bottle. You are going to take a long, hot shower and get to bed. We'll handle the wee one. Well, we'll handle the massive linebacker you've got there. Go to sleep and rest. You're good now. You got him out and now it's time to let me take over."

They presented a united front. All three of them. Nate looked perfectly happy in Avery's arms.

"Okay." She could use a shower, use some sleep she hadn't been able to get while sitting up in economy with a baby in her arms.

She was safe. It was enough for now.

* * * *

Brody Carter set the weight down and stretched one arm over his head and behind, trying to loosen his left tricep.

"I can't believe you're actually up at six in the morning working out." Kayla Summers strode into the gym, wearing pink yoga pants and a tight tank, her night-dark hair in a high ponytail. "After everything you drank last night, I suspected you would be sleeping it off."

"Bastard doesn't sleep," Tucker said as he did what had to be his hundredth bicep curl. The damn boy had been in the gym before Brody and he hadn't broken a sweat. "He parties and he works out. I think he needs a mission."

The man they'd named Tucker had a point. Tucker was one of the six men McKay-Taggart rescued from Dr. Hope McDonald's cruel experiments. The now deceased doc liked to experiment on men. Her drugs had wiped the memories of the men the team now called the Lost Boys.

Thinking about Dr. McDonald made him think of another doctor, a doctor who was the opposite of Hope and her evil experiments. It made him think of a doctor with the sweetest smile in the world.

"Hey, anytime the boss needs me, I'm ready to go. And it's not like I haven't been working. Walt and I just got back from a job in Iraq. That wasn't a piece of piss job. It was serious. God knows keeping Walt alive is work enough."

His normal partner also happened to be the scientist on the team. Walt was brilliant, but he also sometimes was a magnet for trouble. He was far better in the lab than the field, but that meant Brody got stuck there where he knew nothing and ended up surrounded by people who were way smarter than him.

That was his place though. He was pure muscle and he couldn't forget it.

Tucker shifted the twenty-pound weight to his free hand and started all over again. "Well, I would do almost anything to get out of here. Not that here's bad."

Sasha was working out beside Tucker, laid out on the leg press. "Here is no bad. Here is good food and many women to pleasure me. I have been in bad place. Bad place has no women."

His bad place had been torture and drugs that wiped his memories, so Brody was fairly certain Sasha was telling the truth. Sasha had recently completed his training with their boss Damon Knight and been given Master rights at The Garden, the club they all played at. Sasha was there every night the club was open.

Brody spent all his time in the bar lately. Oh, he'd had a few sessions with submissives, but he couldn't work up the will to go any further than a flogging or rigging up a sub for his friends. He'd been a bit like a monk because every time he put on a pair of leathers, all he could think about was how Stephanie had dropped to her knees in front of him, offering up her sweet self.

And then she'd tried to walk away when he wanted to save her. She'd been willing to offer herself up to that bugger CIA guy Ezra Fain, with his perfect looks and polished ways. He'd had a vision of Fain putting his hands on her and he'd made the single, biggest mistake of his life.

He'd given in and let himself go. He'd taken her in a wild frenzy of lust. He hadn't been tender with her, hadn't given her the long hours of lush lovemaking she'd deserved. He'd fucked her hard a couple of times and then snuck out like a bloody coward when she'd fallen asleep.

He didn't deserve a sub. Nope. Not when he couldn't get his head off the one he'd let slip away.

"Is he going to murder someone?" Sasha asked. "I have seen this look, right before someone tries to murder me. This is not old memory coming back. In the bad place, I was nearly murdered many times."

"Yeah," Tucker whispered back. "I remember that, too. Sometimes I wish the doc had done one last memory wipe and made me forget her. But it's like I said, Carter needs a mission to work. He's getting antsy. And since Walt is off his feet for a couple of weeks, I will volunteer to be your partner. I can watch your back and hey, if you want to rough up a few bad guys, well that doesn't need to go in a report, does it?"

"The only thing I'll be doing today is sitting in front of a computer finishing up the details on the Iraq job and making sure Walt remembers to take his antibiotics." It was going to be a dull day, and for some reason he'd been antsy the last two days in a way he wasn't sure had anything to do with Walt nearly getting himself killed because he was far too curious.

He'd been thinking about her for days. Maybe that was because he was surrounded with women planning a wedding. Hayley Dalton was marrying his friend Nick Markovic, and all the women of The Garden were aflutter with the details. There was an incredible amount of lovely feminine energy around him and he couldn't help but think of Stephanie.

Kayla grabbed a bottle of water from the small fridge. "I don't think we have anything exciting right now. I'm working on a couple of corporate cases. Super boring. I don't get to shoot anyone or anything. I was so bored I almost asked for the Loa Mali assignment."

Brody turned to her. "The royal wedding? I thought the Dallas office was handling that. Didn't you sleep with the king once?"

Kayla's ponytail bobbed as she nodded. "Many times. I was undercover. Hence the 'me not getting to go to the beach wedding of the century' thing. Exes. I've found it's totally best to keep that door shut, locked, and the key thrown away."

Ah, words of advice. Yes. That was what he needed to hear. "Because it's best to look forward and not back."

Kay shook her head. "Nope. Because almost all the time I was working the dude over for intel. I've spent most of my adult life making a living as a spy. Dudes get pissy when they find out you didn't give them your real name or your real job and hey, sorry I downloaded your computer and gave all that stolen tech to my government. It's a whole lot of drama. But if I could go back and see Scotty Barris, I would do it in a heartbeat."

"Another spy? Did you have hot time while on the job?" Sasha asked with a wink.

"Nope. He was the president of the chess club and I was the only female member of the chess club," Kayla explained. "One night while practicing he touched my boob and my world changed. Unfortunately, one of my dads walked in and then both my dads were giving me the lecture. And Scotty never touched my boob again. I would go back and ask him to touch the left one, too. I'm a little OCD. It still bugs me."

She was also a little sarcastic. But her words were still true.

He'd shut the door and it needed to stay locked.

It was precisely why he'd erased Stephanie's messages without listening to them. He'd always had someone follow up a few days later to make sure she was all right, but he couldn't listen to her voice and not break down. He had to be strong enough for both of them.

Because that woman deserved the best, and it wasn't him. It wasn't fucking him.

"He looks like he wants to murder someone again," Tucker whispered far too loudly.

He was done. The gym wasn't going to do it for him today. He needed coffee and then he would dive into writing a report about how Walt got shot in the foot because he stopped in the middle of a gun fight to solve a damn equation on a white board. "I'm going down to breakfast. If you see Damon, tell him he'll have his report this afternoon."

Kay gave him a jaunty salute. "Will do. Hey, anyone want to spar? I was going to do yoga but now all the violent talk made me want to punch someone."

They were arguing about who got to punch whom as he strode out the door.

His crazy life. This was the only thing he was good at, stepping in front of bullets so smarter people could live. That was his talent.

He was halfway to the lift that would take him down to the kitchen when his mobile trilled. He pulled it out. He always answered. Unless it was her.

It wasn't. It was a call from the States. From Li O'Donnell, which meant it had something to do with work, and likely something important since it was around midnight in Dallas. With a long sigh, he answered. "This is Carter."

"Ah, good. Now look here, I'm going to say something and I'm only going to say it once. I'm saying it to allow you to get a good head start and because I'm a fair man. I'm coming for you. Did you think you could sneak in and out of her life like that and there wouldn't be any consequences? Did you think because her mum died that no one would stand up for her? You were wrong, you arsehole."

He sounded an awful lot like another Liam. The one who had a special set of talents and murdered people on screen. "Uhm, I think you got the wrong number, mate. This is Carter. Brody Carter. If something's happened to Avery, I'm sorry, but I haven't seen your wife in a long time."

"I'm talking about Stephanie."

He stopped, his whole body going cold in an instant. "Something happened to Steph?"

"Yeah, something's happened to Steph and you damn well know it."

"What? What the hell is it?" His heart thudded in his chest. If some fucker had hurt her, he would have a job to do. A bloody, painful job. Damn it. Damn it. Damn it. He'd known. He'd known that clinic would get her killed one day. "Tell me, O'Donnell."

There was silence on the other end of the line.

"Tell me now!" The waiting was going to kill him.

"You almost sound like you care, Carter."

"I bloody well do care about that girl. More than you can know. Fuck. Tell me what happened. Is she dead?" He couldn't help it. He was practically crying. The idea that she was gone gutted him. And yet wasn't that part of why he'd left? Because she was so reckless?

He should have stayed. This was his fucking fault. He'd been right not to try to be with her. She deserved better, but he'd walked away and left her alone. He'd done that when he knew how reckless she could be. He'd done it knowing how close a couple of her calls had been.

He'd done it because he'd been afraid.

It hit him with the power of a sledgehammer. All this time he'd told himself he'd done it to protect her, to ensure she found someone worthy, but he'd been a sniveling coward protecting himself.

"Brody, she's not dead." Liam sounded calmer, less like he wanted to slice a man open and play in his entrails. "She's alive, though she is in real danger. Why did you dodge her calls if you care about her this much? Don't lie to me, man. I can hear it in your voice."

The tightness in his chest eased. "I dodged her calls because you know how it is with women. They get it in their heads that a man is worth something he ain't. They can give up their lives following a man who ain't worthy of them. I couldn't listen to the messages she left because I knew I would break down and go to her and then she'd be strapped with me for life."

"You're a stupid bastard," O'Donnell said and Brody could practically see him shaking his head.

"Yes, I believe that's my point." He didn't need O'Donnell to tell him something he already knew. "Now tell me what's going on with Steph."

"So, you haven't seen her since the Freetown op?" O'Donnell asked.

Only in his dreams. In his dreams, he wasn't a stupid bloody wanker. In his dreams, he had the kind of job that would make her proud, that they could build a family around. He wasn't the man who'd screwed everything up again and again. He was the kind of man she could depend on. "No. I haven't seen her since then. Haven't talked to her. She called me, but I couldn't... I thought it best we didn't talk. I sent a friend of mine down there to watch after her. He checks in and he hasn't said a thing about her being in trouble."

O'Donnell sighed and seemed to come to a decision. "Understood. Sorry, I was under a mistaken impression. You're right. I am calling the wrong number."

He wasn't going to let O'Donnell hang up. Not until he knew what was going on. "Wait. What kind of danger is she in?"

"Don't worry about it, mate. She's here in Dallas and I'll take care of it. You don't have to be involved at all. I can see that now."

"I want to know what's going on. Damn it. Tell me." He wouldn't be able to do anything until he knew she was safe.

There was an arrogant huff over the line. "You can't be bothered to even listen to her voice mails, you don't deserve to know what's happening in her life. Even when there's an army out there looking to kill her. Bye, Brody. Hope you're happy with your choices later in life. I made a mistake by calling you. I should keep this in the family and you are not in my family. Stay away from her."

The line went dead.

There was an army looking to kill her? What the hell was happening? O'Donnell couldn't leave him hanging like that.

Brody immediately called the number back. It went straight to voice mail. Bastard. He tried to pull up Steph's number. He'd erased it off his phone and she hadn't called him in months. The lift doors opened and Damon Knight stepped out. It was always odd to see his normally perfectly dressed boss in workout clothes, but Brody didn't give it too much thought. All he cared about was what Damon could give him.

"I need Steph Gibson's phone number."

Damon's gaze sharpened on him. "I thought that was over."

He didn't have time to argue, but Damon was his boss and Brody owed the man. "Yes, of course the op is over, but I heard a rumor that she's in trouble. I want to check it out."

"I wasn't talking about the op. I was talking about the affair you had with her."

Did everyone know? Could not a single person keep their mouth shut?

Damon's lips curved up in a smile. "I know what you're thinking. You're blaming the rumor mill. Normally I would as well. Not this time. You're to blame that particular secret got around. You get chatty when you're drunk. If it helps, I think you're wrong to believe you're not good enough for her. Women tend to know what they want. When we tell them what they want, it's called Mansplaining and it tends to get a bloke in trouble. Like when you kindly attempt to help your wife through those first few months of pregnancy by giving her scientific facts about why her hormones are out of balance. Spent a week on the couch for that. Apparently walking off morning sickness isn't a thing."

"Her phone number?" He didn't need to hear about Damon's problems with Penny. Even Brody was smart enough to know that when a woman was pregnant, a man should rub her feet, throw food at her, and pray he survived.

"Ms. Gibson's?" He pulled his mobile out of the pocket of his sweatpants, flipping through the contacts there. "I'm sure I have it somewhere. You said she was in trouble? I think you should call the Dallas office. According to my records, Liam O'Donnell is her primary contact."

Yes, and that had grated on Brody when he was in Sierra Leone with her. He'd been her constant companion, her guard, and her cover, and yet he hadn't been in charge. Not really. Every move he made had to be reported back to O'Donnell, who acted like her dad or something. He'd never truly been in command. "I need to talk to her."

"Here she is." Damon turned the phone his way.

He wasn't wasting a bit of time. He simply took the phone from Damon and pushed the button to connect.

It wasn't more than one ring before a masculine voice answered. "Hello?"

That accent was fairly thick. Definitely European.

Brody froze for the second time. "I'm looking for Stephanie Gibson."

A chilly chuckle came over the line. "Yes, well, aren't we all? Are you a friend of hers? Because we would really like to know where the bitch is."

"Who is this?"

"Let her know she can run, but she can't hide. I know what she has and I'm going to get it back one way or another. I'm going to give her everything I promised her. Tell her if she turns herself over I might go easy on that boy of hers. What did she call him? Nate. Yes, Nate. If she makes me come after her, all bets are off. I'll kill him, too. Real slow like. She's got twenty-four hours."

The line went dead.

Brody immediately tried to call it back. It went straight to voice mail.

What the hell had she gotten herself into? And who was the "boy" that man had mentioned? Had she taken a lover? Someone named Nate? Of course she had. She'd talked that night about how she was sick of being alone and she needed someone in her bed. It had been him for one night and now she'd found someone else and they were both in trouble.

His insides ached at the thought of another man's hands on her, but he'd made that bed and he had to lie in it. He owed it to her. She'd given him everything she had that night and he'd taken her like a rowdy sailor.

"What's going on?" Damon asked. "I take it that wasn't the doctor."

"Not sure yet, but I need to get someone to ping her cell phone and find out where it is. O'Donnell said she's in Dallas, but she didn't answer. It was some arsehole with a German accent. Maybe Dutch. I can't tell. Give me a minute."

He handed Damon his phone and shuffled through his own, looking for Alfi's number.

Damon was already on his line. "O'Donnell, give me the rundown on what's happening with Stephanie Gibson. Yes, I know it's midnight there. I'm aware of the time difference."

O'Donnell wasn't going to be helpful, but Alfi might. The phone rang once and then again and again before the line picked up.

"This is Dauterre. I'm partying right now. This better be good."

Brody could hear loud, thumping industrial music. "Where the hell are you? You're supposed to be in Africa."

"Brody, my mate!" Dauterre's Aussie accent was thick over the line. That's what happened when he drank heavily. "Brody, I was thinking about you. Gosh, mate, you have no idea how much I've wanted to talk to you."

"Are you in a pub? Where the hell are you? You're supposed to be watching over the doctor. You remember her? I'm paying you to check in on her." He was going to kill Alfi. "Where is Steph? What happened?"

Alfi went silent for a moment. When he spoke again, he seemed a bit more sober. "No idea, mate. I suspect she's at her clinic. Ain't seen her in a while. I got things to do with my time, too, you know."

"She's not there. She had to leave in a hurry because someone's trying to kill her. I believe that's a fact you might have mentioned to me."

"Well, then I'm sure she's probably on her way to see that Irishman she always talks about." Alfi sounded tired, his words slurring. "Nice lady, she is. I'll check in on her next time I'm in Freetown. It's probably a misunderstanding or something. Don't be so high strung. The girl is fine. Everything is normal. You know you only told me to call you if something outside the norm happened."

He hung up. Alfi was drunk somewhere and he would be useless until someone sobered him up.

"Bastard." Damon was staring down at his phone. "Told me to mind my own business and then hung up on me. This is my business. That's my name on the bloody door. Arrogant Irishman."

Brody looked at his boss. O'Donnell might have done him a favor. "There's only one way we're getting answers."

"Go there and demand them. Well, you'll be useless until you do. Though you're not using the jet for what will be personal business. You'll have to fly commercial." Damon shuddered as though that was the worst punishment he could hand out.

Brody had only flown private since he'd come to work for McKay-Taggart and Knight. Before then almost all his flights had been in the back of an SASR transport aircraft. "No problem."

"Take one of the lads as backup," Damon ordered. "If the good doctor is in trouble, I have no doubt you'll convince Big Tag to let you work the case. Owen's working with Nick and Robert's acting as Ariel's bodyguard while she's working a case for MI5. I need Kay here in case anything comes up, so it's got to be one of the others."

"I'll take Tucker." He'd said he wouldn't mind turning a blind eye to any random violence that might occur.

"I'll let him know to be ready. I would call Big Tag, but he'll back his man. You'll have to make your case in person." Damon strode into the gym.

Brody walked past the lift. It would take too long. He jogged up the stairs.

He would get to the bottom of this. Even if it killed him.

Chapter Two

Stephanie looked at the laptop screen, slowly scrolling through a rogue's gallery of mercenaries.

"The trouble is we mostly have pictures of these men when they were younger," Adam Miles explained. "Once they join the ranks of soldier of fortune, the dirty ones tend to not let themselves get lined up for portraits we can use to ID them."

"Wouldn't that make the world a simpler place?" Charlotte Taggart set a cup of coffee in front of her before sinking into her seat.

"So says the woman once wanted by every intelligence agency in the world," Liam quipped. "You're a lucky one we didn't have that kind of database a few years back."

Charlotte shrugged. "Yes, well, now I play for the good guys and I totally want a database."

Stephanie enjoyed the easy banter between the employees of McKay-Taggart. Liam had driven her to the office, both babies in the back of his big SUV because Avery was working that day. Nate had gurgled and kicked his fat baby legs and laughed at everything Aidan did. She'd freaked out a little when it had come time to leave him in the nursery. He hadn't been more than a room away from her since he was born, but the women in the nursery had started cooing and ahhing over him and he'd seemed to revel in the attention. When she'd left, Charlotte's twin daughters had been standing over

Nate's crib, making him giggle.

She wished she was in there with him rather than looking through the military equivalent of mug shots.

It hit her hard that she was tired. Tired of working endlessly, tired of never taking a real break. She'd watched Avery and Liam this morning and she'd loved their easy manner with each other. Li had made sure Avery had coffee and Avery had stopped him and redone his tie, ensuring it was perfect. They'd passed Aidan between them, effortlessly tackling all the morning tasks, and then there had been that moment when she and the boys were in the car and Liam had stayed at the front door, kissing his wife like they would be apart for weeks instead of hours.

She'd sighed and longed and was starting to wonder if maybe Avery was right and she could be a good partner to a man. Maybe a man could want her if she let him in.

She forced her mind back to the task ahead of her.

The men in front of her were all hard looking, but mostly clean and neatly kept, wearing various uniforms. "This man was definitely older and he had longer hair and a beard. I don't know. It could be that one. Maybe, but I'm not sure. I was pretty terrified the whole time. I could better ID the man I worked on."

She could ID that dude's liver in a heartbeat. He definitely ate too much fat and drank a bit much since there had been scarring on the liver that hadn't come from the bullet he'd taken.

She sat back. It wasn't going to help. The man was dead and that was precisely why she was on the run. She hadn't been able to save him. The bullet had done its job.

"Do you remember anything else about him or any of his men?" Liam asked.

She'd already told them everything that had happened. She'd gone over it in a dull monotone, keeping all emotion at bay. Ian Taggart had sat in on that portion of the meeting along with his partner Alex McKay. The big guy had sat back, his hands steepled in front of him as though he was already working through the problem. She'd told them what she remembered, which was mostly being terrified for her son and herself and the people around her.

Big bad dudes had come in, brought her a patient, and then told her if he died they would murder her.

The patient had survived the initial operation, but coded shortly after and died.

Her part-time security guy had gotten her out of there before the boss had found out his man was dead.

Thank god Alfi had been there. It was the only piece of good luck she'd had that day. Alfi often was gone for weeks at a time, but he'd been in Freetown the night before and had come to check in on her.

She couldn't think about what would have happened if Alfi hadn't been there.

Steph wracked her brain for anything she could think of. "At first I thought the man he'd brought in was one of his soldiers. I don't see many of those kinds of men where I am. It's actually somewhat peaceful since I'm close to Freetown. Still, there are plenty of Western corporations who basically hire their own armies to provide security for businesses in Africa. They don't exactly have HR departments, and I'm pretty sure they don't care about civil rights."

"You're talking about resource development?" Adam asked. "Mining and oil?"

"Yes, especially the diamond mines are known to violate locals' rights, but that's mostly to the south. Like I said, I'm not used to a bunch of armed men coming in unless it's local police bringing me a patient. They're quite friendly. I've worked in much worse places."

"And they didn't give you the name of the man they wanted you to work on?" Charlotte asked.

"No. They were rough with him. I suspected that the boss himself had shot the man and he was trying to fix the situation." Not that anyone had explained it to her. She flipped through another row of military men on the screen. Nothing.

"All right, I can buy that. Where was he shot?" Liam asked.

"He had a GSW to the abdomen. It's the kind of wound that can certainly kill a man, but it takes a while and it hurts like hell." She felt better talking about the medical stuff. "The bullet lodged in his liver. I had to bisect it, but I thought I might have saved enough of it that he could survive. I suspect he had a massive stroke following the surgery." She thought about what she'd seen while she was operating. "I would say he was in his mid- to late-forties. He was either American or European. Could have been Aussie, but he was Caucasian and First World. Now that I think about it, he was far smaller than the other men. He didn't have their muscle. He was a bit on the soft side."

"Well, soldiers of fortune tend to keep up their fitness routine," Charlotte remarked. "They have to in case they need to run. So, we're thinking this guy might have run afoul of this boss person, and then the boss worried he might get in trouble for killing him."

Liam sighed and leaned against the table. "Have you thought about the fact that perhaps the boss made that threat and didn't mean to follow through? What I mean is that he was trying to use the threat because he was scared of what would happen if the man died. That doesn't necessarily mean he would compound the mistake by also killing you. Sometimes men like that don't handle failure well and can say things they don't mean."

She prayed that was true. There was nothing in the world that would make her happier than finding out she'd completely overblown the situation. It would make for a good laugh if "the boss" was somewhere wondering where the hell the doc had gone and trying to explain to the police why the doctor had run away. "I hope so. Has anyone called the clinic? I had to leave my phone behind. Obviously. Even I know I can be tracked by my phone. I know he can track my credit cards, but that will only tell him where I've been. He might be able to find out where I'm going."

"But the cell will tell him exactly where you are," Charlotte agreed. "Yes, it was good to get rid of that. You're playing this smart. If he's actually after you. If he's not, you're going to have to buy a new cell, and that can get expensive."

"All right, you keep looking at the pictures. I'm going to do some more research," Adam said. "And I'll see what I can find out about your clinic."

"I've been afraid to call." She was worried about her nurses and patients, but she had to protect her son. The boss had only threatened her, and she'd told the nurses to leave. Anya had stayed but she'd had her second nurse flee out the back with the small group of patients that had been waiting on treatment.

She hoped Alfi was safe. He'd left her in Guinea, his flight taking him in a different direction. She hadn't called him either. He'd warned her that they needed to stay far apart until everything shook out, as he put it.

"I can ensure that no one can trace the call," Adam assured her. "Don't worry about anything but taking care of your baby. We'll handle things now. Though you know I'm surprised you didn't go to the London office. It would have been a shorter trip."

"Why would she go to London?" Liam asked, his voice taking on that forbidding tone Steph was sure would one day scare the crap out of his son's teenaged friends.

Adam didn't seem fazed. "Well, like I said, it would have shaved eight hours off her flight. She might have been able to get a direct flight, and Brody's there. I thought she had a… Oh, holy shit. How old is your kid again?"

She felt her skin flush. She should have known she wouldn't be able to keep it a secret.

Liam stepped in front of Adam. "Brody's got nothing to do with any of this, and if I catch you gossiping about Steph and her kid, I'll end you, and not in a pretty way. I know Ian's always jokingly threatening you, but I don't joke around. Not about me family. Am I understood?"

"It's okay." Brody already knew. There wasn't a big worry about him stomping in and demanding to see his kid. He didn't want his kid.

Adam frowned, stepping back from Li and straightening out his dress shirt. "I seriously doubt Brody had nothing to do with that kid, and I wasn't gossiping. I was sleuthing, something we're encouraged to do around here. And now I've solved the mystery of why our client didn't head for London. You know, Li, the older you get, the more you sound like Ian, and that is not a compliment."

He turned and walked out.

"Yeah, well the older I get, the more I understand Big Tag." Liam looked back to Steph. "Are you all right here? I've got work to do and I want to make a couple of calls and see if I can hear anything about a German mercenary who calls himself 'boss.' Can't be too many of those out there, right?"

"I'll stay with Steph. I know Ian is looking into some stuff, too, and I asked Chelsea to monitor the Dark Web to see if there are any rumblings out there," Charlotte said.

"Dark Web?" She'd known that was what the team had used when setting her up as a smuggler during the mission that had saved Theo Taggart. She herself hadn't used the underbelly of the Internet. Chelsea Weston had done that, pretending to be Stephanie and making those connections that had led them to Hope McDonald. Still, she wasn't sure why they needed the Dark Web now.

"Oh, the Dark Web is where they would put a bounty on your head," Charlotte explained with a sunny smile. "Chelsea's going to see if anyone's out there looking to assassinate you."

"Charlotte!" Liam frowned her way.

"Adam's right. You do sound a lot like Ian," Charlotte replied before turning back to Steph. "And it happens way more often than you would think. I've had many bounties on my head and I'm still kicking. It's nothing to worry about."

"Don't use Charlotte as your role model. She's a terrible one." Liam opened the big glass door. "If you need anything at all, I'll be in my office. We'll head for home in an hour or so."

"Thanks for lunch," she said with a smile. Liam had gotten her the most delicious BLT from the deli on the first floor and then he'd sat with her and had his own lunch, talking mostly about their children and all the fun things Avery was doing with Serena as her personal assistant and all-around gal Friday. He'd taken her mind off all the awful things surrounding her and she was grateful.

She'd also thought a lot about what Avery had said the night before. She did need to think about coming home, and Dallas was the best place for her.

"You're welcome. I was happy to have the company." Liam winked her way and walked out.

Charlotte immediately turned in her seat, her face going from serious to excited in a heartbeat. "Wanna have some fun?"

She opened her mouth to thank Charlotte, but to explain that she had to keep searching through the pictures and then she should…what? For the first time in ten years she didn't have a clinic to manage, didn't have patients to oversee. No paperwork to do or grant requests to submit.

"Yes. Yes, I do." Baby steps. She was going to take baby steps in this new life she found herself in.

Charlotte grinned and started for the door. "Awesome! Let's go pick you out a couple of pieces of candy."

She stood up, surprised. "Candy? I'm a little full."

"Oh, you can never be too full of this candy," Charlotte assured her. "We need man candy. It's time to pick your bodyguard. Or guards. Why pick one when you can have several?"

She hurried after Charlotte and wondered if her baby steps hadn't become one giant leap into the big old life pond.

* * * *

Brody woke up with a shock as the car he was in came to an emergency stop, throwing him against the seatbelt. A horn blared and he heard someone shouting.

Tucker turned in his seat, giving him a wary smile. "Sorry. Apparently driving is one of those things that got wiped from my memory." He waved a hand out the window. "Sorry about that! Yeah, fuck you, too! Jeez, I thought people in Texas were supposed to be friendly."

As far as he could tell from Tucker's accent, he might be from Texas. Or someplace in the American west. Brody glanced around. They weren't far from the McKay-Taggart building. Another few lights and one right turn and they would be there. If Tucker didn't get them killed. "They're friendlier when you're not driving like an arsehole with a death wish. You do realize this ain't a road, right?"

Tucker stopped. "What do you mean? The GPS lady told me to turn here."

Did he not notice that people on both sides were looking down at them from the platform like they were idiots? "Nope, she told you to turn on the road. This is where the train runs. In case you've forgotten what a train is, it's a bit like a high-speed bullet that kills everything stupid enough to get in its path."

Tucker's eyes went wide. "Holy shit. Holy shit. We're going to get hit by a train. What should I do?"

Brody yawned again. It had already been a long damn day. Why had he thought bringing the brain-damaged puppy along for the ride would be a good idea? "Probably get off the tracks. Preferably before the train comes. You wait too long and the train will do the work for us."

Tucker gunned it and managed to get back to the actual road. He stopped at the next light, his hands wrapped around the steering wheel like he was afraid to let go. "Maybe you should drive."

"How are you going to learn if you don't do it?" He certainly hadn't brought the lad along to let him sit in the back and eat candy and play on his bloody iPad. He got enough of that back in England.

Tucker relaxed a bit. "You are a weird dude. From what I can tell nothing upsets you. You didn't even wake up when the plane hit that storm. Everyone else was puking their guts up and you were asleep."

"Man needs his sleep." Odd that now that he knew he was going to see her, he'd settled down. It would be all right. She had another man and all he was doing was checking up on a woman he cared about. He would see her, talk to her, meet her new guy, and then he would be able to move on with his life. Whatever trouble she was in, he would help her out, and then he would know everything was fine. He would be able to date other women, women more like him.

Women who didn't make him crazy with lust. Women who didn't haunt his every dream.

"It's unnatural," Tucker complained.

It wasn't for Brody. He'd nearly been killed about a hundred times, and he remembered every single one. He didn't let it get him down. He went into every situation with the same odds. He would either die or he wouldn't. Most days it didn't matter to him which outcome came true.

But the thought of her being killed, that made his heart race.

Couldn't the bloke drive a bit faster? He would feel better once he saw her. Once he laid eyes on her he would remember all the reasons he'd left. All the reasons he'd stepped aside and let some bugger named Nate take over for him. Yes. He would meet the bloke. Nate would be an over-educated arsehole, and Brody would be able to happily step back after he'd fixed this problem for her. He would know that she was fine and had found a man worthy of her. Maybe Nate was another doctor or a scholar of some kind. That was what she needed.

He could have a talk with the man, get him to see that talking Stephanie into coming back to the States would be good for her.

Tucker moved the car along, coming ever closer to the building that housed MT. He might have to fight his way in, but that would be okay, too. It would be good for Big Tag to know that anything that happened with Stephanie Gibson should go through Brody Carter. Not Liam O'Donnell, who already had a family to take care of. Him. Brody. He was her close contact.

He was the one they should call on.

He sat up straighter, watching for the turn since it seemed like Tucker didn't know the difference between a road and a set of train tracks.

"Turn right at the next street," he said a few seconds before the GPS navigator told him the same thing.

Tucker turned. "Way to gang up on a guy."

He had no idea. This was more important to him than Tucker could possibly know. "Did the team find out anything on this bloke she's with? Nate something. Is he a new doc at her clinic?"

"I got a report from Sasha, who told me he couldn't find anything on his travel search. He looked through records for the past year and the only Nathans who came through on his passport search didn't fit the bill. There was a Nathan Conroy who traveled on a British passport for a corporation. Stayed exactly two weeks in Freetown and went home. A Nate Gilliam who appears to be a missionary from Utah."

He could see her building water wells with a missionary group. "Maybe it's him."

"Then she likes them young. He's nineteen."

Probably not. "Tell Sasha not to bother. I'll have an actual name for him in an hour or so. And tell him to keep trying to get in touch with the clinic. I can't get anyone to answer."

"About that, uhm, that's where things get a little weird. You were sleeping again when the drone footage came through. Damon's got spectacular connections in that part of the world. Some of the corporations over there use drones for security purposes. Damon convinced one of them to send the drone over the clinic. I sent the footage to your phone."

Now he was talking. He reached for his mobile, switching it on and pulling up the email that contained the footage.

"Damon had them do three separate flyovers," Tucker explained. "At three different times, a few hours apart."

The buildings were there. Even though they were overhead, he knew the site well enough to pick out the surgery and the clinic. The drone flew over, showing the dusty road that led to the small cluster of buildings. Three cabins that would more likely be called huts by most people lay on the outskirts of the site. There was an outer building where the kitchen was located. Steph and her workers all ate together, each taking turns cooking.

He'd done his part while he was there, though he wasn't the world's greatest cook. He'd taken turns with breakfast, frying up eggs and making a reasonably decent oatmeal. She'd laughed the first time he'd done it. It had been a watery mess, but she'd still eaten it.

The buildings were all there. Where the hell were the people?

The clinic always had someone walking about. Whether it was patients straggling in to see the doc or kids coming for food and water, staying to play football in the lot behind the kitchens, there was always someone milling about.

Not this time. This time the place was eerily deserted. A chill crept up his spine. Something was wrong. Very wrong.

"What time of day did they fly over?" He switched to the

second of the three short videos.

"Noon, three p.m., and just before dusk. That's what Damon said. They could go over it at night, but Damon didn't think they needed to. He says he'll send the intel to Adam, if you like. He might be able to see something we're not."

He didn't want Adam. He wanted his own people. "Make Walt do it. He's going to be resting for a week or so. He can certainly isolate some imagery for me. I'm looking for anything out of the ordinary. We should have footage from the Theo Taggart rescue op. Have him compare the two and give me anything different. If there's a new tree, I want to know where it came from."

"Landscaping. Got it." Tucker sighed. "I think that's it. Should I park in the garage?"

And let them know that he was coming up? O'Donnell had told him he was giving Brody fair warning, but Brody played a bit dirtier than that.

Actually, now that he thought about it, he wanted to know why O'Donnell had decided he needed an arsekicking. Unless Steph had talked about their brief night together. O'Donnell couldn't possibly think he had something to do with whatever had sent Steph and her new boy toy running for Dallas.

A sick feeling hit his stomach. Was Steph talking bad about him? Was she angry he wouldn't return her calls? So angry she would want to get a bit of her own back? It occurred to him that she could make his job difficult if she wanted to. He'd never thought she would. She was too kind, too sweet, but sometimes women changed when a man had his back turned.

"Park in the visitor slot. If we try to get into the covered garage, we'll need a code from the front desk." He would figure this out because he wasn't losing his job over a consented upon one-night stand.

"Are we sneaking in?" Tucker asked. "Because I didn't bring my stealth clothes."

Such a pain in Brody's arse. "You just watch my back, mate."

Tucker parked and Brody got out of the car. It took a moment to realize the bloke wasn't following him. He turned and started to bark at him for not keeping up, but he stopped. Tucker was standing in the middle of the lot, his face turned toward the brilliant sun.

A smile played his face as though he'd never felt that kind of warmth before, never stood in the light and had it warm his skin.

It was rainy and cold most of the time in London. Even when the sun came out it didn't feel like the same sun that would shine down on him in Australia. No. That sun would beat a man down, but it could also warm him, lift him up, and give him energy he couldn't find anywhere else.

Tucker had spent his whole life in the cold. At least all the life he could remember. As far as Tucker was concerned, he'd been born a grown man in a sterile lab where he'd been tortured into submission, and even when he'd been rescued, he spent all his time hidden away in a building in the middle of a city he wasn't allowed to explore.

Brody could give him a moment.

Tucker's head came back down and his skin flushed in a way that wasn't from the sun. "Sorry. It felt nice."

Nice. Yeah, he needed to be nicer to the bloke. "No worries. It's a lovely day. When we're not working, maybe we can see a bit of the city. I've been told there's a park up the road that has something called food trucks."

Tucker's face lit up like a kid being given a treat he'd been sure he would be denied. "That sounds great. I'm starving. Airplane food is terrible. And there was so little of it."

He practically ran up the stairs to the building.

Damn, but he wished he had that kind of energy. Wished the world felt fresh and new. Not that he wanted to get his brain wiped out, but the energy that came from no past weighing Tucker down, that was something he could handle.

He took the lift up. McKay-Taggart occupied the top two floors of the building, with the highest floor used as the main office. He'd only been to the Dallas office on two occasions, but he remembered the way.

Where would he be without this place? And why the hell had Ian Taggart offered him a bloody job? After he'd left SASR, he'd been at loose ends, unwilling to go back to his tiny hometown and work at a station the way his old man had. He hadn't wanted to go home to his mum's place and be forced to look at the room his brother had left behind when he'd been killed in combat.

He'd taken a bodyguard job. Stupidest thing he'd ever done because he'd found himself thinking it would be an easy job. All he had to do was escort a scientist named Walter to meet his contact in Finland. No worries. Except he'd been smack in the middle of a bloody global conspiracy.

He'd screwed up and gotten himself taken, but at least it had been by the good guys.

End of the op, he and Walt found themselves working for McKay-Taggart and Knight in London.

What if he'd taken a different path? He would have never met Stephanie and she wouldn't be a hole in his heart. He wouldn't have flown halfway around the world to check up on her.

The lift doors opened and he followed Tucker out.

"Nice place." Tucker opened the big glass and metal doors that led inside. And stopped, his shoulder dropping down before he walked up to the receptionist desk. Walk? More like strode in, as though he'd managed to transform from curious lad to lothario in a heartbeat. "Well, hello, pretty lady. What might your name be?"

The young woman behind the counter looked up from her laptop. Her glossy red hair was in a high ponytail and she was wearing a pretty blue dress that accentuated her curves. "Sadie. Do you have an appointment or are you bringing in the order from the pie maker? I sure hope you are. He's been in a doozy of a mood this afternoon and his wife is downstairs working with a lady who needs a bodyguard. So the only thing that works is to stuff a lemon square in his face the next time he says something awful. I've had one client walk out and he threatened to cut the man bun off the deliveryman. He had the scissors out and everything. I'm supposed to avoid lawsuits, but how can I do that when the boss is a crazy man?"

So Big Tag was still Big Tag. "Not the pie delivery service, luv."

Tucker's smile was movie star wide and his voice had deepened. "Not at all. I'm a secret agent. I'm so secret no one even knows my name."

Sadie was a pretty redhead who looked an awful lot like her Aunt Grace. From what Brody recalled, she'd started working part time at McKay-Taggart after Grace had joined her husband Sean's growing restaurant empire. They had sites in Dallas and Fort Worth, but Sean had recently been featured on the Food Network and was a rising star in the culinary industry.

"If you don't have anything sweet and lemony, I have no use for you," Sadie said with a frown. She sat down and went back to her laptop.

Tucker frowned and turned to Brody. "I've been told I'm quite attractive. Did the women at The Garden lie?"

Brody stared for a moment. "How the fuck am I supposed to know?"

"Human attractiveness is an easily settled subject, from what I can tell." Tucker seemed tense, his hands on his hips as he worked through the problem. "Symmetrical features are important. Women seem to appreciate a fit body on their men. Do I not exude a willingness to both physically and financially take care of a female?"

Sadie stood back up, her green eyes now wide with obvious curiosity. "Oh, you're one of them, aren't you? Like my Uncle Theo? He's not my blood uncle, but they take family pretty seriously around here. I was raised in Waco by my mom, who was Grace's sister, who is married to Ian's baby brother, who is half brothers with Theo and Case because their daddy was something of a rogue, as my momma would say."

Brody wasn't following her at all. She talked fast, spitting out facts with her down-home Texas accent. "He's one of what?"

"Them. The Lost Boys," she clarified. "Uncle Ian calls them vagrants, but he calls a lot of people that. It's a catchall term for him, really. He will see a perfectly dressed guy and call him a vagrant because he's wearing one of those pork pie hats. I don't see how that's an indication of one's homelessness."

Brody had to chuckle because Ian was a bastard. He put a hand on Tucker's shoulder. "He is one of the Lost Boys. You'll have to forgive him if he doesn't know he's acting like a bloody douchebag."

Tucker frowned again. "I was only trying to test the waters with a beautiful woman. I haven't had a chance to meet women outside of The Garden and the office. Kay told me it's different in the outside world and that I needed practice or no one would ever swipe right. I'm not sure what that means but if I want a woman, I have to ensure that she swipes right."

Sadie suddenly seemed less grim. She looked up at Tucker and gave him a playful grin. "You're quite symmetrical, Mr. Tucker. And women like more than fitness in their men. They like politeness and kindness and a man who'll make sure to put them first in the world. If that happens to come with a nice set of abs, then that's all the better."

Tucker immediately pulled up his shirt. "I know what abs are. I have abs."

Sadie put a hand over her eyes and laughed. "I'm glad I didn't mention anything lower. All right. Since you're not going to help me with my boss, why don't you tell me how I can direct you? Just a pointer, again, if you're here to see Ian, you might wear a flak jacket."

"I was actually looking for Li O'Donnell." If Big Tag had his knickers in a twist, he would avoid the man. Besides, Li was the one he needed to talk to. Li was the one who knew where Steph and her boy toy were holed up. Li could make a meeting happen and then he could put this all to rest. He would get the name of the bloke who was threatening her and he would then educate Steph's new boyfriend on how a man handled himself. If his young charge wanted in on that bit of violence, well, sometimes two sets of hands were better than one.

"Hey, Sadie, has my brother shown up?" Adam Miles walked around the corner.

Sadie frowned at him and pointed a finger his way. "I was warned about you, Mr. Miles. There will be no pranking going on today. I intend to run as tight a ship as my Aunt Grace, and that includes attempting to keep the two of you from doing horrible, juvenile things to each other. You will not touch those lemon squares or I will do something terrible that you will regret for the rest of your life."

Miles smiled her way, a condescending grin on his face. "Oh, I sincerely doubt you could do violence to anyone."

"No violence. I'll call your wife. I have her on speed dial," Sadie threatened, holding up her heavily bejeweled cell phone like it was a weapon of the first order.

Miles frowned fiercely. "That is rude and unbecoming. It was a tiny little laxative. He wouldn't have even noticed. No taste. No odor. We all know how that man likes his bathroom time. I was simply trying to give him more of it."

Well, it was good to know the juvenile pranks weren't limited to the London office.

"That's a good idea," Tucker piped up. "I need to write that down. I'm always looking for ways to liven up a party, if you know what I mean."

Sadie's green eyes rolled and it was easy to see she dismissed the man no matter how nice his abdominal muscles were. If only all young ladies were as practical as Sadie. "Oh, thank god. Macon Miles, you are a life saver." She glanced back as she moved from behind her desk to greet the man who walked into the office carrying a box. "Mr. O'Donnell is in his office. Give me a sec and I'll let him know you're here."

Adam Miles seemed to realize Brody was there. He smiled and held out a hand. "Carter. Hey, man, what's got you…" His face fell before Brody could even grasp his hand. "Oh, shit. This is better drama than I had planned. I'll take you back to Li's office myself."

"I'll hang out here," Tucker offered.

He wasn't sure that was the best idea. Tucker would annoy the hell out of Sadie, but he might learn a lesson. The women of McKay-Taggart could handle themselves, and it looked like Grace's niece was no different. If Tucker found himself with his balls being handed back to him, he would learn a lesson in dealing with the fairer sex. "Don't go too far. We'll be leaving soon."

He started to follow Adam down the hall, his brain making plans. He would need an office and a hotel room. Not in that order. He would pray Tucker didn't irritate Sadie so much she put them in a rattrap. Or should he try to stay with Steph and Nate?

That would be hell on earth, but after the conversation with the man who had Steph's phone, he knew damn well she shouldn't be left alone.

"You know anything about what's happening with Steph?" Brody asked Miles.

"I know I'm deeply interested in what happens in the next few minutes," Miles replied. "And I have talked to her. Unfortunately, she doesn't have a security camera at her clinic. I'm going to have to see if there's anything on the road that leads up to the clinic that I can use. This isn't London. I'm not optimistic."

He wasn't either. If they'd been talking about a hospital in a city, they would already have a dossier on the man and could have gotten full police aid. "Have you run his name through Interpol?"

"No name," Miles replied, turning down the hallway that led to the offices with the big, gorgeous windows. O'Donnell was a founding member of the company and it looked like he'd moved up in the world. "I've had her looking through pictures of known mercenaries and players in that part of the world. We haven't come up with anything yet. So it's been a while since you've seen her, huh?"

"Not since we finished up and got Theo back. No reason to," he replied, hearing the defensiveness in his own tone. He lightened up. Miles was a known gossip. Almost as bad as Big Tag. "She's a nice lady. We got to be friends. Hate to think she's in trouble."

"Friends? Okay," Miles replied. "I hope you're still friends. That makes things easier."

He wasn't sure they would ever be friends again, but that was his fault. He'd fucked up that night. He'd given in when he'd known he shouldn't. "You know anything about this Nate fella she's taken up with?"

Miles stopped, turning in the middle of the hall. "Nate fella?"

He'd stepped in it, but damn it all he wanted to know. "I heard she brought her new man along with her. Just wondering if he's trouble or not. Do we know anything about the bloke?"

Miles stared at him like he'd grown another bloody head. "He's very attached to her. Super attached. He might have cried a bit when she left the room."

Brody bit back a groan. She'd gone for someone super whiny? What the hell? And it had only been a bloody year and she'd already found herself some clinging vine of a man. He should have known. "They meet in Sierra Leone?"

"Yeah, about two months ago," Miles replied. "Maybe two and half, but it's hard to believe. I was thinking more like six to nine months, if you know what I mean."

He didn't, but he wasn't going to stop asking questions to try to figure out Miles's odd brain. So Steph and Nate had only been together for two months, but he'd fled the country with her? Only two months with this man and she was in trouble. It made Brody eager to check him out. "So this Nate fella is here?"

"Oh, yeah. Last I checked he was flirting like a pro with a couple of babes. She should watch out for that one." Miles turned and strode down the hall. "I think he's a player of the highest order."

Brody felt his blood start to boil. "He's doing this out in the open?"

"Oh, I'm pretty sure he's loving the attention." Miles stopped in front of Li's door and gave it a brisk knock. "Li, you have company."

Maybe this wouldn't go well for Nate What's His Name. Did the bugger think the minute Steph left a room he could go from crybaby to some kind of player lothario? He would find out pretty quickly the woman wasn't without protection, and here was the perfect man to talk to.

Brody strode into the room. "Miles tells me her boyfriend is hitting on everything in a skirt and you're sitting in here? I thought you were going to protect her."

O'Donnell sat behind his desk, one dark brow arching over his eyes. "And I thought you were going to stay the hell away from her.

Shouldn't you be back in London?"

"It's a damn good thing I'm not since it seems to me you're not taking care of business."

O'Donnell looked over at Miles. "So young Nathan is hitting on women, is he?"

Miles gave him a sunny smile. "He likes 'em young, too."

O'Donnell shook his head. "You're a bastard, Adam."

Miles shrugged. "It's a talent. I have to practice or I'll lose it and become all sullen and mopey like Jake. There's only room for one brooder in our threesome. So he's in the dark, huh?"

"This is not entertainment, Adam," O'Donnell warned.

"Bloody oath, it ain't. That girl needs someone stable," Brody said. "She needs someone who can take care of her since she's determined to sacrifice herself to the rest of the world. Where is he? I think I should talk to the bastard."

"Use small words," Adam advised. "He's not very well educated. You know the type. Born big on muscles, little on brains."

What the fuck was going on? "I want to see Steph and this Nate person. Now."

O'Donnell held up a hand. "Calm down, Brody. I think everything is all right. Chelsea hasn't found anything on the Dark Web. I think Steph might have jumped the gun running the way she did. I think she was in a situation where she got scared and she took this arsehole too seriously. As far as we can tell he tried to get her to correct his mistake. He was probably afraid if the man died, he would get in trouble, and he likely will. I've got a call in to local law enforcement. They're going to look into it, but I think it's safe to say she's going to be okay. But you do need to talk to her."

"I thought you were going to murder me."

"That was before I realized you're just a dumbass who can't accept the inevitable. Think about it, man. How long did it take you to get on a plane? It's only been ten or eleven hours since we talked. The flight itself is eight. That's not the actions of a man who doesn't care about a woman. Did you take the time to pack?"

Barely, but Li was wrong about one thing. "I don't care what you think you know, the man who wants her dead is real. I talked to the bastard. He told me he was going to kill her and her boyfriend. He was serious, Li. He's coming after her."

Liam stood up. "I think she's with Charlotte. Let's go find her. She needs to be the one to explain to you about Nathan. And then I want you to tell me absolutely everything you know."

Brody followed, ready to face her.

Chapter Three

Steph stopped at the door to what seemed to be a full-on gym, glancing around the room and praying she wasn't drooling.

The room was filled with gorgeous, muscular men working out, several of them without their shirts on.

She'd wondered why the outer office had been completely deserted. There had been plenty of desks, but Charlotte had mentioned that most of the men who worked for this particular division of McKay-Taggart didn't like to be tied down to desks. In deference to their unique natures, Ian had let them put two of the large conference spaces together for a gym.

"It keeps them close to the office," Charlotte explained. "There's also a room with a massive TV and a shocking assortment of video game systems. We've found if we don't keep them engaged, they wander off."

Beautiful, sexy men with distraction issues. "And you want one of them to watch over me? Should I worry about shiny objects?"

Charlotte laughed. "Not at all. They're focused when they work. You have to understand some of these guys take on a single client for long stretches of time. They eat, work, sleep when the client does. It's very involved. It's why they don't want to be tied to a desk when they aren't on assignment. And this is what they do every afternoon."

"I thought I would find you down here, baby," a deep voice said.

She turned and Ian Taggart walked through the door. He was so close on their heels she wondered if he'd found out where they were going and run to catch up with them.

If it bothered Charlotte Taggart, Steph couldn't tell. The woman merely grinned up at her massive husband. "You know I try not to miss the afternoon show."

Taggart made a vomiting sound, but then sighed. "You should be glad I got my fix." Taggart winked down at her and held up what looked like a yellow piece of cake, or perhaps a kind of lemony brownie. "Stephanie, this is what I like to call the full douche."

"Excuse me?" He couldn't have said what she'd thought he said.

"Yeah, you know how a group of dogs is called a pack and a bunch of crows is called a murder. A big group of bodyguards is called a douche," Taggart proclaimed. "Idiots, every single one of them. I have no idea why I hired them."

"You hired them because they're the best," Charlotte explained with a long sigh. "And now we have to pick a couple for Steph."

"You know I could have called them into a meeting," Taggart explained. "They are sometimes allowed to come upstairs to the big kids table, but only if they wear clothes like normal people. Blade! What the fuck is wrong with your pants? They're supposed to be around your waist not barely hugging your ass cheeks, you douche."

A tall, lean god of a man dropped from the bar thingee where he'd been pulling up his muscled body and then lowering it back down. And then pulling it back up and lowering it down. It was hypnotizing. She could watch that all damn day. But now the man turned, putting his hands on his hips. Taggart was right. They did ride low on his hips, showing off those gorgeous notches. She hadn't seen notches like that on a man since…

Well, not since the night with Brody.

The man named Blade frowned his boss's way. "There's

nothing wrong with my pants, Tag. If you want to wear those grandpa khakis around your man nipples, then good for you, but I'm not eighty-two."

Steph waited for Tag to explode but he merely grinned, the expression making him look younger and far less scary than normal. "That's right. I totally hired him because he's a massive asshole. His name is Riley Blade. Yeah, I know it sounds ridiculous but someone put those two names together."

"Yes, my mother," Blade shot back with a roll of his dark eyes. He stepped forward, wiping off his hand with a towel before offering it to her. "You must be Dr. Gibson. It's a pleasure to meet you. Liam called up earlier and told us all to be prepared to take shifts working with you."

She shook his hand. "I appreciate it very much."

"Blade is used to protecting Hollywood stars," Charlotte pointed out. "He worked with Lyle Tarpin on his last action/adventure flick. It was exciting."

"Not as exciting as I would have liked," Blade said with a frown. "And I was a consultant on that, not a bodyguard. I got to tell them all the ways they were fucking up and they still did everything I told them not to do. Now I'm here and I take shit from this guy. But seriously, we all know what you did for Theo. He's one of the good Taggarts. We're all happy to help you out."

"Good Taggarts? What does that mean?" Big Tag asked.

A massive man sat up on the bench press. He had dark, close-cropped hair. "It means he's the least assholey Taggart, though I have a fondness for Sean. Any man who can make a brisket the way he does can be a complete dick and still a good guy in my book."

"Well, all I know is I'm thrilled you decided to cut that hair off," Taggart announced. "He used to have hair down to his shoulders. It took forever to get him to do anything because he had to curl his hair and shit."

Charlotte slapped a hand on her husband's chest. "Stop being such a dick." Her face softened as she looked back at the man. "How are you, Remy?" She leaned over to Steph. "He had surgery to correct a few issues with the metal plate he has covering his brain.

It's an injury he received while serving his country. My husband should be polite about it."

"I'm good. No complications from the surgery and my hair is growing back in nicely. I'll be curling it again soon." He stood and he had to be six and a half feet. Almost as tall as Brody. She barely reached the middle of his chest. He smiled down at her, charm pouring off him. "I'm Remy Guidry. I run this group of crazies. How you doing, chère?"

Oh, that accent. Pure Cajun. It made her think it had been too long since she'd even thought about sex.

"She's doing great. She's got a two month old," Ian pointed out.

"Yes, I heard, and no man," Remy replied with ease. "My own momma was a single mother. Brave and beautiful women. I will try to make your time with me as comfortable as possible. I know you've recently given birth to that beautiful boy of yours. I'll make sure to take it easy. When it comes to the physical stuff."

Wow. There it was. She'd kind of thought all those female instincts in her had died somewhere in the middle of her third trimester, but they were flaring back to life now. Was he saying what she thought he was saying?

Not that she would. She wasn't going to keep her bodyguard so close he would be in bed with her. Though it would make it easier for him to keep track of her…

Nope. Not going there. Never ever again.

Was she going to be a nun for the rest of her life? Did she have to martyr herself because she'd made a mistake? At least this time the mistake had given her the gift of Nathan.

"You do understand that Li considers her something of a kid sister, right?" Ian asked.

Remy actually took a step back and slapped Riley Blade on the shoulder. "I think this is a job for you and Burke."

Charlotte leaned over. "Everyone's scared of Li."

"It's starting to get annoying," Ian admitted. "I'm way scarier than Li."

Blade shook his head. "I worked a protective detail for Serena Dean-Miles at a book convention. She's got a few crazy fans. Avery

O'Donnell is her personal assistant. Jake Dean simply shook my hand, told me to take care of his girl. Adam gave me some pointers. Liam took me aside and explained that if anything happened to either of those women he would kill me, but not right away. He promised to take me somewhere and slowly feed me to a group of mangy dogs he intended to recruit off the street, but he would make sure I was alive as long as possible so I could enjoy my hideous death. He went into great detail about all of it."

"He said that?" She couldn't imagine it. Liam was always nice. Not always. Yeah, okay, she *could* see him saying that. "Well, I'm sure he didn't mean it. You know, it's like the dad who cleans his guns while his daughter's date shows up."

"I would never show that little fucker what caliber of weapons are coming his way," Ian announced. "I will show him the report I have on him, his parents, all those fucker friends of his, and how I can find him anywhere he goes. And Li's totally serious. He's got a notebook filled with all the ways he can get away with murder. Serena's been trying to get her hands on it for years, but he thinks he's going to need it in the end. Probably for Guidry."

A chuckle came from a man in the back. Like his cohorts, he was gorgeous. Steph put his age at roughly thirty. Dark hair and deep blue eyes that seemed built to catch the stare of any woman around. "Definitely Guidry. But he should hurry. I'm fairly certain one of his women is going to take him out first."

The big Cajun rolled his eyes. "That will be the day."

"Nope, it's definitely going to be one of his one-night stands," the man in the back replied. "We voted him the bodyguard most likely to be the subject of a *Dateline* episode. Hey, Taggart, those lemon bars? Why don't you share?"

Taggart's face went a mottled red and he clutched the box close. "Not on your life. These are mine, Landon. You shouldn't have carbs at all. You think I don't see that pudgy midsection you're getting. Go back to working out."

Landon rolled those gorgeous blue eyes and stood, proving there was absolutely nothing pudgy about him. He strode forward, offering her a hand. "I'm Shane Landon. Former LAPD. I left LaLa land like Riley here for the land of heat and sarcasm. It's a pleasure to meet you, Doc. You are looking gorgeous as usual, Mrs. Taggart."

Charlotte gave him a dazzling smile. "Thank you. I try, you know." She looked back at her husband. "So when they try to steal your lemon bars, you defend them to the death, but your wife gets nothing?"

He clutched the box. "The lemon bars are completely defenseless. You are not. I trust you, baby. Any one of these guys tries something on you, you'll take 'em out. And I'll protect the lemon bars."

Charlotte groaned and faced Steph again. "The only two missing today are Wade Rycroft and Declan Burke. They both have assignments this afternoon, but you'll meet them at some point. As long as you're in Dallas, we'll have everyone taking shifts." She glanced down at her watch. "I've got a meeting in ten minutes. Remy, can you go over protocols with Dr. Gibson? Li wants someone with her when she's not in the building. She's staying at Li and Avery's."

That was something that had to change. "No. I don't want to impose on them anymore than I already have. I've got a little money saved. I can pay for a hotel."

Sadie, the receptionist she'd met earlier, strode through the door. "Ian, did you forget your four thirty? Because he didn't forget. He's here. Waiting for you."

Ian grimaced. "It's a corporate client. Tell him I died."

Sadie put her hands on her hips. "I got you the lemon bars. That corporate client pays us two million a year for security services. You take those lemon bars and talk to him, and you will be nice or I will sic your wife on you."

Charlotte slid an arm around the younger woman's shoulders. "Don't let me forget to thank Grace for sending you our way, hon. You are perfect."

Taggart sighed and seemed to know when he was beaten. "Women all ganging up on a man. What's the world coming to? And she's not perfect. We're out of coffee. I am going to fall asleep without coffee."

Charlotte joined him. "Sadie, can you please make a coffee run? I'll stop by the store and pick up a case for tomorrow. For this afternoon, the cart downstairs will do. Tell them he needs at least three shots of espresso to make it taste as harsh as he likes it. No sugar. He's got enough of that from the lemon bars. I don't want him overstimulated."

"Grace's niece is mean," Taggart was saying.

"She has to be, baby." Charlotte patted his back as they walked away. "It's the only way to survive you."

Sadie sighed. "It actually is my fault we ran out of coffee. I was supposed to pick it up this morning, but I got caught in traffic, so I'll make a quick run. You want anything?"

Remy Guidry put a hand on his chest. "Ms. Jennings, I would be forever in your debt if you would grab these guys some coffees. We need to get changed and then we can have an actual meeting with Dr. Gibson. Unfortunately, Charlotte likes to catch us working out. Most of the time we meet with clients in actual clothing. We try to be civilized."

"Except for Burke," Landon argued. "Nothing civilized about that asshole. He punched me in the face for asking about his back tattoo. What guy puts frilly angel wings on his back?"

"The type who punches hard," Blade replied. "Made the same mistake. Damn near broke my nose. I'm hitting the showers and then we can all sit down with the doc and figure out how and where we're going to protect her."

"And I will juggle a whole lot of coffee," Sadie said, her eyes grim with determination.

Remy nodded her way. "We'll meet you in fifteen, Doc."

They filed into the back of the gym through the door that led to the locker room.

"I'll come down with you." It wasn't like she had anything better to do. She could go up and watch Nate sleep, but she didn't want to disturb the nursery. Besides, she'd only been told to not leave the building. And she'd been wondering if Li wasn't right. She had panicked. She'd been afraid for her baby and she'd let Alfi feed into that.

It didn't make logical sense that a man would travel halfway around the world to enact vengeance on a woman he'd barely met, a woman who'd tried her hardest to help him. It was more likely that Liam was correct. The "boss" had panicked and tried to threaten her in order to make her work harder to save the man he'd probably shot himself.

Sadie gave her a grateful smile. "Thanks. They all want those super tall cups and when I have two trays, it's hard to hit the elevator buttons. The last time I tried it myself I got caught in the insurance firm on three's rush. They get out at a quarter to five, and let me tell you, I've never once seen an office empty that fast. They sprint out of here."

Maybe it would be okay to stay at Li and Avery's. She followed Sadie to the elevator, enjoying the easy chatter. She liked the people she'd met. Sadie talked about growing up in Waco and all the friends she had there. She'd gone to college and still kept up with her hometown people.

Steph hadn't talked to anyone from her quiet, upstate New York town in years and years. Not because they hadn't tried to reach out, but because it hurt too much. It hurt to watch them move on with their lives when she was stuck. Not career wise. Avery had taken care of that, but emotionally she hadn't truly moved on.

"A lot of my friends have moved into the military," Sadie was saying as they approached the small coffee cart. The smell of fresh ground coffee permeated the air even this late in the day. "Some of them are at Fort Hood. I'm kind of surrounded by military men, which is how I know I can't show Uncle Ian any fear. You have to be firm with the man and not put up with his shenanigans. Although it really does help if you have something tart to shove in his face."

Would she be around long enough to use that bit of information? "I'll keep that in mind."

She heard Sadie ordering from the barista, but her mind was on the talk with Avery the night before. Was it time to put down roots? Time to try to build something stable? Her clinic moved often. She went where she was needed, and sometimes she got kicked out by various officials who didn't like her helping the poor. It happened far too often. In the seven years she'd had her clinic, she'd moved six times. What kind of existence was that for Nate?

He would probably be an only child. If she moved here, he would have a group of kids to belong to. They might not be blood, but that didn't seem to matter to these people.

She could start a practice here. The poor didn't only exist in Third World countries. There was plenty of need right here in the States, especially in big cities with large pockets of uninsured and homeless people.

She could do good here and Nate could have a semblance of a family.

"You want anything?" Sadie asked.

"Sure. I could use a pick me up. How about a vanilla latte?" How long had it been since she'd had one of those? Her mouth kind of watered. If she lived here, she could go to restaurants and coffee bars. It was hard when the nearest city was thirty miles away and she didn't have a lot of backup.

She could eat and shop and have friends to do girly things with. She could maybe meet someone. Not the bodyguards. They were lovely to look at but she couldn't handle another big, glorious manly man. Nope. She would stick to her own kind. Find a nice doctor or a lawyer who spent more time in the courtroom than a gym. No more notched hips to distract her. No way.

"Doctor? Is there a doctor? I think my friend is having a heart attack!"

Steph looked over and there was a man in the doorway to the building. Several people were pulling cell phones, assuring the panicked man that they would have an ambulance here in no time at all.

But Steph knew any time was too long, especially when she was right here. She ran toward the man. He was in jeans and a T-shirt, his beard a bit ragged. "I'm a doctor. Where is he? Did he collapse?"

"Around the corner," the man said. "We were looking for the parking lot, but he collapsed onto the sidewalk."

She didn't even think about the fact that he wasn't moving to get in front of her, merely pointing her in the direction he wanted her to go. Her adrenaline was already up. People reacted in many different ways when confronted with medical emergencies.

Her mind was on what she would need to do.

ABC. Airway. Breathing. Circulation.

"Was he conscious when you left him?" She ran around the corner and stopped. No one was lying on the ground. They were on the far side of the building, the street blocked by large bushes that also cut the majority of the noise. There was a good three or four feet of grass that ran the length of the side of the building, and there was nothing at all but green.

And she was alone with the man who had run into the building.

She turned, hoping she was wrong.

Nope. Not wrong. The man she'd been trying to help was standing there, holding a gun aimed at her head.

"Hello, Dr. Gibson," the man said, his accent now strong. How had she not heard it before? "My boss would like to have a word with you."

She held up her hands and prayed she survived the next few moments.

* * * *

Brody stepped into the small locker room. It looked like even though this McKay-Taggart office didn't also house a club and living quarters, there was still space to work out. He was sure Taggart himself would call it the dog park and discuss the need for all the puppies to expend energy, or something equally obnoxious.

Liam was by his side. "Guidry? Is there a reason the office is empty?"

Even from where he was standing, Brody could hear that Cajun groan. He stepped out, his body covered only in a white towel wrapped around his waist. "We're getting dressed. Charlotte sprang the doc on us. We didn't think we were meeting with her. Honestly, I thought you would just tell us what we were going to do. I didn't realize the doc had a choice in the matter. I'm a little surprised.

81

You're quite bossy when it comes to your family."

"And that's why you live alone, Guidry," O'Donnell shot back. "You always let the woman think she has a choice. However, you'll find I recently emailed you a schedule for who will watch over her and when and where. I've also sent you protocols you're to follow, but I want you to chuck 'em right out the door."

Guidry's eyes narrowed. "Ah, you've decided this is serious. I got the feeling when you came in this morning that you weren't sure. What's happened in the meantime? And why the hell is the Aussie here? Shouldn't you be back in London?"

Oh, it was time to start letting the whole team know why the hell he was here. "She's my client. I'm running lead on this. You can look at what O'Donnell sent you all you like, but I'll be the one making the decisions when it comes to the doctor."

"Oh, really now?" O'Donnell asked.

"Really."

O'Donnell watched him for a second, but then he softened slightly. "You might find that a harder job than you think."

Probably. The new boyfriend might not like that someone she had a past with was trying to control the situation. He would deal with it. "It's my job, all the same."

"As it happens, I agree with you." O'Donnell turned back to Guidry. "Where is Steph? She isn't in the office, that I can see."

"I told her to wait in there," Guidry explained. "She was talking to Sadie when Shane, Riley, and I hit the showers. She can't have gone far. Maybe she walked back upstairs for a minute."

"She got in a lift with the pretty receptionist chick." Tucker walked in, glancing around at the new surroundings. "Hey, we've got something like this back in London."

"She got in a lift?" Then they were likely right and he needed to go back upstairs. When he got hold of her, he would tie her to a bloody chair and then she couldn't lead him on a merry chase. "I'll try to catch her upstairs. You wait down here. Ping my mobile if you see her first."

He started to turn to go.

Tucker shook his head. "I don't think she was heading up to the other floor. I was kind of wandering around because the cute receptionist actually has quite the bad attitude. I was surprised by that. I read somewhere that women who get employed in her position are generally hired for their welcoming natures. Not so with Sadie. She told me she would find a new home for her letter opener if I didn't stop touching her. I don't think she meant a new desk. I got the feeling she intended to use the letter opener for something painful."

Which proved that the bloke still had good instincts.

O'Donnell's shoulders squared. "You touched her?"

This was why he hadn't wanted to bring one of the lads with him. They weren't good in the real world yet, but they never would be if they didn't get out. He got that. It was up to him to protect the poor bastard until he understood enough of the world to get by on his own.

Brody stepped between O'Donnell and Tucker, trying to ward off what would likely be Tucker getting his arse handed to him. "Tucker, tell the nice Irishman why you were touching her and where."

Tucker was smart enough to stay behind him, but Brody could hear the confusion in the younger man's voice as he began to speak. "I was trying to hold her hand. I read in a book that the way to let a woman know you are truly listening to her is to hold her hand and look her in the eyes when you speak to her."

"Back off, O'Donnell," Brody warned. "He wasn't trying anything perverted. He simply doesn't understand how to behave. Every single thing the kid knows of the world he learned from a bloody book. He's basically a toddler."

O'Donnell seemed to deflate slightly. He looked at Tucker and there was something almost fatherly about him this time. "That kind of advice is for when you're dating a woman, not one you've recently met. It was unnerving for Sadie to have you suddenly holding her hand. Intimacy takes time. And stop reading books like that. You have questions, ask the other members of your team."

"The other members of my team don't know anything either," Tucker replied. "Though Sasha did tell me something about women who will sleep with you for money. I don't have any money. Could I borrow some money? It might be simpler that way. I don't seem to be good at attracting a woman myself."

O'Donnell's jaw dropped. "Is he serious? And you've got five of them?"

"Six, actually, though Robert hides it better than the rest of them. I think it's because he spent so much time with Theo Taggart." Or because, unlike the rest of them who were just horny bastards, Robert had a focus for his longing. He turned back to Tucker. "Let's hold off on the prostitutes for a bit. Where did Steph go?"

"Well, if she was the chick with the letter-opening-loving receptionist who broke my heart, then she went downstairs. I overheard them talking about coffee," Tucker explained. "Actually, I could use some. And all the talk about lemon bars made me hungry. Also, the danger made me hungry."

He nearly groaned. The bloke didn't understand danger yet.

"Sadie was doing a coffee run," Guidry explained. "We're out and being out of caffeine is a serious issue around here. It's okay though. The coffee cart is inside the building. They'll be back up here any minute. The building is perfectly safe. We train the guards. Hell, I'll call down there right now and let the guard on duty know to keep eyes on her. He'll let me know when she's coming back up, if she's not already."

He strode back into the locker room. Hopefully he'd put on some damn pants.

Brody turned back to O'Donnell. "I thought you were taking care of her. I didn't think you would let her run around wild. And where is that boyfriend of hers?"

"He's incredibly concerned about the boyfriend," Tucker offered helpfully. "He's got everyone back in London trying to run down information on the poor man."

"We need to know who's gotten close to the client." He sent Tucker a stare that should have made him think twice.

"I think it's about how close this dude is to the client, if you know what I mean." And there went Tucker's survival instincts.

"The rumor around our office is that Brody likes the doctor but hasn't figured out how to move things to the next level. I believe the next level is sex that happens more than once. Sex that occurs on a regular and much-needed human basis. You see, this is why I read those books. Damon doesn't want to talk to us about stuff like this. Nick screwed up and lost his girl for a long time before getting her back. Kay doesn't do relationships, and Brody is bad at them. Walt is as clueless as the rest of us, though he did offer to try to make personalized musks for each of us. I was reading a book on how animals attract mates."

Walt was an arsehole, and he would have those boys wearing yak urine as cologne and laughing his arse off about it. It might be funny if they wouldn't stink up the place.

"So you're worried about young Nate?" Liam's lips had curled into a slight smile.

"Just how young is he? One of our potentials was only nineteen." Had she gotten involved with a child? Somehow, he couldn't see it. She needed a strong man. She was a stubborn woman, smart and resourceful and pig-headed when she wanted to be. It would take a strong man to put his foot down when she tried to go headlong into danger.

"He's not nineteen, but he's certainly young," O'Donnell explained, his eyes lighter than before. "Seems nice enough, though he needs to keep it down at night. That was quite a racket he made. Our guest room is on the other end of the house from the master and I could still hear him."

Brody's fists clenched at the thought.

"See, he's doing a lot of things right now that many psychologists would call physical tells," Tucker said in a low voice. "Tight fists. Clenched jaw. His skin flushed. Now that could be a sign of anger or embarrassment or even sexual arousal. I don't think it's the third, though, because he seems pretty hetero to me."

"If you don't shut your trap, mate, I'll shut it for you." He should have come alone.

O'Donnell was laughing. "This is the best. I thought it would be a rough day, but this has definitely made it better. Maybe Tucker should stay here with us and irritate the shit out of Big Tag."

Tucker would be dead in a day. Or Big Tag would find him amusing and set him on everyone else.

Before Brody could foist Tucker off on the Dallas office, Remy strode back in and had every single bit of Brody's attention. He'd put on jeans, but hadn't bothered with shoes. He'd managed to throw on a shirt, but it was unbuttoned. None of that set off Brody's instincts the way the Browning pistol in the Cajun's hand did.

"We're on our way down," Guidry was saying into his phone. "Check the security footage. I want to know which way she went and who went with her. And block one of the elevators. I know it's quitting time, but I need one up here and dedicated to getting me down there ASAP. Lock out everyone but McKay-Taggart."

Brody's heart sped up. "What's happened?"

Two new men came out of the locker room. Riley Blade and Shane Landon, if he remembered correctly. Both men were carrying their sidearms. Unlike their boss, they'd managed to put on shoes, though both sported wet hair.

Guidry strode out, obviously expecting everyone to follow. He moved toward the lifts. "Approximately three minutes ago, someone walked into the lobby screaming that he needed a doctor."

"Bloody hell." There was no question in Brody's mind what Steph would do. It wouldn't matter that she was in danger. She would go anywhere, with anyone, if she thought she was needed.

Li had his mobile out, putting it to his ear as they made it to the lifts. "Steph? Pick up the phone. Damn it. She's not answering. I gave her a new phone this morning. I told her to keep it with her at all times."

"Which she wouldn't if she was doing CPR on someone," Blade pointed out. "I'm taking the stairs."

Guidry nodded and pointed to Landon. "Go with him. Hopefully we make it down first, but head out the minute you hit the floor."

"Well, I hadn't gotten to the cardio portion of my day," Landon said before taking off for the stairs.

Brody waited for the lift doors to open, cursing the fact that

Taggart had to have the best views.

That view could cost Steph her life.

"You know she really could be saving someone's life," Guidry pointed out. "Heart attacks do happen. The guards have called 911. We could be walking into a situation where we scare the crap out of someone who's barely holding on to life."

Brody shook his head. He trusted his gut. His gut said this was far too much of a coincidence to be real. "Nah, he found out where she was and he knew exactly how to get to her. He's probably had men watching for her."

"Then we'll pick them up on CCTV," Tucker said, sounding far more serious than he had all day. "We can send every face through the software and maybe we'll get a name."

"Good." His heart was racing, but it came to him in that moment that he'd made a mistake. A horrible mistake that he needed to correct as soon as possible.

When he got hold of her—please, please let her be alive—she would know who was in charge, and it wouldn't be some playboy kid.

He realized in that moment that he'd been so bloody wrong. She did need him. He'd thought all along that she was too smart for him. Nope. Not for a second. Her brain might be brilliant but it had not a single lick of common sense.

"I need you to understand that I'm done playing around, O'Donnell," he said under his breath as the lift doors finally opened. "That woman belongs to me and I intend to let her know."

Li pushed the button that would take them to the bottom of the building. "And I intend to sit back and see what happens. I need the man alive, Brody. If she's been taken, we have to try to not kill the fucker."

"No promises." If the man had laid a hand on her, he wasn't sure what he would do. Except that it would be brutal and painful.

She was his. It all fell into place. He'd been a damn moron to not see it.

The woman needed a keeper. He was nothing but a grunt who'd spent his whole life as cannon fodder, protecting men who were worth more than him.

She was everything to him. Why couldn't he be that for her? Why couldn't he spend the rest of his life protecting her?

He watched in tense silence as the floor number got smaller and smaller.

The doors opened and Brody ran out, hoping beyond hope that there was still time to save her.

Chapter Four

Steph held up her hands, a vision of her son playing through her head. What would happen to Nate if she died here? Brody didn't want him. His father wouldn't take him, but she knew deep in her heart that Avery and Li would welcome Nate into their home. How hard would it be for her baby boy? He wouldn't remember that she existed. How would they legally adopt him? He'd been born at her clinic. She had his birth certificate, but no other legal documents. God, what would happen if CPS took her baby because Avery couldn't prove she had the right to take care of him?

Was this her real punishment? To die not knowing if her child was safe? To die knowing the one man who should take care of him didn't care that he was alive?

"What do you want from me?" She had to ask the question. "You know there wasn't any way to save your friend. I did everything I could. He threw a clot and it caused a massive stroke. It sometimes happens after major surgery."

The man rolled his dark eyes. "I don't care what you did or didn't do for that fucker. I think we both know what my boss wants. The question is what happens to you before you get to my boss. I don't know that he cares about how I deliver you to him as long as I deliver you."

A cold chill went through her. How long did she have before the ambulance showed up? Would they look for her on the steps of the building? Would they search at all? Or suspect the call had been some kind of a joke?

How long would it be before Liam realized she wasn't coming back?

"Turn around and start walking." His voice was rough and she caught the hint of panic in his eyes when a siren started sounding in the distance.

She wasn't about to turn her back on him. If he was going to murder her, he could do it to her face.

"They're coming," she said, willing to play any card she got dealt. "I don't know if you understand how it works here in the States, but it won't only be an ambulance that shows up. The police will follow, too. And there are about twenty security cameras on the building."

"I am careful."

"No matter how careful you are, someone will remember you, and the minute I'm reported missing, my friends will paint your face across the media." She was pleased with how steady her voice was. Inside she was quaking like a leaf, but she forced herself to appear calm.

How far away was the sidewalk? The giant bushes would muffle much of the sound, but if she started screaming her head off, surely someone would hear.

"I'll be out of the country before they even realize you're gone," he promised. "Now move. The car is behind you. Don't think I won't shoot you. I will."

He was lying. Oh, he sounded like he meant business, but something about the way his eyes didn't quite meet hers told her that he wasn't going to pull that trigger. Why? Did the "boss" want to kill her himself? Her dead body wasn't good enough? He needed to see her pain?

She saw a shadow move behind her would-be attacker.

Steph caught her breath as Sadie turned the corner. Quietly and with purpose, the receptionist moved across the grass. There was something in her hands, but Steph couldn't tell what. She shook her head, silently pleading with the other woman to run. She couldn't get Sadie killed. She couldn't handle more blood on her hands.

"Don't shake your head at me," the man commanded. "Move. You're going to get in that car on your own or I'll drag you there." He shifted his gun slightly down. "You can get into the car without a bullet in your leg or with one. This is your choice. You have five seconds to make it."

"Hey!" Sadie yelled.

The man turned instinctively, and Sadie tossed two massive travel cups of coffee right at his face. The man screamed, dropping the gun and covering his scalded skin with his hands.

Steph decided right then and there that she wasn't even going to help him. New rule. When someone tried to kidnap her, they gave up all rights to her skills as a doctor.

Sadie pushed the screaming man, making room for Steph to run her way. "Let's go."

She had no idea whether or not one of his cohorts was about to show up or if they would leave him behind. She started jogging, gripping Sadie's hand.

"Thank god the run was for the boys," Sadie said, glancing back over her shoulder. "The women like Frappuccinos and iced coffees in the afternoon. That wouldn't have worked as well. Oh, no. Duck."

A shot cracked and Steph felt something burn and sizzle over her left bicep.

"Stephanie!" A booming masculine voice shouted her name.

"I'm here!" They were almost to the end. Almost out. If he was going to shoot her now, there would be witnesses.

And apparently someone was looking for her.

She clutched Sadie's hand, her arm burning as they ran around the side of the building and back into the bright afternoon light.

Which was suddenly blocked when a massive figure stepped in front of her.

Brody Carter frowned down at her. "Do you have any idea how much trouble you're in, luv?"

Her head started to spin and Steph wasn't surprised when her vision receded and the world went dark. Just before she slipped to the ground, strong arms picked her up and she was safe.

She let the darkness take her.

* * * *

Brody managed to get an arm around her before her body fell to the concrete.

What the hell had happened to her? He shoved his gun into his holster and hoisted her up. "Steph?"

Liam was already taking charge. "I'll go in the front. Brody, get her and Sadie upstairs. If the police get here, they'll want to take her in for questioning and we'll lose control. I'll handle the police when they show up."

"He shot at us," Sadie said, her eyes wide. "I think Steph got hit."

Brody felt bile rise. Had he been too rough with her? He hadn't seen any blood. What if he was making it worse?

Liam was already moving into the narrow alley formed between the bushes and the wall.

Tucker examined her arm. "It's a graze. It barely burned her shirt. We should go. Those sirens are almost here. Unless you want to turn everything over to the police."

Tucker knew damn well he wouldn't do that. She hadn't gone to the police. She'd come to McKay-Taggart.

She hadn't come to him.

It didn't matter. He had to get her inside and away from prying eyes. Luckily, it seemed despite the chaos of moments before, the men and women in the building had gone back to their regularly scheduled afternoon evacuation.

"Come on," Sadie said. "I know a back way. We'll take the freight elevator. I know the code."

"What happened?" It seemed surreal that she was in his arms. So pale and fragile. She'd gained a bit of weight and it looked good. Still, there was something delicate about her.

"We were getting coffee when this guy comes in, yelling about how his friend is dying." Sadie opened the door and pointed to the small hallway to the left.

He moved quickly, feeling curious eyes on him. He hoped these people were more interested in getting home than figuring out why he was carrying a passed out woman away from the incoming sirens.

Tucker jogged ahead, turning the corner and checking out the hall. He'd kept a cool head to this point. Cooler than Brody's. "We're clear. Let's go."

"You can continue," he said to Sadie. She was the only one right now who could tell him what had happened. Steph had been all alone with no one but a receptionist to defend her. That was going to change.

Sadie strode forward toward the big industrial-looking lift. "I was paying for the coffee when I heard the commotion. I had my hands full when I saw Steph running out with the man. She's a doctor. I get it, but I didn't think that was entirely safe and when I saw her go into that creepy alleyway, I knew I had to follow her."

"Or you could have called on the people who know what they're doing," Tucker replied.

Sadie waved that piece of advice off as she punched in the code that opened the lift doors. "That would have wasted valuable time. Also, I know procedures. The guards informed Remy, who's in charge of actual building security for the company. Remy must have called Li. So I would have wasted a phone call."

The doors opened and he swept Steph inside. She was limp in his arms. Were they sure she didn't need a doctor?

Her eyes fluttered open. "What happened? Where...? Brody?"

Sadie pushed the button and the lift started to rise. "You're on your way back up to the McKay-Taggart office. You thought you were going to save a man, but he turned out to be a massive tool. He pulled a gun on you. I had to leave a full tray of coffee behind, but I was carrying the last two when I followed you. It was a good thing, too. I threw both scalding cups of coffee in his face and we got away. You passed out when you saw this big guy. There. You're all updated."

Tucker frowned. "You threw coffee at that man?"

"Well, I didn't have time to get to my pistol, so I used what I had," she replied. "And that is the last time I don't grab my purse. Everyone told me when I hit the big city there would be plenty of times to use my gun. It's pink. Goes with everything."

Tucker took a step back.

Steph started wriggling, as though trying to find her balance. "Where did he go? Did he get away? He said there was a car waiting for me."

It nearly sent a shudder through him. They'd had a car waiting, and if Sadie hadn't been incredibly brave, Stephanie would have been tossed in a trunk and would be speeding away to god only knew where.

He could have lost her and all because he was a stubborn wanker.

"Just relax," he ordered. It was past time that he took charge. "You can tell us the whole story when we get upstairs. I'm sure Big Tag and O'Donnell will want to hear about it, too."

"Li? Does Li know?" Steph asked. "We don't have to tell him. He would worry."

"Oh, he knows. You'll be lucky if I don't tell him you thought he didn't need to know. He's down there right now, taking care of the problem," Brody explained.

She tried to sit up. "But he could get hurt."

He tightened his arms around her, gently easing her back down. "He's a big boy. He can handle himself and he's got plenty of backup. You are another thing entirely, and we're going to have a long talk about your behavior when all this is over."

"You can let me down now." She'd gone still and now the confusion seemed to flee, replaced with that stubborn look she often got when she wouldn't be moved on something. "I can walk on my own."

"You're hurt. You nearly got shot. We have to take a look at your arm when we get upstairs." He didn't want to let her go. He had no idea how long it would take to get her back into his arms again, so he was going to enjoy the brief moments he had. "And you passed out."

"Well, I had a shock to the system," she shot back. "Sometimes that's the body and the brain's way of saying they've had enough and need to recuperate. But I'm fine now. Though I am wondering why you're here. Shouldn't you be in London?"

"I called your phone and some bastard answered," he replied. She should know how dangerous the situation was and that he was fully intent on taking care of it for her. "He wouldn't give me his name, but I suspect he's this 'boss' person you told Li about."

"He has my phone," she said a little forlornly. "I just managed to pay off that phone and it had minutes still on it."

"Bastard." Sadie seemed good at knowing how to support her friend. Unlike Tucker.

"He told me he was going to kill you and that boyfriend of yours if he didn't get what he wanted." Brody felt the lift moving beneath his feet.

"Boyfriend?" Steph asked, her face clouded with obvious confusion.

Had she hit her head during the fight?

"He's extremely concerned about your boyfriend. Has the whole team working on the issue." Tucker couldn't seem to get off the subject. They were going to have a long talk about what it meant to back a partner up. "You know, the one named Nathan. We don't have a last name. Could you supply us with one? It would be very helpful."

Her eyes went wide and for a moment he thought she might pass out again.

"Oh, that's not her boyfriend," Sadie began. "How can you not..."

Steph shook her head, cutting Sadie off. "He is no one you should concern yourself with."

Her voice had gone cold. Her body had stiffened and he knew they were going to fight it out over the new guy. Was she in love with him? It seemed like yesterday that she'd been all over him and now she'd given her heart to another guy?

"And yet I'm going to concern myself with him," he replied just as coldly.

"Let me down right now, Brody. Or I swear you'll walk into that office with me screaming my head off."

He wanted to argue with her, but he knew that look. She was sweet ninety-nine percent of the time, but when she got truly mad, it was a sight to behold. He eased her down. "Look, I know you have reason to be angry with me, but we're going to talk, you and I. And whatever boyfriend you've dragged along with you is definitely my concern."

She shook her head. "You don't even remember his name."

"Of course I do. It's Nate." He wasn't sure how to handle her. The anger pouring off her seemed a bit much. Was she truly so angry that he hadn't returned her phone calls? He had a lot of making up to do. He tamped down his own irritation. He needed to be calm with her. He was the one who had transgressed. She was in the right.

"He definitely knows the man is named Nate because he's had everyone at the London office looking into him," Tucker replied. "Again, a last name would be helpful."

Steph looked back at him. "His last name is Fuck Off."

"An odd name," Tucker mused. "Does he know that his name is also a curse? Does this get him into trouble? We have to choose last names soon and I think FuckOff would do well for several of my brothers. It would be fitting for them."

"Ignore him," Brody said. "Steph, I know I've been stubborn, but I had my reasons. I'd like to explain them to you. Why don't we sit somewhere and talk for a bit?"

The doors opened. Steph strode out, moving toward the office. "Why don't you head straight back to London? I don't need you and neither does Nate."

Sadie turned to him as well, her face flushed and eyes flashing. "You should be happy I don't have the rest of those coffees because I might be tempted to use them on you, sir. You are a jerk."

He stood and watched the women stomp down the hallway toward the big glass doors that led to the lobby of McKay-Taggart.

"I'm glad I didn't make headway with the redhead," Tucker

said with a nod. "She seems very violent. I'm looking for more of a nonviolent female."

"Good luck." He followed the women out into the hall. "You won't find many of those here."

Steph strode through the door that led into the lobby and he realized if he didn't catch up to her, she might lock herself in an office with that boy toy of hers and refuse to come out.

He walked in, stalking her like a predator. She would find out that she couldn't lose him. Yes, he was tired and cranky, but they were going to have that conversation and she would see that he meant to do things right this time. They'd lost a year, but he could summon up a bit of charm. He would make her see that he was ready to try with her. He could soften her heart. He knew he could.

"Steph, we need to go to the conference room. We have to get everything you can remember down on paper. I need to know every single thing he said to you, everything you can recall about what he looked like," he called out.

She turned down a hall that most certainly did not go to the conference room.

Sadie settled in behind her desk. "I'll call everyone in. Ian's in a meeting but he'll be thrilled we nearly got murdered because it means he can cut it short. For a man who makes his money off corporate clients, he really hates them."

"And get Adam on pulling the CCTV footage." He wanted a face. If he had a face, he would be one step closer to a name. "Steph, I'm not joking. Come on. This is serious."

She merely kept walking, her right arm in the air and middle finger extended.

"That's rude," Tucker commented. "At least that's what everyone tells us when we use that gesture. I thought it was comical in all the movies I've seen it used in."

Steph turned and walked through a door, disappearing from sight. Here it was, the moment he'd been dreading. He was going to meet the competition, the younger, likely less scarred rival who liked to flirt with other women when his girlfriend wasn't around.

There wasn't anything else to do but get the damn introductions over and let the young man know what he thought about how he took care of his girl.

He stopped at the doorway, realizing where she'd gone.

Brody stopped because she wasn't walking into one of the offices, or even the break room. She walked into the large conference room they'd turned into a nursery. He found himself standing on the threshold of a room covered in toys and cribs. Two girls who looked an awful lot like Charlotte Taggart were sitting at a tiny table coloring. A couple of toddler boys were giggling and pushing toy cars along the floor. There was a nursery worker with a tiny baby in her arms, rocking in a rocking chair while she patted the baby's back.

And Steph was standing over a crib.

"He's been such a sweetheart," the second of the nursery workers was saying. "He woke up a couple of minutes ago and he doesn't fuss at all. He's probably ready for a bottle though. He's been trying to eat his own foot. Are you okay? Something happened to your shirt."

He felt like his feet were nailed to the floor. Like he couldn't move at all. What was going on?

Why was she here? The answer played around in his head and made him the tiniest bit ill.

Or a lot queasy. Yeah, it was more like a lot.

"It's nothing to worry about. I'm fine. I just need to see him," she said as she leaned over and picked up whatever was in the crib.

A baby. A freaking baby was in the crib, his inner voice was screaming. A baby. She lifted the baby up. A big baby. A big boy baby. He was wearing one of those blue shirt things mums put their infants in. It snapped together under his nappy. He had white socks on his pudgy baby feet.

Brody had seen that child before. He'd seen him at home, in pictures his mum kept on the walls.

"Nate?" His voice sounded tiny to his ears.

She turned and rolled her eyes. "Yes, I believe I told you in the voice mails I left that I was naming him Nathan. That's his name. Nathan Avery."

Her voice mails. The ones he hadn't listened to. The ones he'd callously deleted so he wouldn't be tempted by her. The voice mails where she told him she was having their child.

"Uh, Brody, you just went super white," Tucker pointed out. "It is not a good look on you. You okay?"

Nope. Not at all. He felt light-headed and he couldn't quite make his feet move. What had he done?

"Did I miss the big reveal?" Adam Miles showed up, a can of soda in his hand. "Damn it. I wanted popcorn to go with the show. Yeah, that's your son, you dumbass. Whoa. Uh, I take it back. Do you need some sugar or something?"

The world spun and Brody felt himself falling. Right on Adam Miles.

He heard Steph cursing, but he was the one passing out this time.

The world blinked out and he found momentary peace.

Chapter Five

"Your ribs are fine," a feminine voice was saying as Brody started to come out of the haze. "Your arm is not broken. I think if you hold a cold pack to your wrist it should be fine by morning."

"No, I can tell that something is broken. I had four hundreds pounds of Australia fall on top of me. I have to have nearly died," Miles whined. "I'm sure he broke my spleen."

He felt a hand on his wrist, soft fingers sliding over to check his pulse.

"Brody? Can you open your eyes?" Steph's voice was strong and clear. The voice of a doctor taking over out in the field.

He opened his eyes, blinking at the lights. What had happened? "I'm fine. I must have fallen."

She frowned down at him. "You fainted."

"You tried to kill me," Miles accused. "You were like a mountain of pain falling on me."

"Good, you arsehole." Brody struggled to his feet. He needed to eat something. It had been roughly twenty-four hours since he'd eaten a damn thing and it was catching up to him.

Then he remembered where he was. "I want to see him."

Steph held a hand out. "Why don't we go talk?"

So she could put him off? "I want to see him. Or are you going to deny that's my child? Because I can get a DNA test very quickly."

"I never once denied it," she replied. "I left you several messages concerning the fact that I was pregnant. I believe I threatened you with lawyers."

"I didn't listen to the messages and I damn straight didn't get any messages from a lawyer. Did you try anything else? Why the hell didn't you come to see me?"

Steph leaned over and gently kissed the baby, who was now being held in the nursery worker's arms, a bottle lodged firmly in his mouth. When Steph glanced back up, there was a steely look in her eyes. "Out, Mr. Carter. We can have this discussion but I'm not doing it in front of the kids. I'm not going to scare them."

He looked around and the older kids were watching him with wary eyes. The Taggart twins were staring up at him like they were ready to jump into action if needed.

He took a step back. "All right, but we do need to talk. Tucker, go find something to do."

Tucker nodded and started down the hall toward the kitchen.

Steph led the way out after assuring Miles that getting a knee jammed into his crotch didn't necessarily mean he could no longer have children.

Bastard.

Steph walked into an office, Li's office. Brody followed and closed the door behind him. They were alone for the first time in a year.

She'd had his baby.

"You didn't even listen to the messages?"

He sighed. "I was afraid I would give in if I heard your voice."

"Give in to what?" Steph asked, obviously exasperated. "You act like I'm some kind of temptress. I asked you to sleep with me once. I agreed to all your conditions. If I hadn't gotten pregnant I would never have called you again."

That hurt more than he'd like. And it was perverse. He'd wanted to disconnect with her and yet the idea that she didn't want him made him ache inside.

She shook her head, leaning against the desk. "Don't. You don't get to look hurt. I was honoring your wishes. You didn't want me to call. I wouldn't have called unless there was an emergency. You couldn't even find out if something was happening to me. That's how little you cared."

"That's not true."

"Oh, the evidence would say differently, Mr. Carter."

He had to get through that wall. "Stop calling me that, Steph."

"I'll call you whatever I like," she replied. "You wanted a polite relationship, this is what you get. We ceased being Brody and Steph the minute you decided to ignore my calls. And don't you dare tell me I should have done more. You want me to show up on your doorstep? With what? I barely had enough cash to get out when someone was trying to kill me. I wasn't wasting what I had on a man who didn't care. And I certainly never dreamed you felt so little for me that you would erase my voice mails."

God, he was in it up to his neck now. "That's not why I did it, luv. It was the opposite. I felt too much for you."

Her eyes rolled. "Yes, that's why you haven't reached out at all in a full year. Well, I feel better."

"The minute I thought you were in danger, I flew here. Doesn't that say something?"

"It's too little too late." She crossed her arms and winced slightly.

No one had even checked her out. Things had moved quickly, and then he'd been a dumb arse and passed out at the sight of his son. God, he had a son. "Let me see your arm."

"I'm fine."

"I said, let me see your bloody arm," he repeated, his voice low. He wasn't going to take no for an answer. Not this time. He'd fucked up horribly, but he was going to take care of her now. A year couldn't have changed the heat between them. A year hadn't changed his feelings for her. For an unknown reason, this woman had wanted him once before. He could find that magic again if he stayed close to her.

Suddenly, staying close to this woman was his main mission in life.

She shrugged out of the plaid shirt she wore, revealing a plain white sleeveless T-shirt underneath. She often wore layers. He could remember vividly sitting up in bed a few days after they'd met and thinking about how nice it would be to peel back those layers of clothing and get down to her skin, to unwrap her like the gift she was.

"See, it's nothing more than a graze," she said, holding her arm out.

He moved behind her because the red line where the bullet had grazed her seemed to start at the back of her arm. He held her in one big hand, gently running a thumb over the raised scratch. "Still needs to be cleaned."

He reached over and grabbed a tissue from the box on Liam's desk, soaking it with the hand sanitizer the Irishman kept by a picture of his kid. She was perfectly still as he touched the cleaner to her wound, though he couldn't miss the hiss that came from her mouth.

"Sorry, but if you think you need better care, I can take you to an ER," he promised.

"I think we're avoiding the ER. Liam doesn't want the police to get involved," she replied, her whole body stilling as he leaned over and blew across the wound, trying to cool the heat from the alcohol. "Li doesn't have a lot of faith that they can handle something like this. They don't have the kinds of contacts in Africa that McKay-Taggart has."

She seemed fragile. Despite the weight she'd gained, she was still dainty compared to him. He could wrap his hand nearly all the way around her arm. This was why he'd been reluctant to touch her at first. He was a hulking beast and she the fairy princess who deserved a prince.

"Are you sure there's nothing else wrong?" Brody asked quietly.

"Besides the fact that I'm tired and I've barely slept because I'm terrified a maniac is going to kill me and my son? I'm great."

He put his hands on her shoulders. She always held her tension there. How many nights had he run his hands along her shoulders, rubbing until she finally relaxed? It had served as a way to quell the deep need to touch her. He let his thumbs slide along the rigid muscles, satisfied at the way she sighed.

"I came as soon as I found out you were in trouble. I don't intend to leave. I'm going to take care of this for you."

"It's fine, Brody. I'm hiring bodyguards and Li is sure that they'll figure out how to handle this man."

"What does he want from you?" He wanted to talk about Nate. Desperately. He wanted to know everything about the kid, but she was talking to him, allowing him to touch her. He wasn't about to stop. They would have plenty of time to talk later.

"I don't think he wants anything but revenge." Her voice was softer now.

He would rather keep that sweet voice of hers softening up. He knew how to do it. She melted when he touched her, responded like no woman ever had to him. But that would have to wait. Li would be back any moment and they needed to solve the problem.

"That's not how he sounded on the phone. He wanted something. He said he knew what you had and he would get it back one way or another." He'd thought about those words over and over again. He'd carefully typed them into his phone so he would have notes on the conversation.

Her shoulders were tight again and she moved away from him. "I didn't take anything except Nate. I barely had time to shove a can of formula in his diaper bag. I left my phone behind, my laptop, everything except my purse. I had to buy clothes and a small suitcase when I got to Guinea. I only did that because I knew there would be questions about a woman traveling to the States without a suitcase."

"That was smart." He kept his voice low and soothing despite the fact that he wanted to shout a million questions at her, wanted to drag her back into his arms. "They likely would have questioned you and that would have cost you time."

"Well, I didn't actually think of it. Alfi did," she replied. "He's another Aussie, believe it or not. I can't seem to find a security guy who wasn't born in Oz."

Alfi. Bloody Alfi. Oh, he should have known better than to

think Alfi could do one favor for him. "What did he do?"

"The boss? I don't want to go through this again, Brody. I'm tired."

"I meant that wanker Alfi Dauterre."

She was quiet for a moment and then her jaw dropped. "How did you... Of course. You sent him. I should have known he was too good to be true when he showed up two weeks after you left and wanted nothing but room and board." Her hands went to her hips. "And you say you had no idea about Nate? Alfi knew. And by the way, if you sent him to take your place, sorry, I turned him down. I'd had enough larger-than-life Aussie sex for a lifetime."

"He did what?" Brody felt his fists at his sides again. "He tried something with you?"

The door opened and Liam stood there. "What's going on? Carter, if you lay a hand on her..."

Steph waved the notion off. "He's not going to hit me. He's pissed that his plan to foist me off on someone else didn't work." She frowned as though something had just occurred to her. "Or maybe it did. You know Alfi could be Nate's bio dad. Maybe you're off the hook."

"Don't you even pretend that boy ain't mine," he growled back. "Don't try me right now, luv. I'm not capable of handling it the way I should. Or maybe it *would* be the way I should. You always were interested in D/s, weren't you? You keep pushing me and you'll find out what it means to be my sub."

Steph started to open her mouth.

Li put a hand out. "Don't. He's been pushed enough, darlin'."

"I thought you were on my side."

Liam turned to her. "Have you figured out that he's a dumb bastard who didn't know about the boy?"

"Like that matters," she shot back. "It means nothing. He didn't care enough to even listen to my voice mails. And according to him, he sent Alfi to take his place. Did you think if I started sleeping with Alfi that I would leave you alone? Seriously? You are one of the most arrogant men I've ever met."

"He's not arrogant at all and that's part of the problem," Liam said, holding the door open. "And I doubt he sent someone to take his place in your bed."

"I bloody well didn't, and when I get my hands on him, he'll find out how little I thought of his help," Brody said between clenched teeth. "He was my friend. We grew up in the same town, went into SASR together. The bastard was supposed to tell me if she needed anything. I sent him to watch over her because I couldn't."

"Wouldn't," Li corrected.

He wasn't going to argue the point now. "He didn't bother to tell me she was pregnant and now I find out he tried to sleep with her. I'll kill him."

"He also managed to get her out of there before she got killed." O'Donnell seemed determined to be the voice of reason. "Now, we're wanted in the conference room. There have been a couple of developments and Big Tag wants to talk about how we proceed."

"I don't want him here," Steph said, her arms crossed over her chest.

O'Donnell's jaw firmed and he pointed her way. "Then you shouldn't have made a baby with the bastard. He is here. He is Nathan's da and you've got to deal with that. Unless Carter doesn't want the boy."

"I want him." He spat the words out as quickly as he could. There would be no doubt as to whether or not he wanted the child. That boy wouldn't spend another day without his father in his life. "I didn't think I was good enough for Steph, but none of that matters now."

"So you're not good enough for me, but you're good enough for Nate?" Steph asked, sarcasm dripping.

"No, I'm not good enough for him, but I got no choice. I'll make myself better. He's my son and I got no choice but to change and be the kind of man he can be proud of. I ain't leaving him. I ain't gonna be my dad."

Her eyes closed and when they opened, they were softer than before. "Of course I want you to be able to see him. You are his father." She sighed and looked back to Liam. "All right. Let's get this done. I need to find a place to stay tonight."

"You'll stay with me." It was said in stereo. Brody hadn't meant to be in tune with O'Donnell, but they managed to say the same thing.

Steph threw her hands up and strode out the door.

O'Donnell shook his head. "You're in trouble, mate."

Like he didn't already know that.

* * * *

Steph eased into her chair and realized she'd made a horrible mistake. She hadn't taken the empty chair between Charlotte Taggart and Adam Miles. She'd decided to sit across from them and that left a chair open on either side of her.

Not for long. Brody sat down beside her, moving the chair closer to hers.

Why did he have to look so damn good? When she'd run around the corner and nearly knocked into him, all she'd been able to think about was that he looked like safety and home all rolled into one gorgeous man package.

I ain't leaving him. I ain't gonna be my dad.

She wasn't going to think about how easily her heart had softened. She'd heard him talking about how he would be a better man for Nate's sake and much of her rage had drained.

He couldn't love her, but if he could love their son, she had to give him the chance to. She had to try to at least be friendly with him.

Remy Guidry strode in with Riley Blade and Shane Landon at his back. "We've handled the police. Told them it was some prankster trying to pull one over on the doc. They were happy to let us deal with it internally."

Because they had a million things to do. If they thought for a second it wasn't serious, the police would move on to real problems.

Of course, they couldn't know how real her problem had become.

"I don't understand why I'm needed in this meeting." Sadie was being herded into the conference room by a steely-eyed Liam.

She knew that look. They were in a whole lot of trouble.

"You're here because I asked Li to invite you, Sadie." Ian Taggart sat at the head of the table, leaning back and looking way more intimidating than he had when he'd been hoarding his sweets. There was no glint in his eyes now. The blue had turned an icy color. "Please sit down. We're going to have a talk. You might not be my niece by blood, but you are family because Grace is my family."

Sadie frowned and sank into the chair on the other side of Steph. "And I love my aunt and uncle."

"Then why do you seem intent on giving them both freaking heart attacks? You do understand that I have to tell my brother what happened here today. I can't get around it." Ian stood, leaning over the table a bit like a cobra waiting to strike. "Coffee? You went after a known killer with two cups of frigging coffee?"

Damn that man was scary when he wanted to be. Even Sadie shrank back a bit.

"It was all I had," Sadie replied.

"Where the hell was the damn pistol I made sure you knew how to use?" Ian asked.

She winced. "I didn't take my purse because it's heavy."

Charlotte sighed. "That was the wrong answer, hon."

"I'll make sure your damn purse is easy for you to carry then," Ian said. "We'll go through it together. You and me. We can dump all the frilly girly shit. Or better yet, Remy, I believe Sadie will be joining you for afternoon workouts from now on. Pay special attention to her shoulders so she can carry her damn bag around."

"Have ya heard the term too stupid to live, you two?" Li joined in, standing next to Ian.

This was what it meant to have an overbearing dad. Yeah, she hadn't had one of those. Her dad had been laid back, allowing her mom to do most of the work. She'd had a mom who'd believed in logic and quiet discussion.

"I am not too stupid to live," Sadie shot back, her former fear seeming to evaporate. "I knew exactly what I was doing. I snuck up on him and made sure he didn't take Stephanie, and now you can totally ID him because he's going to need medical attention. Unless one of the big bad boys managed to catch him."

There was a whole lot of silence from the boys.

Li and Big Tag looked at each other for a moment and then Ian sighed.

"Adam, start checking the ERs." He pointed a finger Sadie's way. "You don't get caught without a gun again. I am responsible for you until your uncle can marry you off. I'm helping him find a list of qualified candidates and everything."

"That'll be the day," Sadie replied, more chipper now. "Now, it's after hours and I have my own things to take care of. I've already typed up a whole report on how everything went down and I think you'll find that it's more detailed than anyone else's. So I think I was good in the field."

"Absolutely not." Ian shook his head in pure horror. "I am not telling my brother that I made his niece an operative."

She stood up and straightened out her skirt. "Someday. Now, I have work to do. Let me know if you need anything else."

Sadie winked her way before she walked out.

Ian slumped into his seat. "That girl is going to kill me. It was easier when Grace was here. She ran the office and didn't once try to take out the bad guys all on her own. I don't understand this generation."

Charlotte smiled. "I view it as practice for our own girls. They'll be way worse than Sadie. Now that the men have stopped yelling, are you all right, Steph?"

"I'm fine." Except for the fact that her biggest mistake was sitting beside her.

Could she trust him with Nate? It wasn't Brody's fault that he couldn't love her. She had to throw away all her anger with him when it came to their son. He hadn't known. He'd been a bastard, but he seemed to want to know Nate.

Could she leave Nate with him while she hid? She was worried about Nate being around her, though the idea of being apart made her heart hurt.

"I'm glad, but you can't do that again," Charlotte said. "I

understand that before we believed the situation might be fluid, but we have solid evidence now and I have to ask you to reconsider your position. There is a hefty bounty on you on the Dark Web."

Her stomach churned but she managed to stay upright. This asshole was offering people money to take her out? Had they put Nate's life up for sale, too? It seemed surreal. Even with what had happened this afternoon, it was hard to reconcile with reality. "For my head?"

"Not bloody likely." Brody's hand slid over hers, warming her skin. "You need to understand no one is going to allow that to happen."

She forced herself to pull away when all she really wanted was to crawl up into his lap and wrap herself around him and beg him to save her, to save their son. But that was a reality she'd accepted long before.

Ian Taggart leaned forward, his elbows hitting the table. "The good news is they want you alive."

"I think he wants to torture me himself." And not the fun torture. No, this would be pain and horror and eventually death.

Did she deserve that? Had the universe merely granted her a reprieve from the pain she deserved for that night when she'd taken lives instead of saving them?

"I don't think that's his point. When I talked to the bastard he said Steph had something he wanted and he was willing to let Nate go if she came in," Brody said. "He wanted to bargain with her. Now that doesn't mean he won't kill her. I won't have her used as bait or a bargaining chip."

He might say that, but she had to seriously consider it. It wouldn't do a lick of good to mention it here though. "I don't know what they think I have to give them."

"That's what we need to figure out." Ian sat back. "I'm hoping that finding out the bastard's name will help point us in the right direction. We've got a few feelers out on the Dark Web. We'll see if we can get someone talking."

"I've already pulled CCTV footage. Hopefully we'll get a face from our would-be kidnapper today if he chooses not to seek medical attention. But I do have a couple of questions that might help. Did the man you were working on pass anything to you?" Adam asked. "Did he say anything at all?"

"He was unconscious when he was brought in," she said, her voice going a flat monotone. She hated thinking about this. Hated everything about it. When she closed her eyes she could see the boss's face, the cruel hard glint in his eyes as he promised to end her. "He had a GSW to the upper right quadrant. I was forced to resection part of his liver and take out his spleen. The operation took approximately three hours. The patient required three liters of blood. Luckily, I had some on hand. He was O positive. I keep that and A pos on hand at all times. He did have a cardiac arrest on the table, but I was able to get the heart functioning again. When I left him, the patient was critical but stable."

"I'm not talking about the operation," Adam said quietly. "I'm talking about before and after the operation. What do you remember about that? Can you tell us anything about him as a person and not a patient?"

She shook her head. "It all happened so fast. I don't remember much. I remember a lot of yelling and one of my nurses was crying. I have two. One fled when she realized what was happening. It was protocol. She was responsible for the kids. We had a small group of pediatric patients. Luckily no one was critical. Uhm, two broken arms and a case of strep throat. She would have walked them to the nearest village. It's about a mile east of the clinic. The children were mostly from that village. They should be safe."

Adam was taking notes. "Excellent. We'll see if we can find her and ask if she remembers anything. What happened to your other nurse?"

Anya Shadrova. God, what had happened with Anya? Guilt pressed on her. Stephanie had fled, terrified for her son. She'd spoken briefly to the young nurse from Ukraine before she got into the car, but Anya hadn't left with them. She'd been all of twenty-four and filled with a need to do good in the world.

Had she gotten Anya killed?

"Anya wouldn't leave the clinic. She stayed with me and

assisted on the procedure. She remained with the patient to monitor him overnight. That was the last time I saw her. That was roughly two o'clock in the morning. I went to sleep and my security head woke me up. The patient had died and he thought we needed to get out of there very quickly. I don't honestly know that I could have saved him even if I'd been in a modern facility."

"What do you remember about the patient?" Charlotte asked.

She closed her eyes and tried to remember. She tried to envision him alive, but all she could see was that shell of a body on the table, the one she hadn't been good enough to save. "He was male, mid- to late-forties. Dark hair. I estimate his weight at one hundred seventy pounds and his height as a little shy of six feet. His skin was a sallow, yellow color indicating jaundice and probably liver damage. I believe that was from the wound. I estimate he'd been shot over eight hours before he was brought to me."

Charlotte held up a hand. "No. No medical terms. Remember everything you can. What was he wearing?"

Frustration swelled, a wave threatening to crest over and drown her. "Clothes. Bloody, torn up clothes."

She hadn't been sure of what color his shirt had been. It had been soaked in blood.

"Hey, I think she needs a break." Brody leaned forward. "She's had a hell of a day. Can we take this up tomorrow?"

"Will she be able to remember tomorrow?" Taggart asked, his eyes narrowed on Steph. "I think we're dealing with a serious case of PTSD. Or she's potentially blocking the information because it's too painful. I'd like you to let Kai put you under hypnosis and walk you through the day."

Walk her through? Walk her through what had been one of the most horrifying days of her life? She shook her head. "I'll try to remember on my own."

"Stephanie, we need to know everything we can," Li said, his voice soft. "I'm worried something's happened at the clinic."

At her clinic? "He came after me. Why would he do something to the clinic?"

"Not the clinic, exactly," Ian said. "It's still standing, but drone footage shows something that concerned me. Our London office had a drone do a couple of flybys, and I found the pictures it took a bit disturbing."

"What?" She had to see them. Tension twisted her spine, her hands curling into fists. What had happened? What had her cowardice cost someone else? "Do you have the pictures?"

"That's not for you to worry about," Li said.

Ian passed her his tablet. "Scroll through the footage. The photo that's worrisome is at the end. The London office isolated the problem areas. Thanks for the heads up, Carter, but until the moment she fires us, this is an American op. I've already talked to Damon and he's forwarding everything to me. As far as I'm concerned, you're nothing more than a friend lending my client support."

Brody had stiffened beside her. "I'm bloody well not a friend and you know it."

Taggart said something else, but she was looking at the pictures on the tablet in front of her.

"You don't have to look at those." Li sat down beside her. "I can take care of this for you."

She barely heard his words. She knew them though. Those words were filled with sympathy and took her back to that moment when she'd woken up in the hospital after the accident. Her mother had been there, promising her it wasn't her fault. Not really. She'd killed two people and the third might not live, but it hadn't been her fault. She'd been tired and distracted. That's what her mother had told her over and over again, as though saying the words would somehow make her magically believe.

She'd heard the same tone in the police officer who'd arrested her. He'd explained that by law, since she had a small but discernable amount of alcohol in her system, he had to arrest her for DUI. In the state of New York, any alcohol level in a person under twenty-one years of age was considered a DUI. She'd barely registered, but the accident had gone from tragic mistake to something that could end her life then and there.

She'd heard it when Avery Charles had stared at her and then quietly come to some place deep inside that Steph had never understood. Some place that made Avery who she was.

So much sympathy when she hadn't deserved any of it. It didn't matter the whys or hows. It only mattered that she'd been driving that car.

She flipped through the pictures until she got to one that showed an aerial view of the cabin her nurses shared. She recognized it because of the flowerpots on the side of the cabin. Anya had loved gardening and said she couldn't live without flowers to brighten her day.

The whole place was eerily empty. No one walked down the dirt paths. No kids skipping in, looking for the candy Steph always kept for them in the pockets of her scrubs. No patients milling about or staff briskly walking to their next task.

It was empty.

Had they all fled? She wouldn't be able to breathe until she got to talk to Anya, make sure she was all right.

She flipped through and this time the photo had been enhanced, the cabin bigger than before. It looked like the door was open, the inside of the cabin lost to the shadows.

She flipped again, the photo becoming grainier as the cabin came closer and closer.

And she realized what Ian Taggart had been talking about. What Liam hadn't wanted her to see.

There was a shoe sticking out of the doorway. One tennis shoe. The photo was black and white, but she knew the shoe itself was pink. She'd seen it many times in real life. Anya wore them because she was one of the girliest girls Steph had ever met. Even her tennis shoes had a hint of glitter to them.

Now one lay on its side and she couldn't see enough to discern whether it was still connected to its owner.

Nausea threatened.

"Damn it, I told you not to let her look at those things," Liam cursed. "She didn't need to see that."

"She needs to take this seriously," Ian shot back. "She needs to understand that she can't run off like she used to. She has to protect herself and that means following orders. Next time around, there won't be a crazy girl with coffee to defend her."

Brody took the tablet out of her hand and stared at it himself. "I can't tell if that's just a shoe or a body. You think that's one of your nurses?"

Steph nodded. "I'm pretty sure it is. I don't suppose she's napping in her open doorway, and she wouldn't have left a shoe behind. How many others died?"

"We don't know that she's dead," Charlotte began.

But the truth was there in her sympathetic eyes. Anya was probably gone and Steph had left her there. Alfi had convinced her that the boss would show up at any moment and kill her baby. She'd made a choice in that moment, one that might have cost Anya her life.

So much of that day was a horrific blur. She didn't want to remember.

"How many others?" She forced the question from her mouth again. When had her tongue gotten so dry? It was hard to talk.

"I don't know," Li replied. "But I'm going to find out. I've got a call in to a friend who's out that way. He's in Liberia with his wife, but I'm sure he'll help us out. I'll have him make his way to the clinic and report back. He'll also go into the village and make sure we can find your other nurse."

"I don't want a friend of yours to walk into something he can't handle," she insisted.

"There's very little Tennessee Smith can't handle," Li promised. "I also called Fain a couple of hours ago. The Agency's interested if there's a new player in that region. It's actually fairly stable, and that's why Fain is a bit worried. He wants to check it out, too, but we need that information from you. I need you to remember everything you can."

Ten Smith? She knew him. She liked his wife. Before she could protest, Brody was speaking.

"Not today she doesn't. She needs to rest and settle in. She's had a shock."

"A couple of them," Charlotte corrected.

Adam chuckled. "Yeah, she's not the only one. Though I should remind everyone that I took the brunt of the Aussie finding out about the secret baby."

She wished they wouldn't joke. She had no idea how they could find anything at all funny at this point.

"I can handle it. Tell me what you want me to do. You want me under hypnosis? I can do it." Her hands were shaking.

Brody stood up. "No. She's not doing shit tonight except having a good meal and cuddling with our son and getting a few hours of sleep. We'll make sure she does what she needs to do in the morning, and we'll send Smith a report before he goes in. Can we stay at the club tonight?"

"I wish I could let you do that, but we already have guests there," Ian explained. "The king and queen of Loa Mali also find themselves on the bad side of someone who wants to kill them. They're in hiding, a fact I know the two of you will keep to yourselves. But I can't put all my chicks in one basket. That's a good way to get the whole client list murdered."

She was incredibly tired. She wasn't even willing to argue with Brody, but there was one thing she was determined to do. "I won't stay with Avery. He knows where I am. He's watching me. He could come and hurt her and Aidan and the baby Avery is carrying."

Before Li could argue, Adam held up a hand. "Stay at our guesthouse. We've got a fence and security that's about as tight as we can make it. Riley, Shane? You up for some night duty?"

Both men nodded. "And we'll make sure Declan and Remy and Wade take their turns, too."

"You have two children in that house." She couldn't stand the thought of someone else getting hurt.

"And I have a partner who hasn't killed anyone lately. It's making Jake cranky. Bring it on. I need that man calm. We've got to present a united front when I tell Serena I want to turn the upstairs game room into a massive man cave. She doesn't understand the need for a TV screen that covers a whole wall," Adam explained.

"We're getting old," Ian offered. "Our eyesight's going."

Charlotte groaned as if she'd had this argument before. "No.

Your eyesight is perfectly fine. The children need a playroom, not a television overlord."

Brody reached for her, gently hauling her up from her seat. "Thank you, Miles. We accept. And I'll put Tucker on duty as well. He can learn from the bodyguards. He's a good bloke, even though you'll find him a bit odd. Excellent when it comes to hand to hand as well."

"I think I should stay at a hotel or something." And then everyone in the hotel was a potential victim. Was there anywhere she could go that she felt safe? Anywhere on earth where her continued existence didn't endanger someone else's?

When she didn't move, Brody leaned over and picked her up like she weighed nothing at all. "Come on, then. We should get settled in. I want someone to follow us, make sure we get there all right. I'll have Steph lay down in the back with Nathan's car seat. Tucker can sit in the front. When we get there, I want a full walk of the property and a report on security."

Miles gave him a salute. "I'll let Serena know we have a few extra for dinner. Don't worry. She'll be thrilled. She's been trying to write an Aussie hero so she'll want you to talk a lot."

"Brody, I said…" She'd said no, but it seemed foolish. Did she honestly want to do this alone? Her choices were to let Brody take some of the burden or let him take Nate and leave it all with her.

She was weak, but she wanted another few days with her son.

"Hush, luv. I've been gone, but it's my turn to take over." He leaned in and she could feel his breath against her ear, the sensation sending a long dormant longing through her body. "It's my turn to handle things. You've done good, Steph. Our boy's alive and healthy. Let me do my part."

She sagged in his arms, his warmth too nice to deny.

It was all she would let herself have. This one moment where she could pretend he was really here for her.

Chapter Six

Brody closed the door behind him, locking them inside. He took a deep breath. He'd left Tucker with Shane Landon, who'd promised not to murder the bloke. Riley Blade hadn't been able to promise the same. He'd taken the first watch outside the house while Shane and Tucker sat in the kitchen, drinking endless rounds of coffee and watching the security monitors.

And Shane was answering Tucker's rapid-fire questions. He hadn't stopped talking all evening. Tucker had been fascinated by the suburbs. He'd finally seen one of the trains and then told the story to everyone about how he'd nearly gotten them murdered by one. He'd gone with Adam to a big box store that he'd described as magical but was really just a place to buy nappies for Nate and some clothes and toiletries Brody prayed would work for Steph. Adam had treated Tucker like a child he was babysitting, buying the bloke lollies and soda Brody was sure would get him hyped up on sugar.

The only person who'd asked more questions than Tucker had been Serena Dean-Miles.

"I was worried Serena would think we were imposing, but she seemed more than happy for us to be here," Steph said, her voice quiet. The sound of a chair creaking rhythmically let him know she was sitting in the rocking chair. "Do you think she understands how dangerous it is to be around me?"

"I assure you she's been informed," he replied. Another deep breath. They were finally alone. After hours and hours of being surrounded by others. They'd gotten stuck in traffic for an hour. Then he'd spent the early evening making himself acquainted with the house and the grounds, walking the security wall to ensure there was no way in. Dinner had been a big affair, with Serena and Steph making spaghetti and meatballs with a big salad. He'd watched them when he could, loving the way Steph relaxed around the other woman, laughing for the first time in hours as Serena made her feel at home.

"Somehow, I think Serena is made of sterner stuff than you think," he replied, finally turning around.

Fuck, but she was beautiful. In the low light of the bedroom, with her hair down, there was practically a halo around her pretty face. Nate was in her arms, looking up toward his mother, and there was no way to miss the utter adoration on the boy's face. One pudgy hand reached up, trying to catch his mother's hair.

"She's a nice lady and incredibly talented." Steph eased a lock of hair out of Nate's grabby hand. "I like her books a lot. They got me through a few rough times. I think she's looking to make you her next hero."

Serena wrote romance novels. He'd never read one, but he'd heard she took heavily from McKay-Taggart missions. "Nah, she's just trying to get a bit of the lingo down."

"She asked you about a lot more than Aussie slang," Steph continued. "You never told me you served in Afghanistan."

At least she was talking. She wasn't talking about what he wanted, but she wasn't trying to throw him out of the room, either. "Yeah, I went into the Army right out of school. The minute I was allowed to sign up, I did. I joined up right before 9/11."

"Right before the world changed," she said quietly.

"Yeah. My brother was already a legend by then. When the war in Afghanistan came around, I was in one of the three combat units that went. Was there for a couple of years." He stepped closer, well aware he was moving from the shadows into the light. He did better in shadows, but he couldn't hide there any longer. "He's so small."

She chuckled. "You're joking, right?"

He shook his head, staring down at the baby. His baby. Tiny and fragile.

"Brody, he came out of my body weighing ten pounds. Ten freaking pounds. You do understand that most babies come in at seven pounds, maybe seven and a half. I practically gave birth to a toddler."

"He looks pretty small to me."

"Do you want to hold him?" She asked the question with the cautious tone of a woman who wasn't sure she wanted to know the answer.

He was scared to. Nothing in his life had scared him quite like that tiny boy in her arms. He barely remembered his father, and most of those were ghostly visions of a monster who used his fists to do his talking. His father had been a drunk and an abusive arse who'd left his mum with two kids and piece of shit station that she'd had to make work.

"Brody, it's okay." She stood, easily moving with the baby in her arms. "Sit down to hold him at first. It's fine. You're not going to drop him."

"What if I hold him too tight?" There were plenty of things he could do wrong. He was big and clumsy at times.

A smile curled her lips up as she offered him the chair. "Then Nate will let you know. He's not one to suffer in silence."

"He's barely made a sound all night." Brody worried about the chair. It looked somewhat delicate, too. He didn't want to break it.

"The chair is solid, Brody," she said with a shake of her head. "You know you're always worried you're too big for furniture. Get over yourself. Yes, you're all big and muscley, but most furniture is still going to be able to handle you. If my crappy folding chairs in the mess hall could take you, I think you're fine in a rocking chair."

There was something about the saucy way she teased him that got his motor running. Most women didn't tease him, didn't turn their tart tongues on the scarred bloke who looked like he'd killed many times. Women either saw him as a challenge or they were intimidated by him and stayed away. Only Steph had ever managed to get close to him, to show him she wasn't going to take his shit, that she saw right through him.

He gave the chair his full weight and let himself rock gently. She was right. It wasn't going to crumble under him. Another couple of pounds of baby boy wouldn't change things. He nodded her way. "It's solid. I think it's safe."

"Nate's solid, too," she promised him. "He's not going to break. Have you never been around babies before?"

"Not until I met you. Not until I was in the clinic, and even then I tried to stay away from them," he admitted.

She stood over him, though even standing while he sat, they were practically eye to eye. "I did notice that. I thought you didn't like kids, but then you blew that all to hell by spending all your time letting the older kids treat you like a jungle gym."

He smiled at the memory. He'd let the older ones climb him like a tree at times. One boy in particular. Ardu had a bum leg, the bones in his left leg shorter than his right, so he didn't grow the way other kids did. They'd made fun of him for being short and one day Brody had lifted the kid up and settled him on his shoulders, letting him see the world from a different point of view. He'd walk for hours with Ardu hanging on, the boy's wonder at the different view making any annoyance evaporate. "I like kids, Steph. Just never expected to have any of my own."

"Well, sometimes plans change. Here's your son, Brody Carter." She eased the boy into his arms.

Whoa. The boy was staring up at him, his blue eyes wide, and for a second he was worried the kid was going to cry at the sight of his father's face. He knew he wasn't the prettiest man in the world. He had more than a few scars. He wore his hair too short. He thought he looked a bit cruel even when he wasn't trying to.

And then the most heartbreakingly gorgeous toothless grin broke over the boy's face.

Tears clouded his eyes. There was no way to hold them back. He reached down and touched that baby-soft skin. Nate's cheeks were fat and precious. The baby reached up and gripped his father's index finger in his hand, squeezing with surprising strength.

He was completely, utterly, madly in love.

"I think he likes me," he managed to say.

Steph moved in behind him, putting a hand on his shoulder. "Of course he does. He knows his father. I'm glad you're here, Brody. I'll go get his bottle. If he eats, he might sleep longer than a few hours."

She moved away, and he felt the loss of that connection.

"Call Tucker. He'll bring you one," he said. He couldn't, wouldn't take his gaze off her.

She turned, both brows rising over her eyes like he'd said something truly ridiculous. "Seriously? That man barely knows how to open a can of soda, much less how to make a bottle."

"Then I'll come with you." He was afraid of getting up and jostling Nate. The boy seemed perfectly comfy. He was wriggling, bouncing in Brody's arms as he held on to his finger.

She was already in motion, reaching into her diaper bag and pulling out a smaller bag. "Do you think I'm not ready? I've raised that boy in a place where if I needed to go to the kitchen to get him a bottle in the middle of the night, I would have to walk a quarter of a mile and deal with a bunch of critters who hunt at night. I've learned how to use a cold bag and a bottle warmer."

She plugged something in and settled the bottle inside the device.

"I'm sorry, but I think it's best we stay together and in one place." He rocked Nate, watching his every expression.

"So what does that mean for tonight?" Steph asked.

Damn it. He was kind of hoping she'd be so tired she wouldn't fight him. He'd thought she might even let him in bed because the bed was pretty big. It wouldn't be his fault if he rolled over and they ended up pressed side by side. If his arms wrapped around her, would that be such a bad thing? "Steph, I'm not leaving this room."

She nodded his way. "I figured that's what you would say. It's all right."

Excellent. "I'm glad you're being reasonable."

"Serena told me where the extra sheets and blankets are. There's a linen closet in the bathroom. I'll make up the sofa for myself."

"You bloody well will not."

She glanced down at the bottle. "You won't fit on the couch. I will. Besides, I can be closer to Nate that way."

"Nate's crib is right across the room. You'll be plenty close in the bed. And the bed is big enough for both of us," he replied, cuddling closer to his son.

"You honestly believe I'm going to sleep with you?"

So much for her being reasonable. "Stephanie, we have a kid."

"Yes, and I was on birth control at the time which proves that your sperm are dangerous and they're not coming anywhere near my ovaries again. I'm worried that simply being in the same room with you might be too close for comfort."

"I know it's soon, but do you want him to be an only child?"

Her eyes went wide. "What is that supposed to mean?"

"It means a boy needs siblings." He could be stubborn, too. "I know you didn't have any, but you have to understand that brothers and sisters are important to a kid. I don't know what I would have done if I hadn't had Harry in my life."

She held a hand up. "No. You're not going to distract me. Brody, what do you think is happening between the two of us?"

"I think it already happened."

Nate started to frown as though he'd realized something terrible. His little mouth opened on a low moan.

Brody stared down at him, his heart starting to race. "Did I hurt him?"

Steph took the bottle out, testing the liquid against her wrist. "Nope, that is the calm before the storm."

Another moan, this one starting to have an edge of anger to it. Nate's mouth screwed up and then his whole body seemed to tighten, his skin turning red before a wrathful squall seemed to shake the walls.

Steph shoved a bottle in Nate's mouth and he started to suck furiously.

"He's a drama queen," she said with a shake of her head. "And he goes from perfectly content to oops, there's a small place in my stomach where food could go, and then he's like a starving demon.

There's only one thing to do and that's shove food in his mouth. See, back to being a perfect angel. You have to hold the bottle at the right angle or he gets frustrated."

What the hell had happened? Nate was back to staring up at him like he was completely fascinated and now content to relax and get to know his dad since Mum had been smart enough to know how to soothe the tiny beast.

"Brody, we need to talk."

He knew that tone of voice. This was the part when she told him he'd fucked up and wouldn't get another chance. He knew that was what she was thinking. He had to get her thinking something else. Anything else. He said the first thing to come to mind. "He's my mum's first grandbaby, you know."

He watched her struggle between continuing the conversation she knew she should have and asking the questions she'd always wanted. All those months they'd spent together, he'd dodged all questions about his past and his family. When she would ask, he would turn the conversation back to her.

"You never talked about your mom. I wondered if she was still alive."

Win. "My mum is alive and kicking. Strongest woman I know. She still lives back on Wanga Woo."

"Excuse me?"

He felt himself flush a bit. "Wanga Woo. Hey, it's not the worst name in Australia. We've got towns like Humpty Doo, Mount Buggery, Dismal Swamp. Quite descriptive if you ask me. Wanga Woo was founded by a couple of brothers who got themselves transported over from England for stealing. Then they got kicked out of Sydney for the same reason and finally found a bit of fortune in Western Australia. What you would call the Outback. They named their station after a particularly punchy kangaroo. And yes, those brothers were Carters. I'm directly descended from them and no, we don't fight kangaroos anymore. Well, at least we don't go looking for it. Some of the buggers will find you though."

She sat down on the edge of the bed. "Your ancestors fought kangaroos?"

"Some people think that's what went wrong with our brains," he said.

Nate giggled around the nipple in his mouth.

"That's right, little fella. Your nanna put a right stop to that. She told me and your uncle that she wasn't going to stand for none of that kind of roughhousing. She's a lady, she is." At least she'd always seemed that way to him. He looked up at Steph. "Not that anyone else would think that. My mum ain't the kind to wear nice dresses and stuff. She had a station to run, but she always made sure that our bellies got fed and that we went to church every Sunday all clean like. So she's always a lady in my mind."

"She sounds like a lovely lady," Steph replied. "I'd like to meet her someday. Well, as long as the kangaroos won't attack."

"Nah, they're all right. For the most part you leave them alone and they'll let you alone. And the snakes and spiders are way overblown. Again, you leave them alone and you'll be fine."

"And the crocs?"

He snorted. "I'm talking the Outback, luv. Two kinds of crocs in Australia. The saltwater crocs are the dangerous ones and they're not in the Outback. We've got a couple of freshies in what little water you can find, but they're small and shy. One brushes up against you in the billabong and you give that old boy a good punch on the snout and he'll slink away. Hell, my brother and I named the one in the river that ran through the back acreage of our station."

"That is disappointing. I thought Australia was super deadly."

"The sun'll get you," he said, turning his attention back to his son. "So will the quiet sometimes. Being isolated like that, well, it works for some, makes others mean. The heat can make a man crazy. One of the best things I've done since joining up with McKay-Taggart is being able to buy my mum a reliable air conditioner. Had to talk her into it though. She was sure it would make her soft."

"Why did you leave? You didn't want to work on a station?"

"By then she'd sold off most of the land. She doesn't make her money that way anymore. She married a man who worked with a mineral company. He had stock in the damn thing and made a mint when they hit natural gas. She'd been working to feed and clothe us all by herself since I was six or seven." That was when his mum had enough. He wasn't sure why she'd done it, what had broken her resolve to keep them together despite the fact that his dad had been a piece of shit. He suspected that dear old dad had threatened something Mum had loved far more than her husband. He wasn't sure, but one day his father had been gone and a year and a half later, the police had shown up to inform his mum that Dad had been killed in a bar fight in Coober Pedy. "My biological dad was a worthless bum who beat the shit out of me and Harry but saved the best for my mum. My stepdad is a vast improvement. He's a really good man."

His mother had wept when his dad had left, but he rather thought they'd been tears of relief.

It'll be all right, Mum. I can help.

Oh, we'll be all right, my lovie. Don't you doubt that and don't think we need him for a moment. You'll be a better man without him around.

Did Steph feel the same way about him?

"I'm sorry about your dad, but it's good your mom found someone new. I wish mine had. I was close to mine for a long time and then we kind of drifted apart," she admitted. "My mom died a few years back. I don't talk to my dad anymore."

"Why is that?"

"I made a mistake back in high school," she said, her eyes on the ground.

He knew her story. He'd been given background on her and her association with Avery and Liam O'Donnell. "That was an accident. No father should drop his baby girl because she makes a mistake."

"It was a big mistake."

"Ain't no mistake that big. You tell me if there is anything this boy could do that would make you turn from him. I just met him and I can tell you I'll stand by him for the rest of his life. He might disappoint me, but he's my boy. He's mine and that means I will be at his side even if the worst happens."

She looked up finally, tears in her eyes. "I won't leave him either. Not for any reason."

"Yeah, I think you and my mum will get on just fine." He rocked and Nate's eyes were starting to close.

"I'm tired, Brody. I think I'll get dressed and go to bed. I'll be out in a minute to put him down."

"I can handle it. You take a nice long shower. I've got the boy. And I'll take the couch."

She stood up. "It's fine. It's a king-size bed. I'm sure we'll survive one night. And thanks for telling me about your mom. I know you don't like to talk about the past."

"All that's changed now," he told her. "Anything you want to know, I'll talk."

"Brody," she began.

"No. No matter what happens between us, we have to be friends, and I didn't treat you like a friend back then."

"It felt like friendship."

"It was more but I was too stupid to see it. No more talk. Go and relax. We'll get a good night's sleep and things will look up in the morning. That's what Mum used to say. I'm not calling her now because they could be monitoring us, but I hope you'll let me send her pictures when this is over."

"Of course." She glanced at the bathroom. "If you're okay taking care of him, maybe I could take a bath. It's been a long time since I had access to a tub, much less one the size of a small pool. I wish I was married to Serena."

He smiled at that. And got hot at the idea of her in that tub. "Go on then, luv. Take as long as you like. We'll be fine out here."

She leaned over and kissed Nate's head then disappeared into the bathroom.

A sense of peace came over Brody, unlike anything he'd felt before. It was settled. He was a dad and now he knew he had work to do. Why had he avoided this all his life? This boy in his arms gave him purpose and meaning he hadn't found before.

There was only one thing wrong now.

"Your mother thinks we're going to be friends, but I've got a secret for you, son." He gently pulled the bottle out of Nate's mouth since his whole body had gone slack with sleep. "We're going to be a family. She's going to marry me, and I finally know what to do with my life. Make her happy. Some people, they have great callings. Like your mum. She's a special person and I thought that meant she needed another special person to be with her. But I can see that was wrong. Two people with great callings have to focus on their callings, on their careers or work. But with me, well, she'll be the reason I'm special and I'll make sure she has everything she needs. What she needs is a dumb grunt who loves her so much he's willing to give everything to her and their family. I promise you, Nathan. By the end of this, we're all going to be together."

Or he would die trying.

He thought briefly about putting the baby in his crib and trying to get a bit of work done, but it felt better to sit, to rock with his son in his arms.

For the first time in forever, he knew what peace meant.

Chapter Seven

Steph breathed in the warm air, steam rising from the tub as she lay back. The Dean-Miles clan knew how to take care of themselves and their guests.

So warm. How long had it been since heat had sank deliciously into her skin? Since she could take a moment to indulge in something as simple as a bath? Far too long. She didn't indulge. At first it was because she didn't feel as if she deserved indulgence of any kind, and then medical school trained it out of her. It had become habit to work and work and sleep and work.

Then she'd had Nate and the world seemed to slow down, to become softer and harder at the same time. Her personal world had become one of stolen moments with her son. Those beautiful moments when she looked at him and everything seemed fresh and new.

But then she would look outward and realize the world would come for him and she was afraid.

She wiped a tear away and took another breath, letting the sound of the rocking chair creaking lull her. As long as that chair was rocking, Brody was here with their baby, and he wouldn't let anything bad happen to Nate.

She closed her eyes and relaxed because she wasn't alone for once.

She would rest for a minute and then get going. Maybe the superhot water would help her sleep. Maybe not being the only one responsible for Nate would do the same.

She relaxed and found herself in a different world.

Driving, her hands on the wheel, music in the background. Just a few more months and high school would be done. No more teachers. No more books…until college, of course, but that felt like Disney World.

She yawns, the lateness of the hour pressing in on her. She knows she should have left that stupid party hours before but Kyle had been there and he'd brought her a beer. She didn't like the taste, but he'd been so insistent that she'd found herself slowly drinking it down.

She'd liked the taste more when it had been on his lips. She feels her whole body flush. He'd kissed her. Not the first time, of course. She's been kissed before, but this was different. This had sent a forbidden thrill through her system.

Like the big guy. Big gorgeous Aussie with hands that could cover her whole breast.

No. That was wrong. He wasn't here.

She's driving and she's young. Whole life ahead of her. Wasn't that what that light ahead meant?

The light, so bright she's momentarily blinded, and then she's flying. The car her dad had fixed up for her sixteenth birthday wasn't supposed to fly, but here she was. A flash of light, a scream of metal.

Somewhere in the distance she heard crying. Wailing.

A mother's loss. A wife's pain.

Pain. Yes, she felt it flashing through her. This was what she deserved. This was why she'd been born. To ache. To hurt.

She tips the bottle back. She paid some asshole older guy to buy it for her. Naturally he wanted more than cash and that shame was on her, too. It doesn't matter. There are no more Kyles with sweet kisses that end in promises of dates. There is no more future, nothing beyond the harsh burn of cheap vodka that dulls the sound of those sympathetic voices.

The angry ones she can handle. The yelling, the name calling, they all feel like home to her now. It's her mother's voice telling her it wasn't her fault that makes her sick.

If it wasn't her fault, then there was no meaning to be had. If it was, then she knew what to do. Punish herself since no one else would.

She looks at the knives in her mother's kitchen but that would be far too easy. Somewhere across town there's another woman and she's lying in bed, her legs useless because an idiot kid should have left the party an hour before.

She can't end her own suffering while Avery Charles is still in pain.

I don't recognize you anymore. I can't look at you. Where is my little girl?

Can't he see she's buried under three tons of guilt and keeps piling it on because it won't ever be enough? There is no redemption. None.

Her father walks out and she knows that it's right and good and she thinks about how she can hurt herself tonight.

A warm hand encloses hers. It's only for the mission. It's their cover, but her heart still skips a beat the minute he touches her. She does good now. She's found her mission, her purpose.

Does it make up for the wrong she's done? His hand squeezing hers feels like a gift she'd never expected. Brody. Even his name is masculine.

Would it be different with him? Would she feel clean? Or would it be one more way to degrade herself?

The baby's coming. Yes, this pain was deserved because she'd been stupid enough to think she could steal a moment's pleasure. Stupid enough to think the punishment was over. She screams and wishes she'd never put on that ridiculous gown and tried to seduce Brody Carter into staying with her. There is no fooling herself in this place. As the pain wracks through her body, threatening to split her in two, she knows she's lied to herself, to him. She loves him. She wants him.

This is her punishment, to know he can't love her back.

And then she holds him. Not the father. No. She won't hold the father again. He is lost to her, a silent figure, but the son isn't silent.

He blinks open his eyes and she finds her purpose.

I am going to gut that kid of yours. Do you understand me, girl? I'll do it in front of you if you don't get what I need out of that fucker.

"Steph?"

Cold air shocked her, her whole body shaking. Nate. He was going to kill her son and she didn't even understand what was going on. Terror flooded her system. She wouldn't be able to save him.

"Nate," she said, but it came out as a whisper, her voice hoarse as though she'd been screaming and couldn't do it anymore.

"He's fine. He's all right."

The dream had her in a fog. Why was she wet? And naked. She was naked and Brody was lifting her up.

He held her close. "Hush, luv. You're going to wake the baby and have every bodyguard in the area running in here. I don't want to have to punch the men we're paying to keep us safe so stop fighting me. It was only a dream."

A dream. A waltz through Hell was more like it.

What would he think if he knew the things she'd done? How she'd punished herself, tried to obliterate herself? Would he think he wasn't good enough for her then? Or would he look at her like her father had? Would he figure out she was nothing but a piece of garbage to sweep under the rug and out of his life?

"Come on. You're shaking. Can you stand?"

He was holding her and getting soaking wet. She was making a fool of herself. She slowly nodded, trying to get her mind off that terrible dream. She could still feel the wretched heat coming off the boss's body as he'd leaned in and explained how he would kill her precious baby if she didn't perform. She could smell the acrid scent of the cigar he'd smoked the whole time he was there.

Cool tile steadied her as Brody eased her down. She covered her breasts, wrapping her arms around her body in an attempt at modesty.

Brody stepped away for a moment and she was left shivering with the memory of how that man had stormed into her clinic, brandishing guns and knives and threatening everything she held dear if she didn't help him.

"He told me I had to get him what he wanted," she said quietly.

Brody came back, a big, fluffy towel in his hands. He wrapped it around her, his arms following and pulling her back to the comfort of his body. "Did he say what he wanted?"

She shook her head. "No. I don't know. Maybe, but I don't remember right now. I think Taggart's right and I need someone to walk me through it. God, Brody, I want to forget."

"I know, but you have to remember. Not tonight though. Tonight you need sleep. Try not to think about it."

How the hell was she going to do that? She couldn't get the vision out of her head.

"You're fine now." He held her tight, his voice whispering against her ear. "You're safe and here with me and Nate's sleeping. We're all safe. No need to be afraid."

She loved how strong he was, the way his arms seemed to cage her in the most delicious way. There was safety in that sweet cage.

But she had to remember that he'd made his choice long ago.

"I'm all right. I'll get dressed now. Thank you for waking me up." She made the words as polite as possible.

"You could have drowned."

That was a bit of a stretch since her hair wasn't even wet. "I'm good now. Like you said it was nothing more than a dream."

"I don't want to let you go," he whispered.

Would it be so bad to let him kiss her? To spend another night in his arms? Maybe if she let Brody make love to her, she wouldn't think about that terrible dream. Maybe he could tire her out and then she could sleep.

She knew it was wrong and there was a part of her that wondered if this wasn't another sick way to punish herself more. She wasn't planning on a life with Brody. He could be in Nate's life and not truly in hers. But maybe she could let herself have one more night with him.

"What if you didn't?"

She felt him go still behind her. What if he'd been joking? What if those words had been nothing more than a way to try to make her feel better about herself, and now he was going to turn her down again?

A sick feeling lit the pit of her stomach as she waited for him to let her go.

Then she felt him press a kiss to the top of her head, his hands moving to turn her around. "You won't regret this, Stephanie. I promise. It won't be like last time. Last time I was quick and rough and I didn't give you what you needed."

She let him turn her, staring up at the most gorgeous man she'd ever seen. "I got an orgasm, as I recall. A few of them. I think that was what I needed."

"Tell me you didn't want D/s sex." He was staring down at her, but there was no hesitation in those warm eyes now. His hands came up to cup her cheeks. "Don't lie to me. I'll know if you lie to me and it won't go well."

Wow. There it was. There was that dark, deep voice he used when he wanted to get something done. When he needed her to obey him while they were in the field, he would turn that rich-as-honey voice on her and she would find herself nodding and doing what he told her to.

But she wasn't going to open herself up that much. She couldn't, not when she knew that tomorrow morning they would be back to caution. "I read too many of Serena's books. That's why I did what I did. It's okay. The sex was great."

It had been the best sex she'd ever had. Since the majority of sex she'd had before hadn't been about finding pleasure. It had been about escaping, and she hadn't cared if she felt anything at all. Sex had been dirty, but then she'd been dirty, too.

So the sex she'd had with Brody had at least been for the right reason, to bring pleasure to them both.

"It wasn't. Oh, it got the job done, no doubt," he rumbled as he stared down at her. "But it didn't fix my soul or yours. It didn't connect us the way it should have. I want that connection. I want to feel you, and not only in a physical way. This isn't playing. Playing is a silly word for what I want from you."

"What word would you use?"

"Everything. I want everything."

She couldn't give him that, but she could give him tonight. Well, she could be with him for as long as Nate would allow. He slept fairly well, but certainly not through the night. What was she doing? "Nate's going to wake up."

His hands tightened slightly, gently forcing her to look up at him. "And I'll feed him and change his nappy and rock him back to sleep. And then I'll get back to making sure his mum can sleep, too. I've been gone and it was wrong of me. Let me make a bit of that up to you."

"Brody," she began because she didn't want to lead him to believe this was really going anywhere beyond tonight.

"Don't think and don't argue. Let me take care of you. Let me show you everything is going to be okay."

"For tonight," she insisted.

"If that's all you can accept," he allowed. "But we're going to do this my way."

His head lowered down, sensual lips brushing hers. A rush of heat flashed through her body and it felt like her skin was alive with sensation. Even where he wasn't touching her, her skin was primed, like a flower that knew it was finally going to get some love from the sun.

He kissed her, his lips moving over hers in a slow, methodical fashion. It was far from the way it had been the first time. The first time, he'd gone fast, passionate, like he couldn't wait to swallow her whole.

This was different. This was thoughtful, meditative.

Was he taking his time because he felt differently about her now that she was a mom? Was she not as sexy as she'd been before Nate? Her body had changed. She hadn't shed all the pregnancy pounds yet. She wasn't a supermodel with two trainers, a nutritionist, and a chef.

"Stop thinking," he whispered. "I know that big brain of yours is working. I can feel it. Stop. There's no thinking tonight. No analyzing. There's just you and me and what I can do to your body. Drop the towel, Stephanie."

She bit her bottom lip. "Maybe we should go to the bed."

"Because I turned the light off so Nate could sleep? I didn't. The light on the nightstand is still on and if it wasn't I would turn it on. I'm not fucking you in the dark. You're going to look in my eyes and say my name and I'm going to do the same. It's going to be you and me, and no pretending it ain't exactly what it is. Drop that towel and let me look at you. I close my eyes every damn night since the day I met you and do you know what I see? I see you. I see you laughing and frowning, and they're equally beautiful because they're equally you. Since the night when we made Nate all I can see is you sleeping in that bed. I didn't sneak out right away, you know. I stayed for three hours. I held you for the longest time and watched you while you slept. I only left when I had to and I did it because I thought it was best for you. You've been a ghost haunting me every night since that one."

Somehow she couldn't believe that. She'd been the one who sat up every night thinking about him. He'd been in his happy London club. "Somehow I think the subs at The Garden took care of you. It's all right, Brody. We weren't together. It was one night and it didn't change anything."

One hand tugged the band out of her hair, spilling it across her shoulders. "I think the baby sleeping in the next room is evidence that night changed everything. And I'm trying to tell you that I haven't had another woman since I left you. I wasn't off gallivanting around and forgetting you. I spent every moment of our time away from each other miserable as hell. So let that towel drop and give me what I've only seen in my dreams for a year. Let me see you."

She wasn't sure why she did it, but her feet moved. She stepped back, putting a small but critical distance between them as her hands floated up and she dropped the towel.

The offering of a submissive to her chosen Dominant.

The towel hit the floor and she felt herself flush. She wasn't as pretty as she'd been the first time. Now she had stretch marks that spoke of her pregnancy. Her belly was still rounded, her breasts not as firm.

"Stop it," he said. "Don't you think about anything but how the air feels on your skin. Don't you think about how you look. I'll tell you what I see. I see the most beautiful woman I've ever known. I see that my dreams of her were nothing compared to the real thing. She's stunning and my heart aches at the thought of her not understanding how beautiful she is."

"Brody, I still haven't lost the weight I gained with Nate," she said, trying not to let his words affect her too much. She was already on the verge of tears, and she'd cried enough.

"You get one," he said, his voice deep. "One time I'll let you get away with saying something like that, but now you know the rule. You are beautiful and thinking or saying anything else about yourself will end in discipline."

"You can't control my thoughts." But she could feel her lips curling up at the very arrogance of him thinking he could. This was the Brody she'd fallen for. She'd known his larger-than-life, damn the torpedoes attitude had been half truth and half cover, but she'd adored it when he would walk in, take control, and do something or say something ridiculously over the top to make her day better.

"Watch me," he replied. "After I've spanked the hell out of that gorgeous arse a dozen times, you won't think that way again. I'll tie you up and torture you until you agree with me that you're the most gorgeous woman on the earth."

"Fine, I'm gorgeous." She didn't believe it, but standing here felt weird. "Shouldn't you get undressed? Or did you change your mind?"

His eyes roamed over her body, not missing an inch. "I didn't change my mind at all. I told you how this is going to be. The first time we did this, I let you push me."

"The first time we did this, you didn't want to."

His eyes narrowed. "You know damn well that's not true. Turn around and put your hands on the side of the tub."

"Why would I..." The answer hit her with the force of a steam engine. "You want to spank me?"

It should have come out in that horrified, I'm-a-feminist, shocked tone she often used when a random asshole told her she was cute to think she could be a doctor but they would prefer to see a man for their medical needs. Nope. It came out all breathy and porny. The porny part might have been because when she watched porn—rarely—she gravitated toward the movies where the big, dominant man spanked his lover to orgasm.

Which likely was a myth. Like most porn.

"Yes, and every second you make me wait is another smack to that pretty arse of yours." His hands were on his hips, his jaw squared as he looked her over. "If you push me too hard, I'll find a way to clamp your nipples and *then* I'll spank you."

What was she doing? She was standing here naked with a man who'd broken her heart once already.

"Tell me you don't want to know what it feels like." His voice had lost its harsh edge, sliding into silky smoothness. "Tell me you don't want to try it once. You're the woman who was brave enough to get on your knees and present yourself to me like the sweetest treat I've ever been offered. Do what I'm asking. You can always stop me. One word will work tonight. No is all I need to hear. If you say that, then I'll get you dressed and I'll sleep beside you so you know you're safe. But I think you're braver than that. I think you're still a woman who knows what she wants."

"How do you know I haven't already tried it?" The minute the words were out of her mouth, she wanted to call them back. She'd spat them out to protect herself, as though saying cruel words to him could throw some sort of force field around her.

Because deep down she did know what Li had been trying to tell her. Deep inside she knew Brody wasn't as arrogant as he seemed sometimes. Under that blustery exterior, there was a man who wasn't sure of how smart he was, how worthy he was.

Before she could apologize, he moved into the space again, a sad smile playing on his face as his fingertips brushed over her cheek. "I know because you wanted me and then you were pregnant. I know because you wouldn't have changed your mind and heart that quickly. I was stupid to think you had a boyfriend, but then I was blindly jealous, and I hope you can forgive me for that. Hell, luv, I need you to forgive me for a lot of things, but we can deal with that another time. For tonight, let me give you what you want. Let me do what I should have done that first night. Let me show you how good this can be."

She was afraid. Afraid to want him. Afraid to hope that this could be something good.

She let it all go and focused on him.

"Tell me something, luv." He leaned over and kissed her forehead, the light touch of his lips making her shiver. "Are you thinking about anything but me right now?"

She wasn't now. Everything else had melted away and she realized that she needed this. Needed him. Tomorrow would make sense of itself. Tonight she was going to know what it meant to be his sub.

She turned and placed her hands on the side of the big tub. At some point he'd pulled the plug and the water was all gone now, but the whole place still smelled like the lavender bath salts she'd used. She breathed it in, letting the comforting scent wash over her.

She heard Brody moving behind her and tried to relax. She'd made her decision—to give him control, to let go for once in her life. She wasn't in charge of this. He was. She had to trust him.

"Now that is a beautiful sight." His voice seemed to roll over her skin like a warm wave, warmer than the water she'd sunk herself into. "This is what I missed out on. How much sex have you had, luv?"

She tensed, a vision of the ways she'd degraded herself flashing through her.

His hand steadied her, pressing on her lower back. "I wasn't asking because I care how many men you've had. I don't. I was asking if I was the only man you've had in the last couple of years."

That was better. She had a good answer to that question. "Before you I hadn't had sex in four years."

He groaned. "Well, I'm going to make up for that because this is how it's going to go. It's going be long and slow and I'm going to know every single inch of this beautiful body like it's a map I need to memorize. I'll be able to close my eyes and know how many kisses it takes to get from your mouth to your nipple to your sweet belly to that pussy I'm going to eat like a starving man."

Every word seemed to turn on an invisible switch in her body, winding and winding her up until she was sure she would uncoil the moment he touched her again. She managed to hold perfectly still as he traced the curve of her spine with his fingertips.

"This is a spankable arse." He cupped her cheeks in one big hand. "Hold on to the side of the tub and try not to scream. Don't want to wake the baby now, do we?"

Scream? She was about to ask why she would…and then a crack resounded through the room and she bit her bottom lip, biting back the cry that threatened to erupt. Pain blistered across her backside, the sting hard on her skin. He slapped her ass five times in rapid succession and then soothed his hand over the tender flesh.

"I know it hurts right now, but give it a moment. Let it work its magic." His hand held the heat in. "Do you have any idea how lovely you are to me right now? You're always stunning, but like this you take away my every worry until all I can think about is how I'm going to take care of you. How I'm going to make you crazy for me."

That shocking pain was turning into something else. Heat and ache. It sank into her muscles and she could feel herself getting wet. She could feel arousal start to pulse through her system and she breathed a sigh of relief because she hadn't been entirely certain she would ever want sex again. Since she'd been pregnant, she'd felt sexless and more like a mother than a possible lover. She'd worried something about Nate's birth had burned out her sex drive.

Nope. It was good. That sex drive was roaring back to life, and she realized it had nothing to do with time or healing and everything to do with this one man. No one in her life had ever made her hotter than Brody Carter. All he had to do was walk in a room and her hormones lit up.

Another smack cracked through the air. One and two and three and she couldn't hold back a low moan.

"Can you handle more?" Brody asked.

It would kill her. She would cry. No. She wasn't giving in and crying might be nice. She held it together all the time. She was the one who had to make all the decisions, take all the blame and responsibility. "Yes."

Rapid-fire slaps took over her life and she held on. Nothing mattered except getting through it. She moaned and felt tears slipping from her eyes as he kept up the torture. She didn't count, didn't think about when it would end. She gave over and let it take her, let her body accept his discipline and sensitize her skin.

The room went silent and it took her a second to realize he was done. There was silence between them for a moment, but it wasn't empty. She could feel his hands on her, feel the will he put into them. He wanted her.

"Tell me how you feel." His voice was low as though he was afraid to truly break the quiet communion between them.

"I hurt and ache, but in the best way." She'd never felt anything like it. Yes, there was pain, but this wasn't a wild attempt to release her tension or purge her demons. This was calculated. He knew what he was doing and there was no crazed edge to it. She was safe. She'd gotten to cry, to let some of the toxins in her system go, but in a surgical way.

There was peace to this, comfort.

But mostly a wild need she'd never felt before.

"Come here. We're done with discipline." His hands curved up and he helped her balance as she stood on shaky legs. He gently turned her around and she was hauled up against him.

So big. He was six foot seven inches of pure muscled male, and he overwhelmed her every sense. Even as she felt the ache in her backside, her pussy was warm and soft. Her body felt languid, but she managed to let her arms float up around him. One big hand was on the back of her neck, the other steady against her spine. She was pressed to him, her nipples rubbing against the soft cotton of his shirt. She felt the cool of his belt buckle brush against her belly and the denim of his jeans tangle with her legs as he lowered his head once more.

His tongue invaded, warm silk stroking her lips and then deep inside her mouth. She didn't need to breathe. She needed this. She needed long, slow kisses that seemed to go on forever, as though he'd become as important to her as air or water. Every kiss took her higher.

She needed him.

The thought scared her, but she pushed it aside. This was for one night only. Tomorrow they would go back to being wary co-parents, but tonight she was taking what she needed.

He kissed her until she was breathless and then she found herself turned in his arms, her back to his front. His arms wound around her, sliding down her body in a slow exploration. She let her head drift back, resting against his chest as she let him have his way. His callused hands cupped her breasts, testing their weight and learning her curves.

He rolled her nipples. "How sensitive are you? Tell me if I hurt you. I don't want to hurt you. Nate's only two months old."

The only way he could hurt her now was by walking away. "I'm fine, Brody. His birth was natural, and despite the fact that he was as big as a freaking linebacker, I didn't need surgical intervention. Please touch me and don't make me explain things like episiotomies to you right now. I didn't have one, by the way."

"I don't want to know," he vowed. "I only want to know that you're healthy and you want this."

His big hand covered her belly, easing down her body, inching ever closer to the part of her that needed the most attention.

"I want it. I want you," she managed to say. All thoughts of anything but that hand and its destination were gone, banished to the dark regions of her mind.

"I want you more than I can say. Let me show you how much. Let me show you what I want. I want this pussy soaked for me. I want it warm and wet and ready. I want you to see me walk in a room, remember what I can do to you, and have your whole body make itself ready for me."

Every word was a drug working on her system.

"Please, Brody." She wasn't sure how long she could hold out, and that suddenly seemed like a joyous thing. In her daily life she measured time and duties, often merely counting down time until the next day or duty presented itself. Life had become something to be endured rather than celebrated, but she couldn't wait for this. She needed this more than she needed her next breath.

She stiffened when she finally felt a single finger slide over the pad of her clitoris.

"Relax, luv," he whispered. "Let me get you started and then I'll show you what I can really do. Can you be good for me? Can you hold still and not scream when you come? Because I'm about to make you come. I'm going to fuck your pussy with my fingers and you're going to come all over my hand and then we'll begin again. Do you understand me? But it all stops if you try to take control. This isn't the clinic or an operating theatre. This is *my* place. This is where I'm the king and I make the decisions, and you're my precious submissive who takes all the pleasure I can give her and serves her Master."

"Yes. Yes, Brody." She was shaking with desire and for the first time wondered if she knew what she was getting into. The first time they'd made love had been the best sex of her life, but it had been quick and he hadn't talked much. He'd inhaled her, but he hadn't made a slow, decadent meal of her the way he was doing now. He hadn't tortured her with promises and teased her with words.

This was so much better. This wasn't a random body in bed, giving her incidental pleasure. This was Brody and he was focused on her, only her.

"Put your left foot on the tub," he ordered.

That would leave her completely exposed. It would open her up to him in a wholly vulgar way. Of course, it was all about perspective. It could be vulgar or it would open her to a way that led to an orgasm. What was vulgar about that? It was all about intent. This wasn't a crazy attempt to degrade herself. She didn't want to punish herself. She wanted connection. It might be an infinitely more dangerous thing to seek, but it was all she could think about now. Him. Brody. He'd haunted her dreams since the moment she'd laid eyes on him.

She brought her foot up, giving him the access he wanted, and immediately was rewarded with the feel of his fingers sliding through her labia. She was slick and he moved easily.

"That's what I want. Yes, I want this sweet pussy ready for my cock." His hips moved, rubbing his erection against the small of her back. "Can you feel me? Can you feel how much I want you? Do you know why I'm going to make sure you come before I touch you with my cock?"

"Why?"

"Because you're going to feel so good wrapped around me that I don't think I'll be able to hold back. I think you're going to be hot and tight and my dick won't be able to hold off. I'll thrust in and nothing will stop me from filling you up with my come."

She shivered as one big finger eased inside her. His thumb was on the button of her clitoris, rotating and pressing down as he began to ease that finger in and out of her pussy. She sighed and let him hold her up as he started to fuck her with purpose.

His mouth was on her ear, tongue licking along the shell. "That's right. Give over. Let me control this. All you have to do is take what I give you."

He added a second finger, curling up deep inside her. Pressure built, pulsing up like a bottle of champagne waiting to be uncorked. She rode the wave, letting it take her higher.

"Let go. Give it all to me. You're close. I can feel you clamping down on my fingers," he whispered. "Let go. I'll catch you."

He rubbed someplace deep inside her and she couldn't hold back. The orgasm exploded through her, starting in her core and blasting outward. She started to yell out, but he bit her ear, a sharp, stinging rebuke that somehow amplified the pleasure coursing through her system.

"Quiet," he admonished. He continued to rub, bringing her down with ease. "We're not done and I don't want to take a break to get the lad back to sleep. Hush and let the calm take you."

The calm. Yes, she'd never had this sense of peace and calm after sex with anyone but him. Of course, the first time she'd fallen asleep with dreams of forever in her head, but this time she was smarter.

And what the hell. As long as they were both single, why couldn't they be co-parents with benefits?

Yes, that made sense. Her brain was pleasantly fuzzy as he eased his fingers out of her and kissed her shoulder.

"Now it's my turn," he promised.

He picked her up and Stephanie knew his turn was going to be good for her, too.

* * * *

"Now, it's my turn," he managed. What he really wanted to say was something about how now she'd done it. She'd given herself to him and he wasn't about to give her back. She was his and he would prove it to her over and over again. By the time he was done with her she wouldn't have the energy to fight him.

Brody picked her up, loving the feel of her in his arms. He knew he was a big bastard and could lift about anything he needed to, but there was something about being able to pick up Stephanie and haul her up high that made him feel like a true blue man.

Unfortunately, he also knew he'd fucked up royally and that she thought this was a one-time thing. There wasn't even the hope in his heart that she was surrendering to him for good. But perhaps if he showed her exactly what he could do for her, she would change her mind and forgive him.

He opened the door as quietly as he could. It had been a miracle that her screams hadn't woken Nate, but there he was. His son was asleep in his borrowed crib, one tiny fist up by his face as though even in sleep he was ready for a fight.

His dad was, too. He was ready for the most important fight of his life.

Steph looked up at him and he could see that she was coming out of the sweet fog of the orgasm he'd given her. He would never forget that moment when her whole body had tightened and she'd clamped down on his fingers.

That was going to be his dick soon, and he couldn't wait.

He eased her down on the bed, leaning over to brush his mouth against hers. "Keep quiet. I turned on the white noise app on my phone, but I think his mother crying out would still wake the lad up, and I'm not done with you yet."

She looked up at him, uncertainty clear on her face. "Maybe we should…"

"What?" He whispered the words against her jawline as he started to kiss his way down her body. "Go find another room to do this in? I think the bodyguards would be surprised, to say the least. We could always have one of them come in here with Nate, but I swear Tucker would show up and ask a million questions. He's like a horny teenager except he's never had anyone give him the full birds-and-bees talk. I think it's best we keep this private."

He heard her take a breath, knew she was going to argue with him now that the first rush of pleasure had come and gone. Now she would go back to all the rational reasons they didn't work—namely he'd been a blind arsehole and he'd hurt her terribly. He wasn't good at talking. It was one of the dumb reasons he'd had for staying away from her in the first place, but now he could see talking wasn't at all what she needed.

"Brod…"

He licked her nipple, curling his tongue around the bud. Whatever she'd been about to say seemed to die on her lips. "You've got the most beautiful breasts. I can't get enough of them."

"Brody, we should talk." The words came out breathy.

Even as she said them he was moving to the other breast. "You can talk but quietly. Don't wake the baby, luv. As for me, I'd rather not talk unless I'm talking about how gorgeous you are and how much I missed you."

"You can't have missed me too much," she whispered back. "Since you knew exactly where I was and how to get in touch with me."

That had been a miscalculation on his part. No more talking about the past. He'd fucked up in the past. He needed her focused on the now. The future would work out. He would make sure of it. Now that he was here with her and the baby, he knew one thing. He wasn't leaving them again. Not for anything.

He got up on his knees. He had a few weapons in his arsenal. He wasn't sure why, but Steph liked the way he looked. He thought he was a grim-looking bloke, but her eyes always lit up when he took off his shirt. Distraction. That was what he needed to give her.

He pulled his T-shirt over his head.

"That's not fair," she whispered, her eyes steady on his chest.

He wasn't going to play fair. Not when it came to this. He would use every trick he could find. He pulled his belt free and unbuttoned the fly of his slacks. "Nothing fair about this. This is about what I want. What I need. And I need a taste. I didn't get a proper taste of you and I can't get that regret out of my head. Do you have any idea what it's like to sit up all night long trying to come up with how your pussy's going to taste on my tongue? Will you be sweet like fruit? Or rich like cream?"

"You need other things to think about," she said, but this time her lips were curling up. "I sit up at night thinking about what I need to buy for the clinic."

He shifted his body, getting down to his belly and laying a sweet kiss on hers. "No, I like my nightly ritual better."

He ran his tongue down from her belly button. This was where she'd carried their son. The bittersweet thought ran through him. If he'd been with her, he would have kissed the growing mound, measuring it with his hands and giving her comfort while they waited for their boy.

He wanted to apologize, but she wouldn't listen to him. Not yet. Oh, she might say all the right things, but he hadn't earned her forgiveness, so those words would be meaningless.

He breathed in her scent. Sex and soap and a sweetness that made his cock tighten. Her pussy was a thing of beauty. Smooth and ripe as any peach. She'd either kept up her grooming routine or at some point had that perfect piece of flesh lasered to perfection. "Don't move. I don't want to stop and have to discipline you again. I would rather spend my time doing this."

He set his mouth on her, loving the way she squirmed under him. She made mewling sounds that went straight to his cock. He could feel himself pulsing even as he tongued her clitoris, rubbing that nub over and over. She was the most delicious of desserts. He could taste her arousal, the lush flavor of her orgasm. It coated his tongue and left him desperate for more.

Her legs spread wider, practically begging him to keep up his torture. He had no plans to stop. Certainly not until she'd come all over his tongue. That was what he needed. He needed to show her all the ways he could take care of her. She might be smart and quick and capable, but she couldn't do this to herself. She needed him.

He parted her labia, sucking each side gently and leaving not an inch of her feminine flesh unloved. He let his thumb find her clit, pressing down and rotating in time with his tongue. So much sweet cream and it was all for him.

She was all his, and though she might not know it yet, she was staying that way. She was staying that way forever.

He speared her with his tongue, letting that glorious arousal coat him like honey. He felt the moment she gave over again, letting the orgasm take her. She was quiet, but he could hear her whimper and felt the way her hands found his hair, sinking in and twisting as though she needed to keep him where he was.

He could have told her he wasn't going anywhere, but he was far too busy enjoying her. His whole body felt alive, every inch of his skin lit with the pure need to connect with her.

Since the moment he'd realized she was asleep in that tub and known some kind of horror movie was playing out in her head, all he'd been able to think about was getting her out of that place. He wasn't sure what she'd been dreaming about, but he'd known it was bad. His heart had ached and he'd realized that his connection to her was about much more than lust. Sex with her could be more than it had been that one night when he'd first taken her. Sex could be more. They could be more.

But that was a thought for another time. Now he could have her. He'd done his job. He pushed himself up to shove down his pants and get inside her.

He stopped, the image of his normally upright and slightly prissy doc making him freeze. Her body was flushed with orgasm, her face relaxed. Her hair was spread out over the pillows and her body lax and beautifully wanton. She didn't look like the woman who competently handled everything from broken bones to viral outbreaks. She looked like a woman who'd been well loved.

That was what he could give her. That was the one thing no one else could give her. No one on the face of the earth would love her as long and well and devoutly as he would.

Her eyes opened and he saw doubt creep back in. "Brody?"

He shook his head. "I'm memorizing this moment. I never want to forget how beautiful you are right this second."

When she was eighty, he would look at her and see her like this.

Her lips curled up. "Stop memorizing, Carter. I want you. I need you. Come down here and kiss me again. I want to feel you inside me."

That was an offer he would never again refuse. He'd been stupid to have wasted all the time they could have been together. He should have gotten on his knees the first night they'd met and begged to be allowed into her bed.

He shoved his slacks and boxers down, freeing his unruly dick. After fishing out a condom and rolling it over his cock, he eased her legs apart. He rubbed himself against her pussy before gently starting to press in.

Her arms reached up, closing around his waist. "Be close to me. I won't break, Brody. I want you on top of me. I want to feel warm and surrounded by you."

He didn't want to hurt her. He was big and she seemed petite and delicate next to him, but she'd had their baby and done it all without any help. She wasn't a delicate flower that would wilt at the slightest provocation. She could handle him.

He lowered himself down, letting his chest find hers. He was taller, but with a little maneuvering, he managed to plant his mouth on hers as he held his cock deep inside her. He forced his hips to be still when every instinct inside of him screamed to move, to thrust, to fuck her hard. Instead, he kissed her, giving her time to adjust to his size, the feel of his weight on top of her. Her arms wrapped around his chest and her legs around his waist. He was the one who was surrounded. He was lost in her silky skin and the heat of her body, the sweet smell of her flesh and their sex mixing to make a heady perfume.

"You feel so good," she whispered. "Please, Brody. I can't believe it, but I'm close again."

It was a good thing because he knew he wouldn't last long. She felt too right around him, too tight and perfect. His cock was already pulsing, moving toward the inevitable. He kissed her one last time and then moved, dragging his dick out even as the small, strong muscles of her pussy worked hard to keep him in.

He felt the hard drag of her nails in his back, but it did nothing but enhance the feeling of being inside her. This was what he wanted. He wanted her fierce and fighting for her pleasure. He wanted her to know that he could handle everything she had to give him.

She tightened around him. He gave over and lost his careful rhythm. He fucked her hard, loving how she held on to him, riding out the storm.

He gritted his teeth as the orgasm poured through him. Pure pleasure like nothing he'd ever felt before made his whole body stiffen and then relax.

He felt boneless as he let her take his weight. He knew she wanted it, could handle it.

She was his woman.

After a long moment he moved to the side. She turned toward him, cuddling close to his body.

"I don't think you should sleep on the couch," she murmured even as her eyes were closing.

He kissed her and then eased off the bed. She was asleep and it looked like no bad dreams were taking over. He'd tired her out. She looked like a sleeping, satisfied kitten. He dragged the blanket up and over her and then went to the bathroom to clean up.

How had he walked away from her? He'd thought he couldn't handle her. Yes, it had been there that she deserved more, but now he could also see that he'd been a fucking coward. He didn't want to love her because she was so reckless. He didn't want to love her because if he ever lost her, he would be devastated.

But wasn't that what life was about? Loss only hurt if you loved the thing you lost. He looked at himself in the mirror and for the first time in forever didn't see only scars and regret.

Somehow when he looked in the mirror this time, he saw the Brody he'd been. The kid who'd tried and failed and got up and tried again.

The one who'd loved his brother and lost him to a war.

The one who could be brave enough to love his wife and son even though there would be no promise that he could keep them.

He took a deep breath. His path was set. There was nothing to do now except crawl back into bed and enjoy these hours before she woke and fought him again.

Because there was no doubt in his mind that she would do that.

A cry that rattled the walls made him rush back out to the bedroom. Nate was red in the face and he'd kicked off his blanket. And damn but the boy smelled to high heaven.

He'd never changed a nappy. He reached for his shorts, pulling them on.

Steph rolled over, her eyes tired. "I'll get him."

He lifted his son up, trying hard not to breathe. He knew where all the stuff was. "No, luv. Sleep. We'll be right back."

He grabbed the nappy bag and was rewarded with a sweet sigh as she turned back over.

He turned off the light and closed the door behind him.

"Everything all right?" Shane was standing at the end of the hall.

His son had what might be the world's worst-smelling bottom and he had no idea how to change a nappy. Someone wanted to kill the woman he loved and they might have to go on the run with an infant. He was beyond tired, and in the morning he would likely go back to war with his soon-to-be bride. Mostly because she wasn't going to want to be his bride.

"Everything's perfect."

Life was pretty damn good. Now he just had to figure out the nappy thing...

Chapter Eight

"It was the single most horrifying thing I've ever seen and I was like born in a creepy lab where a doctor conducted experiments on us," Tucker was saying. "But that had nothing on the way that kid squirmed and managed to get poo everywhere. I think I have PTSD, Doc."

Steph glanced around Kai Ferguson's office. It was a Zen paradise complete with a soothing waterfall on one wall. She felt pretty safe ignoring Tucker since she wasn't the doc in question.

"You do realize you weren't actually born in that lab," Kai said, his deep voice curious. "You were born somewhere else. We assume you had a human mother and father and were a lot like young Nate here at one point."

Tucker shrugged one shoulder. "All I can remember is the white light and being told I should meet my brothers, none of whom were babies. Everything else is foggy. You know one memory I'll never get rid of? What that baby did with all his poo."

"See, this is why I have dogs," Kori Ferguson said as she walked in with a tray of tea in one hand. Kori was Kai's wife and she ran his office. She was a lovely woman with a halo of brown and gold hair and a smile on her face that told Steph she didn't take the world too seriously. "You open the door and they happily go poo in the yard."

"Could we do that with the baby?" Tucker asked. "Because I

think free range is the way for that kid to go. I did not know there would be baby changing duty when I signed up for this sucker."

"It wasn't bad," Brody said, the deep rumble of his voice sending a thrill up her spine.

And reminding her of every single dirty, nasty, glorious thing he'd done to her the night before. Just hearing his voice sent a tug deep inside her core and she knew it wouldn't take much more than the touch of his hand for her to get warm and ready for him again.

What the hell was wrong with her?

"He's a cutie," Kori agreed, smiling at Nate, who seemed perfectly happy in his father's arms. "But I'm happy with my French bulldog."

Kai frowned. "The asshole dog who pees in my shoes?"

She gave him a brilliant smile. "It means he loves you, babe."

The psychologist gave his wife a quick nod. "Excellent. I now know how to prove I love you. I thought you had said it was a hard limit, but we both know how much you need love and affection."

Kori's eyes narrowed. "Oh, you stop right there, buddy. Hard limit." She winked his way. "And I'll keep Gideon out of your closet, I promise. I left the paper on the coffee table for later. Call if you need me. I'll be out here with the hot bodyguards. Hey, Riley knows your brother."

"Has he talked to him lately?" Kai asked, a frown crossing his face. "Because Jared isn't returning my calls."

"I'll see what I can find out," Kori promised.

She walked out the door and Stephanie sat down on the couch. She could use a cup of tea. And a couple of the cookies Kori had put on the plate. After a few days of being too sick to her stomach to think about eating, her appetite was back. She'd woken up this morning and eaten everything Brody had put in front of her.

She'd woken up alone in bed and for a moment she'd wondered if the night before had been a dream. And then she'd wondered if she'd been a complete moron once again because she'd slept with the man and he'd snuck out—again. Only this time, she'd been left with a baby to deal with. Except Nate's crib had been empty and she'd found her baby boy cuddled up against his father's chest while

Brody managed to flip a pancake with a spatula.

"I'm not making my son some kind of free-range child, Tucker. It was my bloody first time changing a nappy. I think I did a good job. Oh, we both needed a shower afterward, but we managed." Brody looked down at Nate. "Now this morning we should talk about because it's not funny to hit your old man in the eye with your bodily fluids."

Tucker laughed. "No, that part was hysterical."

"You have to be fast," Steph said quietly. She wasn't sure what was going on. Nate didn't mind other people holding him for brief periods of time, but he always cried for his mama after a few minutes. She'd been shocked to wake up to sunshine, as Nate had never once slept through the night. He woke up screaming for her, but not this time. Nate seemed to have a never-ending fascination with his father, though. It was mutual because Brody had barely put Nate down once all day. When she offered to take their baby, Brody would shake his head and tell her to get some rest.

Somehow, she'd thought he would try to talk to her about what had happened the night before. She'd woken up and once she'd realized he was still there, she'd started getting her arguments ready.

She wasn't going to have a relationship with him because he'd been right all along. They were opposites.

She certainly wasn't going to get serious with him simply because they'd had a baby. That seemed like a terrible idea that would lead to heartache for all of them, Nate included. It was best that they began as they meant to go—friendly co-parents.

"Should you drink that?" Brody asked, standing over her.

She looked down at the cup she'd poured for herself and realized what he was talking about. Tea could be a stimulant and she was about to begin a therapy session that required relaxation. She looked up to Kai. "Is this black tea?"

"It's a tea specifically formulated to help with relieving stress." Kai looked very professorial in his white button down and khaki slacks. He did not look like a man some had called a sadist, and yet she'd heard the rumors. In his normal life he was kind and caring, giving his time to his patients, many of whom could not pay him.

At night he let his other half out to play.

When she thought about it, it was actually pretty healthy. Could she view the previous night as nothing more than her sexual side needing a release? There wasn't anything wrong with indulging that side as long as she was doing it for the right reasons.

She took a sip. She had lots of stress right now.

"Why don't we clear the room?" Kai asked. "I think this is going to be much more effective the fewer people we're surrounded by."

"I'd like to stay," Brody said.

She shook her head. She had no idea what would come out of her mouth. She'd never been put under before and she didn't want Brody learning all her secrets. "Someone has to stay with Nate."

"Kori can watch him," Brody assured her.

"I want you to do it," she insisted. "Also, it's not fair to assume that Kori will watch the baby simply because she's female. Don't you think that's a bit sexist?"

Kai's eyes lit up and he looked to Brody. "Yes, I would love to hear your answer to this as well."

Brody clutched Nate like he would protect him. "I wasn't being sexist. I wasn't going to hand him off to Kori because she's female. I was handing him off to her because she's the most competent person here. Should I give our boy to Tucker?"

Tucker shook his head. "I'm not competent at anything. Damon says I'm like a Labrador retriever, constantly distracted by squirrels. I like squirrels. They're fun to watch, but I'm far more distracted by women. A good-looking woman walks by and I'll probably try to trade your baby for sex... You know, I actually could probably handle him for a little while. I mean, you changed him already, right?"

Brody's head shook. "This is what I put up with and thanks for making my point for me. Come on then. We'll sneak over to the club. I need to make a few calls anyway. Riley and Shane are posted around the building and there are two other bodyguards next door guarding the king and queen of Loa Mali. We should be relatively safe, but if you feel even slightly uncomfortable, call and I'll be here."

She nodded his way.

He leaned over and before she could protest, he'd brushed his lips against hers, the move so sweet and affectionate it hurt her heart.

"Be good, luv," he said before turning. "Come on, Tuck. Let's go and see if you can annoy royalty. I think you can."

They strode out and the door closed behind them, but not before she had a glimpse of Shane Landon's broad back, reminding her that she had two bodyguards with her at all times. The door closed and she was left with Kai and his peaceful oasis.

"I wasn't aware you two were together." Kai sat down on the couch across from her. Though there was a big desk in the room, he'd explained he preferred a more casual setting when it came to actual therapy.

"We're not," she replied, her eyes still on the door. "I think he misunderstood something that happened last night."

"Like sleeping together?"

He was going to try to put her in a corner. She'd been to enough damn therapy sessions to know where this was going. "We both had a long, trying day. Our emotional states led us to reach out to each other for physical comfort, and I'm worried that he's translating that into something it's not."

"Or you're deflecting."

"I'm not here to talk about my relationships, Dr. Ferguson."

"Avery thinks you need to." If Kai cared about her short tone, he didn't show it. His words were calm and measured. "She called me yesterday morning to set up a few sessions for you. You know she still sees someone. Not me. She prefers a female therapist, but she still has monthly sessions. Just to talk and make sure she's all right."

"What does Avery have to be anxious about? She's got the perfect life."

"And she's had something like it before. You know there's nothing even close to perfection, and you know that it can all go away in an instant."

There they were—those tears that seemed to be at the edge of her consciousness all the time now. She was being a selfish bitch. "Of course. I'm glad she's seeing someone. She deserves every bit of happiness she can find. I love her very much. I'm not myself right now."

"I don't know. I think maybe you are," Kai pointed out. "There's nothing wrong with being jealous of someone like Avery. I wish I had half her faith in the world around us. I envy her that every day. I have no idea how I would handle the things the two of you went through."

"She went through it. I caused it. There's a difference."

He pointed her way. "Ah, there it is. That's what she's afraid of, you know. That you can smile and still hold such self-hate inside you. Tell me something—when this latest incident happened, what was the first thing that ran through your mind?"

She hated shrinks. "Well, he pointed a gun at my face and my first thought was I hope he doesn't murder me."

"Is that really what you thought?"

She shook her head. "I don't remember a lot about it. I was terrified. For me and for my people, and definitely for my baby. But I got through it."

"All right. We'll see if we can recover that memory as well," he said. "Are you ready to start? We could talk more. I worry this is going to be a dark place we go to. If you want to relax and have some more tea, we can talk about other things."

Shrink things. Talking to a man like Kai in a setting like this would never be as simple as discussing the weather or what TV shows she liked to watch. He would be probing and trying to find all her vulnerabilities. "I think I'd rather move on. I want this mystery solved."

"All right." He stood up and moved to the wall on the left side of the office. He closed the blinds, the natural light blinking out and leaving them in a twilight dim. He grabbed a candle and matches, lighting the flame and then dousing all other lights with a flick of the switch.

She watched him move in the gloom of the office, knowing that

it was brilliant daylight outside. In here there was one light source—
that candle that he placed on the table between them.

"This is your focal point." He shifted back and seemed to move
into shadows, his face disappearing as she stared at the candle. "I
want you to stop thinking about anything at all except the sound of
my voice and the light from the candle. It's warm and inviting."

It could burn her. If she did this, how did she know she only
went back to what happened last week? How could she be sure he
wouldn't take her further, back to when she'd truly discovered who
she was.

"I need you to relax, Stephanie. You're in control of this."

She shook her head, but she couldn't make herself look away
from the candle. Something about it called her in. Like a moth to the
flame. "I don't feel in control."

But last night she had. It was perverse that giving up control
had made her feel strong. She'd decided on her path and then
followed it, trusting Brody to catch her if she fell. She'd fallen, but it
was the most magnificent fall ever.

"That's better. You're thinking of something that makes you
calmer. Can you tell me what it is?"

She thought about lying, but she needed this to work. "Sex."

"Ah," he said, a chuckle to his voice. "Sex is as good as
anything else. It can be a safe place when the partner is right. You're
warm and safe and in his arms. I want you to keep that thought in
your head. If the memory is too much, you come back to this place
where you're wrapped up in him. He's there with you, even while
you're in the memory. He's waiting for you."

Brody. Brody would be there. She stared at the flame, but she
could feel his big hands on her. "All right. What do I do next?"

"You listen to my voice and let your mind open. Let all the
other sounds fall away. You can select them out like turning off
lights. Turn off the switch that allows you to hear the hum of the air
conditioner."

In her mind's eye, she flipped the switch and the sound faded.
She did it again with the sound of trickling water from the fountain,
bringing down the distractions one by one until only his voice was

audible.

An odd sense of peace settled in her limbs. Her muscles felt relaxed, her whole body soft.

"I want you to open a door for me," Kai said quietly. "We're going to walk down a corridor and when we get to the end, we'll open the door and you'll be back in Africa, back at your clinic. We'll walk out into the day that the soldiers came."

"Yes." Somehow the candle flame became a long corridor. She walked down it. The first door she came to pulsed with life and beckoned her. Her safe room, the one where Brody made love to her again and again. She could come back here and find respite.

She touched the door but didn't open it. Stephanie forced herself to move, walking past other doors. Some she knew she would never open again. They were best locked and barricaded. But there was one at the end of the hall. Light came from under the door, streaming in enough to show her the way.

"Have you found it?" Kai's voice seemed to come from far away at first.

"Yes. I think this is the one." She touched the door. It was warm and there was a white flower on the floor in front of it. They grew all over in the woods outside the clinic.

She was here.

"Open the door and step through. It's all right. This is only memory and nothing on the other side of that door can hurt you now. You're not inside this memory. You're on the outside and you're looking in."

She knew what he was doing, trying to give her a bit of psychic distance. It was exactly what the hypnosis was supposed to do, allow her to relive the memory without feeling all the pain, allow her to be objective.

She didn't want to go. She glanced back down the hall and wanted to run back to the room where Brody was.

She had to be stronger. Braver.

There was nothing inside that could hurt her. Not now.

She opened the door.

White-hot heat blasted against her.

"What do you see?" Kai asked and he was suddenly beside her, as though her mind couldn't quite stand the idea of some voice talking to her like a heavenly overlord. He was standing there in his khakis and button down looking completely out of place in the Sierra Leone heat.

She looked around. They were standing in the courtyard. "I'm in the clinic. At least I should be at this time of day."

"You are wherever you were. This is a movie that's going to play out the way it happened. You're merely an observer."

"Then I know what happens next." As if on cue she heard the squeal of tires and the rumble of a huge engine. "They pulled into the courtyard. I was standing inside with both my nurses. Anya and Keniyah. We heard the sound of a Humvee. Two, actually. We looked out the window."

She glanced over and sure enough, the thin curtains pulled back and she could see her own face staring out. Her eyes widened in pure fear and then another odd look came over her.

She shivered even in the heat of day because she remembered what she'd thought.

"What happened next?"

She suddenly found herself inside the clinic, the scene shifting with the ease of a movie.

"Keniyah, get the children out," she was saying in a firm voice.

The nurse nodded and hauled the child they'd recently vaccinated up into her arms.

The back door opened and a handsome man strode in. He was roughly six foot two and had a broad build and sandy blond hair. There was normally a wide, expressive grin on his face, as though he found the world continually amusing, but today he frowned.

"What's going on, Doc?" Alfi Dauterre asked, glancing out the window. "Shit. Those aren't locals." He squared his shoulders. He was dressed for the bush, intending to go out hunting later in the day. He pulled his Tilley down over his head and made sure his shoulder holster was secure as the door burst open.

There he was, the "boss."

"Hey there, mate." Alfi stepped in front of them. Keniyah had gone out the back and Steph remembered praying they were already making their way to the road that led through the woods and to the village. "What's the problem?"

The "boss" was dressed in fatigues, his face scarred, but he looked perfectly clean. His uniform appeared to have been pressed and his beard was neat and trimmed. "I hear there's a doctor works out of this clinic. Got a man down. Need to see him."

"I'm Dauterre, Alfred Dauterre," Alfi said. "And you are?"

The man ignored Alfi's outstretched hand, preferring to pull a gun on him. "I'm the man who will murder you if you don't present the doctor. Did you call yourself the doctor? I can barely understand you Australians."

"I'm the doctor," she said, stepping forward.

She turned to the Kai in her head. "I introduced myself."

"You didn't think about pretending you are a nurse, or maybe be a patient?" Kai asked.

She could see herself talking to the big man with the gun. He was telling her about a patient. A man. "No. He came in pointing a gun Alfi's way. I couldn't let him shoot someone. At the time, I thought the patient might be his son or someone close to him. He seemed desperate though cold. Some people have that reaction. They detach themselves so they don't have to feel too deeply. I thought that was what was happening, but I quickly learned something different."

"Where was Nate?"

A shiver went through her. "He was asleep. He naps for long periods of time during the day. I'd just fed him and I had a baby monitor on him. I thought at the time that Keniyah had gotten him out, but I realized later she hadn't. I think because he wasn't in the clinic she either forgot about him or couldn't make her way around to get him out. I don't blame her."

"You're not angry?"

She shook her head. "I gave her a lot to do. Likely she thought I would get him out."

"When did you realize he wasn't safe?"

The scene shifted and suddenly she was in her operating room.

She and Anya were working on the man. Anya sucked away much of the blood and Steph could see the wound more clearly.

"I was working on the patient and I heard Nate through the monitor. I had my hand inside the man, trying to get the bullet free, and I heard my son wake up."

She watched herself falter, the horror of what was happening dawning on her face.

"Don't you stop, Doctor." The boss was standing right outside the room, looking inside. "I'll take care of the child. It's a good trade-off, you see. You take care of this man, ensure he doesn't die, and I'll do the same for the child." He turned back and shouted. "Find the baby."

"That must have been a horrible moment," Kai said.

One of many. "He'd already explained to me that he would kill me and my nurse if we didn't save the patient. That's not what he called him. No." Her mind was working. He'd called the man something else. Something weird. "Verse…something."

"Go back to that moment. This isn't the real world. This is your movie and you can fast forward or slow it down. You can select the scene. Go back to when you first spoke to the boss. Run through the scene again. Concentrate on that moment."

He'd called the man something else. Not a name, but a word. It had been all jumbled up in her head, but now she thought it was important. He'd spoken in English most of the time. But this once, the word seemed to fail him and he'd spat out something in his own language.

What language was it?

"I'll write it down and we'll figure it out. Stop trying to force it. Let it slip and flow," Kai ordered, his voice as calm as the world around her was chaotic.

Because Alfi was trying to step in front of her, putting a hand up as the boss got in her face. She could still feel the tension of the moment, waiting for the small room to explode in gunfire.

"Step back, mate," Alfi was saying. "This doesn't have to get violent."

"If I have to kill you, I will. Do you understand me?" The

boss's face had turned a florid red, and now she was surrounded.

"They were all around me," Steph told Kai. "They flanked us like they were setting us up for slaughter. I was strangely calm about it. I knew he wanted me to save someone, but Alfi was being overprotective."

"It sounds like Alfi was being properly protective," Kai said. "How often do you get armed men threatening you?"

"In that part of Sierra Leone? Almost never," she admitted. "I set up the clinic there as a base camp of sorts. I did it because it's stable. So I knew I would have somewhere to go back to. The problems are to the east and south, mainly. We do have issues with emergent diseases. We had an Ebola epidemic, but we don't have mercenaries normally."

"Yet you had a plan in place for how to deal with them. You didn't wait to send your second nurse off with the children," Kai pointed out.

"I've been in much darker places. I've learned to be prepared." She watched as Alfi finally put his hands up and let her take over. It was obvious Alfi had run out of options besides being horribly murdered, and the man loved his own face far too much to allow that to happen. "This is where the boss threatens me. He's good at the intimidation thing."

The boss was looming over her, his accent thick as he spoke. "I need this man alive. Can you understand that, Doctor? If you can't save him, no one will be able to save you."

He turned and walked away.

Steph looked to what appeared to be the second in command. "Is this his son? Someone close to him?"

The man shook his head. "*Verslaggever.* Don't know the word in the English. *You* need to know the word alive. He will kill you. We must to keep this *verslaggever* living."

"Excellent," Kai said. "I've got it. We'll run it through a translator after we're done here. What happened after the surgery?"

She let the scene shift to the small room where she and Anya had taken turns watching over the patient. "He was still critical, but for several hours we had him stabilized. Once the boss saw that all the monitors were functioning and he had one of his men confirm that it seemed like the patient would live, he gave Nate back to me."

Steph stood outside the room, Nate swept up in her arms. She was talking to Anya, though tears were running down her face. Yes, she remembered that moment. Once she'd had Nate in her arms again, she hadn't been able to stop crying.

"He's awake?" Anya was asking, her voice hushed.

Steph looked around as though trying to make sure they were alone. "Briefly, but his pain was intense and I had to give him something. He wasn't speaking English. I think he speaks the same language these guys do. I tried to talk to him, but his blood pressure spiked. He needs rest."

"The boss has already been in here demanding to speak to him," Anya explained. "I had to tell him that if he tried to wake him up too soon there could be dire consequences. I don't think he cared. The only thing that stopped him was one of his own men. I wish I knew what he'd said. I don't speak Dutch."

Dutch. Anya had believed it was Dutch they had been speaking.

"Very good, Stephanie." Kai's voice encouraged her. "That's important information. Do you have any recollection of speaking directly to the patient?"

"Only the once before I gave him pain meds, and I couldn't tell you what he said. Shortly after that Anya and I talked, and then I fell asleep with Nate. I woke up to Alfi telling me the patient had died and we needed to run before the boss found out."

The scene shifted to a small room in the back of the clinic. She hadn't been allowed to go back to her cabin. The soldiers had told her they needed to keep an eye on her. She was fairly certain the soldiers had taken her bed and the one she'd had brought in for Brody. That was where the boss had disappeared. She hated the fact that he was sleeping in Brody's bed.

She watched as Alfi entered the room, Nate's diaper bag already in his hand.

"Stephanie, wake up," he said, not bothering to turn on the light. "You gotta wake up. We have to get the hell out of here. He's dead."

Steph sat up, trying not to disturb Nate. "What?"

164

Anya walked in behind him. "It's true. I think he threw a clot. I tried to save him, but he's gone and any minute now the guard will walk back by. I have to be there to tell him everything is fine. He's an idiot. He won't notice. Come on, you have to go."

"At the time the words didn't make sense to me," Steph explained to Kai. "I was very tired. I understood that the patient was dead, but now I remember that Anya knew I was leaving. It happened quickly. Alfi hustled me out to the car and we left then and there. I think Anya believed the guard would do what he'd done all night. He'd been checking in and then doing a long perimeter sweep so he could smoke. She could have snuck off then, but she was trying to give us some cover."

And she'd probably died for it. She'd gone from being a brave young nurse with an infectious smile to being a dead body in a doorway.

What had happened to her before she'd died? What horrors had she gone through?

"Stay with me, Stephanie." Kai's voice soothed her and she forced herself to focus.

"The only people who were alone with the patient were me and Anya," she said.

"What about Alfi?"

She stopped. How could she have forgotten about Alfi? "Yes. He sat with the man for a little while. But he didn't say anything about the patient talking."

"All right. I think we're in a good place but I need you to do one more thing for me," Kai said. "Go back. Go back to that first moment when the boss strode in."

She let the scene shift and flow back and she was standing in the lobby of the clinic again, in that moment right before the day had gone to hell. She was talking and laughing. She watched herself look up, see the problem coming, and go into action. "I'm there. What am I looking for?"

"I want you to think about that moment when you realized this was serious," Kai explained. "That moment when the boss strode in and you knew he could kill you."

What was Kai looking for? She let the moment happen, running up to the second that the boss had looked at her with cold, dead eyes. She watched as a blank look came over her own face. "I'm there."

"Tell me what your first thought was."

Without thinking, she spoke. "I thought I'd been waiting for this moment since I was sixteen years old. I thought finally, I get what I deserve."

The memory fell apart and she was back in the present, staring at a flame. Her heart seemed to seize as she acknowledged the truth.

Kai touched a button and daylight started to stream in.

Why had she told him that? "I don't really feel like that. It was a momentary lapse."

Kai turned to her, his intelligent eyes narrowing. "Oh, I doubt that very much. I think that was the most honest you've been with me and yourself in a long time. This is what your friends are worried about."

She knew it was what Avery was worried about. "I'm fine, Doc. I might have those feelings from time to time, but I'm not punishing myself anymore."

"You used to?"

"I was behind the wheel in an accident that killed two people and left one without the use of her legs for years. And I barely had a scratch on me. Yes, I punished myself. When I was younger I did it all, Dr. Ferguson. I used hardcore drugs, drank anything I could get my hands on, and I don't remember all the times I used sex to try to obliterate myself."

"And now you're involved with a man who enjoys a particular lifestyle."

She wasn't going there with him. "Oh, don't you even judge him for that. It's not the same thing. Not even close. I've hurt myself in an attempt to kill whole parts of my soul, and that is not what happens between me and Brody. It's not about pain or hurting myself. It's about connecting and the fact that only that one man in the world can give me relief, can make me feel safe enough that I can let go. I've been out of control before and I know what it feels like. It's nothing like being with Brody. When I'm with him, I can hand over control knowing he won't use it against me and I'm safe. I'm surprised that you would even think that way. I thought you were in the lifestyle."

A smile spread over his handsome face and she realized she'd been perfectly manipulated. "I am, and you explained it quite properly to me. You're cleared for play at Sanctum if it comes up. Now let's look up that lovely word of yours. Dutch, you said?"

She stopped, confused at his turnaround. "I didn't expect you to say that. I thought we would have to have more sessions."

His eyes came up from the tablet in his hands. "You know what your problem is. You admit you made a mistake. I can't force you to forgive yourself. You know what you have to do. You have to find the meaning in what seems meaningless. I personally would say you've done that. You've worked tirelessly to save people who wouldn't have been saved if your life had taken the path it would have without the accident. But I don't think you're at peace with it. You can't be if that was your first thought when confronted with a monster. It wasn't that you would save your son. It was that you had been waiting for this, deserved this."

She felt tears gather. "I love my son."

"I believe you, but Stephanie, how will you teach him to love himself if you can't do the same? Forgiving oneself is something you have to decide to do. I'm here if you want to talk, but I otherwise think you're doing fairly well at handling things. When you find the true meaning in what happened to you, that's the moment you'll forgive yourself."

Meaning. There was no meaning in what had happened. There had been only death and pain and long years of misery. Avery thought saving people in Africa made up for the horror of that night, but it wasn't true.

It wasn't a calling. It was penance.

Did she intend to force Nate to live in her version of Purgatory? She'd stayed away from the States because she could pretend to be someone else when she wasn't here. She could separate Stephanie, the idiot teenage girl, from the selfless doctor, but something had changed when she'd met Brody. She'd wanted, really wanted something for herself. For the first time, she'd wanted to be free of the cage she'd put herself in.

Avery had opened the door years before. The cage was no longer locked because Avery's kindness had busted it open.

But Steph was still inside. She might always stay inside. Could she keep Nate in there with her?

"Ah, there it is." Kai turned the tablet her way. "Journalist. *Verslaggever* is Dutch for journalist or reporter. Now that's interesting."

It was, but her mind was somewhere else. She tried to shove all the dark thoughts back and concentrate on the problem at hand.

"Can we call Adam Miles and see if he can run a search to see if anyone's missing a Dutch journalist?" Steph asked.

"I'm on it." Kai smiled like this was going to be a fun afternoon.

She wasn't sure about fun, but she'd learned a lot. Not all of it welcome. She turned to the job at hand, trying not to think about the future…or the past.

Chapter Nine

Brody nodded at Wade Rycroft as the door swung open, allowing him into Club Sanctum. The big dark-haired former cowboy was not only a bodyguard employed by McKay-Taggart, but he served as the club's Dom-in-residence.

"Carter, good to see you." He started walking up with his hand out but stopped as Brody walked in and he got a good look at the fact that he wasn't alone. "Whoa. When did you have a kid, man? Or is that a new fashion accessory?"

Taggart had sent over something called a sling. Naturally, because he was a bastard, the sling was pink. "Big Tag swears by the sling. This is my son, Nathan Avery Carter."

"Except his last name is actually Gibson because he refused to call the mother of his child back," Tucker explained. "He's not good with women."

"And this is my…partner while I'm over here. He's one of the lads from Dr. McDonald's experiments. Apparently, we can't lock them up forever so I had to take this one out in the field. Ignore him completely," Brody said. "I was told I could set up in the conference room for the afternoon while Steph is working with Kai."

Wade nodded. "Sure thing. I think I've got that information you wanted, too."

"I thought you were protecting the royal couple." Brody followed him through the lobby, hearing the locks on the front doors resetting. Anyone else coming in would need a key card, or someone with access to one. Not that he expected guests. The club had a gate around it as well. Having the first Sanctum blown up by a double agent had obviously taught Tag a thing or two about security.

"They're not as exciting and fun as I'd expected a king and queen to be," Wade said as he moved toward the big conference room. "They mostly watch movies or work out. Never together. They eat meals as fast as they can and then go back to doing things alone."

"And when they think no one is looking, they stare longingly at each other," a new voice said. "It kind of makes me sick. Shouldn't arranged marriages be less emotional? I kind of thought that was the point."

"Brody Carter, this is our resident romantic, Declan Burke," Wade said with a bite of sarcasm. "He's got day duty with me and then he's providing security for the party tonight."

"Because what you need when you're hiding from royal assassins is a play party," Burke replied. "You think if the assassins show up, Big Tag wants us to spank 'em?"

"You know he's doing this because Kash is going stir crazy," Wade replied.

"I think Tag is doing that thing where it looks like he's doing one thing, but he's actually being a gossipy matchmaker. Again, didn't realize this job would be so touchy-feely." The big guy's brow rose over one eye. "Or that there would be all those babies. What's up with all the kids? Most people leave them at daycares or something."

"He just found out he has a kid," Tucker offered helpfully. "So now he's afraid to put the kid down in case the mom runs with him again. Not that she really ran. She didn't have to. She left him a voice mail saying she was pregnant, but Brody here erased it without listening to it and now she's twelve kinds of pissed, except she's also horny and apparently big Aussie dudes do it for her."

He sent Tucker a dark look. "Do you mind?"

Tucker shrugged. "Not really. Although all that moaning and screaming made me think about hookers again. I don't think it's normal to go without sex for your whole life. I'm a virgin. I don't think I want to stay a virgin."

"You're not a virgin," Brody pointed out. "I'm sure you've had sex before."

"I don't remember it so it didn't really happen. That's the hardest part. I can't remember if I'm a tender lover or like a sex machine. It haunts me."

Burke stared at Tucker for a moment and then a smile of pure joy crossed his face. "All right, he can stay. He amuses me. Come on, weirdo. I've got to do a perimeter sweep. You can tell me all about the things you can't remember."

"And Burke can tell him about how he sees things that don't exist," Wade said with a shake of his head.

"Just because you can't see them doesn't mean they aren't there, asshole." Burke put a hand on Tucker's shoulder. "Tell me about the hookers, buddy."

"That is one weird dude." Wade opened the conference room door. "Big Tag finds him amusing, but I worry about that kid. Kai claims he's perfectly sane, but he talks in his sleep sometimes. I have no idea what language he's speaking and he claims to have zero memory of any dreams."

Brody laughed. "Oh, I thought you were talking about my weird dude. Tucker's good enough as they come, but he's got no life experience. He's like a six-foot-three-inch toddler with the sex drive of a porn star. What have you got for me?"

"Remy explained that you wanted someone to do a rundown on a man named Alfred Dauterre."

"And what did you find out? I know the background material," Brody said. "He was born in the same town I was in Western Australia. Went into the Army at the same time."

"So you're friends."

"I thought we were. I need to know what he's been doing since he left the service. I know what he's told me he's been doing, but I don't trust him anymore." How could he? Alfi hadn't bothered to tell him Steph was pregnant. They'd talked several times and never once had those words come out of his mouth.

"From what I can tell, he's done a lot of odd jobs," Wade explained, his fingers typing on one of several laptops around the room. "He spent time in his hometown. Looks like he went home for a couple of months and then his mother passed away. That prompted him to start to wander. He set up shop in Darwin as a security consultant. That's where his business is still based. I use the term 'business' loosely. I think a better word for it is mercenary."

"I'm sure he would call it soldier of fortune or some nonsense." Alfi was forever trying to pretty up the dark side of life with fancy words and phrases. He had quite the imagination.

"And he had his fingers in a lot of pies, as far as I can tell," Wade said with a shake of his head. "Did you know he was hauled in by the police for fraud? He's been accused of running cons in a couple of places, but nothing stuck."

Brody sighed. "He was always trying to make a quick buck. Hell, he conned me right and good."

And that hurt. He had to wonder why. He knew Alfi had been upset when he'd left the Army, but they'd still been friends. How could Alfi have kept that secret from him for all those months? Had he meant to ever tell him?

Worse, he was starting to worry that Alfi had used the job Brody had been paying him to do to facilitate his never-ending quest for cash. Steph would never forgive him if he'd sent in a man who'd worked with those criminals and gotten her friend killed. "I sent him in to check on Steph after my mission was over."

"Yes, you were the one who facilitated the rescue of Theo Taggart. I heard stories about that, though I'd only started in at Sanctum at the time. I wasn't working for McKay-Taggart proper yet. It was a long-term op, right?"

"Exactly six months, four days, and eight hours undercover." How that half a year, four days, and a few hours had flown by. He'd dreaded it in the beginning, but known he was the best man for the job. He had no ties to Theo at all. No ties to the Agency, and he'd been quiet about his work in London.

"That's a long time to work with a woman. Seems odd that you would duck her calls afterward."

"At the time I thought I was saving her from something. Well, I thought I was saving her from herself, I guess. I wasn't good enough for her. It made sense to me. She's a doctor. I barely got an education. I didn't see what I could give her."

"You gave her working sperm."

Brody had to chuckle at that. Proof of what he brought to the table was currently sleeping against his chest. It was easy to put a hand on his son's back and feel him breathing, feel how small and warm he was. "It's odd how the world changes. One minute I was miserable and the next I looked down at him and I couldn't be miserable anymore. I couldn't think of all the reasons I'm not good enough. I can only think of how to be better. And how to murder my former best friend for not bothering to mention I was going to be a father."

"Any chance he didn't know?"

"Not at all." Brody was certain of that. "He knew how much I cared about her. It's why I sent him, and he was supposed to tell me if anything happened to her. I think having a baby qualifies as something happening."

"So you hired him to watch over her?"

"Not exactly. I hired him to check in on her," he explained. "I wanted to know if she needed anything."

"But you weren't willing to check in yourself?"

"Again, I was a bloody wanker and I'm paying for it now. She's certain there's no future for us. Looks like I convinced her."

"Hey, I think that means you're good at something," Wade quipped. "You know if you were that good at ignoring her, you could be even better at chasing her down. I've found there's very little in this old world that can't be fixed with hard work. At least that's what my dad always used to say."

It was good to know someone was optimistic. "The good news is I've got a reason to stick around her."

"And hey, you're around her enough to make her scream, so there's that." Wade's mobile chirped and he pulled it out of his pocket, staring down at the screen. "She in the lifestyle?"

"She's certainly curious about it." It was another thing in his favor.

"Then bring her by the play party tonight." Wade typed something on the screen. "You can even bring the kiddo. They have nursery workers on play nights. You should totally come out. We're doing a whole costume-fantasy theme. Make her forget everything for a while."

"I thought we couldn't come here because of the royals." Having a few hours where she was under his command might do them both good. He had Master rights at Sanctum and she wasn't a club member. She would likely be allowed in the club because of her relationship with Avery and Liam. But if she wanted a Dom patron, she would have to look to Brody.

Sex was how he could win her back. Sex and pure groveling, if it came to it. He could grovel. He could be the best fucking groveler in the world if it meant getting his girl back and keeping his family together. He was in the wrong here. It didn't matter how it had started. He should have answered that call. He'd owed it to her.

"We couldn't put you up here because the royals are taking up the rooms that work as bedrooms, but if everyone's at the party, there's no reason you shouldn't come. Besides, then we don't have to split our resources. We can have the whole team watching one building instead of two. I can talk to Remy about it, but I think we would all feel better protecting you at Sanctum."

"I don't want to bring the royals under any more danger than they already are."

"Good, then don't break up the team," Wade insisted. "This will be the most secure place we can keep the two of you. I suspect the king and queen will hightail it out of here the minute Simon and Jesse figure out who the traitor in the palace is, and then Big Tag will want to move you two in here anyway."

Brody held a hand up. Wade was right. "We'll be here. I'm sure Serena's got something Steph can use as a costume. Now, have you found where the bastard is? The last time I talked to him he said he was in a pub somewhere."

He'd been partying. Steph had been on the run and Alfi had been living it up.

"Yeah, I got him," Wade said. "I tracked him out of Guinea. He headed straight for Berlin. From there I lost him for a bit, but I picked him back up when he hopped a plane in Brussels for...wait for it..."

"He's coming here." The fucker was coming for Steph. There was no other explanation. The question was why was he coming to see Steph and who else was he working for?

"He landed forty minutes ago," Wade replied.

Brody needed to get to the airport. How far could he have gotten? He needed to drop Nate off somewhere safe. "I have to get to the office."

"Why? Remy's bringing him here. I thought you would want to talk to the guy so I sent Remy out to nab him the moment he gets off the plane. He texted me two minutes ago and he should be pulling in now. You want me to tell him to turn around and head back to downtown?"

There was a brief knock and then the door opened.

"Hey, mate, no need to push. I'm perfectly capable of walking and..." Alfi walked in, Remy's big body pushing him along. He stopped when he caught sight of Brody and his expression changed. "Brody! I'm right happy to see you." He frowned back at the Cajun guard. "Now you're in for it. That's Brody Carter and he's been my best mate since we were kids. He's not going to let you push me around. Bloody Americans. What the hell has happened to your country? Bastard shows up and doesn't even offer me a meal. I'm starving. Do you know what airplane food is like? And I had to fly bloody coach. Got wedged in between a grandma who smelled like spearmint and tried to convince me to date her spinster daughter and a man I'm pretty sure was really a shaved bear."

"Does he ever shut up?" Remy asked, the end of his patience obvious.

Nope. Alfi never shut up. He could talk for hours and hours and he could make himself sound like an expert at almost anything. Mostly because he never let anyone get a word in edgewise. Only one thing ever managed to make the man go quiet.

Brody stepped up and popped his former best friend right in the face.

Nate gurgled and seemed to giggle, obviously enjoying the way he bounced from the activity.

Alfi yelped and covered his nose. "Damn, mate. What was that for?" He frowned and then sighed. "Fine. I probably deserved that. Is that the little nipper?" He was back to grinning. "Aw, you remember me. I'm your Uncle Alfi. Looks like you finally met your dad. Now, is there any food around here? Man needs to keep up his energy."

Remy shook his head. "Can I gag him?"

Brody sighed. "Won't work. He'll find a way to be annoying. Besides, I could use food, too. Come on, then. Let's sit down and you can explain why you're such a bloody bastard."

"Or I could shoot him," Remy muttered under his breath.

Alfi was on his feet, trying to follow. "No need to get violent. Besides, I got intel. I can be helpful. Hey, tell me there's decent beer here. The plane was a barbaric place. Did I tell you about the hairless bear I was forced to sit next to? Oh, that man smelled to high heaven, I tell you."

Alfi followed Wade out and Brody kind of wished he'd let Remy have his way.

Twenty minutes later, Brody leaned over and kissed his son's sleeping forehead. He'd found the fully functional nursery while Wade had taken Alfi to the small kitchen, which was well stocked since there were two guests somewhere else in the building.

He picked up the mobile part of the baby monitor and made sure it was on. He looked around the room, wondering if he should stay.

He had a job to do. He'd never hesitated to do his job. Not once. He would toss his personal life aside in a heartbeat. He'd broken dates, hung up on his mum (which never ended well), and once left a doctor's appointment in the middle of an exam because his job had called him. But Nate wasn't his personal life. Nate was his son. Nate was more important than any bloody job. Nate *was* his job now, the only one that mattered beyond taking care of Steph.

"It's perfectly safe," a soft voice said.

He looked over and a lovely woman with pitch-black hair was standing in the doorway. She was dressed in cotton pants and a long tunic that looked comfortable and oddly exotic. There was only person she could be. "Your Majesty."

The queen of Loa Mali stepped into the room, a book in her hand. "Please, call me Day. I'm not used to the royal thing. You must be Mr. Carter. I was informed you might be in and out of the club. And this young man?"

"My son, Nathan. Nate. I'm worried about leaving him alone. His mum might get upset."

The queen smiled, a peaceful expression. "Well, the good news for you is I happen to have a bit of time. I'll stay and sit with him."

Was it a trap? "You shouldn't be expected to do that simply because you're a woman."

She laughed, putting her hand over her mouth to stifle the sound. "Well, you're a well-trained one, Mr. Carter. Perhaps you can spend some time with my new husband and train him." She sobered. "It would be my pleasure. I would find it peaceful. I happen to adore children. Whether or not that has anything to do with my gender, I don't care. I've found a woman can be many things as long she accepts herself."

If only his woman could do that. "Yes, I'm sure that solves a lot of problems."

"Well, it solves the ones I can handle myself. Getting acceptance from others, that can be the hard part." She settled into the rocking chair. "Go on. The quicker you deal with the charmer in the kitchen, the faster my life goes back to normal. The last thing I need is my new husband trying to deal with a serial flirter. Not that he isn't one himself, but I've found we're less tolerant when we find our own foibles in others."

"Opposites attract, huh?" Brody asked quietly. She seemed easy to talk to for a royal. Not that he'd ever met one.

"I think it's important that we find our natural mirrors," she said with a sigh. "Someone who can show us who we are when we forget. Of course, if that person can't also see or accept who he or she is, well, that's when the trouble occurs."

"And if they can never accept themselves?"

"We must always have hope." But there was the saddest smile on her face. It made Brody wonder if there was more trouble than an assassination attempt in her marriage. "And we must know when the time has come to move on. Not everyone can be saved from themselves. And you have a greater duty now. You have a son. Everything changes when you have to raise a child. Children learn how to live from us. They learn our good points, but they also come to accept as normal things they shouldn't."

"I won't have my son growing up believing he ain't good enough," Brody swore. "But that means I have to feel like I'm good enough. That could take a bit of work."

She smiled and this time it was a brilliant expression. "But you're ready to take it on, aren't you, Mr. Carter?"

"Don't have a choice, the way I see it." Boys needed their dads. No. Children needed their dads and their mums, or however that love showed up. They needed someone who could put them first always.

Could Steph do it? Or would her penance always come first?

"I won't be long and I'll be sure to explain to Alfi that you're off limits," he said, her words playing through his brain.

"Oh, I can handle him, but like I said, my husband is itching for a fight. I would not give it to him." She turned back to her book.

Brody walked down the hall. He knew after last night that he could be enough for Steph, but did she know it? Did she understand what they could have together?

He had to come to terms with the fact that he might have to give up the one thing he loved. His job. He might have to sacrifice his job to make sure she didn't kill herself while trying to make up for something that had happened when she'd been a kid, something that had been a bloody accident.

He let the thought drift away because Alfi was holding court.

"So I'm walking along the beach when I hear this terrible scream. Naturally I stop everything and start running toward the sound. That's what we do, right? This saltwater croc is coming up on a gorgeous blonde. Well, she was far too pretty to become some nasty croc's dinner, you know. So I jumped right on its back."

Such bullshit. "He sure as hell did not. Those fuckers are twenty feet long and they'd swallow him in a heartbeat. He did save a pretty blonde when she got stung by a jellyfish. He peed on her. That's about the extent of his beach heroics."

Alfi puffed up a bit. "Hey, the lady was in pain. I did what I had to do."

Tucker frowned. "You should have found a bottle of vinegar. Peeing on a wound like that won't actually help and the pH balance of the urine changes from human to human, depending on diet. You need a heavy acidic pH to neutralize the alkaline nature of the jellyfish venom." He sat up, a surprised look on his face. "How do I know that?"

"You read a lot," Brody pointed out. "Now, can I have a moment alone with Alfred?"

Wade stood up. "Are we keeping him here?"

Not after what he'd found out from the queen. "No, he can come back to the guesthouse with me, but he's staying around until I figure out exactly what part he's playing in all this. However, if the bullets start to fly, you can duck behind him. After all, he's bulletproof, as I'm sure he'll tell you."

"I'll make sure there's room in the guesthouse. He can bunk with Shane and Riley. They'll make sure he doesn't wander off," Wade promised. "I'll be around if you need me. Come on, Tucker. You can meet the king. I think he'll find you amusing."

The minute the swinging door closed, he turned to the man who'd been his best friend for most of his life. "I thought you were my friend."

Alfi shoved the chair he'd been sitting in back and strode to the sink, tossing out the contents of his mug. "You know I am." He picked up the kettle and filled it. "You want a cup? The American microwaved mine. Barbarians."

"I don't want a cup of tea. I want answers."

He chuckled, though it wasn't an amused sound. "Oh, Brody, I don't think you can handle the answers, though they've always been staring you in the face. You're too noble to see it, I suppose."

He turned the range on and set the kettle on it before turning to prepare two mugs.

"Too noble to see what? I gave you one job and you couldn't do it. One fucking job. You weren't ever going to tell me about my own son, were you?"

"You didn't want Steph. You didn't want Nate either. You sent me there to fix all your problems. I was doing you a favor." He kept his back to Brody.

"I sent you there to look after her. I sent you there to protect her if she needed it."

"You sent me there to ease your bloody conscience and that was all." He turned, his eyes looking far older than they had the last time Brody had seen Alfi. "You never intended to talk to that woman again. You tossed her out like a bit of rubbish."

His hands fisted but he forced them to his sides. "I wouldn't send my best mate to check in on rubbish, you fool. I was trying to save her. I thought I was wrong for her."

"You are," Alfi said, his voice dark. "What on earth makes you think you're good enough for that woman? She's practically a saint. She's gorgeous and she's smart and she's capable. You don't think she needs someone better than you?"

He let out a deep breath. Something was going on with Alfi, but it didn't have to enrage him. He knew the answer to all of Alfi's nasty questions, and now he got why his old friend was asking them. "I think she needs me because no one on this planet is going to love her more than me, is going to see her the way I can. I love her. I thought that wasn't enough, but it is. And she deserves me because she picked me. She wanted me and I was a fool to question it. I should have gotten down on my knees and thanked god that she had bad taste in men."

"Not bad enough."

Yes, there it was. "You fell for her."

"Not that it did me any good," Alfi admitted. "It was always you. She didn't say your name to me, but I stood outside surgery when she was giving birth. She cried out for you. I was planning on going in and offering her my hand. I thought maybe if I was there when her boy was born, she would see me differently. But all she could do was cry out for you."

A sick feeling hit the pit of his stomach. "I would have been there with her if you hadn't been such a selfish git."

He would have been standing there, lending her his strength. He would have been there to hold Nate when he was born, to help her, to make sure she didn't find that trouble that always seemed to be looking for her.

"You think I don't know that?" Alfi sounded weary. "I was selfish and it didn't matter. Once again the great Brody Carter wins."

"Wins? There's no win here. I missed the birth of my child, Al. I might never win that woman back."

He shrugged. "You'll do it. You always do."

"What the hell is behind all this? Why on earth did you agree to look after her if you hate me the way you do? Never thought you would hate me. Damn, mate, we were like brothers."

"Brothers don't leave each other behind. Brothers don't walk away from each other."

What did he mean? "I didn't leave you. I…after Harry died, I couldn't stay in the Army. I tried to go home, but I was lost."

"Maybe you wouldn't have been lost if you hadn't chucked me out with the rubbish."

He groaned, trying to find a way to make Alfi understand. "I didn't. I needed to be alone. I needed to deal with what had happened to Harry."

"I loved him, too, you know. Your family was like mine. Your mum…well, she was better than mine. At least she was around. She cooked dinners and made sure you had everything you needed. Mine, if she showed up, was drunk half the time." He shook his head. "Not that it matters. I missed Harry, too, but I didn't stop caring about everyone else."

He softened a bit, their shared childhood sitting between them. "I'm sorry. I didn't mean to leave you behind. Like I said, I needed to figure a few things out. I drifted for a while."

"You played around for a couple of years and then the best job in the world dropped in your bloody lap. You moved to London, found a new best friend, and didn't call again until you needed old Alfi to help you out, check in on a girl."

"So this was payback." He could believe that of Alfi. If he thought he'd been betrayed, he would look for revenge.

"No. It was desperation. It was… I'm not a good man, but I wanted to be around her. I liked her. I liked how selfless she was. She cared about the people around her. She gave them everything she had. And she could use me," he pointed out. "She needed security, especially when she leaves the clinic and goes out into rural areas. She needs someone looking out for her, making sure she don't get hurt. I didn't see why that couldn't be me."

"Because she loves me. Alfi, I'm sorry. I didn't mean to leave you alone like that. I got caught up in a new life and London was far away. I think I needed it at the time." Was he going to be happy leaving London? Could he live the rest of his life running around Africa? Never having a real home? How would they raise Nate? Would they be able to have other kids?

If he had his way, he would raise them in Chelsea. Close to his friends, who'd somehow become his family. He would buy a townhouse, one close to his work and a park. He would take his kids to museums and historical sites. He would take them with him sometimes when he traveled so they could see the world.

He would take them home to visit his mum and stepdad.

He wanted roots. He craved them, but he would give it all up if she would say yes. He would find a way to make it work.

"Well, she didn't want me. Never did. I tried everything I could, but none of it worked. Like I said, she wanted you."

Did she still? Oh, he knew she wanted him in bed, and that was what he had to build on. "You had no right to keep Nate from me. I would never have done that to you. Not for anything."

"Yeah, well, I'm not the perfect one, am I?" The kettle started to squeal and he turned again, pouring out the boiling water. "If the shoe had been on the other foot, I'm sure you would be married to the lady by now."

"Why did you come here? You seemed to be having fun the other night when we talked."

Alfi shook his head. "I wasn't. I was in Berlin. I was a bit pissed that night. I'm afraid I indulged in wine, women, and song after my meeting with those bastards. You know when you think of big, bad mercenaries, you don't think of bloody Belgians. Shouldn't they have been picking tulips or some shit?"

"You knew who they were? Where they're from? You didn't bother to tell me?"

Alfi set a mug in front of him, shaking his head. "Like I said, I was a bit on the drunk side, and I still couldn't believe it had happened. One minute I was talking to Steph, the next I had a gun at my head and they were going to shoot her. Why couldn't she have told the arseholes that the doc was out of town? Why couldn't she play dumb? We might have gotten out of it."

"She would never do that. She certainly wouldn't do it if she thought for a second someone's life was on the line. That's not who she is."

Alfi popped two tea bags in the hot water and placed one in front of Brody. This was the civility they'd been taught. Tea cured all ills. "She has to think of the boy now. She has to have a sense of self-preservation. I damn near had a heart attack when she stepped up, pretty as you please, and said 'I'm the doctor.'"

A bit of unwelcome sympathy reared its head. He could see Alfi falling for her, maybe should have expected it. He'd also thought that their friendship would let Alfi know Steph was off limits, but then Alfi didn't believe in things like rules. Perhaps his chaotic childhood had taught him something different. "I can see that. I watched her run into the middle of a skirmish between government and rebel forces once. I was sure she was going to die. She doesn't value her own life."

"Because of what happened when she was a kid?" Alfi asked.

Brody nodded and hated the way his spine was easing. It felt good to be with Alfi. They'd known each other so long that it felt right to be sitting here with him and discussing Steph.

183

Had he left his friend behind? He hadn't meant to. He'd been utterly lost after he'd gotten the news that Harry had died. He hadn't thought about the fact that Alfi would miss him, too.

Was he always this selfish? Again, not something he tried to achieve, but something a man had to look at and examine as he grew older.

"I don't think she's ever forgiven herself."

"I looked into her after I met her," Alfi admitted. "I ran a pretty thorough trace. She killed two people in that accident. Do you think anyone gets over that?"

"I think she didn't mean to do it, and it solves nothing and serves no one at all if she throws her life away."

"But she's not. She's trying to save lives."

"At the expense of her own," Brody shot back. "It's why I walked away. I can say I was trying to spare her all I like, but it was a selfish act because I was in love with her and I couldn't watch her die. But she gave that up the minute she chose to bring Nate into this world. She can't not care about herself anymore. She's his mum. She's everything to him."

Silence descended while Alfi added two packets of sugar to his tea. "You can get by without a mum. God knows I did."

"Nate's not doing that. Nate's growing up with two parents, and if I have my way, he'll have brothers and sisters."

Alfi huffed. "You want him to go through what you did? Brothers can die. It might be better to teach him to rely on himself."

Brody shook his head. "Been thinking about that too. I hated how I felt after Harry died, but I wouldn't take back a single second. I loved my brother. That's what I was trying to do with Steph. I was trying to protect my own selfish arse."

"Yeah, you were, and you were doing the same thing when you walked away from me, you arsehole." He sighed and slumped back in his chair. "And I decided to punish you by keeping Nate a secret and trying to take your girl. Though I do care about her. Hell, man, I started out thinking you deserved not knowing since you wouldn't even accept her calls and then time moved on and I didn't know how to tell you."

"Phone call would have worked." He took a sip, breathing in the smell. P&G. Not the brand he expected to find here in the States, but it was familiar and soothing.

"Yeah," he replied. "I'm sorry, Brody. I can't say more than that. You know I'm a selfish bastard, but I did get her out of there. I didn't fail you when it came to that."

"Why didn't you fly back with her? Or call me?" He was calm, but his anger was simmering. He could understand that he had some culpability, but Alfi had taken it too far. "Anything could have happened to her."

"I thought it best we split up. I was worried they might have recognized me. I was hoping if they were going to follow, they would come after me."

He wasn't sure he believed that, but he wasn't going to argue. He needed information. "What do you know about them? And how could you have left that poor nurse behind to die?"

Alfi went white and his body stiffened. "What do you mean?"

"I'm talking about the nurse. Anya. We sent a couple of drones to get footage of the clinic and it looks like she's dead."

"You saw her body?"

"We saw what looked like a shoe in her doorway. Can't tell much more but the way it's sitting, it seems like it's attached to something. Probably a body."

Alfi shook his head. "Anya was supposed to run. She promised me she could make the machines look like they were working. That fucker wasn't supposed to be back until morning, but he had a couple of men working the perimeter, keeping the locals out and us in. She can't be dead. I left her there because she had the keys to a Jeep and she was going to sneak out and get to the village where we'd sent Keniyah. Hell, I was sure Keniyah would have sent the local police by morning. Damn it, she can't be dead."

His head fell forward and Brody sighed. Alfi was a bastard, but he did have a heart.

"I'm so sorry. God, I'm sorry," he said.

Brody got up. They were going to need something far stronger than tea. "Come on, let's get you back to the house. We'll settle you in for the day and we'll talk more."

And he would wait for Steph to see how his night would go.

* * * *

Steph stared at her former head of security. She'd been a bit surprised to find him sitting in the kitchen of their safe house when Shane had driven her back. Actually, she'd been completely surprised because she'd expected Brody to wait for her, but he hadn't been in the car that picked her up.

Now she knew why. He'd been here spending time with his bestie. His lying, sneaky, asshole of a bestie.

"You're an asshole." It was all the welcome Alfi Dauterre was going to get from her.

Alfi grinned, his eyes a bit on the cloudy side. "Yeah, but I'm also a charmer. It's how I get through life, lovie. And I'm quite an attentive lover."

She frowned Brody's way. It looked like they'd been doing more than sitting around talking. "You had to get him drunk?"

Brody shrugged. "He's impossible when he's sober. Actually, now that I think about it, he's spent most of his adult life drunk. A lot of our adolescence, too. Not a lot to do in Wanga Woo."

Alfi slapped the table and held up his now empty glass. "To Wanga Woo. Damn but I miss that piece of shit town."

"Did you get anything out of him?" Steph asked. She'd been with Kai for hours, patiently looking through European news sites, trying to find out if one was missing a reporter. They'd gotten someone named Penelope Knight to call around and see if she could find out any information from the big media outlets in Europe. And Liam had come to the office and set up a video meeting with Tennessee Smith, the former CIA agent who now worked odd jobs for several agencies, including McKay-Taggart. She'd met Ten and his wife, Faith, whom she'd worked with on occasion. Faith Smith was a doctor who'd worked on various charities over the years, several in Africa. It was a small world. Ten was trying to find the name of any Dutch mercenary groups working in the region.

And Brody had spent the afternoon watching Alfi get his drink on.

"I actually found out quite a lot," Brody replied, bringing her out of her dark thoughts. "I found out Alfi here kept the secret about Nate's birth because he fancies himself in love with you."

She had to shake her head. "What?"

"Totally in love, luv," Alfi affirmed with a brilliant smile. "Marry me. You don't want that big bastard. He takes up all the space. Can you imagine what doing his laundry is going to do to you for the rest of your life? I'm much more reasonably sized, and honestly I don't change clothes all that often."

What the hell? "That is not a point in your favor." She turned back to Brody, who looked so deliciously large and muscular that she really was trying to think of a way to get his arms around her without having to ask for it. If she didn't ask for it, then she wasn't leading him on. She was simply taking what he offered. It had been a long day and she wanted nothing more than to sink into him, to let him take over and take care of her. But she had to remember that she was alone and she had to maintain control. "And don't play innocent here, Brody. Alfi didn't keep the secret from you. It wasn't a secret at all. A secret is something no one talks about. I told you on several occasions that I was pregnant. Alfi isn't the reason you didn't know about Nate. You are."

Alfi nodded. "There. What the girl said. Another reason to marry me. I answer my mobile. Well, when I've paid the bill and it's on, I answer it. Mostly."

Brody sent his friend a look that should have had him running scared. Maybe it would have if the man could move. "You stay out of this." He looked down at her. "Yes, that part was my fault. I was stubborn and selfish. I figured out a lot about myself sitting here and talking to Alfi this afternoon. I didn't run away from you because I was trying to protect you. I did it to protect myself."

She shook her head. She couldn't deal with this right now. The last thing she wanted from him was a well-rehearsed speech meant to get her to forget that he hadn't wanted her before she'd shown up with his spawn. "Doesn't matter. That's all in the past."

"Doesn't feel like it is," he said, suspicion plain in his voice.

Alfi was shaking his head. "Women are like elephants, Brody. They never forget. One misstep and you'll get hounded with it for the rest of your life. Like that little thing in Melbourne. You remember her. One mistake and she broke my heart."

"You slept with her sister," Brody shot back.

Alfi put a hand to his heart. "They looked a lot alike in the dark. Her mum did, too. Glad she didn't find out about that until we were gone. Good times, mate. Such good times."

Brody's hands came up. "I had nothing to do with that. I was in town to see my aunt and my mum thought it would be smart to take that arsehole with me. I spent all my time taking my elderly Aunt Rose to various bingo parlors."

"It doesn't matter, Brody. I'm focused on the now not the past. So you got nothing at all out of him about why a crazy Dutch dude is trying to murder me?"

He grinned and pointed her way. "I did find something out. Dutch was the language he was speaking. Alfi knew that."

"My brain did, too," she shot back, frustrated as hell. "I spent all day staring at a candle with a shrink tromping through my head and Alfi knew all along. He's a giver."

"I do try, luv," he said solemnly. "But they weren't Dutch, you know. I was with 'em while you were working on the patient and I heard them talking about going home to Antwerp. That ain't in the Netherlands. Those boys were from Belgium."

She sort of growled his way. "Thanks for that because I've been working on the theory that we're looking for Dutch dudes."

Alfi didn't seem at all deterred by her show of rage. "Not a problem. Anything for a pretty lady."

Brody ignored him, his big hands coming out, cupping her shoulders. "Was Kai hard on you? Come here. I bet it was rough to have to go through all of that again. I wish I could have stayed there with you."

There it was. She sighed as she let him pull her close. His big arms wrapped around her and she felt safe and warm for the first time in hours and hours. He'd started it. She hadn't promised him anything. It was perfectly all right to revel in it. She let her arms drift up and around him. He was incredibly big, but she could clutch him and hold on. She felt him kiss her hair.

"Kai wasn't bad," she admitted. "He's just a normal pushy shrink. They kind of have to be. At least I figured out a few things. We know the patient was a journalist. They called him that in Dutch. We have someone from the London office calling around the big European news agencies trying to see if they had any male reporters working on a story in Sierra Leone. We don't know if the journalist was Belgian or from the Netherlands, so we'll look all over Europe."

Brody tilted her head up. "That'll be Penny you'll be working with. She speaks all the languages. She's a good one."

"Is she part of his fancy-schmancy London team?" Alfi asked.

Brody groaned and rested his head against hers. "He doesn't like my new career. Apparently I was supposed to join him in dashing about the globe doing odd jobs, some of which I'm fairly certain involve criminal activities."

"Do not...mostly," Alfi shot back. "My point is, you ran off to England and became a pommy git who can't even be bothered to call his friends. Or the woman he knocked up. He ain't ever going to traipse around Africa with you saving babies and stuff. He's too posh for that."

"Shut up, Alfi," Brody growled. "She's not marrying you. Leave her be."

Steph pulled away, not wanting to, but they'd introduced a word she simply couldn't handle right now. That word needed to be avoided at all costs. "Could we get back to the actual job at hand? And where's Nate?"

"He's over at the big house with Serena and Adam and Jake." Brody looked like he wanted to push her, but he seemed to back down. "We'll go over and get him in a bit, and then I want to talk to you about going to the club tonight."

Kai had mentioned that she was welcome at the club. Sanctum. She'd heard a ton about it, but she'd never been inside. Avery was fairly open about the lifestyle and how she and Liam played, but everything Steph knew came from books. The night they'd made

Nate had been quick and passionate, but there hadn't been a lot of D/s. Only the night before had given her a hint of what the lifestyle could offer her.

She shook her head. "I need to be with Nate."

"He'll be in the daycare with the other kids," Brody promised. "Wade doesn't want to split the guards up tonight. If you don't want to play, we'll take a couple of movies with us and sit in the conference room, but there's a big party going on. Don't you want to have some fun?"

That kind of fun was dangerous. That kind of fun led to getting naked and giving her body over to her Master. Oh, there it was. She was thinking of Brody that way and she shouldn't. Though it was only for play. Only for a night.

She clung to the only reason she could think of to tell him no. "I don't have the right clothes."

"Serena's going to find something for you. It's a costume party. It should be loads of fun," Brody promised.

"What are you going as? James Bond? Got your martini all ready?" Alfi asked, his voice harsh. "I mean you probably own a tuxedo now."

Brody's eyes rolled in perfect disdain. "Pass out, mate. You would be doing us all a favor."

"I've the constitution of a rutting rhino. A bit of drink can't keep me down," Alfi vowed. "Am I going to this party?"

"No," they said at the same time.

Alfi frowned. "What if I get murdered here?"

"I'm willing to take that chance," Brody replied. He pulled his cell phone out. "I'm going to make a few calls and then we'll go over and pick up Nate. I think we're having dinner at the main house before we head to the club."

"Brody, I think we should talk about this," she began.

He leaned over and planted those big, sexy lips right on hers. Any thought of protest fled her brain as she felt his hands cup her neck and his body press to hers. The kiss was swift and devastating, and she was lucky to find her balance when he pulled away. There was the most arrogant smirk on his face as he stared down at her.

"Don't think, luv. Let me take control and I'll show you what it means." He started for the kitchen door. "If that one gives you trouble, murder him. He's not worth it."

He was typing on his cell screen as he walked away, and she was left with Alfi and a million questions.

"Why didn't you tell me they were speaking Dutch?"

He shrugged. "Didn't think about it. That day was a mess, Steph. It all happened so bloody fast and I could barely keep up with it."

"I don't know about that. You were the calm one."

He huffed. "I was not. I was terrified. Don't think because I spent years in the Army that I don't get scared. Spent half my life scared out of my mind and finding ways to make it look like it don't matter. That's how you survive. You were the cold one that day. I barely saw your hands shake until you realized they had Nate. Did you think Keniyah had gotten him out?"

She nodded. "Yes."

"So as long as the nipper was all safe and sound, nothing else mattered, right?"

"It wasn't like that. I was very dedicated to making sure no one died."

"Anyone but you." Somehow he made it almost seem like an accusation. "You know protecting everyone was my job. You didn't let me do my job. You should have told them you were a volunteer and that the doctor was in the city for the day."

"And let that man die?"

Alfi's hands fisted on the table. "He was going to kill everyone, Steph. That damn journalist didn't have a chance. He would have been questioned and once the boss had what he wanted, he would have killed him. Then he would have killed us. All you were doing was putting off the inevitable. I could have come up with something, but no, you step up, pretty as you please, and walk into the croc's mouth."

"I couldn't let him die. Not when I could save him." She'd taken an oath when she became a doctor and she took it seriously.

"You couldn't save him. That's what I'm telling you," Alfi shot back.

She wasn't sure what his point was or why he was angry with her. "I doubt that me telling that man there was no doctor around would have made him go away."

"We'll never know now, will we? You should have left it to me." He let his head fall forward. "I thought Anya would get out."

Her stomach clenched. "I should have thought about that. I should have stayed there with her or sent her out."

Those red-rimmed eyes rolled when he looked back up at her. "God, Steph, does it all have to be about you? Are you the only one in the world who gets to be wrong?"

"What is that supposed to mean?" She'd never seen Alfi like this. He was always charming. Smarmy at times, but charming. He never raised his voice unless he was playing football with the local kids, and then he merely shouted out encouragements. He was a rogue, no doubt, but she'd never seen him so dark.

"It's pretty fucking arrogant, you know. Everything bad is your fault. Like you're some kind of goddess on earth. It's not always about you. I can make big fucking mistakes, too."

"Well, on that we can agree."

"You're making another one," Alfi insisted. "If you let that man go, you'll regret it for the rest of your life."

"I thought you wanted me for yourself. Which is utterly ridiculous."

He shrugged. "Yeah, but now that I'm here and thinking about it right and proper, I can see maybe I was right. Maybe we're more alike than you and Brody. He spent all that time thinking he was bad for you. Maybe you're bad for him. Maybe you're the one who would drag him down and not the other way around."

Wow. That hurt more than she'd thought it could. "It's good to know how you think, Alfi. When all this is over, don't feel like you need to check in on me again. I'll be fine."

He sighed, a hand scrubbing through his hair. "Damn it, you don't understand a thing I'm saying. You'll drag him down into the mud with you because you're too daft to see that you don't belong there. You think I didn't run a check on you? I know all about what happened. I'm sure Brody thinks he knows, too, but I would bet he knows nothing about what you did in the years after the wreck."

She felt her whole body flush with shame. "No, I suspect he doesn't or he wouldn't think I was too good for him."

Alfi groaned. "That's where you're underestimating him. He won't care. He won't care how many men you tore through trying to forget. He won't care what drugs you did in an insane attempt to make things right with the universe because you think someone somewhere got it all wrong. He won't care what you did in the past. He'll try to make it so you never feel that way again. He'll love you if you let him and when that man loves... I've never known a better man than Brody Carter, and that's why I wanted to take you from him. I thought if I could make you love me instead, maybe I'd be more like him. I ain't going to change, luv. I'm going to die exactly who I am right now—a good for nothing player, but I do care about him. If you're not going to change, then you should walk away from him."

That was the whole problem she found herself faced with now. "I can't walk away from him. We have a child. And I have changed. I don't do self-destructive things anymore. I'm over that."

"You have a child who almost got killed out there, so I beg to differ. I watched you. You didn't care about anything until you realized Nate wasn't safe."

He wasn't right. She didn't believe it. "I did, too. I cared about everyone in that clinic."

"Not yourself. You didn't give a bloody damn about yourself, and that's what will kill Brody. His brother died and I thought he would lay down and die with him. What's going to happen when the only woman he's ever loved dies because she needs to martyr herself more than she needs to live?"

"Hey, I think you should go sleep it off, mate. Now." Brody was standing in the doorway, a forbidding expression on his face.

"I've said what I needed to say." Alfi stood up and made his way to the door. "I'll bunk in with the crazy one. Tucker whatever his name is."

"Why did you come here, Alfi?" Brody asked.

Alfi stopped, one hand on the door, holding it open. "Didn't know where else to go. If everyone I know is going to get themselves murdered, thought I probably should, too."

He walked out, but Steph still felt a hole in her gut.

"What did he say to you?" Brody asked. "I didn't catch anything but his tone and the look on your face. Should I talk to him?"

She shook her head. "No. He didn't say anything I didn't already know. I'm going to get Nate."

"I'll go with you."

"I can handle it."

He stepped in front of her, looming large. "Sweetheart, he said something that upset you. I wish you would talk to me about it. He's pissed. You can't listen to him." One big hand came out to smooth back her hair. "He's also jealous as hell. I can't blame him. You're a beautiful woman."

Tears sparked behind her eyes. "I can't do this with you right now."

"Do what?" He moved closer, drawing her in. "Do this? Take comfort from someone who cares about you? You had a rough day. Let me take care of you. You can't be all wound up around our boy. He'll sense it and it'll affect him, too. Come here and let me take some of this burden from you."

She was enveloped in his arms again and she couldn't find the will to break away. He was right. It had been a shitty day at the end of a string of shitty days, and he was safety and warmth and pleasure all wrapped up in one gorgeous man package. Despite the fact that Alfi's words and what she'd realized in the shrink's office that day were plaguing her brain, she couldn't force herself to move away from him.

"That's better. That makes me feel better," he whispered against her ear. "I had a nice day with Nate. He's a good kid. I might have called my mum and told her about him. Took a couple of pictures and texted her. I hope you don't mind."

Those stupid tears were playing at the corners of her eyes again. "She's his grandmother. She should know he's alive. I never…"

"Shh, I know you never tried to keep him from me, but I'm stepping light here. You've had all the responsibility for two months, and I can't come in and ride roughshod over you. I should have asked, but I wanted to talk to her. I didn't know what to do with the tube of white stuff and then Tucker opened it and it got all over him and it wouldn't come off."

She laughed at the thought. "It's diaper rash ointment. It's not easy to get off. He's like a large puppy, you know."

"You're telling me," he replied. "Mum cried. Said he looks just like me. Said you deserve a medal for pushing out that…well, she's got a mouth on her."

"For pushing a giant baby through my hoo haw? I got a mouth on me, too, and it was horrible. I have no idea how I managed that. Could you make smaller babies?"

"I'll try," he promised.

She started to pull back, realizing what she'd said. "Brody, I didn't mean that."

He held her close. "I know. I'm not taking anything seriously. You need time and I'm going to give it to you, but Stephanie, we're stuck together for a while. We're going to be living in the same house, spending a lot of time together until this gets sorted out. There's no reason for us to not sleep together and play together and be kind to each other. Can we do that? No expectations of what happens when the case is done and you're safe."

She wanted to believe him. "None?"

"None except that I want to be in his life. I want to be his dad. God, Steph, I didn't think I wanted kids until I picked him up and held him. Now there's nothing I want more than to be around him."

"Of course, but I have to go back and you'll be in London." Did she have to go back? That part of her that had held things together for the last decade screamed yes. She'd promised Avery that she would do good.

Avery thought she could do good here.

"We'll talk about that when the time comes," he promised. "For now, we're not going to look past tonight and having a good time while we wait to see what happens next. Can you do that with me?"

She should say no. She needed to listen to what Alfi had said. Maybe he was right and she was the one who wasn't good enough for Brody. Distance. She needed some, but she still found herself lifting her head and nodding. "Only while we're stuck here."

"Only while we're stuck here," he agreed.

So why did being stuck here suddenly seem like something she could do for a very long time?

Chapter Ten

A few hours later he stood outside the locker room, waiting for that moment when she would walk out and he would get a glimpse of her.

Alfi, the fucker, had at least one brilliant idea.

"Nice tux." Big Tag strode out wearing a long blond wig, red bandana, and leather pants. "You a maître d?"

"You a heroin addict?" He could give as well as he got.

"Definitely at some point." And Big Tag could take what he shoveled out. "Dude, I'm Axl Rose. Do you know who that is? Do they have music in Australia? I know they have that diggery doo thing, but I'm talking about rock 'n' roll."

"It's a didgeridoo and I might have heard of Guns N' Roses somewhere." He wasn't giving Tag anything. He was too happy tonight. Steph was here and he got to play with her all night long. Or at least until the party was over and they had to pick up their kiddo and head home.

Yeah, he liked that thought, too.

"Got to love a costume party." Tag patted him on the shoulder. "You sure about that other guy?"

There was only one person he could be talking about. Alfi. Well, he might be talking about Tucker, but Brody doubted it. "Am I sure about him? I'm sure he's an arsehole. Do I think he'll hurt someone? No. I've known Alfi all my life. He'll do a lot of stupid things but he's never cruel. He can be mercenary, but if he truly understands how he's hurting someone, he'll stop. He's angry with me."

"Because you walked away after your brother died?"

Naturally Tag knew about that, but then he would have done a thorough investigation before he brought Brody on the team. "Alfi thinks I abandoned him. I had a shot at getting out of the Army. He reupped because he thought I would. Spent another year in while I kind of roamed the world until I met Walt."

And Walt had led him to a ship called the Royale and the Taggarts. And they had led him to his home in London and the job that brought him to Steph.

"Any reason you didn't tell him?" Taggart asked.

He sighed because he was done lying to himself. "Yeah, chaos follows Alfi and I needed a couple of months of peace. I had to figure a few things out. I grew up with that man, but sometimes it's hard to be his friend. He can be very self-centered, and he doesn't always see it. I'm not saying he's a bad guy. But he's difficult. We weren't on the same team. Even when we were in the Army we wouldn't see each other except when we were on leave or happened to find ourselves on the same base."

"Was the Army good for him?"

"Kept him out of trouble for the most part," Brody admitted. "But I don't know how to deal with the fact that he didn't tell me about Nate."

"You know what would make you feel better?"

Brody could think of a few things. "Hanging him by his arms and slowly feeding him feet first into a vat of piranhas? Or lowering him into a nice pool that contains that South American worm thing that slips up a man's willy and hooks his way in?"

"Dude, that's brilliant." Taggart pulled out his mobile, touching the screen. "Note to self, arrange to buy South American penis barb worm and slip it into Adam's daily rose-scented bath. I'm sure he has one." He clicked it off. "I like you, Carter. You're mean. I was merely going to suggest negotiating a series of punches or bitch slaps to be used randomly over the next couple of years. Made me feel better about Ten. Friends are hard things. Women are even harder. Ah, you're Pierce Craig. I should have known. Steph, you make a lovely Genie. You know Geneva Peretti is based on Charlie, right?"

Brody's breath caught because Steph had walked out and she was wearing a teeny tiny white bikini that showed off her graceful figure. On her right thigh there was a holster that held a wicked knife. He figured she was a surgeon so he didn't have to find a fake knife.

Damn, but she was gorgeous.

Charlie was behind her, dressed as Wonder Woman and looking every inch the superhero. "She's a Bond girl, Ian."

Tag shook his long blond hair. "Don't know who that is. Only one true fictional super spy and that's Pierce Craig. Come on, baby. We've got some work to do tonight. Brody, before you head in, Adam is going to meet you in the conference room in a while. He's got questions for you and Ten's on the ground in Sierra Leone. He's calling in from there."

Charlotte took her husband's hand and winked Steph's way. "Have fun."

Steph frowned at him. "Why do you get a tux and I get two inches of Lycra and a big knife?"

He couldn't help but grin at her. "Because that's how Bond girls get their Bond, luv. You look absolutely delicious. And I promise there will be people here with far less on. That swimsuit doesn't even qualify as fet wear. If tonight were different, I would have you in a gloriously tight corset that would push your pretty tits up, and the only other thing you would wear would be a teeny tiny thong that wouldn't even cover your lovely cheeks."

"Put that way, I think I'll take the swimsuit. Sounds way more comfortable," she said.

He moved in close, staring down at her. There was a faint flush to her cheeks that let him know she was aware of him. He wasn't sure if she was embarrassed or slightly aroused, but he intended to turn her toward arousal. After they dealt with Adam and Ten. He took her hand and started moving toward the conference room. "Who the hell is this Pierce Craig person? And how does Taggart not know who James Bond is?"

She laughed, the sound magical to his ears. "You don't pay a lot of attention to pop culture, huh? Serena wrote a book called *Love After Death*. I've been told it sounds suspiciously like Ian and Charlotte's real love story, complete with a sarcastic, Viking-like hero named Pierce Craig. It was made into a movie. I think Big Tag likes to pretend like he doesn't know it's him, but surprisingly enough he talks about how cool Pierce is."

"Ah, that thing Kay's always talking about." Kayla loved her romance novels and didn't mind telling off anyone who said they weren't worthy fiction. "She's a big fan of Serena's."

"Kay?" Steph kept walking, but her voice had gone stiff.

Ah, sweet jealousy. "She's a coworker in London. I think of her like a little sister."

He opened the door to the conference room. It was empty. Looked like Adam hadn't gotten here yet. That was all right with Brody. He didn't mind having her to himself for a few minutes. It would give him a bit of time to lay out rules for the night's play.

"I find the female agents a bit intimidating," she said, glancing around the conference room. There were a couple of laptops humming along and a printer. "Erin, in particular, scares the crap out of me."

"You would like Kay," he replied. "And Erin and you actually have quite a bit in common. You were both forced to give birth without your men."

That was a mistake. He knew it the moment the words left his mouth, and definitely the second he saw fire light in her eyes. "Her man had been stolen away by a crazy doctor who performed experiments on his memory. You're just an asshole who can't check his voicemail."

He held his hands up in pure defeat. "Yes, I am. I'm a coward who doesn't deserve you even looking twice at me again, but I intend to make up for that."

She shook her head. "We're not talking about the future. Nothing past tonight or tomorrow."

He conceded because the last thing he intended to do tonight was fight with her. "Tonight, I'm afraid all I can think about is how beautiful you are. Are you cold?"

She shook her head. "Surprisingly no. They keep it warm in here. I'm surprised you're not hot. Though I have to admit, you look amazing in a tux."

Oh, he was hot, but he wasn't about to change since she seemed to like him all posh. "I'll wear one more often if you like. Perhaps after all this is over, we can go somewhere nice and fancy."

"No talk about the future."

"All right, let's talk about tonight." He leaned against the conference table. "Do you want to watch or participate?"

"I'm not sure. I haven't done anything like this before."

"What are your fantasies like?"

A sweet blush crossed her face. "I don't know. Private, mostly."

She wasn't getting out of this so easily. "Nothing's private here. Not really. Oh, there are privacy rooms, but they're off limits tonight because the royals are staying here for a bit. They've been turned into a large suite of rooms for their use."

"So we can wait and have sex when we go back to the guesthouse."

"If you like."

"But you don't want to wait?"

"I can wait for as long as you like, but I would rather get you so hot and bothered that you can't wait to have me inside you. I want to watch a couple of scenes, maybe perform one of our own, and at some point I want you so wet, so damn aroused that you can't take another second without my cock inside you."

She put her hands on her cheeks, a sure sign of her embarrassment. "How can you talk like that?"

"It's easy when I'm talking about you," he admitted. "I think about fucking you all the time. It's been pretty much all I thought about the last year. And you should know when I use the word fuck, I mean more than that. I think about holding you and kissing you. I think about waking up next to you in the morning and going to sleep with you at night. But I definitely think about getting inside you and making you scream."

She turned for a moment, but not before he saw how hard her nipples had gotten against the thin material of her bikini top.

He moved in behind her and put his hands on her shoulders. "Normally we would sit down and negotiate a contract about how we'll move forward."

"I signed the contract Jake brought over." She leaned back against him. "I read it. Most of it. I understand I'm supposed to respect the other patrons and behave in a manner that won't embarrass my Dominant partner. I'm to be quiet and respectful during scenes and to leave the dungeon floor if I find I cannot be. It also said a bunch of stuff about obeying you that I'm pretending doesn't bug me."

"It's only on the dungeon floor," he said, kissing the top of her head. "No one expects you to do it outside this club. Well, unless you're in danger, and then you'll obey me or there will be hell to pay."

"Because you're the man?"

That was one trap he didn't have to set off. "Because I'm the one who's been trained to protect. I promise I'll let you top the hell out of me in the operating room. I mean it, Steph. I expect you to do everything the bodyguards tell you to do if I'm not around. They're in charge of your safety."

"Even Tucker? Because I think I'm way smarter than Tucker. When we left he was pouring chocolate syrup on microwave popcorn. He called it his grand experiment."

"Even Tucker," he replied. "Tucker might seem like an idiot, but he's actually quite smart and he knows his job. He knows how to protect you and he'll do what it takes. But we're not out there in danger right now and we're definitely not in an operating theatre so that means that I'm in charge."

He was satisfied by the shiver that went through her.

"What did you want to do tonight, Sir?"

"First, I want you to call me Brody. I don't like Sirs or Masters. That's up to each couple, unless the idea of calling me Sir trips your switch and then I'll allow it."

"I like your name," she admitted. "I like saying it."

This was where he needed her to be. Talking about the future put her on her guard, but this was a place where she could be calm and let herself feel. He wanted her to spend all damn night feeling. "Then Brody it is. You'll say, yes, Brody. I do want you to touch me. Yes, Brody, I like the way your hand spanks my arse. Please tie me up, Brody, and blindfold me because I don't want to think about anything at all except the way your hands and tongue and cock feel."

"Yes, Brody." She turned and looked up at him, her eyes cloudy with desire. "Do I go with the flow or can I make requests?"

"Always." He never wanted her to feel like she couldn't talk to him. Even when they played around with ball gags. "This is play, luv. It's play that's meant to help us explore sex. It's meant to show you what you like and what you don't, what your boundaries are. It's also meant to bring us closer, so you can always ask me."

"Will you kiss me, Brody?"

That was one request he would always honor. "Of course. Don't you ever be afraid to ask me that."

He started to lean over, ready to plant his lips on hers and begin the evening right.

The door came open and Adam Miles strode in wearing a perfectly pressed suit. "Hey, guys. How's it going? Steph, looking good there. I like it. It's very Bond girl. The sexy, dangerous type. Feel free to wrap your legs around Brody's head and try to kill him that way. That would be an awesome scene."

All right, he now understood why Big Tag always wanted to kill the bloke. He had the worst timing. "I think we'll avoid the more dangerous scenes and skip to the part where they're all safe and have some time to relax."

"Boring, but probably your best bet." Miles walked straight to the larger of the laptops and flipped the lid up. "Let's make this quick. I've got a naughty schoolgirl to discipline and Jake will kick my ass if I make him wait too long. All right, Tennessee Smith. Let's see if you are where you said you would be."

The screen flickered and suddenly filled with bright light and a man with golden brown hair, a lean face, and startling blue eyes. "Miles? That you? Ah, there you are. Well, well, well. Dr. Gibson. You are looking lovely. Is this a pool party or something?"

"Costume night at Sanctum," Adam replied.

"Damn it. I miss all the fun stuff." Ten Smith had a slow Southern accent and an easy charm that belied what she knew was decades of work for the Central Intelligence Agency. "Ah, well, Faith isn't ready to play yet anyway. She's having too much fun with our baby boy."

"How is he doing? You named him Grant, right?" Adam asked.

Everyone was having babies these days. It seemed a new one popped up all the time. Soon Brody was going to need a chart to remember which poop maker belonged to whom. "Congrats, Ten."

Ten grinned. "Yes, Grant Matthew Smith. And I hear congrats are in order for you and the doc. Can't wait to see that boy when we're back in the States. Now, I went into the clinic. Took a bunch of pictures, but I was surprised by what I saw there."

"What did you see?" Steph asked. "Did you find Anya's body?"

His head shook. "I saw nothing, Doc. No bodies. Not of your nurse or of the patient you talked about. I also didn't find any evidence that you had worked on a patient at all. You clean up real nice, Doc."

"But I didn't," she replied. "It was late and we were tired. I was worried about the patient dying. Anya and I did basic cleanup, but it was still a mess in there. We hadn't sterilized any of the equipment."

"And yet that place was sparkling clean when I walked in. It was like it was sitting there waiting for the next emergency," Ten explained. "The whole place was like that. You said the men slept in a couple of the cabins, but every one of them was neatly made up. Not a blanket or pillow out of place."

"They cleaned up after themselves. They didn't want to leave any evidence behind which tells me this is serious and not contained to Sierra Leone." Brody considered the problem. Most mercenary groups didn't give a crap about making sure they left a place untouched. They were there to destroy. It all came down to who they were working for and what the job was. If the client wanted discretion, then they would attempt to please them, but this level seemed out of place. "Mercenaries don't usually care, but then this one brought you a journalist. We have to assume the boss, or whoever the boss was working for, is nervous about the press. Maybe our journalist knew something he shouldn't. And likely about someone important, hence the whole cleanup project."

"That was my first thought," Ten said. "But I'm surprised because of the location of the crime. Sierra Leone is peaceful compared to a bunch of places on the continent. ISIS and al-Qaeda don't have a big foothold here. Poverty is a problem, but the government is stable."

"You think they took Anya's body?" Steph asked.

He slipped his hand into hers, satisfied when she didn't move away from him.

"All I found was a shoe," Ten explained. "The nurse's cabin was the only one where not everything was perfect. The door had been left open and it looks like she lost her shoe while they were taking her out of there. I talked to a couple of the village kids who saw the group as they were leaving town. One of the kids said there was a blonde in the Humvee and she looked scared. I don't think they killed your girl. I'm going to look into her and make sure there's no way she's got something to do with this."

"Anya wouldn't," Steph shot back. "They've got her and I need to figure out what they want and give it to them so we can get her back."

"We will," Brody promised.

"Bingo," Adam said, looking up from the second laptop. "I think I've got a name. Is this our guy?"

Steph looked down and the minute she saw that face, she backed up. He moved behind her, letting his arms go around her.

"Is that him, luv?"

She nodded. "That's him. How did you find him?"

"You found him," Adam replied. "You let Kori sketch him this afternoon. She's not as good as an actual sketch artist, but she's good enough for a piece of revolutionary software."

A groan came over the line. Ten was shaking his head. "Stop the self-congratulations, Miles. Who is it?"

Adam frowned. "But then she wouldn't understand how perfect the match is. You see I took that sketch Kori made and put it through my own proprietary software. This sucker is why the company Jake, Chelsea, and I are forming along with Si, Jesse, and Phoebe is going to be the premiere missing persons firm of the future."

"I don't care why it's perfect," Steph said. "I just want to know his name."

A long sigh issued from Adam's mouth. "Fine, but the source code on this sucker is brilliant and no matter what she says, Chelsea did not take the lead on this."

"Adam," Brody began.

"His name is Hans de Vries," Adam said as his fingers clicked on the keyboard. "He's a Belgian national. He was in their Army."

"Aww, I know the man." Ten groaned over the line. "Damn it. I need to study this more. De Vries left the Army and almost immediately started up a mercenary unit. He's worked around the African continent and some in the Middle East. He's usually got about twenty men on his team. I've got files on most of the mercenary groups, but they change up pretty fast. I'm never completely current. I need to figure out who he's working for right now."

Brody had worked on the continent enough to have an idea. "If he's Belgian, he's likely working for a diamond company."

Ten nodded. "Yeah, that was my first thought, too. I think we should expand the search a bit. I would bet that journalist wasn't actually working on a story in Sierra Leone. Not if de Vries is working for who I think he's working for. I'll call Penny and tell her to start asking around Antwerp."

"You think they were working for a company?" Steph asked. "Not one of the governments? I've seen a lot of the governments hire outside mercenary groups as security."

"I don't think that's the case here." Brody's mind had hooked the likeliest suspect. "In that part of the world, they're most likely muscle for a corporation. Since they're Belgian, likeliest bet is some form of resource mining."

"Diamonds is what he means," Ten said, scrubbing a hand through his hair. "Antwerp, Belgium, is the diamond capital of the world. Everything runs through the big diamond merchants. If you buy an engagement ring in the suburban US, you can bet it came from Africa and went through Antwerp."

"I think you're right," Brody said. "We'll call Penny in the morning. She needs to know we're searching for someone who was looking into the diamond mines. Maybe the journalist's editor will know something."

"I'm sorry I haven't been able to get anything off the sketch of the journalist." Adam stood up, shrugging back into his jacket. "I'll narrow the parameters, but given the damage to his face, it could be difficult. Pair that with the fact that sometimes journalists go off the grid for months at a time and we're going to have trouble. Our best bet is Penny. If he wasn't supposed to report in for a while, no one is missing him yet. And we have zero idea what his nationality was."

"He never spoke to me in English," Steph said. "He said something to me while I was working on him, but I have no idea what it meant."

"I'm betting on European," Ten replied. "Given what I think he was researching, I'm betting these boys spoke a similar language. I'll start poking around here. My bet is he started somewhere in the south and was trying to make his way back to Europe. They caught him in Sierra Leone."

"And I was the closest clinic," Steph surmised. "But why does de Vries think I have something?"

"Likely he was trying to get information out of the journalist and he thinks you're the only one the man could have passed it to," Ten replied. "Look, I'm going to make a few calls. I don't understand exactly why this has escalated the way it did. That's not how these men tend to work. They'll do their jobs, but they try to keep things quiet. They don't want the kind of scrutiny that would come from killing a journalist. Unless whatever he had could kill corporate profits. I would bet we're not looking for a diamond. We're looking for information. We're looking for his report."

"I don't have it." Steph leaned back against him and Brody could practically feel her fear.

He had some serious work to do. How could he have ever thought for a second that he didn't have something to give to her? He'd been blinded by his own insecurities, too wrapped up in his bloody self to see what she needed—and that he was the man who could give it to her. She spent way too much time in that pretty little head of hers. He needed to get her to let go and feel. "It's going to be all right. We've got a name now. We can deal with this."

"He's right," Ten replied.

"But he's got Anya." Steph's voice shook. "We have no idea what he's done to her, what he could do to her."

Adam smoothed out his jacket and looked to Brody. He seemed to understand what Brody was asking. "Well, I think my job is done here. Why don't you allow me to escort you into the lounge, Dr. Gibson? I think you could use a drink. You're only allowed two and I usually have one before and one to wind down."

She looked up and Brody nodded. "Go on. I'll be with you in a second. I want to make sure Ten has everything he needs."

She bit her bottom lip, as though trying to decide whether or not to leave.

"We can look in on the kids before we go up," Adam offered, proving he was a smooth customer. "There's a window we can watch through. It's fun sometimes to see how they act when we're not around. I know you've got a newborn so he mostly kicks his legs and poops, but let me tell you once they start crawling, it's a whole new world."

Adam continued talking as he led her out of the room.

"Tell me about this Anya person." Ten seemed to know exactly what he wanted to talk about.

"She's fairly new to the clinic. She'd recently come on when I was about to leave. Steph's nurses come and go. Same with other doctors. They're usually there for anywhere from six weeks to a couple of years. I met Anya a couple of times. She seemed nice enough, but she's got a few shady relatives back in the Ukraine."

Ten's head fell back and he groaned. "Tell me they're not mob."

"Wish I could, mate." He'd started vetting her nurses, though she had no idea and would probably get mad pissed at him if she did. It was one of those things she didn't need to know about. "Her brother has close ties, but according to everything I can tell, she's not involved directly. Otherwise, she's clean. On paper it looks like she's there because she cares about the world and the people in it."

"And have there been any problems around the clinic? Any odd losses of vaccines or meds?"

The mob was known for stealing medicines from charities and reselling them on the black market.

"Not according to Alfi, but he's a son of a bitch who lies a lot." Still, he didn't think Alfi hated him enough that he would let someone hurt Steph. "I don't think so, but I'll ask him about it. I have to watch Steph carefully because she'll sacrifice herself if she gets the chance."

"Tell her about the mob connections," Ten urged.

He wasn't sure that would work. "I don't know that she'd believe me, or even if she did, it wouldn't matter to her. I think she's been looking for a way to sacrifice herself for a long time now."

"I don't have any idea why she would do that, but she's got a baby. She has to think about herself. Even Faith's toning down her work. She's heading her charity organization, but she knows we're going to stay in Dallas most of the time. Grant needs roots and family around him. Oh, I'm sure that kid will see a whole lot of the world before he's five, but he'll know where home is. Let me tell you, man, becoming a parent is the single scariest thing I've ever done, and I've done some scary shit. Tag's right. Family men are crap when it comes to field work."

"Because we can't think only of the mission. Yeah, I already got that." He could see what Damon went through. Why he was happier behind a desk now. Because every second he was out in the field he was thinking about what would happen to his boy if he took another bullet, if he was unlucky in a fight. "I think I'll work corporate cases from now on. Gotta come home to my boy."

"And if she doesn't feel the same way?" Ten asked. "What if she's unwilling to change?"

He wasn't even going to think about that right now. "I'm taking it a day at a time. Right now all I want is to make sure she doesn't attempt to sacrifice herself for a woman who might not deserve it."

"I'll do some checking and get back to you. I'll talk to the other nurse. She's been in the village outside the clinic for days now. I'll have her walk through and see if she sees anything I don't. 'Night, brother."

"'Night." He flipped the laptop screen shut and sighed.

What would he do? Was he willing to leave London? He might be willing to move back to Australia, but he wasn't sure he wanted to roam around Africa for the rest of his life, and he wasn't sure how that would work for Nate. The truth was he had found a second family in London and he loved them. Funny how easy that was to admit now.

Fatherhood was making him soft.

He walked out the door. It was time to start softening her up, too. He was going to show her what he could offer her, and perhaps she would come around to his way of thinking.

The one thing he knew he couldn't do was let her go.

* * * *

Steph stared through the window, alone now after assuring Adam he could go and enjoy the evening. He was somewhere in the dungeon looking for his wife. Steph couldn't help but smile as she watched her son. Nate was in a bouncy chair surrounded by little girls. Kenzie and Kala and Carys Taggart all seemed fascinated by the newcomer. One of the twins was gently holding his hand while her sister showed Nate how the toys dangling above him rolled and whistled. Carys bounced and clapped. Nate was grinning like he knew he was the center of the universe.

She'd been all right with dying as long as he was okay. What kind of mother did that make her?

He was so sweet, so perfect. Was she going to be the one who screwed up his life?

"Ah, look at that boy. He's already surrounded by gorgeous women." Brody moved in behind her, his hands warm on her shoulders. "That's Papa's boy there."

Brody was already madly in love with their son. He seemed to ease into it with a confidence she couldn't feel. "I think it's easy to see he's not missing us at all."

"That's a good thing." Brody's hands skimmed down her arms, leaving trails of heat wherever he touched her. "He should be confident enough that we can leave him with people we trust. It means you've done a good job and he thinks the world is a place where he's safe."

"We both know that's not true." Nate simply wasn't old enough to understand it.

"He doesn't need to figure that out yet. This is what a childhood is. This is what we can give him, years and years where he's certain he's safe and loved. That's what forms the base of who we are."

Did it? She'd had two loving parents, a classic picture-perfect childhood with trips to Disney World and Sunday dinners with family. One mistake and it had all fallen apart. Her father had left because he couldn't handle watching his only child disintegrate and her mother had gone to Avery Charles in desperation.

"Sometimes you can have everything and that base still breaks, Brody."

"Then we build it all over again," he said. "We build it stronger than before. Still might get a couple of cracks in it, but we fill those in. We don't give up. No one gets through life without scars. That's what we teach our son. No matter what happens, we'll be there for him."

Would she? Or would she lead him to a place where she couldn't save him? Where she thought to let someone else take care of him so she could fulfill some dark destiny?

"I thought we weren't thinking about the future," she said quietly.

"We can never not think about his future. Ours can wait, but you have to know I won't disappear."

All this talk was making her nervous. "I don't have to know that. I don't have to know that at all."

He turned her, looming over her with that perfectly shaped jaw of his. "I left you. I shouldn't have. I won't again. I'm a simple man and I thought that was a problem. But, luv, you're so bloody complex there's not room for more than me. I never lied to you. Not once. Might have lied to myself a time or two, but never to you."

He hadn't. He'd been upfront and honest about what he'd wanted, and that was precisely why she was in the bind she was in. She could trust him when he said he would be there, but that was about their baby, not her.

At some point she was going to face a terrible decision and she had no idea what she would do about it. And she felt stupid standing around here in a bikini. It was ridiculous and she wasn't sure what she'd been thinking. "I'm going to go change. This is silly. We need to be back at the guest house working on this problem, not playing dressup."

He took her hand and she found herself back in the conference room. "You want to go and get dressed and sit and watch a movie you won't be able to remember tomorrow because your mind is on something else? Because we're not going home until this party is over. All the bodyguards are working overtime. This was a chance for a few of them to get a break. Do you want me to call Remy and tell him the men need to come back in?"

She shook her head. "I'm not trying to be a pain. I'm just not into this."

"Because you're not giving it a chance." Brody walked over to the wall and used the dimmer switch. The room's harsh lighting immediately softened. "I want you to stop panicking and take a deep breath."

She hadn't taken a deep breath all day. Not since last night when Brody had taken her to bed and she hadn't been able to think about anything except him. "I'm not panicking. I'm worrying. Anya's out there. It seems wrong that I'm playing sex games in here while she's missing."

He stared down at her. "We haven't even started yet. Would you prefer I got you a hair shirt to wear? It won't look as good on you, but it will irritate your skin, make you feel like shit. Maybe I could find a nail for you to sit on?"

"Don't be condescending."

He shrugged slightly. "You're the one who seems to think you have to martyr yourself to the universe or something. Now if you tell me you're scared and all you want is to cuddle up somewhere and talk about it, then I'll do that. But that's not what this is about, is it?"

"Maybe I don't want to spend time with you." The words sounded stubborn even to her own ears.

His lips quirked up in a lopsided smirk. It was wrong that she found it incredibly sexy. "Then you probably wouldn't have asked me to kiss you before. You wouldn't have practically melted in my arms."

"I did not melt." Except she'd felt kind of melty. She felt that way every single time they were in a room together, and that was part of the problem. She was fairly sure melting around him was a bad thing. Even if it felt good and right to be in his arms.

"Oh, you were close to it." He leaned over, brushing his nose to hers. "This close. One second more and you would have been limp and warm and submissive, and all those things that would make this a lovely night. But that's what you're afraid of. You're afraid to enjoy yourself because you think somehow that your suffering is going to help your friend. It won't."

"It feels wrong." She couldn't help it. He was right. There was something deep inside her that thought she didn't deserve any of this, that she was still somehow stuck in a dark place where she needed to withhold the good things of the world from herself.

"No, you're not feeling at all right now. You're thinking," Brody corrected. "Getting you out of that head of yours is my number one job tonight. You did good, Steph. You got out and you made it to the safest place you could. Anya knew what she was doing. She was trying to do good too, and we're going to do everything in our power to get her back as fast as we can, but you can't help us at all if you don't rest, and you can't rest if you never relax."

How long had it been since she actually relaxed? Well, besides the night before? The night before had been heavenly, and now she was wondering if she'd deserved it at all. "How can I relax when someone I know is going through something awful?"

His eyes turned warm and serious, staring down at her like he was trying hard to figure out how to handle her. "I want you to answer a question and if you can answer yes, then I'll tear this whole party down and get you home. I won't care what anyone else says or needs. I'll do it all for you. If you answer no, we do this my way. Can you agree to that?"

She saw a problem with his scenario. "What if I simply answer yes and get my way no matter what?"

"Then we'll know more about how we work as a couple."

No. She couldn't go there. "We're not a couple."

He delicately pushed back a strand of her hair, tucking it neatly behind her ear. "Oh, we're a couple. We're a couple of parents. We're a D/s couple until you tell me we're not. We could be more, but we're not deciding that tonight. The parent thing will never go away, Steph. Even if you wish you had never had a child with me, we can't change it. He's ours and he will have both parents in his life."

She fought hard not to cry. Motherhood had turned her into a weepy mess of a woman. "I didn't... I wouldn't take him back, Brody. Not for anything. And I wouldn't change his dad. He would be different if someone else had been his father, and he's perfect the way he is. I wouldn't change it. Fine. Ask me the question. I agree to your terms."

"Will you giving up our play session tonight do anything at all to help Anya?"

Damn him. She tried to come up with a million different ways to say yes, but he was right. She was falling back into old patterns, hurting herself because she didn't think she deserved anything at all good in life. "No."

A satisfied smile crossed his face. "Then you're mine for the

214

night and you will follow my every instruction. The only reason for you to stop our play is because you're frightened in a way that overwhelms you, you're hurt in a way that doesn't enhance the pleasure, or you don't want what I'm doing to you. In those cases, all you have to do is tell me to stop and I will. But for now, you'll kiss me and we'll start the night properly."

She was in a corner and she could fight her way out or she could understand that this particular corner was nice and safe and warm. This corner was filled with him and his unique sexuality. One more night with Brody. That was how she could look at it. One day at a time. One sweet night at a time.

She went up on her toes and did what came naturally. She pressed her lips to his and let her arms float up. His hands went to her hips and all thoughts of how crappy it was to wear a bikini when it wasn't sunny outside flew out the window. Heat scorched her where he touched. Now she understood why he'd picked this particular "costume" for her. He could touch her pretty flesh, remind her constantly of how good it felt to have his hands on her.

His tongue swiped across her lower lip before delving deep inside. He kissed her long and slow, every velvet touch of his tongue making her heart speed up.

He finally put some small distance between them, though he lowered his forehead to touch hers. "Perfect, luv. Now turn and hold on to the conference table. I want your arse in the air, and plant your feet shoulder width apart for me."

She was confused. One minute he was kissing her like he couldn't breathe without her and now he wanted her backside in the air. She still had to get used to him using the word arse as though it was something sexy. "What? I thought we were going out to the club."

"We will, after we get a few things done," he promised.

"Brody, I'm good. I'll follow your lead."

"You'll follow my instructions or things are going to get worse for you," he said, his tone low.

"All right." He looked super serious about the instructions thing. But he also looked intensely sexy. The low growl that was coming out of his mouth sent warmth straight to all her female parts. "I promise I'll follow your instructions."

She turned and started for the door.

A big arm went around her waist and hauled her back against his body. In a second, she felt his hand at the back of her neck and her bikini top dropped, baring her breasts. Before she could protest, his hand covered her right breast and she felt him catch her nipple between his thumb and forefinger. He twisted, hard. She stiffened and bit back a cry.

Pain shot through her and then a ridiculously warm sensation. She knew enough about sexual arousal to know this was something that would only work if she was already aroused. If some asshole walked up to her and pinched her nipple, she would punch him in the face and call out his assault of her person. This was different. Because of the numerous hormones flooding her system, that rough tweak to her nipple made her eyes watery and her pussy go super soft.

"You don't listen well, luv. I gave you specific instructions as to what you're supposed to do. You've ignored each and every word, and that's something we're going to have to fix." He tweaked her other breast, tugging and then twisting. She shivered and bit back a low moan of pure sensual excitement.

"I'm sorry. I didn't understand. I thought we were going out to the club."

"Because you're thinking again and that ain't your job tonight. Tonight you're going to wipe that brilliant brain of yours clean and leave everything to me. You're going to obey your Master and let him take control." Both hands had come up, rolling her nipples softly, but she knew what he could do if he wanted to. There was a delicious menace to that touch. "You're going to spend the rest of the evening thinking of nothing but pleasing me. Now do as I bloody well asked or I'll find a way to make you remember."

That sounded like a deliciously dirty threat, but she was fairly certain she'd pushed him too far already. There was a whole night to get through.

No, there was a whole night to enjoy. Why did she think that way? Why was everything something to get through and not something to experience and enjoy?

She moved to the conference table, not bothering to retie her top. Her breasts were out, but somehow that felt right, too. He hadn't given her instructions to fix the top so she left it as it was. Her nipples were still hard and aching and the cool air seemed to soothe them mightily. She placed her hands on the flat top of the conference room table and moved her feet until they were shoulder width apart. What else had he commanded? Arse in the air. Yeah, she could do that.

Breathe. Forget about everything but this moment. She took in the way her muscles stretched and how it felt when Brody's big hand covered the small of her back, the way her breasts dangled. Nothing else mattered but how her body felt, how she obeyed her Master.

Hours of respite. That was what he was offering her. Hours where she didn't have to worry about anything but him, and he wasn't anything to worry about. He was Brody Carter and he would never hurt her.

A loud smack broke the silence and she nearly howled at the pain.

Well, he wouldn't hurt her in any way that didn't do something for her. The slaps to her cheeks made her body heat in a way she hadn't thought was possible.

"Do you understand why I'm spanking you?" Brody slapped her cheeks, a nasty swat that made her whole body tighten.

She knew she should probably say something submissive about disobeying her Master and this was the only way she could learn, but she knew that wasn't the real answer. "Because you think this is the only way to get me out of my head, to force me to let go of all the crap that drags me down all day long."

Another whack, this one right on the split of her cheeks. His hand lingered, one finger pressing slightly against the swimsuit bottom, making her aware of her ass. "Yes. Because this is fun. Because this is play. Don't you ever think for a second I don't respect the hell out of you. Don't think there's anything dirty about this. The last thing I want is to give you something else to feel guilty about."

"I kind of like the thought that it's dirty, Brody. It feels dirty, but not in a bad way. Believe me, babe, I know what it feels like to be dirty, like nothing in the world can clean me up. This isn't it. This is different." He'd told her what his fear was—that he would drag her down, too. She couldn't let him believe that. Not even for a second. Not even with everything between them. "I'm not trying to get you to hurt me for any reason other than this feels good. I like it. I know what it means to try to punish myself and this isn't even close. I know what to do to make it stop."

"I want to give you what you need," he said, an ache in his voice. "But sometimes I worry about what you think you deserve."

"I agreed to agree with you all night. I deserve this. I deserve this playtime with you, Brody. I want it more than I can say." Which was exactly why she'd tried to get out of it, but she had to change her thinking. She couldn't go through the rest of her life like this. She could see that plainly now.

Life often didn't give her choices. Sometimes she felt as though she moved from one crisis to another, swept up in all of it. But perhaps that was the choice. Like Avery had said. She had to choose how to react to the things that happened to her, around her. She was being offered a choice now. Brody was giving it to her.

For the first time in forever, she wasn't going to overthink it. She was going to grab it with both hands.

He slapped her ass another five times and then she felt him kiss the small of her back. "Stand."

She eased herself up, her body alive and aching with need. She suspected this was the real torture her Master intended to inflict on her.

He retied the top of her swimsuit, but not before he'd kissed the nape of her neck and worked his way across both shoulders. "Better?"

Considering the fact that her whole body was relaxed, her muscles eased, she only had one answer. "Yes, Brody."

"Excellent. Let's go and see what sparks your interest." He

turned her around and didn't try to hide the massive erection that pressed against the fly of his slacks.

"That sparks my interest." She glanced pointedly to his enormous dick. She was soft and warm and ready for a massive throw down. It was probably a good bet they wouldn't be the first couple to do it in this conference room. From what she could tell, Big Tag and Charlotte had a never-ending quest to have sex in every possible place they could. They were like horny rabbits trying to mark their territory.

It wasn't a terrible idea.

"You like what you see?" Brody asked, his voice deep.

Such a vain man. He knew how gorgeous he was. "You know I do."

"Then think about it while we watch a few scenes. Think about the fact that I want nothing more than to bend you over and force my cock inside. I don't think it would even be a hard thing to do at this point. I would bet if I had you get up on that table and spread your legs for me I would find that pretty pussy of yours is wet and ready to take me. Is that what I would find?"

Her first instinct was to hop on the table and show him. She could drop the bottoms and climb up and spread her legs wide. Then they would see who could tempt whom.

But that wasn't being obedient. That was manipulating him to get what she wanted. Suddenly what she wanted was far more than an orgasm. She wanted to please him, to play this game by his rules and see what happened. Even though he'd left her once, she still trusted him.

"You would find that I have become extremely aroused," she replied with a smile. "I could go into all the hormonal reasons that under the right conditions a spanking can make a person sexually aroused, but I think I'll take the short cut and admit I'm a bit of a pervert when it comes to you."

His smirk turned into a brilliant smile that kind of lit up the whole room. When Brody got to smiling, his face lit up and it took her breath away. "That's good to know because I'm a complete and utter pervert when it comes to you. Now let's go and figure out what your particular brand of perversion calls for. We'll stay away from Jake and Serena and Adam though. I'm not sharing you with anyone."

She was perfectly okay with that. She let Brody lead her out, ready for the night to begin.

Chapter Eleven

Brody led her past the scene where Jake and Adam were supposed to be two teachers or something and Serena was the deliciously naughty schoolgirl. Something had gone awry because Adam was attempting to beat the shit out of his partner.

"I told you to wait for me." Adam ran at his best friend, his fist up.

Jake really was the more physical of the two. He evaded Adam. "That's not what you told Big Tag."

Serena's eyes rolled as they walked by. "Yeah, keep moving. This scene is not going to be fun for a while. I swear, I'm going to kill Tag. He's behind this."

He probably was. Big Tag liked to play the trickster. "You want me to stop them?"

Steph's eyes lit up like she would truly enjoy that. His girl had a little blood lust in her, or perhaps she simply enjoyed how big he was. Back when they'd first met, he'd realized all he had to do to get her eyes on him was pick up something heavy and offer to move it for her. Or chop wood. She could watch him do that for hours.

Serena shook her head, looking back at her men. "Nah. Sometimes they work things out by punching each other. Adam's been a beast lately because of the new company. It's all starting up soon and I think both he and Jake are nervous about leaving McKay-Taggart. It's made them antsy and irritable. They kind of need this." Her lips curled up. "And honestly, after they're done with each other, they'll have a go at me. So I won't kill Big Tag. He's like a big, sarcastic genie. He probably overheard me saying that I wished they would just beat the crap out of each other and he found a way to make it happen. I will admit that sometimes I wish we could keep him in a bottle though. It would be nice to only take him out when we need his unique brand of help."

Somehow Brody didn't think that would happen any time soon. "Do you know of any interesting scenes?"

"Charlotte's planning something with Mistress Day that might be interesting, but it's suspension. If you're looking for impact, Simon and Chelsea are playing with floggers somewhere. I heard Alex was planning on lighting Eve up tonight."

"Lighting her up?" Steph asked.

"Fire play," Brody replied.

She shrank back slightly. No fire play for her. That might be a bit adventurous for her first night. "Come on. Let's watch the suspension play scene."

He led her to the main stage and settled in to watch. He was incredibly surprised when the woman in leather and thigh-high boots who promised to suspend her bigger, heavier male sub turned out to be someone he'd met before.

Steph gasped. "Is that...?"

He leaned over and whispered. "The queen of Loa Mali, yes. Well, I'm sure it's been an interesting time over here. Let's watch."

Twenty minutes later he realized something was wrong between the royals that wasn't going to be solved with suspension play. And Steph hadn't relaxed once. They'd stood there and studied the diminutive Domme suspend the big strapping king and Steph had watched silently, not moving an inch, her shoulders bunched up. He'd tried to put his hands on her, but he could still feel the tension.

Mistress Day was explaining how she could make the sub feel safe even suspended over the ground, but Brody realized his sub wasn't at all feeling what he'd meant her to.

He was pushing her too fast. They'd made love twice and now

he had her in the middle of a sex club. She could be insecure.

She was curious about this world, but watching a scene where the Domme and sub weren't in synch wasn't going to help. Then there had been Jake and Adam beating on each other. She hadn't seen the best Sanctum could offer.

It was up to him to save their night. His submissive needed privacy in these first days. She needed to focus on the two of them, not the outside forces around them.

He leaned over to Big Tag, who was standing beside him, keeping his voice low. "Hey, I don't think this scene is helping Steph ease into anything."

"Yeah, this scene is a clusterfuck," Tag agreed quietly. "You know I give great advice. I should be a motherfucking relationship specialist, but no one listens."

So Big Tag had been getting up in everyone's business tonight. That was par for the course. "Can I get into the training room?"

Tag's eyes flared briefly before he reached into his pocket and handed him a key card. "Sure. I hope one of the clients has a fun time tonight. I'll let the full douche know where you are."

Poor bodyguards. "Thanks, mate."

He slid his hand into Steph's and started to lead her away.

When they were far enough from the crowd, he turned to her. "Come with me. I want to show you something."

She followed dutifully behind him, but there wasn't the joy she'd had earlier. She might never be a club girl, but that was all right. He didn't need to fuck her in public to feel like a man. That was fine for the exhibitionists, but his sub needed something different.

He would have beaten himself up for not seeing it, but somehow the last few days had taught him something. There was only room for one broody, moody arsehole in this relationship, and Steph had a lock hold on it.

Sometimes relationships were about adaptation. He needed to adapt to fill in her weaknesses, and vice versa.

He found the door to the training room and slid the key card in. He opened the door and turned on the lights. As with most rooms in

Sanctum, this one had a dimmer switch, and he slid it to a nice, warm light that wasn't too bright. The room was neatly kept and set up for a scene. Likely someone would be using this room in the next few days. There was a large massage table with a quilt over it and several pillows and blankets to make things comfortable. There were discreet lockers he knew were stocked with all kinds of impact play toys. One was filled with floggers and paddles and canes. There were whips in another.

"Is this a privacy room?" Steph asked. She already seemed more comfortable. Her curiosity was back now that they were alone. She walked around the room, brushing her fingers over a plush whipping bench.

"No, this is a training room." He was grateful he'd spent time here and he knew the lay of the land. "This is a room where one of the tops who teach or mentor a D/s couple have sessions."

"I thought they had training classes for that." She walked around the room, stopping to examine some of the equipment.

It gave Brody time to get things together. The training room was ridiculously well stocked. Big Tag was a perverted Boy Scout. He was always prepared, which was precisely why this was the best idea Brody'd had all day. He opened the small toy closet and found a series of sealed bags.

"They have group training classes for singles. This room would be for couples who want to explore or couples who are having trouble. I think it's safe to say the royals could use a little time in here." Despite the fact that Wade Rycroft now ran the club, Big Tag's fingerprints were all over the place, including the pre-prepped perv packages, as the shelf was marked. Each bag included pre-sterilized small toys and everything the top would need to use on his or her sub. He glanced through a few of the packs—*Grease 'er Up* had several kinds of lube. *Pup-Town Girl* had a crystal encrusted water dish and bedazzled collars and leashes for puppy play. *Gimps Need Love, Too* included a few items Brody wasn't even sure about.

"I don't know. He seemed very uncomfortable. If he's an actual submissive, I don't think he wants to be. It's hard to move when you hate the core of who you are."

"Is that what our problem is?" If she was willing to start a discussion about it, he was more than willing to talk. He knew what was at the core of their problems, but she needed to acknowledge it, too.

Her guilt. His insecurity. Neither of them had a place in their world anymore.

"No, our problem is that you're a jerk who can't figure out how to answer the damn telephone," she said, but she chuckled before sobering. "I don't mind being a sub. Sexually that is. Honestly, even in some things outside of the bedroom, I wouldn't mind giving over responsibility to someone I trusted."

"I know you don't trust me, but I need time to change that."

She finally turned. "I trust you with my life, Brody."

"I want more than that."

"Then you should have answered the phone." She turned again, the distance between them more than the few yards of floor he could cross in a second.

Words were not going to fix this. He wasn't sure he *could* fix it, but he had to try. "All right, let's start small. Do you trust me in this room?"

She leaned against the large massage table in the center of the room that would also serve as a bed when it came to sex. Like a lot of the items in this room, it would have more than one purpose. It would serve as a convenient bed, a flat surface to hold on to, a nice space for aftercare. He had to view himself like that table. He served more than one purpose. She wouldn't allow him to play the doting lover, the indulgent and sweet boyfriend he wanted to be, but she needed more than that. Perhaps today she needed the Dom.

"I trust you with my life, Brody. I certainly trust you with my body," she admitted. "But I felt odd out there in the club. Last night was perfect. I didn't think about anything but you and me and what we were doing. Tonight, when we're with other people, my mind wanders. It's hard to stay focused."

"Hence we're now alone and I expect your focus to be entirely on me. In here we're nothing more than a D/s couple who needs a bit of time to work out what we like, what works for us, what brings us closer together as a Dom and a submissive."

She was silent for a few seconds, but then she nodded. "All right. I think that might be a good place to start."

At least she'd used the word *start*. It was the right word. They needed a new start. He knew what she was thinking. He'd given her another way to view their relationship, a less scary way. She thought if she could put their relationship into a D/s box, she might get the sex and pleasure she wanted without all the emotional connection that would frighten her.

Such a naïve thing. She really hadn't had a deep sexual relationship before him or she would know what kind of threat he posed. He wasn't about to tell her. This was one trap he fully intended to spring on her.

"Take off your clothes and kneel in the center of the room. When we begin a session, this is how you will greet me. Naked, hair down, knees wide, with your hands palms up on your thighs."

"And you'll be dressed?" She managed to make it sound like that would be the worst thing in the world.

He was willing to bend. After all, this was a consensual act they should agree upon. Also, he loved the fact that she liked his body. It was big and scarred, and he often thought he was more beast than man, but she made him feel worthy. And maybe that was a start. The last few years of working for Damon Knight had done something to his brain. He couldn't merely look at the things she said. He had to view her as a whole, and oftentimes the way a person treated others was a tip-off as to what they themselves needed the most.

Maybe he wasn't such a dumb grunt anymore.

"How about I promise I'll start with my shirt off," he offered. "I assure you I'll be naked at some point in time because there's nothing I love more than feeling your skin against mine."

She flushed, her color going a lovely pink. "Yes, I think most men like that feeling."

And so she ducked and feinted. That's what they were doing, Brody realized. They were in a fight, and for him that meant jabs and feints and uppercuts. This fight was all about words and emotions. He'd made a direct hit and she was trying to take the point away from him. What did a good fighter do? He certainly didn't go back to his corner. He came back out punching.

"I'm sure they do, but it's different when it's my skin against yours. I still remember how you smell and how your hair tickles against me. It goes everywhere when you wear it down. It's like a gorgeous, soft net catching me and pulling me in. I won't make more of this relationship than is there, but you can't make less of it."

She flushed again, a sure sign he was getting to her. "I think you're the one making more of it. Not on my side. I know how nice the sex was, but you've had more relationships than I've had."

She wanted to do this now? She could do it on her knees. "You want to talk about my past relationships, I'm willing, but you'll obey me first or we'll get dressed and go home and maybe if neither of us can sleep we'll have plain vanilla sex that we'll tell ourselves doesn't mean anything. Does that sound better?"

Her hand went to the top of her neck and she undid the knot of her swimsuit. "You know it doesn't. And all I'm saying is you've had way more sex than I have in the last couple of years."

She had to try to win. That was the funny thing. Somewhere under all that guilt was a competitive alpha bitch who never quit, and damn but he wanted to meet her. "You think I'm some kind of playboy? The James Bond thing is nothing more than a fun costume. The reality of my work is long hours spent in a car with Walt and a bag of stale chips, following around a suspect."

The top came off and she handed it over to him. Despite her breezy, couldn't-care-less nature, her nipples were hard points. Those beauties were pink and tight, as though begging to be tweaked again.

"Somehow I think there's more to it than that." She unhooked the thigh holster and handed that to him as well.

"Yes, that's when the people we've been watching figure out we're watching them and they start shooting," he agreed. "That's the excitement I get."

"You live over a BDSM club in one of the world's greatest cities," she countered. But he didn't mind the argument. She was more animated than she'd been all night. Her mind wasn't going over the collection of ways her world could go topsy-turvy.

"First of all, it's only a club a few nights a week. I spend most of my time in the bar. And in the last year I haven't touched another woman sexually. I've performed my duties as one of the tops in the club, but I haven't taken any gratification from a single submissive because I couldn't have the only one I wanted." He saw the way her eyes lit up and realized he would always have to add on to this line of thought. "I couldn't have her because I was a bloody wanker who couldn't answer my mobile."

Her mouth firmed as though she was considering continuing on, but finally she sighed and hooked her thumbs around the last bit of clothing she had on. The bikini bottom slipped off and she offered it to him. "Though you shouldn't think you could have had me. I was merely calling because I thought I owed you the courtesy of telling you I was pregnant."

He placed her clothes and the prop on one of the prep tables. "Well, I was already missing you something fierce by then. A situation that would have been remedied if I had picked up my damn mobile." He turned back and she was on her knees, adjusting herself to fit what he'd commanded. She wasn't the most graceful sub he'd ever seen, but she was the loveliest. Why this woman? Why this stubborn, difficult, self-sacrificing martyr of a woman had to be the one who held his heart, he had no idea, but there was no way around it. No chance that he could wriggle out of the trap, and he didn't want to. He simply wanted her stuck in this happy trap with him. "I didn't think I was smart enough for you."

"That's ridiculous."

It occurred to him that he had an enormous amount of power here. In this room. At this time. He should use it because she had the power everywhere else. "Hush, luv. We're in the training room and we're in a training session. That means you only talk when I give you permission."

Her head came up. "Seriously?"

He selected a nice flexible crop and let it slap against his hand with purpose. The sound cracked through the air and her eyes widened. "Seriously. Look, Big Tag even left this in case it becomes difficult for the sub to remember."

He held up the small, clear plastic bag that contained several different size fresh and ready-to-use ball gags. *Silence Is Golden* the bag was titled. With the subtitle, *Or your butt is red...*

She started to open her mouth and then it closed, though there was pure fire coming from her eyes.

He was all right with that. She was lovely when she was angry. He put that one back on the shelf, but kept the crop. "Excellent choice. See, I would have named that bag *To Drool or Not to Drool*. Because that really is the question. Those damn ball gags make a man drool like a bloody idiot."

He should know since the first time he ever met Big Tag, the arsehole had been shoving an incredibly large one into Brody's mouth. They'd quickly overcome that mistake, though Brody would never forget the copious amounts of drool associated with one of those things.

He set the crop down for a moment because he'd promised her something, too. He shrugged out of his tuxedo jacket and went to work on the tie and shirt as he talked. "I thought you deserved better than an Army grunt from nowhere Australia who barely had an education. The funny thing is, I've realized how little you need a man with a highbrow university degree who would likely do nothing but make everything more complex. You can do that all on your own. You need someone with street smarts. Someone who understands that when the bullets start flying, it's smarter to not run right toward the man with the gun because you think he might be hurt."

That mouth firmed again and he was sure she had a few choice words for him.

They could wait until later. He slid out of the shirt and her eyes heated. "See, there it is. That's what I need. You need someone who looks out for you because you don't ever look out for yourself, and I need that look in your eyes. I need to know I'm not some ugly beast who's good for nothing but throwing his body in front of bullets for his betters."

"That is so untrue, Brody. And you can spank me for that. It's worth it to say it."

There was his Steph. There was the woman he'd fallen completely in love with. Champion of the underdog, willing to take all the punishment of the world if she thought the cause was worthy.

He needed to take that impulse and excise the guilt from it. He didn't want a Steph who didn't fight for the world around her. He merely wanted her to know that she was worth fighting for, too.

And that he was her champion.

"I can be reasonable. Since what you said was sweet and not bratty, only one swat."

She started to lean forward.

He brought the crop out, stopping her forward progress. "No need. I didn't say I was going to swat that pretty bottom. Get back into position and spread your knees wide."

He loved how her eyes flared and she bit her bottom lip. Her mind was working but there wasn't worry for her life or brooding over the past in there now. Nope. Now she was worried about what lovely piece of her flesh he was about to torture.

When she was in the proper position, he stepped in close and brought the crop up to her chin, gently bringing her head up. "Do you have any idea how good you make me feel? When you look at me like you could eat me alive, I'm suddenly the luckiest man in the world." He traced a line down the center of her body, a light touch that made her shiver. "When you look at me, I'm suddenly not a mass of scars. I'm…handsome."

"Pretty. You're pretty, Brody."

"That's two. Again, because what you said was sweet just an extra one, but soon we're going to have to talk about that ball gag."

She pressed her lips together as though promising she wouldn't do it again.

He let the crop slide lower, skimming over her belly and the faint silvery lines that hadn't been there before. Stretch marks. Signs that his baby had grown inside her body. They only made her more beautiful because they were signs of her strength and her resolve. "You are even more gorgeous than before. You're stunning to me and I realize that all those months I spent wanking my own dick to the picture of you in my head were wasted because nothing compares to how lovely you are in real life."

He skimmed the crop down to the mound of her pussy, noting the sharp intake of her breath and the way she tensed.

"I missed everything about you. And yes, I wouldn't have had to if I'd answered the phone. But I realize now I should have done other things with it as well. I could have taken pictures of you so I could always see you. Pictures of your pretty face and your breasts. Pictures of your perky arse, and definitely a picture of your pussy. I'd have you spread your legs and I'll take a picture when you're ripe and wet for me, and then I'll have something to remind me of what I'm really missing every single second I'm away from you."

"You can't take a picture of my cootch," she said.

Ah, finally something he could punish her for. He brought the crop back and up in a short, sharp arc right on the object of their current contention.

Steph gasped but managed to hold her position.

He slapped that sweet pussy with a flick of the crop that made her eyes water. He made sure he was using the soft leather tip of the crop. Her whole body braced itself for the next blow and he gave it to her. Harder this time, the sound reverberating in the silence of the room. Another and another, because her final stolen words hadn't been sweet.

Brody rubbed the leather tip of the crop over the flesh he'd tortured. Gently now, because he was testing a theory. He eased the tip over her swollen flesh, all the way from the top of her mound down between her legs. Those palms that had previously been relaxed on her thighs were now tight fists, and she gasped as he gently eased the tip through the folds of her pussy.

"What do you think I'm going to find when I bring this crop back up, Stephanie? Do you think I'm going to find it unaffected, dry as the leather it is?" He chuckled because she remained silent this time. "That's a direct question. You can and should answer it. Unless you'd like to see what else I can do with this crop."

"That crop is not going to be dry, Brody. It's not. I'm having a definite physical reaction to you slapping at my female parts.

There's a rush of hormones running through me right now that I would have thought could wait for a bit. This is why some women end up with back-to-back babies. I thought my sex drive would take a while to come back online, but nope. It's a perverted sex drive."

"It's a perfect sex drive." He eased the crop up and sure enough, she'd left her sweet mark on it. He breathed in the scent of her arousal. It was the most perfect smell in the world. It got his dick hard and made his head a little fuzzy. She intoxicated him. "But it's going to have to wait. I think you've used that mouth to say many things I don't like."

She sat up straighter, and he could see the desperate need to defend herself. Why couldn't she do this in the real world? Why couldn't she see how deserving she was?

"Would you like to know what I'm talking about? I'm sure you would. I can see it in your eyes. You see, that's how close a Dom and his sub can be. You don't even have to talk and yet I know what you're feeling. *Brody*, you would say if you could talk, *please explain how I say things you don't like. Because I never want to disappoint you.*"

The cutest frown covered her face, yet she managed to remain silent.

Likely because she knew damn well he got her point. He wasn't going to admit it though. After all, they were playing. He wiped off the crop with the handy box of wipes someone had labeled *Bacteria Isn't a Fetish*. She watched him, every move he made. "Saying things like I'm not sexy when you obviously are. Saying you're not lovely and beautiful when you are, that upsets me."

He moved around her, letting the crop drift over her skin again.

"Furthermore, I hate it when you act like you don't deserve to be happy. I won't stand for it in here. I can't force anything on you outside this space, but inside it, you will acknowledge the truth." He stared down at her. "You will say, *Brody, I am good and worthy.* You may speak."

Her head came up and her eyes shone with tears. "Even if I don't feel it."

"Even if you think it's the biggest lie in the world. You'll say it for me. Say it."

She breathed in and took her time. "I am good and worthy."

She didn't sound like she believed it, but they could work on that. "And you're not allowed to degrade yourself. Tell me you're sexy."

Finally a hint of humor. "Well, I feel that way around you, gorgeous."

"How do you feel about using that mouth of yours for good?"

Her lips curled up. "If you're asking if this poor submissive would like to ensure her Dom that her mouth can do good things, too, then yes. I would love to prove that to you. Can you think of a way I could make that happen?"

His dick was dying. "Unzip my pants."

She breathed again. This time the sigh seemed to be filled with relief. An eagerness lit her eyes as she got up on her knees and started working open his belt. In short order she was drawing his zipper down.

Brody bit back a groan as his cock bounced free.

This was something they'd never done before. He'd taken control of their first encounter and he'd been focused on her the night before. Now he wondered why he'd wasted all those months. They could have been playing for almost two years now if he hadn't been such a broody bastard. He could have been there with her, finding out she was pregnant, holding her hair through the early days, rubbing her feet and putting his hand on her belly. And all the while they would have had this.

"I want you to touch me. I need you to touch me." So much time wasted and he couldn't stand the thought of wasting a second more. He needed to feel her mouth, to make the deep connection sex could bring them.

She reached out, her fingers brushing over his cock and making him bite back a moan. He wanted more, wanted her mouth sucking him deep, but he was going to give her this time. He was going to let her explore since he hadn't done that the first time. He needed her to understand that if she was his, then he was hers. One hundred percent.

She seemed to want to explore. She ran her fingertips over his skin, pulling the foreskin back and revealing the head of his cock. He watched as she leaned forward and he could feel the heat of her breath. A drop of pre-come pulsed from the tip, and he nearly lost his cool when her tongue came out, delicately lapping it up.

"Will you let me make you come, Brody?" Steph whispered the words against his flesh, each one a butterfly on his skin. "You've made me come. I want to do the same for you."

Well, if it was what she wanted, he could make the sacrifice. Besides, he would be hard again a few moments after he'd come because he seemed to have an endless appetite for her. He had been the one in control of everything during their two encounters. She needed to know the effect she had on him, too. "Do it. I want to come down your throat. I want you to love the way I taste as much as I love yours."

The tip of his dick disappeared inside her mouth, a light touch that made him long for more.

He watched as she began to work his cock over. Her tongue rolled along his skin as she started to stroke him. She pulled back the foreskin and laved the stalk of his cock with affection.

Over and over she rolled her tongue around him. Every touch and caress made sparks shoot through his system. He reached down and threaded his fingers through her hair, wanting more of a connection. If he could, he would touch her everywhere, surround himself with her.

She settled in, taking his cock behind her lips and beginning to eat him up. He watched as she worked every inch of his dick inside. She sucked him hard, her hand stroking him as her mouth pulled.

He let her go at it, the hands in her hair merely there to keep up his connection. He wanted her to go wild and she did. Her tongue whirled and he felt the heat of her mouth give way to the soft place at the back of her throat. She swallowed around him and he couldn't hold back a second more.

He came in her mouth, his vision going soft as the pleasure poured over him.

She lapped him up, not losing a drop, and when she sat back, she looked like a cat who'd gotten all the cream. Confidence was there in her face.

Yes, this was the way to get to her. And now it was time to pay his sweet sub back.

* * * *

Steph watched as Brody slipped out of his slacks. He'd kicked his loafers off and gotten rid of his socks. He folded the slacks and placed them on the table where he'd put her clothes. If they could be called that.

Though as she sat and watched him, she realized she wasn't bothered by her nudity. It had been weird at first, but now she was comfortable. More than comfortable, actually. She felt good, aware of herself in a way she normally wasn't. She could feel the cool air on her skin, the hardness of the wood floor on her knees. Her nipples tightened in arousal as she watched that man uncover his magnificent body.

Scarred beast? She wasn't sure she could handle him without the scars. He would be too perfect.

Not that he *was* perfect, and that was something she needed to remember. He was a man who had turned her away for the silliest of reasons. He was a man who could cut her to the quick.

All of this was just fun. It was a way to get her mind off her troubles. That was all. Now she knew the score and could properly play the game. Pleasure was the end, not a deep emotional bond.

Even if she felt it.

"Tell me how you're feeling?" Brody asked.

Like I want to stay here for the rest of my life. Like I need nothing more than to be naked with you. Like I want this to be real. "Good. I liked sucking your cock. It made me feel sexy."

She was going to concentrate on the sexual aspects of this session. Sex was safe. Sex was good with Brody. She was far from that child who had tried to destroy herself by debasing her own body. This was something different. This was empowering.

Because she'd chosen this for the right reasons.

Because she loved him.

She let that thought go and concentrated on the man in front of her. He was six foot seven inches of muscled perfection, with a jawline that looked like it had been carved from the finest marble. Or out of a mountain. He was a mountain of a man.

He moved to another of the closets and opened it, pulling out what looked like a long bar with shackles on either end. They were thick leather and seemed to be padded. "You should feel sexy. You're the sexiest woman I've ever met."

Steph definitely wasn't sure about that, but then they were playing. She shouldn't take anything he said too seriously. When she thought about him not touching another woman because he'd only been able to think about her…well, it was better to put that in the play category. Very romantic but not to be taken literally.

"Thank you, Brody." She wasn't going to argue with him. Arguing with him got them nowhere at all. If he did feel that way, then that was nice.

If he thought she was sexy, then that was his business. So why did the words make her sit up straighter?

She licked her lips, trying to make sure she hadn't missed any of him. That had made her feel sexy. Taking that massive cock into her mouth, letting it stretch her wide and still managing to get her tongue all around him. Yes, that had done something for her.

"See, how can you even doubt it?" Brody glanced down at his own cock. "Man my age should take a bit of time in between bouts, but this fella is ready to go again. So come now and let me help you up."

He held a big hand out and she rose to her feet. Her body brushed against his cock. Yes, it was doing exactly what he'd told her it was doing. That big dick was lengthening and getting hard and ready to fuck again. She let one hand dip down to cup his heavy balls, loving the silky smooth skin.

Brody groaned, but his lips lifted in the sweetest smile. "I can see I'm going to have to take care of those hands of yours if I want to stay in control. Or perhaps I should look for a different path to take. Hop up on the bed and spread your legs. How do you feel about anal sex?"

She stopped in the middle of doing his bidding. Of all the crazy shit she'd done in an attempt to punish herself, she'd never done that. "I don't know."

He frowned her way. "I gave you a specific order. Unless you're afraid of the bed."

He had to be literal. She climbed on the bed with its silky sheets. Steph lay back, resting her head against the pillow. It seemed like the submissives at Sanctum got the best of everything. "I'm not afraid of the bed. I'm a little afraid you have depth perception issues."

He moved to the foot of the bed, easing the long rod between her ankles. He adjusted it so her legs were spread as wide as they could go without hurting her. "What is that supposed to mean?"

"It means I'm not sure that big cock of yours can fit inside me that way. I'm fairly certain that is a small hole. Not that I've looked or anything. But it feels really small."

He laughed, the sound booming through the room. "We'll have to work on that." He wrapped the restraint around her ankle and secured the binding. "I would like to play with your backside a bit this evening. But despite my rough talk, I won't do anything to you that's not consensual. You have to give me permission to torture that sweet hole."

That didn't seem fair at all, but strangely she didn't hesitate. "Do your worst."

He wouldn't hurt her. Not for anything in the world. Actually, when she thought about it, he'd tried his damnedest not to hurt her the first time around. He'd tried to stay away from her because he'd known he didn't love her. She'd been the one to push him.

So giving him control over this wasn't hard. He wouldn't take more than she could give, wouldn't give her more than she could take.

Except maybe he thought she was more flexible than she was. There was a delicious stretch to her legs as he shackled her into the spreader bar. She was completely on display.

Brody stared down at her. "You have no idea what I can do to you. I think a safe word is in order."

"I thought we were using no tonight."

"I think you might overuse that word tonight if I let you. I want you to give everything a chance. You can tell me no all you like, but I want you to think about stopping the play. If you want to stop you'll say zebra. I would have used kangaroo, but that would make me too predictable. Now lie back."

She couldn't help but grin. She stayed up on her elbows, wanting to see what he was going to do. "Can't have that now."

"Did I stutter, luv? I asked you to lie back."

She did as he asked. "Sorry. I'm trying to figure out what this thing does besides hold my legs open. I can do that, you know."

"Let you take control for a few minutes and you get a smart mouth on you. Let's see if I can handle that." He took the bar in one hand, lifted it, and flipped her neatly over in a show of strength that made her heart race. He talked about being a beast, but he couldn't know what that did for her. She loved how strong he was, how he could pick her up and carry her around. She found herself face down on the bed, her fingers clutching the sheets.

"The spreader is convenient for me," Brody explained. "I can shift you around and you can't fight me. Think about that. Think about the fact that there's nothing for you to do except lie there and take everything I have to give you."

Nothing else to do. He was strong enough to handle her. Nate was being taken care of and they were in a safe space. She didn't have to think, only give over to him. "I'll watch my smart mouth."

"And I'll watch this pretty arse." The words came out on such a sweet and loving tone that she screamed when lightning flashed across her butt. His hand came down in an arc of fire. One and then two and then five or seven. She couldn't keep up with the times he rained fire down on her flesh.

The sensation was overwhelming. Tears jarred her sight and she couldn't help the sounds she made. Still, the words "no" or "stop" or even the very stupid word "zebra" didn't cross her lips. There wasn't even the brief thought of saying her safe word.

She lost count of the smacks. The count didn't matter. All that mattered was the feeling—pain and heat and an odd resilience. She could handle this. Steph clutched the sheet and let her thoughts float.

His hand covered her aching ass as he eased up on the pace. She moaned every time his hand raised and came back down. "How do you feel?"

A little floaty. A lot hot. "Relaxed. My backside hurts, but it's okay. It's okay for it to hurt."

Sometimes hurting was a good thing, if she didn't fight it. If she let the pain flow over her because it was normal and natural to feel it. When she didn't fight the pain, it could morph into something else.

"Excellent. I'm going to pull you down a bit. Tell me if anything is uncomfortable."

She felt herself sliding along the sheets as he used the bar between her legs to maneuver her into position. Her feet hit the floor, the bar keeping her spread wide. Her chest was on the padded table, but her still aching ass was in the air.

"Yes, that's exactly what I want," he said from behind her. A big hand touched her between her shoulder blades and smoothed its way down to her backside. "I want you relaxed, waiting for whatever I'm going to do next, ready for anything I want."

Because what she knew he wanted more than anything else was her pleasure.

"I'm ready for anything you want, Brody."

"I doubt that, but it's a start. I think you're ready for this." His hand slipped between her cheeks and she shivered as he touched her there.

He was going to play with her ass. She forced herself to remain still as he touched her. A light caress of a single finger brushing over her. Still, her heart rate shot up at the forbidden sensation.

"This is going to be cold, but it's all right. I'll warm you up, luv."

She gasped as his words were proven true. Something cold hit her sensitive flesh, and Steph bit her bottom lip to keep from calling out.

"It's all right." His tone was soothing and he massaged the cool lubricant against her, rimming her with that big finger of his.

Why did that sensation seem to go straight to her pussy? It was odd. If he hadn't warmed her up before, she likely would have protested it, but now there was something sexy about this intimacy.

"You're gorgeous everywhere. This was the mistake I made that night. I was too eager to have you. I should have taken hours and hours. I should have explored every single inch of you, and then by morning I wouldn't have been able to leave."

She didn't want to hear him talk like that. It hurt to hear those words and think about what might have happened. "You're dangerously close to me saying my safe word, Brody."

"I'm hurting you?" His hand moved away in an instant.

"Not physically, but I can't do this with you. You promised me this wasn't some way of working out our problems. We agreed to no past and no future."

She could practically feel his disappointment, but she wasn't going to waver in this. Pleasure was all she could take from him and all she was willing to give.

His hand was back, this time pressing her against the padding as something hard suddenly rimmed her. "Only this. But you should know, this is me preparing for the future. If all you want of me is the Dom, then you better be prepared. I'll take what I can get. I'll make you my sweet submissive, and one of the things my sweet sub will do is take my cock anywhere I want to fuck her with it. And I'll definitely be taking this gorgeous hole."

The plug pressed in, and Steph let out a shaky moan.

"Relax." Brody moved the plug around and around, sinking deeper each time. "Don't try to keep me out. I'm getting inside."

He was. He was pressing in and there wasn't anything she could do. She was trapped and it felt good. The plug stretched her wide, a sensation on the right side of pain.

The plug slid in and she could feel the base against her backside. It felt huge inside her, but she knew he was bigger. How would it feel to take Brody deep inside her? To have him in a way she'd never had a man before?

"Don't you move." His voice was rough and she felt the loss of his hand on her skin. "If you lose the plug, we'll start all over again and we'll start with a spanking that you won't forget. Do I make myself clear?"

His voice was harder than it had been before, devoid of the emotion that had flowed between them only moments before, but it was for the best. This was the only kind of affection she could take from him. This was all they could have, but he would see it was for the best, too.

She heard the sound of water running and held her place. *Don't think. Don't think. Don't think.*

Don't think about what happens when he gets tired of how stubborn you are.

Don't think about how you'll feel when he moves on and finds a woman who can give him what he needs.

Don't think about how much you love him.

She felt him move behind her, felt his thighs touch the backs of her legs as he moved in.

"Look up. Eyes forward."

She tilted her chin up and saw what she hadn't seen before. There was a mirror in front of her and she could see his big body behind her, the erotic image searing into her brain. She looked small and vulnerable compared to him. Helpless.

And yet she was the one who'd hurt him.

His jaw was tight as he opened the condom in his hand and rolled it over his cock. There was no teasing hint of a smile, no look of comfort in his face.

This was the Dom and this would be an exchange. She'd done as he'd asked, allowed him to shove a piece of plastic up her ass, and now he would service her.

This was what she'd watched between the king and queen of Loa Mali, though she rather thought their positions had been reversed. Mistress Day had seemed almost desperate to reach her husband and he'd been wooden and cold. Uncomfortable in his own skin.

She didn't have a problem with her skin. She could be naked all day, but his words…

She was uncomfortable with her own soul. Wasn't that infinitely worse?

She was giving him no past. No future. No connection except a sexual one, and it was stamped right there on his face that he needed more.

He was here now and he'd been right about one thing. They couldn't play these games when it came to Nate. She was putting off the inevitable moment when she had to decide how they would work together.

Did she want Nate growing up with two parents who couldn't come together for anything but sex? Sex that she would attempt to pull all the emotion out of?

"Watch in the mirror." His voice was a monotone, as if he was going through a checklist of what to do with his sub.

She stared forward as she felt the head of his cock at her pussy. "Would you have put me in a spreader bar while I was pregnant? If you'd stayed?"

He stopped, suspicion on his face. "I would have done a lot of things. I definitely would have done this for as long as I could."

His cock breached her, the sensation different because she had that plug taking up space. She had to force herself to breathe, but it was good. It was right. When she stopped punishing him, she could feel how right it was to be here with him.

"I got so big, Brody. I was huge."

There was the face she loved. He softened around her. He could look cruel and masculine, and yet when his eyes went soft she realized he was a big old teddy bear. With spectacular abs and the most amazing cock in the world.

"You were beautiful." His tone changed and he held himself inside her. One hand moved up, caressing her and making her feel warm and wanted again. "I can only imagine how gorgeous you were."

She'd been a whale, but he wouldn't have seen that. He would have seen her differently, as he'd always seemed to see her. "Tell me why you left me."

"Because I thought I wasn't good for you. Because I never

loved another woman the way I loved you and it scared me."

He never lied to her. Why would he start now? She couldn't offer him anything more than she'd offered him then, with the singular exception of their son. "I won't ever keep you from Nate. You have to know that."

He dragged his cock back out, his face flushing with pleasure. "I know that, but I want us to be more. You don't have to answer me tonight, but give me a chance to show you how much more we could be. We could be a family."

She couldn't respond, the picture of a family with this man far too sweet. It brought tears to her eyes, but she couldn't think for long because he was moving inside her.

Brody let himself go, pounding in her, brushing his cock over and over her sweet spot. Between his cock and the plug in her ass she was full. It was like nothing she'd ever felt before.

He pulled on her hips, going deeper, and she flew over the edge.

Gripping the sheet like a lifeline, she watched as Brody's head dropped back and he pulsed inside her.

Her heart seemed to skip a beat as she watched him. He fell forward, his front resting on her back. He looked down at her and she wanted to be able to see herself through his eyes.

"Stephanie," he began.

She knew what he was going to say. It was there in his eyes. *I love you.*

And for a second she was ready to say it back.

A loud knock disrupted the moment.

"Mr. Carter," a masculine voice said. "I'm afraid we have a situation. I'm sorry to interrupt, but we need to get the doc to another secure location."

Brody stood up, heading for the small bathroom. "We'll be out in five minutes. Steph, luv, give me a second and I'll have you out of there."

He disappeared into the bathroom, probably to get rid of the condom.

Steph set her head down and remembered all the reasons she hadn't wanted to think about the future.

Chapter Twelve

Brody stared at the package on the table and wished like hell that the bodyguards on duty this evening had thought to keep this discreet. They could have said anything to have gotten him out of the training room, but Steph had known something was going on.

Then again, it was really Tucker's fault. He had Tucker to thank for accepting the package, opening the package, and freaking out about the package.

If it had been one of the bodyguards who had been given the package, they likely would have calmly called in and explained that a box had been delivered and Brody should probably come and take a look at it. If it had been Shane or Declan, the two guards who would come back with them tonight, Steph would not be staring down at that package, her face white as a sheet. He would have gotten her home and put her to bed and she could have been blissfully unaware.

"Did it come with a note?" O'Donnell had changed out of his earlier costume and now was dressed in jeans and a button down, his hair slicked back from a shower.

Brody wished they'd had time to shower. He hated the fact that he'd had to hurry her along. At least she'd had street clothes to change into.

"Of course it came with a note." Taggart hadn't changed, though he'd pulled off the long blond wig and bandana. He frowned Tucker's way. "Unless the puppy forgot the note in his mad dash to erase any and all evidence we could have gotten off this thing."

Tucker was pacing the floor, a frown on his face. "Well, I'm sorry. I'm not used to opening boxes and finding…that. I'm used to opening boxes and finding pizzas. Or cupcakes. Good things are supposed to come in boxes that are delivered to your front door. Damn it, I tipped that guy. I tipped him and he gave me that."

"What is it?" Steph asked.

Tucker started to open his mouth and then closed it. "Maybe Steph shouldn't be here."

It was far too late for that. There was no way Stephanie would let him ease her out of the room and allow him to handle this. No way.

"Steph should probably be receiving aftercare, from what I understand," Taggart shot back. His voice lowered and he leaned toward Brody. "Did you find the '*anal*-gesic' packs? It's perfect to ease the way after a good plugging."

"Focus, Taggart." The man had no discretion.

"Is it a body part?" Steph moved toward the conference room table, her voice a bland, flat tone that told him she hadn't heard Taggart.

"It's probably a bad sign that I have boxes of these here." Taggart dragged a pair of latex gloves over his hands. "Let's see exactly what we're dealing with. Still, at least I won't be leaving fingerprints everywhere. We might have to rethink leaving the police out of this. Maybe I should call in Derek."

Brody was not interested in dealing with the local police because he knew exactly where that would lead. "It won't be Lieutenant Brighton who handles this case and you know it. First they'll call in the FBI, and then Interpol will want a piece of it, and potentially whatever the hell agency Ukraine has to track down kidnapped citizens."

O'Donnell stepped in beside Taggart. "I'm with Carter. We

can't let this leave our house. We'll lose control of both the case and of Steph's protection. We wouldn't be consulted at all if they decide to take it out of the US. We don't know that the mercenary team is even still here."

"We can call in the police if it means saving Anya." Steph hadn't moved. She hadn't smiled or held his hand since that moment when she'd realized the future wasn't going to leave them alone. At least Brody thought that's what had happened.

She'd opened up to him. Something had happened when he'd forced her to meet his eyes in the mirror. She'd softened and been willing to talk about what she'd gone through all those long months that he'd been gone. The connection that had always been between them had flared to life and he'd held on to it with all his strength. He'd known he'd gotten to her and that they could talk. She might listen to him, might understand his apology went far beyond words.

One knock on the door and she'd folded back in on herself.

"It won't save Anya," Brody insisted. "In this case, bringing in a bunch of feds and different international agencies will only complicate things. We have no idea which corporation is involved in this or how far reaching their influence goes. If you were on your own, yes, you would call in law enforcement, but you're not. You're surrounded by some of the smartest men in the world when it comes to intelligence and security. Let us do our jobs."

Her arms came up, crossing over her chest. "I want her saved. I'm the client. I want saving Anya to be made a priority over everything else. Unless that's a head in the box and she's already dead."

"It's not a head." Tucker sounded horrified. "I wouldn't have brought a head in here. I don't know what I would have done if it had been a head."

Sometimes Brody thought Tucker had been a mistake on Dr. McDonald's part. All of her other experiments had been warriors, and they still acted like it for the most part. Though Robert was calmer than the rest of the Lost Boys, there was still a deep darkness in the man. Tucker seemed so close to the light that he wondered if it was a part of the bloke or if the drugs had so thoroughly wiped his memory that he couldn't conceive of the world he'd landed in.

"It's a digit. In my opinion it's the fifth digit of the subject's right hand. It was excised at the distal phalanx. I would be way more freaked out if it was a head." Tucker continued pacing.

And then there were times that he thought Tucker remembered far more than any of them imagined.

Taggart glanced up at Steph. "Distal phalanx?"

"He means it's only the tip of the finger. The digits are composed of three segments called phalanxes. He's referring to the portion of the finger that contains the nail. They cut off the tip of her pinky finger and sent it to us in a box." She'd paled, but her tone remained calm. "He's had medical training. Likely a lot of it if he recalls those kinds of facts easily. I know doctors who would have called it the pinkie finger. His training was hardcore."

Taggart lifted the box lid and looked inside, his expression never changing. "Well, we're still learning a lot about the drugs that were used on him. The doctor who experimented on those men was a genius. An evil one, but a genius all the same. She managed to wipe out personal memories without getting rid of important functions like language skills and how to fight. And it seems like a good portion of the puppy's medical training stuck, too."

"Personal and emotional memories are stored in different sections of the brain," Steph replied. "She obviously figured out how to chemically alter the section that holds personal memories."

"She messed with my limbic system," Tucker said with a shake of his head. "That just came to me. Limbic system. I know that's the word to use. How do I know that? How do I know what to call a pinkie finger in a box, but I can't tell you who my mother was? I'm sorry. This trip was apparently more stimulation than I was ready for. I'm sorry I screwed up the forensics. I should have known better."

O'Donnell had pulled on a pair of gloves, too, and now he reached into the box. "Not as badly as you thought you had. You missed something in your very reasonable reaction to receiving a body part in a box. There aren't many people who wouldn't have a reaction to that."

"Seriously?" Taggart threw his old friend a questioning look. "You're getting soft in your old age."

"He's practically a toddler, Tag. We have to go easy on him. He's not a hardened agent." O'Donnell pulled out a small piece of paper. "And he didn't lose the note."

"O'Donnell's right. We're actually lucky it was Tucker and not one of the others who came with me. If it had been Sasha or Dante, they would have played with the damn thing." Brody tried to move closer to Steph, but she stepped away. He thought about forcing the issue, but decided to wait until they were alone. She responded better when they were alone. "We don't know that's Anya's finger."

"According to the note it is." O'Donnell's eyes shifted as he read the note.

"Could you read it out loud?" Steph asked. "I get that you think I'm a delicate flower who's never seen a lopped off body part, but the least I can handle is reading a few words."

"They know you're not a shrinking violet, but they also know it's different when you know the person." He wasn't sure how to deal with her. She seemed to have distanced from everything and everyone.

O'Donnell held the note in his gloved hands. "It's from de Vries. He says he's got Anya Shadrova and will exchange her for the thumb drive you took. If you don't give him the thumb drive by midnight tomorrow night, he'll send a bigger piece next time. If we call in the feds or any reporter, he'll put us all on a hit list."

Taggart rolled his eyes. "Like that's never happened before."

"This is serious," Steph said.

Taggart shrugged. "You're used to body parts. I'm used to people trying to murder me."

"Did he leave us a time and place to meet him?" Brody would be there. Eagerly. Happily. He was ready to get in a room with that fucker.

"There's a phone in here along with his present," O'Donnell explained. "It's a burner and he says he'll only talk to Steph. If anyone else answers the phone, Anya...well, we all know where that's going. He claims he'll call sometime in the morning and set the meeting for tomorrow night. He won't tell you where until thirty minutes before."

"We'll figure it out before then. There are only so many places he can go," Taggart pointed out. "Now that we have a name, we should be able to find the fucker. We need time though."

"I won't let anyone die because of me." She'd gone even paler than before and her voice finally shook.

"No one's going to die," Taggart replied. "And Anya will get a discount on future manicures if that's hers in the first place. I don't know. I don't like her Ukrainian mob connections. It feels awfully convenient."

Steph straightened up, her eyes narrowing on Taggart. "It wasn't convenient for me. And I don't have a thumb drive. I don't know what they're talking about. I didn't go through the reporter's things. The situation was urgent. We cut his shirt off and cut off the khakis he was wearing. We would have thrown them out as medical waste. They were covered in blood. I never saw any piece of luggage he was carrying. No backpack. No wallet."

A nasty theory was playing through Brody's head. There was something convenient about all of this, but it didn't have anything to do with Anya and her mob connections. He didn't want it to be true, but it was far too important to put his head in the sand and pretend. Besides, his loyalty had shifted somewhere along the way. "Remind me of something, luv. Was Alfi ever alone with the journalist?"

Steph turned his way. "Yes, but he wasn't conscious. Alfi said he never woke up."

Yes, but Alfi had been known to lie.

"Fucker," Taggart spat, obviously picking up on Brody's thought process. He pulled his mobile. "Shane, I need you to take Declan and haul ass over to the safe house. Bring me the Aussie asshole. No. Not that one. He's one of ours. The other Aussie asshole. Yeah. You don't have to be tender with him either."

So he'd been a big hit with the bodyguards. Well, he'd been called worse.

"Why would Alfi lie to me?" Steph asked, finally stepping close to him. Her chin tilted up and for the first time since they'd walked into the room he saw some vulnerability in her eyes.

For a hundred reasons, but he could only think of the one that might make sense to her. He smoothed back her hair, desperate for a physical connection. "If he thought he could make money off that thumb drive, he would do it in a heartbeat, the bastard. He would take the drive and get the hell out of there until he could figure out what he had."

"But he wasn't at the house when I left," Tucker said. "He said he needed to go buy a six-pack."

"So he walked to the store?" Brody asked the question, though he was afraid he knew the damn answer. He should never have left Tucker alone with Alfi. He should have known Alfi had come here with nefarious purposes, and leaving Tucker behind to watch him had been like leaving a child in charge of the house.

Tucker's cheeks had gone a nice shade of red. "He promised to grab me a couple of bags of chips if I let him borrow the car. I was super hungry. I ate supper at like five. I need to eat every couple of hours or I get low blood sugar."

"Then why the bloody hell didn't you go with him?" Brody was ready to throttle the kid.

Tucker winced. "Because *American Ninja Warrior* was on and I don't know how to work the DVR."

O'Donnell stepped in between the two of them. "Now, Carter, take a deep breath. If we murder our young we're no better than animals."

"Also, Charlie had the carpet cleaned in here a few days ago." Taggart was back on his phone. "Adam, I need you to find an escaped Aussie. Yeah, the one from your place earlier this afternoon. He's in Carter's rental. Check the traffic cameras around your place." Pause. "If I knew where he was going, I wouldn't need you, would I?"

"Why would he come here?" Steph asked. "Unless he's planning on selling the thumb drive back to the mercenaries. Would he do that? If he does, what happens to Anya? He's probably on his way there right now. If they get that thumb drive, they won't have any use for her anymore. They won't want to keep her around."

"Or she's been involved the whole time," Taggart said, hanging up his phone.

"She's not," Steph shot back. "Anya's innocent in all this."

"You can't know that." Taggart was looking down at his phone, texting away.

"Of course I can know it. I can use my brain and logic this sucker out." Steph moved away from him again. "Why would she be involved with a bunch of mercenaries? What does she get out of it? She just happened to get a nursing degree so she could spend a year in Africa waiting to set me up because she knew a journalist would someday get himself shot and stumble into my clinic? And she knew that Alfi would steal the thumb drive and she could be used to get it back. She's a fucking psychic, Taggart. You should put her on the payroll because she could solve all your cases for you."

Taggart stopped, staring at Steph for a moment with those arctic eyes of his. Steph didn't back down at all, but then she'd always had a death wish. Brody got ready to shift, to come between the two of them and let Taggart know that he couldn't top his sub.

Then Taggart sighed. "All right, put like that it does seem a bit on the farfetched side. Score one for logic. Sorry, Doc. I'm used to being betrayed. It's happened almost as many times as I've been nearly murdered. All right. We'll assume Anya Shadrova is an innocent and needs to be saved."

"Thank you," Steph said with a sigh.

"You want us to save the Aussie, too, Lady SoftHeart?" Taggart asked with a wry smile on his face.

"Nope, you can rough him up all you like, but we need to get that thumb drive from him." Steph turned and shook her head, walking toward the door. "I need to go check on Nate. The party was over an hour ago. The staff needs to go home."

"They left thirty minutes ago," O'Donnell explained. "It's Avery and Charlotte in there now and they're perfectly fine. Nate's in good hands. If he's not sleeping, then he's being well taken care of. Now tell me how you're doing. Do you need anything?"

He hated the rush of jealousy he felt. He watched how Steph squeezed Liam's hand. He couldn't help but step up and reply. "I'll take care of her. You go and help Miles find Alfi so I can rearrange his innards. I'll figure out where that thumb drive is."

Steph held a hand up. "Before you guys do anything at all, I need to make one thing clear. Anya comes first. That's the mission. Saving her comes before everything else."

Was she high? Was she still in subspace because she had to be if she thought that was going to work.

"We'll do everything we can," Brody assured her. But that wasn't his highest directive. She was, and he knew damn well it would be O'Donnell's, too.

"She comes before me." Steph looked between the two of them as if trying to figure out exactly what they were doing. Suspicion was plain on her face. "If we have to give me up to save her, we're going to do it."

"Of course," O'Donnell replied. He reached for Steph's hand. "You're the client. We're going to take your direction."

Taggart's eyes had gone wide but his expression shifted the minute Steph looked at him. "Of course. Like Li said. You're the client. If you want to be dumb enough to martyr yourself, who am I to say nay? Can I get a check from you before your inevitable death?"

"Ian," O'Donnell said between clenched teeth.

"Well, you said she was the client," Taggart replied. "Clients usually pay."

Brody ignored Taggart, but the men were onto something. Arguing with her would lead them absolutely nowhere, but he had to play it right. He couldn't simply scream out that he would save her no matter what. She needed a softer touch.

And a shit ton of lies because there was zero chance that he was going to trade her for Anya.

"I'll do everything in my power to make sure we get the outcome you need," he promised. "I know what you want, Steph. You have to know I'll try to keep you safe, too."

She stared at him as though trying to figure out if she should argue or not.

He was saved when the door came open and Adam strode in.

"Turn that computer on to the security cameras. I found our lost Aussie."

Taggart had the screen up on the wall in front of them in a second. "He came here? Why would he come here?"

Steph gasped as the picture became clear. Brody stepped in front of her as though he could protect her from the men on the screen.

"I don't think it was his choice," Adam said.

No. It didn't look like Alfi had a choice at all. He was on his knees in front of the gate, his hands held high. Two men stood behind him, their faces covered in dark tactical balaclavas. He could see rifles in their hands. It looked like a scene straight out of Afghanistan, but it was happening in front of Sanctum.

"All right then." Taggart pulled out his mobile. "Boys, get ready for war."

* * * *

Steph watched the monitor.

"That's a lot of guns," Avery said, leaning in. When the men had gone outside to confront the intruders, Avery and Charlotte had joined her so she wouldn't be alone. Serena had stayed in the nursery, watching over sleeping children while Adam and Jake had taken up positions they claimed would allow them to watch over the situation.

Or in other words, they were in sniper positions. It made her shiver.

Avery was right. It *was* a lot of guns. Moments after the two men and Alfi had shown up in front of the gates, Shane and Declan had been standing on the other side. Four guns pointing at each other. Four chances for someone to die. Although it was certainly more than four chances since any of the bullets could do damage, and there would be plenty of bullets.

Brody was walking out there right now. Brody was striding out with Taggart and Li, and their guns would join the bodyguards'.

"Don't worry. They know what they're doing." Charlotte's

words didn't reassure her.

They did know what they were doing, and she knew they were lying to her. Brody had no intentions of giving her up for Anya. Neither did Li. She wasn't a complete idiot.

"What exactly *are* they doing?" Tucker had stayed behind. He was sitting at the conference table watching the scene at the street play out.

"They're talking first," Charlotte explained. "Ian needs to figure out who he's dealing with before he murders them all. That's lesson number one, Tucker. Always figure out who you're brutally killing and get everything you can out of your victim before you start in on the actual vicious torture and death part."

A car suddenly pulled up behind the men on the public side of the gate and the door was opened by the man on the left. He hauled Alfi up and shoved his big body into the car. The other man lowered his rifle and seemed to be talking to Taggart.

"Wow, I didn't expect that," Charlotte said as the car drove off. She stood up and started toward the door. "I think the war is off. It looks like we're about to have peace talks. Avery, could you go and tell Serena that we're about to have guests. I'm going to request a guard outside the nursery door and another guarding the stairs that run up to the third floor."

Where the royals were staying. Avery strode out the door while Charlotte got on her phone.

"Remy, we have an evolving situation," Charlotte said, stepping away to talk.

"Are you afraid?" Tucker turned in his chair. "Because I don't think you should be. Brody's good at his job. And he told me if I let you get murdered he would do some things to me that shouldn't be done to a human body. I'm planning on not letting you get killed because I don't think my large intestine should see the outside of my body."

She had to talk to Brody about how he dealt with his coworkers. "He won't hurt you and I plan on not being killed."

Planned, but she knew how plans could go.

She'd planned to spend the whole evening in Brody's arms.

She'd planned to let him handle everything.

Her plans were completely blown.

Twenty-four hours and then Anya would lose her life. Twenty-four hours and there would be more blood on her hands. She knew logically that this wasn't her fault, but deep down in her soul she had to ask herself why it kept happening to her. Was there something wrong with her that she kept hurting people?

Would she hurt Brody and Nate simply by letting them close?

"I think he would kill me if I did something that hurt you," Tucker was saying.

She shook her head. "No. I'll talk to him about it. He shouldn't threaten you. I don't want that."

"You don't want someone to stand up for you?"

She couldn't handle the thought. "No. If Brody thinks that's how I want to live, then he's wrong about me."

And that was a good reason for her to not pursue a relationship with him.

Tucker's eyes tightened, his mouth turning down. "I thought that would be a nice thing. The group where I live, they stand up for each other. I thought it was a form of love. You treat it like it's something terrible. Could you explain this to me? I hate feeling confused."

She wished he'd picked someone else to explain humanity to him. "I don't want anyone hurt because of something I did or something that was done to me. Do you understand?"

"So you don't want connections with people? Because if you're connected in a way that's loving and affectionate, you can't expect that person to sit by while you're being harmed. Or threatened."

How did she make him understand? She glanced up at the screen and sighed in relief. The guns were pointed down now and the two men who'd held Alfi had taken off the masks that covered their faces. It looked like they were talking in a somewhat reasonable fashion. "I expect them to honor my wishes. Look, I've hurt people in the past."

"You're talking about the two people who died in the car accident?"

Well, at least he'd done his homework. "Yes."

"So you think because those two people died, that no one should stand up for you. You think you don't deserve love from anyone."

She wished he would stop playing the shrink. "Of course not. It's simply that I think I should be left to handle things. I know best what I want and that's not more people to be hurt. I'm a big girl. I should be able to choose how to live my life."

"And will you teach your son the same? I often wonder what my mother taught me. Of course, when I think about it too hard, I get a terrible headache."

"It's different. He's a child," she argued.

"But children learn from their parents. I've heard this said many times. If someone was hurting your child, how would you handle that? Would you simply ask the person to stop? If that doesn't work, how would you handle that?"

"I wouldn't let anyone hurt my child." The line of questioning was making her anxious. "Are you trying to say I'm a bad mother?"

"No, I'm trying to understand. Brody is my friend and he's in a bad position. He loves you, but I think you don't want him to love you. I think you don't want anyone to love you and that makes me feel sad. Ariel says we should talk about the things that make us sad even if there is no solution." Tucker looked back at the screen. "I want to be there for Brody if he needs me. I think he's going to because I think you're going to break his heart. He's not a man who can allow those he loves to be hurt. Even if they crave the pain of being hurt."

"I do not."

He shrugged. "Sometimes pain is good. I think I miss my pain. I can feel it simmering beneath the surface, but I can't remember why it's there. If I knew what I ached about, maybe I could ease it. Maybe I could find a way to turn it into something else. Is that why you went to Africa?"

She stood up. "I'm not having this conversation with you. It's too personal."

"I'm sorry. I didn't mean to pry. I guess I did, but I didn't mean to hurt you. I was trying to understand more." He flashed her a sad smile. "I've been told I'm annoying."

She was about to agree with whoever had said that when the door came open and Taggart entered.

"Charlie?"

Charlotte nodded. "I've placed guards on the nursery and to watch over our guests."

He lowered his head and kissed his wife. "Thank you. Now for the fun stuff. Introductions. Don't kill the newbies."

Her eyes narrowed. "Not the mercenaries?"

Brody walked into the room, his eyes finding hers.

What would she do if someone was hurting him? Would she stand back and let him handle it because he was an adult and he should have the choice? Or would she stop whoever was doing it at any cost because she loved him?

Love. She loved him and that scared the shit out of her.

"No mercenaries. We have an interested third party." Liam stood beside a tall, lanky man with blond hair.

He looked incredibly familiar. A name came to mind because she was almost certain she'd seen that face before in a photo. "Fedor? Are you Anya's brother?"

He nodded slowly. "I am and you are her employer? The doctor?"

Brody tried to step in front of her. "She's none of your business."

"Yes, Anya works at my clinic." She couldn't seem to get around him.

"You are the one who left her behind to die?" Fedor asked. His friend stepped in next to him.

"Hey," Brody began.

Guilt flooded her system. "I thought she would run. She offered to stay behind for a few minutes and then she would run."

Fedor's cold blue eyes found hers. "My sister is brave. I can see agreeing to risk her own life to save others. You are coward for allowing her to do this. You and the piece of shit I have taken into custody. You both ran and left my sister to take your punishment."

"Ukrainians." Charlotte made the word sound like an admonishment.

"Russian," Fedor shot back. He said something in a language Steph didn't understand.

Charlotte did the same.

Taggart put a hand up. "I didn't even know some of those words and my Russian is pretty good. It's best that I didn't since if I thought for a second that you called my wife nasty names, I would say our peace treaty is over and you should get ready to fight."

Fedor took a deep breath. "I am sorry, Mr. Taggart. And Mrs. Taggart. I am not friendly with your wife's people, as I pointed out before. This is why I will keep the man and allow you to keep the woman for as long as I believe you intend to work with me to free my sister."

"Allow?" Taggart asked.

Brody took her hand and pulled her to a corner of the room while Fedor began to talk to Taggart. "Are you all right?"

Not at all, but there was nothing she could do about it now. "He's right. I should have waited for her."

Brody's jaw tightened. "Damn it, you had to protect our son." He sighed, a long-suffering sound. "That bastard has no idea what it was like and no right at all to blame you. But you won't listen to me about that, will you?"

She felt his disappointment and couldn't understand it. Not at all. "I could have done a thousand things differently. Can't you see that I should have helped her?"

"Can't you see that you cannot save the whole world? You owe Nate. You have to save him first, last, and always, and part of saving Nate is saving yourself. He needs his mum. I need you."

But she would screw it up. She would screw it all up and then where would they be? She wanted to lean into him, to hold on and beg him to make things right for her. For them. She wanted to hold on to him, but she was afraid.

"I need you." Brody stared down at her, his hands on her shoulders, eyes pleading.

The best thing she could do was walk away. Turn and walk out and leave everything and everyone behind. Go back to Africa where she was needed, but not needed. They needed a doctor, not her in particular. She didn't have to be Stephanie Gibson in Africa. All she had to be was a competent doctor, and that might have been how she spent the rest of her life.

But Nate had come along and now she had to be something more.

"I need you, too." The words came out on a whisper, new words that seemed vulnerable. Fragile words. "I need you, Brody."

A shudder went through his body and he dragged her close. "You have no idea how long I've wanted to hear those words. I'm going to take care of this."

Because he loved her. Because people in love took care of each other. Somehow Tucker's words were sinking in and making her ask questions. She'd seen plenty of therapists who had traced the source of her guilt and self-loathing back to the night that changed her life. They'd all tried to ease her through so she could live a happy life. But Tucker had asked her childish questions. Questions her own child would one day ask, and she'd had no real idea how to answer him.

How would she explain to her boy that she wasn't worth saving? That her life had ended that night she'd made the worst mistake a human could make and she was nothing but a shell already serving time in a self-made Purgatory?

His life should be about joy, and if she didn't find a way to change, she had none to give him.

How did she explain that his birth hadn't changed her life? Hadn't made her more than she'd been before? Had shoved her even deeper into a hole?

She didn't know what to do, couldn't trust her own instincts. The surface instincts told her to push everyone away.

What did her deeper instincts tell her? What would the Stephanie who never got in that car and went to that party have done?

She leaned close and wrapped her arms around him. She breathed in his scent. Earthy and masculine and safe.

She felt him kiss her head.

"Don't worry about anything else. Let me handle this." He kissed her again. "Let me take care of you for once."

She found herself nodding against him. "Okay."

She felt him sigh as though relieved.

"It's all going to be all right in the end. We're going to sit down and talk this out with Anya's family," he explained. "We'll exchange all the intel we've gathered. This is a good thing."

Brody was an optimist. "And what about Alfi?"

"Alfi claims he lost the thumb drive. He admitted he took it and thought to sell it back to the mercenaries or the company they were representing or the newspaper the journalist worked for. He wanted to start a bidding war, but somewhere along the way, he lost the damn thing. I swear I'll kill him myself."

She shook her head, but she wasn't going to argue with him over semantics. He wouldn't really kill Alfi. Even if Alfi might deserve it. "Why? Why would he do that to us? He had to know this would go badly."

"Alfi doesn't think. He never has. He sees money in front of him and all his morals go out the window. I'm sure he convinced himself that he deserved the money. Bastard."

"On this we can agree," Fedor said. "Alfi Dauterre is a bastard."

"That doesn't mean you get to hurt him." She faced Fedor.

"I'll leave that to de Vries," he said with a shrug.

Taggart took over, stepping into the middle of the group. "It's late. Why don't you take Steph back home and I'll deal with our new friends. I'm going to have to bring them up to date on everything, but I'm going to do it at the office. This isn't the place for a meeting."

Fedor didn't know his sister had already lost a piece of herself.

Brody's hand found hers, squeezing lightly. It was easy to see they didn't want her around when Fedor lost his shit.

"How are we going to get her back? If we don't have the thumb drive, what are we going to do?" She needed a plan. They were down to twenty-four hours.

"That's what we're going to talk about," Taggart assured her.

"Go and get your son and in the morning, we'll have another talk. We'll find de Vries. Don't think I won't."

"It's going to be fine, Steph," Charlotte said. "I'll come by in the morning and fill you in on everything. And I'll keep an eye on the boys and make sure they don't do anything too dangerous. By this time tomorrow, we'll have your friend back and all of this is going to feel like a bad dream."

She wished she had half of Charlotte's optimism.

Brody led her out into the hall. The group around them discussed going back to the McKay-Taggart building. Adam joined them, explaining how he was going to narrow down the possible places where de Vries could be hiding.

Steph felt removed from it all.

Brody leaned over and brushed a kiss on her forehead. "I'll get our boy. You wait for me here, all right?"

She nodded and moved to the front windows, staring out into the night.

"This is not how I wanted to visit the States for the first time," a deep voice said.

She glanced up and the second man was standing beside her. "I'm sorry you had to come under such terrible circumstances. You know Anya well?"

"She's my cousin. We have—how would say? Very close family. You must understand this."

She didn't. Her family had broken a long time before. "I know Anya talks about her family all the time."

"She's a sweet girl, but Fedor was wrong to allow her to go to dangerous place." His eyes were on the parking lot. "I'm going to tell you what the others will not. This man who has my cousin will not be bought off with the thumb drive. He wants you and the Australian. He believes you have seen what is on the drive, and he will kill anyone who can speak of it."

"I haven't seen anything." She tightened her fingers around her purse, needing something to hold on to.

"That is between you and de Vries. I suggest you make him believe or he will kill you. I intend to give you to de Vries along

261

with Dauterre in exchange for my cousin. I will go along with this farce for now, but I want you to meet me in four hours. I know the address where you are staying."

"I can't do that. Even if I was stupid enough to try to meet you, I don't think my bodyguards would allow it."

"I've slipped you a letter detailing what I want you to do along with the tools to make it happen. If you don't meet me in four hours, I will use my network to ensure that everyone you care about dies in the next year. I know many of the world's finest assassins. I won't hesitate to spend everything I own making sure you lose everyone. Starting with your son and that big bastard you're obviously sleeping with. Do I make myself clear?"

She turned to him, noting that Tucker was watching from across the lobby. "You've made yourself very clear."

He smiled down at her. "Act like nothing is wrong or we'll start here and now. If you tell your friends, they'll be the first to go."

She forced a smile on her face and Tucker seemed to take that as his cue. He sat back down. "I think you're outnumbered here. My friends aren't exactly lightweights."

"I have no wish to get involved in a fight here and now, and perhaps they would win," he allowed. "But you should understand that even if Fedor and I die, we have others to take care of things. My people have long memories and we'll be smart about it. We'll allow a few months to go by, but sooner or later, you will lose them all. We will save you for the last. By the time we're done, you'll beg for death. Do you understand?"

"Yes, you've made yourself very clear."

"Excellent." He stepped back as Brody strode out of the hallway, carrying Nathan's car seat. "I wish you a good night, then. Mr. Carter, we'll see you in the morning and we'll try to find our way out of this, yes?"

Brody nodded. "We will. This is a smart bunch. We'll get Anya back in no time." He put his free hand on her shoulder. "Come along, luv. Let's get some sleep. Tomorrow's going to be a long day, but after things will get better."

"I hope so." She would have to wait until she got home to read the note and the instructions the Ukrainians had left for her.

How would she get by the guards?

"Are you all right?" Brody smoothed her hair back.

She moved into his arms. "Just tired."

He held her and she wondered if it was for the last time.

Chapter Thirteen

Brody put Nate down, laying him in the crib. "We've got to get him into a routine. The last few nights we've put him down late."

"Or early. Depends on your perspective," Steph said quietly. "He's still on African time. He's also very young. He sleeps most of the day. The fact that he was awake at the club and had attention and affection won't hurt him. It means he might sleep a little later in the day. Kids are quite resilient at this age. As long as they have loving human contact they can get through almost anything."

There was something about the set of her shoulders that worried him. She wasn't relaxed and she hadn't been for hours. He strode over to her, wishing they were back in the training room when everything had seemed perfect and possible.

"Do you want to talk about it, luv? We could go to the kitchen and I'll fix us some tea."

She shook her head. "I just made a pot of coffee for Declan and Shane. I got Tucker some, too. I honestly don't want any tea."

He wanted to talk, but maybe they needed sleep more. In the morning, she might be willing to tell him what she was afraid of. "All right. Let's go to bed, but you need to understand that I'm going to take care of you."

She glanced at the clock. "I wonder why you didn't go to that meeting. I get why I'm not there, but I would think if Big Tag and Anya's brother wanted to talk about how they're going to take down de Vries, you should be in on that."

He sat down on the bed in front of her. It was oddly comfortable to share a room with her, like something had finally drifted into place and he was where he should have been all along. "My place is here with you and Nate. Big Tag can take care of Fedor. It's his job and why we're here in the first place."

"I thought we were here because Li and Avery are my only friends."

There was something up with her and he couldn't put his finger on it. He unbuttoned his shirt and tossed it aside while he considered the problem. "You have more friends than you know. And if you had come to England and this was all going down at The Garden, I would still be going to bed with you. I would let Damon handle the big stuff because my main job in life now is to make sure you and Nate are safe and happy."

She moved closer, placing herself squarely between his legs, her hands on his shoulders. "I believe you."

His hands found her hips, eager to recapture the intimacy they'd lost earlier. "Good, because I mean it. I was a blind fool, Steph. I never should have left you much less allowed so much time to go by. You need to know that every single day we were apart, I thought about you. I never stopped." He picked her up and rolled her over on to the bed, putting her on her back. It was exactly where he liked her to be. On her back with her legs spread, welcoming him home. "I have a lot to make up for. I wonder how I can do that."

She frowned. "Brody..."

Damn it. He was being a selfish git. She was probably sore and tired and he was forcing himself on her. He started to roll off her, but her hands came up, holding him in place.

"Don't go." She looked up at him with clear eyes. Such innocent eyes. "I wasn't trying to stop you. I wanted to switch things up a little. I know we have our places in the bedroom, but I want to look at you this time. I couldn't see you tonight except in the mirror and while that was hot as hell, I want to be the top. Is that okay?"

She wanted a bit of control, did she? He leaned over, kissing her nose before easing off the bed. "I think I can handle that. What do you want from me?"

She sat up, a gleam in her eyes that satisfied him immensely. "You, naked on this bed."

That he could definitely do. There was something about the way she ate him up with her eyes that made him feel like he was ten feet tall. He kicked out of his slacks and tossed them aside gently. Every move he made required patience because Nate was sleeping mere feet away.

When he got her back to The Garden, Nate would have his own room and his parents could have some freedom. Well, as much freedom as an infant allowed. He loved the idea of moving her into his flat, waking up with her every morning. If they decided they needed more room or more privacy, they could look around at the pretty walk-ups in Chelsea. Somewhere close, so even when he was out in the field, she would have people she could rely on.

She would get used to having family around. That was something he could offer her, too.

He eased back on the bed, taking up most of the space. Another good thing they would have when they got back to England. His bed was huge. He spread himself out for her as she got up on her knees. She'd shed her jeans and blouse and gotten into one of his T-shirts after she'd showered. Her face was scrubbed clean and she looked even younger than usual. How could he let her know how precious she was to him? How much he regretted the last year? "Do you know how gorgeous you are?"

Her skin flushed and her lips curved in a half smile. "You tell me often enough. Do you know how gorgeous you are?"

"I'm a big dude with a lot of scars, Stephanie. I'm not sure gorgeous is the right word."

Her eyes widened and she swung a leg over his hips, straddling him. Her hands came down on his chest and she gently pinched his nipple between her thumb and forefinger. "I said you're gorgeous and you should thank me for my compliment. Isn't that what the big bad Dom would do?"

He grinned because she hadn't managed to even send him a tweak of pain. "That's right. You tell me, luv. You put me in my place when I need it."

She sat up, her eyes closing as she shifted on top of him. He bit back a groan because her pussy was right on top of his cock and he realized she wasn't wearing knickers. She rolled her hips, rubbing him to a full erection. How was she wet when he hadn't even touched her?

"What the hell were you thinking of in the shower?" He whispered the question, rolling his hips in time with hers.

Her eyes opened, seduction plain in her gaze. "I was thinking about you. I was thinking about how much I loved what we did earlier tonight. I loved being completely under your control, but I also wanted to have time where I got to touch you to my heart's content. Do you know what I felt when you put me in the spreader bar and I couldn't do anything but accept what you gave me?"

He hoped she'd felt his desire, his overwhelming love for her. "What did you feel?"

"I felt like I was the center of the universe, like I mattered, and often I feel like I don't." She leaned over again, brushing her palms against the muscles of his chest. "I felt sexy and beautiful. I want to make sure you feel that way, too. If there's one thing I can give you...well, I want to make sure you know how I feel."

He reached up, gripping her left hand and bringing it to his lips. They seemed to have made a real breakthrough this evening despite the fact that the Ukrainians had almost wrecked it all. Taking her into that training room and lavishing her with sex and affection had done wonders for his girl. "You make me feel like I've never felt before. Anything you want, all you have to do is ask."

"All I want is you." She straightened up and pulled the T-shirt over her head, unveiling the beauty of her breasts, how graceful her curves were.

The words felt like a balm to his soul. They didn't feel like something she meant only in the moment. They felt like words that promised a future. He knew what he'd told her, but he was already thinking about marrying her. He couldn't help it.

"All I want is you," he whispered back. His cock was so close. All it would take was the right angle and he would be inside her.

And then he would make the same mistake he'd made before. Not that he could be unhappy about it. Nate was the best mistake he'd ever made. No. Nate hadn't been a mistake. He'd been fate. That tiny bundle of humanity was the reason two people were going to be together.

Still, as much as he wished he could have been there for her while she was pregnant, he couldn't do that to her again without careful planning.

"We should get a condom." He couldn't let things get out of control.

She stopped, frowning as though shocked she'd been the one to forget. Then she shook her head. "Yes, you're right."

She rolled off him and the bed, going to the kit he'd carried with them to Sanctum. She was back in seconds, but she didn't pass the foil packet to him. "Spread your legs for me, Brody. I want to do this."

He might not survive, but he wanted her to have some time. She'd given him everything earlier in the evening and he was intent on paying her back. He spread his legs and watched as she crawled on the bed, kneeling between his thighs.

She reached out, skimming over his cock with her fingers.

He bit back a groan.

"Did you know that many men don't have live sperm in their pre-ejaculate?" Her words were low, and somehow she managed to make the question sexy.

As if she'd called it out, a drop pulsed from the tip of his dick. She swiped it off with her finger and brought it to her lips. "That's why it's difficult to get pregnant from pre-come. Unless you're Brody Carter, of course. That's how it happened, you know."

He could barely breathe. How did she do this to him? He'd had her already tonight, but he wanted her so badly he couldn't see straight. "I won't apologize. I know it makes me a bastard, but I'm glad it happened. I'm glad we have Nate."

I'm damn glad I have another chance with you.

She sucked her finger into her mouth and smiled a mysterious smile. "I wouldn't take it back. Not for anything in the world. That night was the best night of my life and you should know that."

"Best night of mine, too." When he thought about it, it was the start of his life, at least the part that had true meaning. He'd rambled through life, drifted through his childhood allowing one day to flow into the next. The only reason he'd joined the Army had been because his brother had and he tended to follow Harry. He'd stumbled into his job, but Steph was different. Steph and Nate were precious. Some men found their passion in their jobs or in hobbies.

He would find his true calling in taking care of his family, the family he would have with Stephanie.

"I didn't get to look at you enough that night." She ran her hands across his chest and down his abs, following the neat line of hair that led to his cock.

He forced himself to focus because her hands felt too good on his body. He wanted her to touch him everywhere. "That's because I went too fast. I wanted you so badly I couldn't stop myself."

She wrapped her hand around his cock, starting to pump up and down in a methodical fashion. "You should know I lied to you that night."

He thought he knew what she was talking about. "You were never going to look for Fain."

She sighed, a resigned sound. "Well, I tried to look like it didn't matter. Guess I did a poor job. No, I wasn't going after Fain. If you had turned me down, I would have gone to my cabin and cried. And I really would cry now, Brody, because now I know what I would be missing."

This woman knew how to make him feel good. "I don't think I would have walked away. I don't think I could have, but it saved us an hour or two. God, that feels good."

"This should feel even better." She leaned over and took the head of his cock in her mouth.

It was hard not to scream out. He held on to the sheets as she worked his cock. This was sweet torture and she would find herself on the other side of it soon. He would take everything she had to give and return it all back to her once Nate had a proper nursery. He would tie her up and not let her go until she begged him. He would give her so many orgasms she wouldn't be able to remember a time when she wasn't coming for him.

She cupped his balls, gently rolling them in her soft palm. She sucked him, and just when he thought he would come against her tongue, she sat up. Yes, this was definitely torture.

"I'll get you back for this, luv. You wait. I'll spend the next few days planning all the ways to make you as desperate as you're making me."

A cloud passed over her face, but she seemed to shake it off. If she was afraid, then he would show her there was nothing to be afraid of. He would take care of her in every way possible.

"Why don't we worry about tonight first," she said and tore open the condom wrapper. She started to roll it on his cock, taking care with the tip. "Do you have any idea how wet I am? You make me crazy. All you have to do is walk in a room and I want you."

"That's good because I want you all the time."

She moved over him, mounting him. "It's not a good thing, Brody."

He held her hips, her heat starting to surround his cock. "What's bad about it?"

She groaned softly as she slid down. "My panties are always wet."

He had a good solution. "Stop wearing panties."

She grinned down at him and then the expression morphed to something full of complex emotion. She leaned over, never losing his cock, and kissed him. "I'm crazy about you. I'm sorry if I ever made you feel like I wasn't. Even when I was so angry with you that I couldn't see straight, I was crazy about you, Brody Carter."

This was what he'd been waiting for. For her to give over and see what they could be. One day he'd get an *I love you* out of her because that was what she meant. But he could be patient as long as she was here and trying. As long as she stayed with him and toughed it out, she would find him the most patient of partners.

And if she needed to go back to Africa, he would go with her. He would give it all up for her if she needed him to. All she had to do was trust him.

He watched as she started to ride him. Her head fell back and he let her set the rhythm. He held her hips, keeping the motion with her. In too short a time, he felt himself tightening up, ready to go off.

He found her clit and started to rub.

She clenched around his cock, her orgasm forcing his own. He dragged her close so he could drink down her cries. He kissed her while the orgasm coursed through him.

She slumped down on his chest. "I can't believe we didn't wake the baby."

He smiled. "We're getting the parenting thing down, luv."

And they were getting the couple thing right, too.

* * * *

Steph rolled out of bed, trying to move as quietly as possible. Trying not to make a sound that might wake the people sleeping close to her. Brody slept on the side closest to the door and Nate's crib was near her. She glanced at the digital clock. She couldn't put this off a second longer or her chance would be lost.

"You all right?"

She closed her eyes briefly and wished Brody wasn't such a light sleeper. She hadn't wanted to lie to him. Not that sneaking out in the middle of the night wouldn't upset him enough. Somehow, she'd hoped to get away without the blatant lie. "I'm fine. Just need a glass of water. My throat's dry."

"I'll get it for you," he whispered and started to stretch.

She couldn't let that happen. She leaned over and planted her lips on his, putting her hands on either side of his handsome face. "It's okay. I'm going to the bathroom anyway. You go back to sleep. We have a long day tomorrow."

In the low light she saw his lips curl up in the sexiest, sweetest grin. "I need it. You're a tireless woman."

When they'd climbed into bed, she'd known she couldn't leave without being with him one last time. She'd kissed her way down his chest, trying to memorize every inch of his skin. She'd worshipped him the way he worshipped her. And when he'd rolled her over and pulled her into his arms, she'd known she would never love anyone the way she did this man.

He was the one for her. If only she'd been the one for him.

"I'll be back in a few minutes." She didn't want to leave him. She wanted to climb back into bed and tell him everything that had happened. She wanted to hand it all over to him and let him deal with it. That was what she'd promised him she would do. Not a few hours before, she'd let him hold her and told him she trusted him with this problem. He would take care of it.

And then a bunch of Ukrainian assassins would come after him. Yes, he was trained to handle things like this, but she couldn't risk his life. Or Nate's.

She slipped into the bathroom. She'd stashed a pair of jeans and a T-shirt she hurriedly dressed in. Her purse was out on the bar in the kitchen, and that was where she needed to go next.

Calm. She had to stay calm. This was stupid. It was stupid but she couldn't think of another thing to do.

You could trust him. You could have a little faith.

She eased the bathroom door shut and was confronted with the reason she couldn't take the chance. Nate was lying in his borrowed crib, his face peaceful as he slept.

Her baby. Her own sweet boy, and he deserved the best she could give him. The best world she could give him didn't include his young, fragile life ending far too soon.

Steph took a deep breath. She didn't want to leave them. Her boys.

What would her life have been like if she'd stayed home that night? If she'd decided to study instead of going to that party? Would she have still found these two? Her lover and her baby boy. Would she have found herself in Africa?

Probably not. She would have followed her father's advice and gone into plastic surgery where she could make bank and live a beautiful life. She wouldn't have known Brody Carter or any of the people she'd met along the way. Avery's daughter would be halfway through high school.

But her son would never have been born.

Liam would never have met Avery and never have changed.

Brody rolled over and Steph froze. He seemed to sigh in his sleep and she knew the time had come. No more waiting. Besides, she'd put this plan into motion an hour ago when she'd been kind enough to deliver coffee to the bodyguards on duty. She doubted Brody would forgive her for that. Hell, Liam wouldn't forgive her for that. He would be angry that she'd put his employees in that position.

Maybe they hadn't drank the coffee that she'd laced with the strong sedative Fedor had slipped into her purse along with instructions on how and when he would pick her up.

What the hell was she doing?

She loved Brody. It was right there in her heart, but she couldn't trust it. Her world simply didn't work in a way that ended with her happy.

A vision of his big, warm body gone cold in a coffin assaulted her. Would she bury him beside their son? Was this the universe's way to find balance for what she'd caused before? This time she would be the one to lose her husband and child. She only thought she'd felt the worse pain imaginable, but it was still out there, lurking and waiting. Biding its time until the moment was perfect to strike.

It was here now. The time to pay for all her sins, and her whole body ached with what would happen next.

She forced herself to walk into the living room, trying to keep her step as light as possible. The lamp in the living room was on, illuminating her way. There was Shane. It looked like he'd tried to call someone. His phone was on the floor in front of him, but he hadn't made it out of the comfy chair he'd been sitting in. The coffee was next to him, half empty, and his chest was moving up and down in the easy motion of sleep.

She'd made sure of the dose. Luckily she'd known the pharmaceutical well. She'd taken it herself before she'd gotten pregnant. Dreamless sleep was what it offered.

Declan was on the sofa across from him. Thank god. She'd been worried he would have time to start his rounds. Declan walked the grounds at least once an hour, and she'd been afraid she would find him passed out on the grass. She couldn't leave him out in the elements, and that would have slowed her down.

Tucker had likely taken his back to his bedroom. He would wake up in the morning with no bad effects. He would wonder what had happened and why she'd done what she'd done.

Everything had worked perfectly. All signs pointed to this plan coming to fruition. The plan where she sacrificed herself for her son and Brody.

She picked up her purse and took the cell phone that de Vries had sent to her. Shane and Declan had been tasked with keeping it close and monitoring it, but she couldn't leave it behind. She was the one who had to answer that phone when it rang, even if she had zero control over what happened in the next few hours of her life. Perhaps the last few hours.

It didn't matter. She shoved the cell phone into the purse and wished she had time to leave a note. She wished she could say all the things she wanted to say, that she was sorry she hadn't been better, sorry she had to make this choice. But when she thought about it, it had been made long ago.

There was no time. If she didn't show up, Fedor would put his plan in motion.

"I'm sorry," she whispered, wishing she could hold them both one last time.

Steph strode out the door, resolute. This was for the best.

Brody would wake up in the morning and he would take care of their son. Eventually he would take Nate back to London where he would be raised in a normal way. He would go to school and have friends. He wouldn't spend all his time in a clinic. He wouldn't have to worry about the next medical crisis or whether or not the ground beneath him would shift and he would end up in the middle of a civil war.

He would have a happy life.

Tears blurred her eyes as she rushed to the gate that led to the sidewalk. She tried to push through the gate but it held.

She pushed again. It didn't move. Where was the latch? There had to be a way to open it. Of course they would lock it from the outside, but she hadn't thought about it not opening from the inside.

"It's locked."

She nearly screamed when she watched Tucker peel away from the shadows. He'd gotten dressed again. The last time she'd seen him, he'd been in pajama bottoms and a T-shirt, his shoes off. He was ready to be outside, his sneakers and jeans back on.

"Don't try to stop me. You don't understand what's going on." Pure panic threatened. All Tucker had to do was shout out and Brody might hear him. There was no way she could outrun Tucker.

He stared at her for a moment. "You drugged the coffee."

"You didn't drink the mug I brought you." She'd handed him a mug after making sure it had the ton of sugar he seemed to require. He'd thanked her with a smile. She hadn't thought to watch him drink it.

"I didn't trust you," he admitted. "I don't know why, but it felt odd for you to do that. Your hand was shaking when you passed the mug to me. Not much, but enough to make me curious. I wanted to see what you were doing. Now I realize you could have killed Shane and Dec. At the time it only occurred to me that you were going to attempt to run away, but I should have thought about more nefarious purposes. Please tell me you didn't kill them. That would make it my fault, too. Brody says I never think. He was right. How will I go back home and explain that I let men die because I thought you wouldn't really hurt them?"

"I didn't kill anyone. It was a sedative. They'll sleep a nice eight to ten hours and they'll be fine in the morning. Please, Tucker. You have to let me go." Why hadn't she thought about the gate? How was she going to get out of here? She had minutes to get to the car that would be waiting for her. Minutes before she would hear it drive away and the decision would be made.

She could put her baby into hiding, but how could they fight the entire Ukrainian syndicate? All they needed to do was get lucky once and she would lose everything. Was that any way to live a life? Always running and hiding.

275

She couldn't breathe. It was like someone was sitting on her chest. In her logical mind, she understood that she was having a panic attack, but her heart was seizing.

"Why? Why are you doing this?" Tucker asked.

"Because they'll kill my baby if I don't. They'll kill Brody. They'll hurt everyone I love. I have to."

"That's what he was saying to you." Tucker sounded perfectly calm. "Again, I should have read that better. I'm not good at reading body language. I thought something bad was going on when he was talking to you by the window. But then you smiled and I thought it was okay. You're an excellent liar."

She doubted it. "Please let me go. I have to do what they want or they'll hurt my son."

How long did she have left? How much time was there? Tucker was close, so close he could reach out and grab her. She didn't have anywhere to run.

"Tucker, you don't remember the people you loved, but can you imagine that you did love someone? You know what it means to empathize, right? Think about how it would feel to love someone with your whole heart. What if the only way you could save that person is to sacrifice yourself? Would you do it? Could you live with yourself if you didn't?"

He moved to the gate and for a moment she was afraid he would reach for her and haul her back to the house.

His hand moved over the electronic lock and it popped open. He shoved the key card back into the pocket of his jeans. "I suppose I couldn't. I'll probably get in trouble for this. I need a good cover story or they'll kill me."

"They won't kill you. They'll understand." She wasn't as sure, but she knew Brody wouldn't truly hurt this young man. She took a deep breath and put a hand on his face. He was taller than she was, a good half a foot, but he seemed so much younger than she. Oh, she knew he was likely in his mid- to late-twenties, but there was something about the openness of his handsome face that made him seem almost innocent. "Thank you. You can't know how much you've done for me. Please give me a few minutes before you wake

Brody."

"I won't. He's extremely cranky when he doesn't get his sleep." Tucker stepped back, allowing her access to the now open gate.

She chuckled but knew that was a lie. As soon as he could, he would run to wake everyone and they would be after her. "Tell them you saw me leave but couldn't catch up. Tell them anything you need to in order to keep yourself safe."

"Why would I do that?"

She barely heard his whispered question as she turned and ran down the sidewalk, her feet pounding against the pavement. Fast, she had to move fast and pray she wasn't too late. One block and then she turned. Right or left? Left. He'd said left. The neighborhood was affluent, with big, sprawling homes and plenty of old trees. No one was out at this time of the night. The whole world seemed dark and peaceful, perfectly quiet save for the sound of crickets chirping. She could hear her own heart beating as she tried to make it to the meet-up point.

She turned down the next street and in the distance could see the lights of downtown. Brody would be there in the morning, working at the office, trying to find her. Or perhaps he would be so angry with her, he'd simply take Nate and walk away.

Where was it? Had they already left? What would she do? She sniffled, trying to stop the stupid tears from running down her face.

There it was. A big van sat at the end of the block, its brake lights a beacon in the darkness. Like two red eyes watching for her, waiting in the darkness to scoop her up. Once she stepped into that van, she wouldn't see her son again. Wouldn't feel Brody's arms around her. She would be alone for the rest of her short life.

But Nate would live. Brody would live. He would get over her and find a proper mother for Nate. A mom who could teach him joy and happiness. A mom who would love him with her whole heart because she knew Brody wouldn't choose anyone else.

Her son was safe with him.

The door to the back of the van opened. A tall man wearing all black stepped out. "I was beginning to worry you would not show, Dr. Gibson. We were about to leave without you."

She stopped in front of him, trying to catch her breath. "I want you to promise you won't hurt my son or Brody Carter."

Fedor Shadrova bowed his head slightly, a courtly gesture. "We had a deal. I always honor my deals. No harm will come to your loved ones. And you should understand that if something goes wrong, I will consider all the responsibility on de Vries. You have honored our deal." His arm came up, gun metal flashing in the low light. "Although part of that deal was you coming alone."

She turned and Tucker stood behind her. His hands came up, showing that he carried no weapons. "What are you doing?"

"Yes, I remember you from the club. You did not come back to the office with us," Fedor said. "I assumed you weren't an important employee."

"I'm not. I'm not even an employee," Tucker replied. "I'm more like a burden."

Why was he here? Did he think he could take on Fedor and his men all alone? "He's no one. He's not important and he won't hurt anyone."

"Excellent." Even in the darkness she could see Fedor's predatory smirk. "Then no one will miss him."

"I know where the flash drive is," Tucker said, his tone perfectly calm.

Fedor stopped, going still. "The one they wish to exchange for my sister?"

Tucker stood tall. "Yes, that one. But I'm only going to talk to de Vries. Take me to him and we'll all get what we want. You get your sister. Stephanie gets to be a martyr, and I get what I want, too."

"And what is that?" Fedor asked.

"A shit ton of cash. Lots and lots of cash," Tucker replied.

"I should kill you where you stand," Fedor said.

Tucker's head shook. "And then you'll never get your sister back because if you think de Vries is going to be satisfied with the doc and Alfi Dauterre, you're wrong about him. He wants everything. He needs everything. His employer won't be satisfied without it."

"You seem to know a lot about this." Fedor's gun didn't waver.

"I listen. Even when people think I'm not listening, I get the gist of what's happening. A smart man knows how to handle his responsibilities," Tucker replied. "And don't bother searching me. I put it in a safe place."

"Get in," Fedor ordered. "We'll see how you handle torture."

Tucker's lips quirked up in a savage grin. "I think I'm a professional at that. I don't know. Sometimes it's hard to remember, but I think I'll be good at this."

Fedor pulled her into the van and she realized he wasn't alone. There was a man driving, and two more inside.

Was Tucker telling the truth? He knew where the drive was and he wanted money? It wouldn't be the first time she'd been betrayed, but she couldn't stand to think about how Brody would take the news. He would be devastated.

All this time Tucker had been pretending to be his friend.

She heard the sickening sound of bone meeting metal and when she managed to turn, Tucker's unconscious body was being hauled in.

The doors closed again and the van started to pull away.

She tried to glance out the window, but she couldn't see anything.

"Time for you to rest as well, Doctor. I don't like it when my plans are upended." Fedor's voice came out of the darkness and then something came down hard on her head.

Pain flared, but it was only for a moment. Then darkness was all she could see.

Chapter Fourteen

"Someone got to her." Liam O'Donnell paced the floor of the conference room. "That fucker Ukrainian did it. Sometime last night, he got to her and he convinced her to do this."

Brody sat back in his chair, his son wrapped up in his arms. Somehow he hadn't been able to drop Nathan off at daycare when Liam had dropped off Aidan. Since he'd woken and found the bodyguards drugged and Stephanie missing, the only way he'd been able to keep himself together had been focusing on Nate.

He'd woken to Nate crying out, needing a change. He hadn't been shocked that Steph wasn't with him. He'd rather thought she'd gotten up to prep the morning bottle their son's endlessly hungry gut required. He'd changed the nappy and gone looking for Steph.

He'd found what looked like bodies at first. It had taken him a moment to realize they weren't dead and Steph wasn't among them.

Nate had kept him calm, kept him from raging the way he wanted to.

Nate had kept him from walking out because he was so bloody angry that he wanted to.

"I didn't leave her alone for more than a few minutes, O'Donnell. I scarcely think he had time to hatch a plan with her," Brody replied. "More than likely this was her plan in the first place and she somehow convinced Tucker to take her where she needed to go."

Which was probably wherever de Vries wanted her to go. Somehow she'd figured it all out and decided she didn't trust anyone but herself to save Anya.

"Why the hell would Tucker do that?" O'Donnell asked.

"Because he's an idiot." Brody could feel how tight his voice was, but he managed to keep it low, not wanting to frighten his son.

His boy. Steph had left him behind too. She'd walked away from them both because her guilt meant more to her than her family.

Anger welled, but there was something deeper, something he couldn't acknowledge because if he did, he might break into a million pieces.

Grief. Grief that she couldn't love him the way he loved her. Grief that she would rather die than fight. Grief that they couldn't have the life they might have because she had never forgiven herself.

That was what it came down to.

"What do we know?" Taggart strode into the room. "I've been trying to get those fuckers on the line but surprisingly the number goes straight to voice mail. I think we can conclude that last night's cooperation was complete bullshit. I've loaded that voicemail of Fedor's up with graphic stories about what I plan to do to every man in his syndicate if Stephanie isn't back here safe and sound in a few hours. I hope they understand English because they were highly descriptive words."

Brody could only imagine what Taggart had threatened them with. It wouldn't matter if Steph had done all of this on her own, and he needed to point that out. "And if she chose this path?"

O'Donnell put his hands on his hips, staring down at him. "She didn't choose this."

"Uhm, then who roofied me?" Declan asked with a groan. "Because I didn't do it myself."

"I'm with Dec on this one," Shane added. "I seriously doubt the sedative she gave us accidently fell into my coffee mug."

The doors to the conference room opened and Avery walked in. The rest of the office was quiet, with only a few of the operatives in. Jake and Adam were somewhere trying to go through security footage. Charlotte was making calls to her contacts in Russia to see if anyone could get a read on Fedor Shadrova or de Vries. A few of the bodyguards had taken an early flight to Loa Mali with the royals to deal with a crisis there.

Brody felt oddly alone without Steph or Tucker. Bastard. He'd grown fond of the bloke and now he was going to have to have a long talk with Damon about him. He was dangerously unstable if he could be convinced that this was the way to handle a situation where a client made a mistake.

A mistake? Or had she been looking for a chance like this for a long time?

"You two should know better," Taggart said with a frown.

"Know better than to drink coffee when we're trying to stay up all night?" Shane asked.

"I told you I can do the same thing with Scotch, and I'm way friendlier. I'm good after a couple of drinks. Better shot, too," Declan added. "Also, I have my own flask, hence not a chance of getting my ass roofied."

"Or you could roofie yourself until your system gets used to it. You should do that with a list of frequently used poisons as well if you're going to survive in this business. If she'd tried that shit with me, she would have had a very different outcome." Taggart sat back like he'd imparted great wisdom on the world.

"I fear what your liver looks like." Shane took the mug Avery offered him. And then stopped, staring at her for a moment.

"Avery didn't roofie the coffee," Liam said with a long sigh. "And I assure you Big Tag doesn't have any more tolerance for that shit than you did. He makes crap like that up all the time to scare the newbies. Ninety-nine percent of what comes out of his mouth is pure bull."

"But the one percent that's real is deadly, boys. And good luck figuring it out." Taggart thanked Avery for his cup of coffee. "Avery, do you think there's any possibility that Stephanie ran off herself? Is there a possibility that she might have found that thumb drive and she's trying to make a deal for herself?"

Brody knew the answer to that one. "She wouldn't do that. She wouldn't do it for herself."

"He's right," Avery replied. She'd come in with her husband, unable to stay at home for fear that her friend was in trouble. "There's no way Stephanie does this for money or to save herself. She's the single most selfless person I've ever known."

"She's always looking for a way to save someone else." Brody stared down at his boy. Nate was looking up at him, his hand around Brody's thumb. "I think she's got a death wish, but she can't go out in some random way. She's gotta give her life to save someone else's."

"You have to understand," Avery began.

He looked up, feeling his eyes narrow. "I understand. I understand it all. I understand that she promised me she would let me handle this and then turned around a few hours later and drugged the bodyguards hired to protect her. She lied to me and she left our son behind."

Now he understood why she'd climbed into bed with him and offered herself up like the sweetest treat he'd ever had. She'd been oddly aggressive. It hadn't put him off at all. At the time he'd thought he was seeing a different side of her, an interesting, hungry side. He'd lain back and allowed her to kiss and lick and lavish affection on his body. It had been a delicious test of wills since Nate had been sleeping only feet away and he'd been forced to stay as quiet as possible.

He'd felt loved. Wanted. He'd gone to sleep thinking about their future.

She'd been saying good-bye, getting one last round out of him before she went off to find her fate.

"That's not how she sees it, Brody." Avery's eyes were red rimmed and Brody wondered how long she'd cried when she'd discovered what Steph had done. "She's never moved on. It's hard. You can't understand it until you've been through something like it."

"I've been through plenty of firefights." He hadn't lived a safe life where his only worry was what to eat for supper. "I watched several of my closest friends take bullets and a few of them die."

"Not everyone processes survivor's guilt the same way," Avery argued. "Some people can handle it. Steph struggles. She was young when it happened. Her vision of how the world was supposed to work was still being formed. I think she struggles with a couple of things she's not willing to admit to. I know before she came to me, she spent a few years doing self-destructive things. A lot of people who go through what she's been through end up escaping their pain that way. They keep going until they find the wrong drug to take or finally meet the person who'll give them the fight they need. She stopped that when she realized helping other people filled the void in her life."

"She can't live that way." Li ran a hand through his hair and it was obvious this wasn't the first argument they'd had about Steph. "She needs to find a way to forgive herself and allow herself to live a normal life. If you let her, she'll either drag Nate around the globe or she'll decide she's needed in some place with a bloody Ebola outbreak and she'll have to leave him behind and she won't know her son the way she should."

"I won't let her take him somewhere dangerous." He was the one with the crazy job, but he would sit behind a desk for the rest of his life if it meant his son having a stable home. "I'm not going to be separated from my son. He's coming back to London with me."

"You can't take Nate away from her." Avery sounded horrified at the thought.

"She left him with me. She left both of us." As far as he was concerned, she'd made her choice. The idea of never seeing her again kicked him in the gut, but he had to stay strong for his son. Nate needed him now.

He needed Nate, too.

"I saw her talking to one of the Ukrainians as we were breaking up last night." Declan sighed and sat back. "It was when you went to get your son. She was waiting by the front window in the lobby and he walked up. I think that's when he got to her."

"And told her what?" Brody wasn't sure he even cared about excuses. She would always have one. It would always be about saving someone else. She would die for anyone. Why couldn't she find a way to live for him? For Nate? "Told her to sacrifice herself? We were handling the situation. What exactly does Anya's brother believe he can do that we can't?"

"Well, I'm sure he thinks he can exchange Alfi and Steph for his sister. That's got to be his plan. No one knows where the damn thumb drive is," Tag offered. "Unless they were lying about that and then the fucker now has absolutely everything he needs to get his sister back."

"Stephanie wouldn't want to leave anything to chance." Avery's hand closed over her husband's, squeezing tight and finding obvious comfort. "If that man threatened you or Nate, then she would have done anything to make sure you were safe."

"Threatened me?" He was floored at the thought of tiny Steph thinking to save his big, bad arse. It was ridiculous. "If you haven't figured it out by now, I can take care of myself. I was in the SASR. I didn't get there being weak and vulnerable. What the hell would he threaten me with? I could kill the man in a heartbeat. He wouldn't win a fight with me."

"Oh, but the fight wouldn't be fair, Brody," a feminine voice said. He looked up and Charlotte was standing in the doorway. She leaned against the open door, her arms over her chest.

"I can handle myself in an unfair fight, too." He'd seen his fair share of pub brawls. He and Alfi used to think that was what made a good Friday night out.

Charlotte's eyes seemed to go cold. It was odd because Charlotte was always so warm around him. "You know nothing about this particular world, Brody. Trust me. I do. I grew up in it. My father would have made Fedor look like a choirboy. I know what I would have said to Stephanie if I needed her to turn herself in to me. You see, Fedor would have studied her. I assure you he had an enormous amount of information on the woman who employed his sister. He would have known Stephanie in all the ways that are important because he's a man who views other human beings as nothing but things to manipulate. That's how the syndicate works. He can love his sister, but anyone outside his family isn't really human to him. It's how he can do what he does. And what he does is kill."

He appreciated that Charlotte had come from that world, but he couldn't see her point. He'd dealt with mobsters before and he was still alive. "Charlotte, I can protect myself. I know I'm not a mob assassin, but I do have training."

"Ah, but I wouldn't come after you today. Or tomorrow. I would wait. I would bide my time and learn everything there is to know about you. I would know your habits. I would know how often you eat lunch out and what days you tend to stay in. I would spend months or maybe even years learning you. You would forget me, but I wouldn't do the same. You would be my obsession, my only reason to live. And then one day when your son is older and you've moved on, when you think the world has shifted into a happy place, I would find you. I would make it random. Perhaps you're on holiday and you stop at a petrol station. I would be waiting in the restroom and I would kill you there. I wouldn't need you to see me. I wouldn't make it a grandstanding thing. You wouldn't hear me. I would be there and you would be dead. And then your son, I would come for him, too."

"Jesus, Charlie." Taggart's eyes had gone wide.

"Well, that's what Fedor likely said to her. I know because I grew up in that life. I know what he's capable of. Brody thinks because he's brave and strong and bigger than a damn bull that he's bulletproof, but he's not. If evil comes for him, evil can win, and Stephanie knows that," Charlotte said quietly.

Avery looked his way. "What would you do for that child in your arms?"

He stared down at Nate. Those big blue eyes were staring up at him, a tuft of hair on his otherwise bald head, and his heart constricted. "I would do anything."

"And so would she, but she's thinking about you, too," Avery said. "You're looking at this from your point of view. You know you're strong enough to save yourself. Steph isn't. Not physically. All she can see is that she's got the power to save you both."

"If that's what happened." But his mind was already bending, his heart aching for the woman he couldn't quite seem to grasp. She was always a couple of inches away from his arms, and he worried she always would be.

"She doesn't trust the world," Liam explained. "She certainly doesn't trust herself and she's never forgiven herself. Until she can do that, I don't know that she understands the value she has. If you give up on her, she might never understand."

He'd given up on her once. "Part of the reason I left her the first time was she scared me. She scared me because she's reckless at times. And she scared me because I don't know if I can reach her."

"You can't." Taggart had stood up and joined his wife, his hand curving around her body to rest on her hip. "Believe me, I've figured this out. You can't fix someone. That's not what love does. Love can make a person want to fix himself. That's the key." He frowned at his wife. "I said love. I want to vomit."

She smiled up brilliantly at him. "You go ahead, babe. I know how hard that is for you. But you're right. You couldn't force me to walk into the light. I lived in darkness, but when I met you, I wanted that light. I wanted you so badly I had to fix my world to have you."

"Sometimes I forget how dark it was for you." Taggart leaned over and kissed his wife, the passion between them a palpable thing. His voice went low and Brody almost missed his whispered words. "Because you're my light now."

"You could be Stephanie's, Brody," Avery said, and now she wasn't even trying to stop the tears. "I think she needs you. I think you might be her last chance at really making a life for herself. She's given up enough. She could be happy with you and Nate. But she can't if you give up on her. You're the one for her."

Her light. Could he be that? He'd never once thought of himself as being someone's light.

Nate pulled his finger down, drawing it closer and closer to his mouth. Everything went into that boy's mouth. He grinned up, the expression so sweet and innocent and full of joy that Brody felt his heart break.

How could she not see how much Nate needed her? How much he needed her? He wasn't sure they could have what the Taggarts had. What Liam and Avery had because Stephanie didn't think she deserved it.

"I can't promise anything." He stood up. He couldn't walk away and that meant putting aside his pain and getting to work. "But I know I can't leave her out there no matter why she did what she did. We have to find her and fast. De Vries will get in touch with either Fedor or on that phone he left for Steph, and if we don't find her by the time the switch happens, we'll lose her."

De Vries would take her, smuggle her out of the country, and he would keep her alive until he was satisfied she knew nothing. Then he would kill her and get rid of her.

He might be left without even a body to bury.

"Awesome." Shane stood up, carrying his coffee with him. "I'll start looking. I don't know where but I'll get on social media at this point and start asking around."

Declan was right behind him. "Me, too. Though not the social media thing. What are you? A soccer mom? I'll troll the Dark Web or something. Anything to get out of the couples therapy session I find myself in. I'm never getting married if I have to be someone's light or something. You all have read way too many fucking romance novels. I bet you believe in faeries and guardian angels, too. Brody, I'm going to give you some actual manly advice. You had a baby with her. She's a fucked-up chick, but you knocked her up and now she's yours. Stop with all the overthinking and go get your girl."

"What he said," Shane added, heading for the door. "Tag, let us know when we can shoot something. Or preferably someone."

The bodyguards strode out.

"I think I figured out how to scare the newbies. That group has been difficult to intimidate. I'll threaten them with group therapy," Tag said, kissing his wife again. "You know how we do it. We can put it into the opening day training package. An hour with Alex going over all the benefits, a tour of the office, and group therapy for the first month. Then maybe they won't complain so much about the…"

Tag stood up straight.

Charlotte put a hand on her husband's shoulder. "About the…?"

Ian looked over at Liam. "What do we do to all the new puppies, Li? Whether they're on the payroll or not."

Li's eyes widened. "You don't think that's why he did it, do you?"

The answer hit Brody with the force of a hammer. A fucking hammer made of hope. He winced inwardly. He was getting syrupy in his old age, but he was going to find her, and Tucker wasn't getting murdered. "That's exactly why he did it. I take back everything I said. That kid is brilliant."

Li pulled his wife's hand up to his lips, kissing it with deep affection before running for the door. "I'll get the London office on the line."

Brody looked down at his son. "I'll bring her back to you. I promise."

And where they would go from there, he would have to see.

* * * *

Steph put a hand to her head and tried to stifle a groan. Her brain was fuzzy and there was a dull ache at the base of her skull. What had happened? "Brody?"

"Ain't here, luv, and I, for one, am happy about that," a deep voice said. A familiar voice.

Alfi.

It came rushing back to her. She wasn't safe and in bed with Brody. She'd given all that up. She'd walked away and she would be shocked if Brody ever spoke to her again.

Not that he would get that chance since she was likely going to die soon.

"Where are we?" Her throat was dry, the words hard to get out.

"No idea." Alfi was sitting across from her, one knee up as though he was casually relaxing on what looked like a concrete floor. His back was against a bare wall, his eyes on her. "I suspect we haven't gone far though. They tried to knock me out, too. Picked me up in front of the petrol station. I bet they drank my beer, too. Anyways, after they showed me off for the cameras, they shoved me

289

in another car, and that's when I got the old head swipe. Lucky for me, I got a really hard head, but I kept quiet. Let them think it worked. We couldn't have gone more than twenty minutes from wherever the hell I was."

"Sanctum." It was all coming back to her now. Every bittersweet moment. "They took you to Sanctum, which means they know a lot about me and who I was with. They knew we would be at the club."

Alfi winced. "Well, I might have mentioned that, but they didn't say that's where we were going. Well, they might have said it, but I don't speak whatever the fuck they're speaking. Then we got here and they tossed me in. It's some kind of a warehouse. There's one window, but it's too small for me. I might be able to save you if I can figure out how to shove you up there."

She looked around the room as her vision cleared. The floor was concrete and the walls completely bare. There was nothing in the room at all save for the blanket she was lying on and a couple of bottles of water. A shaft of light came from above. There was a small window up at the top of the wall. Maybe twelve or fourteen feet up. But she rather thought Alfi was underestimating her curves. Besides, he didn't know what she did.

"I can't leave. I made a deal with Anya's brother. If I let him trade my life for hers, he won't kill Brody and Nate."

"Bastard," Alfi spat. "First off, Brody's a hard man to kill. Second, what kind of a person threatens a baby?"

"I don't know. What kind of a person steals a thumb drive off a dying man?" Alfi wasn't innocent in this, and she had a few questions for him.

Alfi sat up straighter. "Well, it wasn't like he was going to do anything with it. And he asked me to take it. Begged me, really. He woke up and I was the only one there. He told me where it was and begged me to keep it safe."

"And your version of keeping it safe was trying to sell it back?"

"Didn't get that far." His voice went low. "I never even got to look at the damn thing. I tossed it in the back of the Jeep and I don't know what happened to it."

"Why would you do that?"

"Because I thought I heard 'em coming and I didn't want it on my person. I rather thought I was keeping it safe at the time. If they'd caught us, they would have searched me," Alfi argued. "Anyway, by the time I got you to Guinea and I had a chance to look for it, it was gone. I don't know where it is. When I realized that de Vries had figured out my name and that I had something to do with you getting away, I decided to come to the States. I found out Brody was here and decided sticking close to him was my best bet. Knew he wouldn't let you die. Except apparently he has."

"Brody didn't know a thing about this," Stephanie explained. "I made the choice to trade myself for Anya."

A low chuckle came out of his mouth. "Should have seen that coming. You've got a death wish, Doc."

"I don't." Maybe she had before, but all she could think of now was seeing Brody and Nate again. It was all she wanted in the world. One more day. One last hour. One more minute with them. "And I don't know if I would have traded myself in if it had just been about Anya. I promised Brody I would let him handle that."

"But the bastards told you they would hurt him and the kid. Yeah, I get that." He let his head fall back. "Well, we're all in for it now. I think they're planning on making the exchange sometime today."

"Where's Tucker?" Memories of the night before were coming back to her now.

He looked down at her, his confusion easy to read. "I would assume he's back at the house. I left him there. He's probably pissed at me for not bringing him back chips and lollies."

She shook her head and then winced because that hurt like hell. "No, he was with me. He followed me." There was more. There had been something that she'd found hard to believe. "He said he knew where the drive was and that he'd exchange it for cash."

Alfi looked at her, his gaze incredulous. "Are we talking about the same bloke?"

He'd seemed different when he'd stood up to Fedor. Stronger. More sure of himself. "Yes. Tucker claims to know where it is and he wants cash for it."

"I find that hard to believe," Alfi replied. "How did it get from my Jeep in Africa all the way here and into Tucker's hands? It makes no sense."

Not a lot of what Tucker did made sense. Still, in this case, she couldn't see another reason for him to have done what he did. It made far more sense for him to turn around and run back to get Brody. Or to have pretended nothing happened at all. He could have easily walked out and said nothing to Brody. It would have been the simplest thing to pretend like she'd stolen his key card and he hadn't seen her at all.

Why follow her? Why put himself in danger? Unless he was telling the truth and he wanted to exchange the drive for cash.

"I don't know how he would have gotten his hands on the drive, but somehow he did." She forced herself to stand on wobbly legs. What time was it? When would de Vries call and set up the exchange?

Was Brody out there right now searching for her, or had he given up on her? It might be better for all of them if he took Nate back to England this minute and started their lives.

She missed her baby. It was an actual ache in her chest.

The door slammed open, jarring her.

Fedor strode into the room, the phone she'd brought with her in his hand. She could hear it ringing softly. "I believe you're supposed to answer this. Explain to him where you are and then hand the phone back to me."

Her hands shook as she opened the burner. "Hello?"

"Ah, Dr. Gibson," de Vries said over the line. "I'm surprised they allowed you to answer. I suppose the entire team is listening in. I've been looking into Mr. Taggart. Formidable allies you have, but I have some pull of my own."

"I'm not with the Taggarts anymore," she admitted. "I'm with Anya's brother. He wants to talk to you."

There was a pause on the line. "I believe I said I would only deal with you."

"He's interested in getting his sister back. He's got me under his control. I don't even know where I am, so I'm afraid you'll have to deal with him." She pulled the phone away from her ear and handed it to Fedor. "I've done my part."

He nodded. "You've done well, but until you hand yourself over to de Vries, it's not over." He held the phone to his ear. "Mr. de Vries, I believe I told you I would be coming here. Now I have everything you want and you have three hours to bring me my sister."

He started walking out the door, but it didn't close immediately. Steph watched as one of the other men hauled Tucker inside. His shirt was torn and they'd taken his shoes. He stumbled inside, dropping to his knees the instant his guard let go.

He was bleeding from a couple of places. His shirt was torn and Steph could see burn marks on his chest. Taser marks from where the darts had penetrated his skin.

He'd been tortured.

The guard shook his head, staring down at him. "He was right. He is professional when it comes to pain."

"Told you, motherfucker," Tucker managed.

Fedor looked back, the phone still in his hand. "We'll do the exchange here in a few hours. Try to see that he lives. He wouldn't tell us anything. I'm going to turn him over as well and let de Vries deal with him."

She dropped back down to her knees and put a hand on Tucker. No matter what he'd done, he was a human being and she couldn't leave him like this. "I need a first aid kit."

"No, you don't. He'll live," Fedor replied. "I wasn't about to damage the merchandise. He's fine. I didn't even touch his face. I thought I would leave that to the next lucky man." He frowned. "Despite what you might think of me, I don't enjoy hurting others. I find it necessary. I had to try to get the drive, but turning him over will do. Be patient, Doctor. It will all be over in a while."

The door closed and she heard the heavy thud of a lock sliding into place.

"Why didn't you tell them where the drive was?" She looked over his chest. There were several places where they'd used Tasers on him.

"It's hard to talk with all that electricity running through me." Tucker's eyes closed.

"Damn, what did they do to your feet?" Alfi moved for the first time, getting on his knees to loom over Tucker.

"The feet are actually quite sensitive," Steph said, examining Tucker's. More burn marks, though it appeared they'd also used blunt force on his feet.

"Yeah, tell me about it," Tucker managed. "They knew what they were doing. All the pain and not a lot of bloodshed. One of those assholes is extremely good at popping joints in and out of place. My shoulders ache like nothing else. Managed to get most of my toes and fingers, too. Damn, that's painful."

It would have been terrible pain. "Why didn't you just tell them?"

"I know I'm curious about how you found the damn thing," Alfi added.

Tucker smiled, a weak expression. "I didn't. I have no idea where it is. Luckily, I knew enough to know what they were looking for. I had to come up with it quickly or they would have left me behind."

"More than likely they would have killed you." Steph looked back to Alfi. "I need your shirt. I need to immobilize his arm."

Tucker groaned and shook his head. "No. Can't, Doc. I need to be able to fight if I have to. I didn't come all this way to be a burden when the time comes. It's back in place. When all this is over, I want some really good pain meds."

"I sincerely doubt de Vries is going to help you out," she replied, feeling utterly helpless. She needed to get him sitting up. Ice and compression were called for, but she had absolutely nothing here to work with.

"Ye of little faith." Tucker took a long breath, his eyes remaining closed. "Let's make a bet, you and I. If I'm right and we get out of here, you have to go to whatever therapy is going to fix you."

"Fix me?"

"I wasn't born yesterday. It was more like a year ago or something, but even I know you're crazy fucked up inside, Doc."

"He's right about that," Alfi offered helpfully. "You have serious problems."

She wasn't sure this was the time or the place to talk about this. "You would have them, too, if you'd done what I did."

"Nope," Alfi replied, settling back in. "I've been in battles and I've killed many men. Don't bother me at all."

"I wasn't a soldier."

"No, you were a kid in a car and you made a mistake." Tucker seemed to brace himself. "Again, even I can see that. If I'm right, you get to see a shrink. It's not bad. I quite like mine, but then she's pretty hot. Second, if I'm right, you can't push Brody away anymore. You have to be with him and marry him and all that stuff. Maybe you should even ask him. And do it right. Men need to feel loved, too."

"How hard did they hit your head?"

His lips curled up briefly and then he rolled over with a long groan. "My brain has been trashed in so many ways, it's hard to imagine, Doc. But I'm right about this."

She should probably play along. "All right. We live, I marry Brody, and live happily ever after."

"And see a shrink."

She sighed. "And see a shrink." Like she'd never done that before. "And what do I get if we die?"

He groaned again as he managed to sit up. She had no idea how he was moving. The pain had to be incredible. "I don't know. I'll figure something out, but I promise, it won't come to that. We'll be home in a few hours. I don't think I like the Ukrainian mob. They're very unpleasant."

"I think all mobs are like that. Please let me immobilize that arm for you." She hated seeing him in pain and worried he was in for a whole lot more of it. De Vries wouldn't believe him. He would torture Tucker until he died.

"Why did you come with me?" She had to know.

"Might not know who I was, but I know who I want to be," he

whispered.

"How are you sure we're getting out of this?" No one knew where they were and she'd taken their best bet with her when she'd fled. She'd taken the phone and now Brody had no way to even talk to de Vries.

"I know something you don't know." Tucker put his back to the wall. "But it's best you don't. Be surprised."

Alfi was staring at him. "You're not worried?"

"I'm worried about you," Tucker admitted. "I'm worried I read you wrong and you're a bad dude, but someone else will take care of that. I've been told I should sometimes let karma handle things. I think Brody will be your karma."

"I didn't mean for things to happen like this. I truly didn't. I wanted to see if there was anything I could do with the thing. Man's gotta jump on the opportunities the world gives him," Alfi said stubbornly.

"Yep, Brody's going to kick your ass." Tucker's eyes closed again.

Alfi looked her way. "When the time comes, you stay close to me. After Anya's safe, I'll do what I can to get you out. I promise. I'm not such a bad man that I wouldn't try to help you, Steph. I like you quite a bit."

She was fairly certain that by the time Anya was safe, there would be no way out. "Don't risk your own life."

"But you would," Alfi said. "Do you know how brave you are? How much I admire you? I don't care how or why you became the woman you are, I just know a whole lot of people who are grateful you did."

"I tried to help."

"You did more than help. You saved a lot of people. Let me try to save you. Let me try to do one good thing with my life."

"So much drama and it's all for nothing," Tucker said under his breath. "We're getting out of here soon and I'm telling Brody you were hitting on her."

"He is not," she shot back. Why couldn't he be serious?

Alfi shrugged. "Kind of was. I mean, if we're about to die, do you really want to go out in anger and fear? Or should we celebrate life one last time?"

Not a one of them could be serious.

The door crashed open and she was reminded that not all men joked around. Fedor strode in, followed by a couple of his cronies. They were all massive and armed to the teeth. One of them reached down and hauled Tucker up.

Tucker went pale and moaned, but managed to get to his feet.

"It's time," Fedor said.

Steph stood up and hoped and prayed that Tucker was right.

Chapter Fifteen

Steph stumbled out into the hallway, trying to keep up with her captor. It was the same man who had spoken to her the night before. The cousin. She didn't know his name, only knew that he spoke for Fedor.

How many were there? Three had come for them the night before, and those three walked them down the hallway. Up ahead she could see a fourth man, smoking a cigarette as he leaned against the wall. He shouted out something in either Ukrainian or Russian.

Fedor nodded and replied.

She hated this, hated the fact that she was vulnerable. She couldn't even understand what they were saying around her.

They turned a corner and she realized Alfi had been right. They were in a large warehouse. There were big boxes stacked all throughout, a veritable labyrinth of cardboard. Thick yellow and green and red lines on the floor seemed to point the direction to various parts of the warehouse floor, if one knew the code. Which, of course, she didn't.

There were two more men in this large space, both smoking and looking vaguely bored with life.

"What is this place?" She couldn't help but ask the question. She knew the answer. It was her Waterloo, but it would be nice to know a more literal name for where she was taking her last stand.

"It's a shipping station for one of my many businesses. This one is completely legitimate," Fedor explained. "I hate using it like this. I try to keep the legitimate and the not-so-legitimate in their own pretty boxes. I had to shut down operations this weekend. I'm sure there are some employees out there who are happy to have the time off."

Well, at least something good had come of her eventual murder.

"I thought you were a full-time mobster," she said under her breath.

"You thought wrong." Fedor glanced down at his watch. "Where I come from, the syndicate is one of the only ways out of poverty. My father was strong man. He lifts us up, allows Anya to go to school. Allows me to learn how to be a legitimate businessman. In a few years, I'll switch everything over and we'll make our money in the proper ways. I'll leave the syndicate to my cousin Petor."

The man with the reptilian smile nodded her way. This was the man who'd told her how her world would shatter. "I have no desire to be legitimate."

Yes, he would make a spectacular mob head.

"You planning on shipping us to de Vries?" If Alfi was bothered at all by the gun to his back, it didn't show in the bland expression he wore. Alfi had an air about him, like this happened regularly, just another event in the life of a handsome rogue.

"They'll be here in a few minutes. After that, you're his problem. I'm certainly not helping him smuggle you out of the country." Fedor moved to the center of the warehouse floor. The building had to be as large as an airplane hanger, the walls swooping up to what looked to be four floors. They were in the center of the building, the ceiling high above their heads. "Both of you on your knees."

Steph started to drop, but Fedor held her up.

"I meant the men. I know you won't run." Fedor glanced around as though doing one final assessment. "You will not believe this, but I actually wish I didn't have to give you away. I know how much Anya cares for you. She speaks of you often."

"Anya will be a problem," Petor said with a shake of his head.

"You should let me put her out. I have plenty of drugs that would work. I fear what she'll do when the time comes. It might be better to deal with her when we get back home."

Anya could be vocal about her opinions. She was strong willed, but Steph knew that even the strongest of wills could be broken. God only knew what had happened to the lively blonde while she'd been in de Vries tender care. She hated the thought that Anya's spirit might have been dimmed by these days spent in captivity.

"She'll do what I tell her to do," Fedor replied with the supreme confidence of a man who was used to getting his way. "This will have taught her that I was right all along. My father was overly indulgent with her. She will come home and marry a proper man and I won't have to worry about her anymore. I'm done with this experiment. She should be settled down with children by now."

"Good luck with that," Tucker said. "Women don't like it when you tell them what to do. That's one of the first things I was taught after I woke up. Well, after I went to The Garden. Kayla gave us a list. Rule number one. Don't be a douchebag."

"Can you shut him up?" Fedor asked.

Maybe it was time she found a bit of Anya's stubbornness. They'd left her on her feet. She needed to use all the advantages she had. She moved in front of Tucker's kneeling form. If they wanted to hit someone, they could hit her. He'd taken enough. "He's in pain. Let him be. If you need to torture someone, do it to me."

Fedor chuckled, a humorless sound. He moved in, looming over her. "Do you think I cannot break you, girl?"

"I think I don't care," she replied. "You've already ensured that I won't ever see my son again. I don't care what you do to me now."

Fedor frowned. "You make me sound like a monster. I am doing this for my family. You would do same. Your man would likely do the same if he was smart enough to catch me."

She shook her head. "I wouldn't. I would find another way." Avery's words floated back through her head, their meaning so much more precious in this moment. "Sometimes the universe deals us shitty cards and how we handle it is how we'll be judged. I think this is exactly who you are, Mr. Shadrova. I think you enjoy killing.

I don't know why or how or what turned you, but since you and Anya came from the same place, I have to wonder who was the strong one. Actually, I don't have to wonder at all. Whatever broke you, whatever transformed you into a man who could turn over three innocent people to someone who will torture and kill them, it didn't break her. She would never do this. She wouldn't stand for it."

Fedor looked her over. "So the mouse has a backbone? Funny thing you should show it now."

She was sick of that attitude. "You think because I don't shoot people that I don't have a backbone? That shows me how small-minded you are. The strongest woman I've ever known has never lifted a gun in her life. I've survived more than you can ever imagine."

It struck her as the words rolled out of her mouth. She had. She'd survived. She might have made a lot of mistakes along the way, but she'd survived and come through the other side.

She'd become a woman who thought of others first, who put kindness above self-interest. Who sacrificed herself.

Who needed to let a man love her so all those good things she did didn't mean she gave up a life of happiness.

"Perhaps you will survive this, too." Fedor moved away, his hand on his cell phone. "They're almost here. We will move quickly. And you're wrong about one thing. You say I'm giving up three innocent people, but these two are guilty. You are guilty. You ran. Deep in our hearts, we're all dark. You left my sister there."

"You ever tried talking your sister out of something?" Alfi asked. "Who do you think came up with the bloody plan in the first place? It sure as hell wasn't me. Anya made sure I got Steph out. Anyone's at fault here, it's me. I wanted to see if I could make a few bucks off that drive."

"You see, not innocent at all." Fedor glanced down at the phone again.

"Have you thought about the fact that someone might blame you if she dies?" Tucker said. "Steph has people who care about her. Strong people."

"Yes, I was surprised that the mouse had ties to a man like Ian

Taggart," Fedor agreed. "But this I do not worry about. He is a man I can handle. He will play by his rules and they have nothing to do with mine. Besides, I believe her ties are as a client. He won't come after me over a client. She has no family."

Oh, but she did. It brought tears to her eyes to think of it. She had Avery and Liam and Aidan.

She could have Brody if she was only brave enough to really love him. Not in a passive way, as she had since the moment she met him. She'd always known she couldn't have him, and that made loving him easy.

But real love, honest deep-down love required something more than sacrifice. It required her to live, to believe, to have faith.

Tucker looked up at him, his eyes steady. "She has more family than you can imagine. You think family is blood and some oath you make because you have a mutual need to make money and pretend you're doing it for the right reasons. You don't know what a family can be when it's truly chosen, when it has nothing to do with need and everything to do with the fact that the people around you give a shit. You think she's a random client. She's not Brody Carter's client. She's his lover and he won't forget her. She's not Taggart's fucking client. She's his friend, and I've learned that some people can do remarkable things for their friends. You think you can toss us aside, but friends keep up with friends in my world. Friends find a way."

"Well, good for you. Perhaps Mr. Taggart will find you before de Vries kills you. I wouldn't be surprised. You're quite good at handling pain." Fedor glanced over and said something in his native language that had all the men standing taller. All the guns came out and Steph knew they were close.

There was a loud slam as a door came open and a group of men strode in, all wearing black and carrying weapons that were banned in most countries. She didn't know much about guns, but these looked state of the art. The team moved in like a well-schooled predatory flock.

Outnumbered. There had to be fourteen, maybe fifteen, versus Fedor's six or seven. And it was a military crew against Fedor's mobsters. A chill went up Steph's spine.

"Mr. de Vries, where is my sister?" Fedor didn't seem at all fazed by the fact that he was outnumbered.

De Vries glanced behind him and nodded. A man from the back pulled along a woman with a cloth bag over her head. Anya. Steph recognized the blue scrub pants she'd been wearing that night and the top with pink and yellow flowers that had caused the kids of the village they served to call her the Flower Lady. Flowers and bling and glitter. Anya loved anything bright and cheerful.

It would bother her that she'd been forced to wear dirty clothes. Anya loved her girly products. Even when they would go deep into rural villages, Anya would carry small tubes of body lotion, shower gel, and dry shampoo so she could stay clean and sweet smelling.

De Vries took hold of her elbow and pulled her up. He dragged the bag over her head. "She's right here. Now give me what I want or I'll take you all down."

"Fedor?" Anya blinked, though the lights weren't bright in here. She squinted and seemed to be trying to focus. "Fedor, what have you done? Stephanie? Is that you?"

"Everything's all right," she called out. "You're going to be okay."

Fedor held up a hand. "Both of you be quiet. Say another word and I'll have you gagged."

"Like I haven't heard that before," Steph said. Yes, she'd said that out loud.

Petor put a hand on her arm, but she was already thinking. If she let them get her into the car, she wouldn't see Brody again. The minute Anya was safe with her brother, all bets were off. Somehow, she had the feeling that Fedor would honor his agreement since she'd upheld her end of the bargain. Now she had to find a way to get herself and Tucker out.

Could she really leave Alfi? Maybe. He was a dick. He was the kind of man who slung Nate's diaper bag into the backseat of a Jeep without closing the top so everything went everywhere and then complained about it later. He'd bitched until she'd gotten in the back and shoved it all into her bag without even organizing it. It still wasn't organized.

Oh, god. She knew where the drive was. He'd tossed it in the back after he'd thrown the bag in. She remembered the moment clearly. They'd been rushing to the Jeep and she'd been locking Nate's car seat when Alfi had told her to be quiet. They'd stood there in the darkness, holding their breaths. After a moment, whatever had spooked Alfi was gone and they'd driven off as quietly as possible.

She'd had the damn thing all along, buried under rattles and diapers and wipes.

How could she use that to get them out?

"You will send my sister over and then we will back off and you can take these three with you," Fedor commanded.

De Vries's eyes narrowed. "If you so much as breathe the wrong way, I will kill you. Is that the man who says he knows where the thumb drive that fucking journalist had is?"

Steph kept her mouth shut because she was fairly certain she wasn't up for as much physical pain as Tucker had been. It wouldn't help to admit she knew anyway. It would only make Tucker useless to them, and that would get him a sure bullet to the brain.

Fedor put a hand on Tucker's head. "It is, but you should know he's hard headed. I tried to get him to tell me. I think he wants to go with the girl."

"He'll tell me," de Vries promised. He eyed Alfi. "And you are merely coming along because I need to give my men someone to torture."

"Excellent. I always knew I was the pretty one." Alfi took a deep breath. "But I would leave the doc behind if I was you. She knows nothing and she'll be more trouble than she's worth. Let Fedor take her back to her people. Ain't no one coming after me or the pup there, but they will come after her."

"I've already tried this line of thought on them," Anya said. "Neither one of us knows shit, but this one doesn't understand. He is very thick in the head."

"Do you want me to take another finger, bitch?" de Vries growled.

Fedor's gun was up and aimed in a heartbeat.

Anya raised a hand, showing him her wrapped right pinkie finger. "He didn't even get that right, Fe. He left me this one. Fuck you and whatever happens, know you deserve every bit of it. I can't wait to see what Carter does to you. He's going to take you apart and eat your intestines."

She walked toward her brother, her middle finger shoved in the air.

Not broken then. And it was good that Anya had some faith. Steph looked at her friend. "He might pull his intestines out, but Brody would never eat them. He's a gentleman."

"Not so much a gentleman that he didn't knock you up," Anya replied. "As I'm being held prisoner by the cavemen, all I think of is the good thing that will come out of this is Brody will pull his head out of asshole and man up, as you Americans say."

"Do the women ever shut up? And who the hell is Carter?" de Vries asked.

"He's the man who's going to kick your arse, as *we* say Down Under," Alfi replied.

Fedor's group closed ranks around Anya as she made it to their side. Anya put her hand on her brother's arm before reaching for Steph.

"Come along. He's not going to let them take any of you," Anya whispered. "He never was. Now he will kill them all and we need to take cover."

Fedor's eyes never left the other team, but his lips curled in a way that let Steph know he'd heard his sister and was happy she knew him so well.

He hadn't meant to let them go?

"Bring over the younger one," de Vries commanded. "Something about him is familiar to me."

"I think perhaps I will keep them to ensure that we are allowed to leave this place," Fedor replied. "When I know where this drive thing is, we can talk again."

"Shadrova," de Vries yelled.

The guns came up and that was the moment that Steph heard

something she didn't expect. A low, familiar baseline wailed from the speakers on the walls.

Everyone froze, looking around, trying to figure out what was going on.

Was that Guns N' Roses?

"You see, that's where you assholes always go wrong." Ian Taggart strode out from behind one of the islands of crates awaiting transportation. "You got no style. You need a theme song."

The men seemed to move in perfect accord, all guns trained on the new guy. Taggart was a massive presence wearing all black, a Kevlar vest over his big chest. And he wasn't alone. Li O'Donnell was right beside him dressed exactly like his boss and friend.

"Don't take him too seriously. I'm pretty sure he stole those lines from a kid's movie. And I thought 'Sweet Child o' Mine' was your theme song," Li mentioned casually as he carried a big-ass gun like he meant it. "Isn't this 'Paradise City'?"

It was. And it was surreal because no one seemed to know what was going on. Even the big bad mercenaries didn't seem to know how to react.

How the hell were they here? How had they found her?

"It is indeed, my old friend," Taggart replied. "'Sweet Child o' Mine' is my sweet, sweet lovemaking song. This is the one I kill assholes to. GN'R provides the soundtrack to my whole life. Hello, Fedor. I thought I told you we would meet again. You have something of mine and I'm here to fucking take it back. You boys might not give a shit about your people, but I'm smart enough to microchip all my puppies. Tucker, you brilliant motherfucker. You get all the hookers you want, my brother. I'm paying."

She looked down at Tucker, who was staring at de Vries, seeming not to hear Taggart. That was why he'd come along, why he'd allowed himself to be tortured? Because he'd known he could be the beacon that brought their people here. He'd had little time to figure out what to do, but he'd offered himself up in an instant.

"Perhaps we could talk, Mr. Taggart," Fedor said, his voice steady. "My sister is right. I was about to murder them all and give you your people back."

"You're outnumbered, you idiots," de Vries yelled.

Taggart smiled, the pure, happy smile of a predator about to get a meal he'd long been denied. "Not on your life, asshole. You see, you forget. I came prepared. I brought snipers to the party. Hello, boys."

Suddenly the room seemed filled with red laser lights painting the chests or heads of every man in there.

"Speaking of parties, I'm supposed to be at one in about five hours," Taggart said, glancing down at his watch. "So we should get this one started."

"Aye, I'm double-booked, too, brother, and I have to be there to work the grill." Li continued on as though they were talking about a damn hair appointment that was running long. "Adam can't do medium rare to save his life. He overcooks everything."

She gasped as an arm curled around her waist and started hauling her back.

"Time to go, luv."

Brody. It was Brody. He was here. Oh, god, Brody was here and he was taking her away from the brink of what would have been death and pain, and she wanted to turn and hold on to him and beg his forgiveness.

That was when she noticed Brody wasn't alone. Theo and Case Taggart had his back, providing him with access to move to her and start to drag her away.

"Anya, I think you should go with the doctor's friends," Fedor said, never taking his eyes off Taggart. "I don't believe they'll hurt you."

"I think I better stay here and try to explain that you are an idiot, but you don't deserve to die," Anya replied.

Alfi got to his feet. "Bloody hell. Save me from stubborn women. I'll take her."

Before Anya could say another word, Alfi had her in a fireman's hold, walking her back to the McKay-Taggart line.

"If you think we're going down without a fight, you better think again," de Vries promised.

"You are going to run to the back of this bloody building and you're going to hide," Brody whispered into her ear. His voice was cold as ice, his hold on her not at all lover like.

He was angry. So angry. She could feel it.

"I can walk, Brody," she said, trying not to be a burden.

"Alex McKay is back there along with Erin, and they're going to get you someplace safe. I want you safe. I can't do my job if you're not safe. Is that clear?"

She was going to have to handle his rage at another time. Now wasn't the time to argue or to explain that she'd seen the light.

She hadn't meant to hurt anyone. She'd only wanted to go to a party and see her friends. That had been the reason, the motivation behind her crime. It hadn't been the same for de Vries. De Vries meant to kill them all. His sin was an act of evil, hers of youth.

She might never be able to find the meaning in it that Kai and Avery talked about, but maybe she could try to have something good in her life, try to forgive herself enough to be worthy of them.

"Yes, Brody. You can let me walk. I'll go back there. Tucker needs help. They hurt his feet."

"Can't worry about Tucker because I can't trust you," he whispered back. "Get behind me. Something's wrong."

She found herself pushed behind Brody's body. Theo Taggart moved in behind her.

"I've got her back, Carter," he promised. "But you're right. I got a feeling de Vries won't go down and Big Brother is going to get his firefight."

"Why don't we get the women and hurt puppies out of here and then we'll talk?" Taggart seemed tenser than before, as though he'd realized what his brother had as well.

"The puppy? Are you talking about that animal there? Now I recognize him." De Vries was staring at Tucker. "Since when do you hire true mercenaries, Taggart? I didn't see it at first. He's cut his hair. What the hell are you doing here, Razor?"

Tucker managed to get to his feet, his face contorting with pain. "Razor? Are you talking about me? Do you know me?"

"But you already know all of this, Taggart. We call him Doctor Razor because he cuts so deep. I find it interesting that he is here with your doctor. You like to experiment, don't you? What were you doing with this one in Africa? Something terrible, I assume," de Vries said.

Tucker shook his head. "No. I wouldn't do something like that. I would never hurt someone."

A low laugh came from the mercenary. "Very cute, Razor. And you call me a monster when you're harboring the worst I've ever seen." De Vries took a step back. "I think we'll call it a day. Don't think this is over."

"Taggart, take her," Brody ordered. "I've got a better chance at getting Tucker out than you do, and this is about to all go to hell."

Steph looked up at him, trying to memorize his face. "Please don't make me leave you."

His jaw hardened, his eyes flinty as he looked down at her. "Go, now."

Theo Taggart took her by the arm and started to lead her back. "Hurry, I need to drop you with Erin and get my ass back out here. Please don't give me trouble."

She kept up, but turned to see Brody's big form becoming smaller as Theo led her away.

Through her tears she wondered if the battle had already been lost before she'd even started to fight it.

* * * *

Brody shoved down his fear, trying to stay cool and calm. All these years of fighting and he'd never once had his heart in his throat the way it was now. He'd been trained to handle the anxiety, the pressure, the fear of having his life in danger. It didn't bother him. Most of the time he welcomed the adrenaline rush, sort of lived for it.

Not this time.

He had no idea how to handle losing her. This was everything he'd thought it would be and more. And this was what it would mean to be with her. She would never take her own safety seriously. Every single day would be a fight to curb her self-destructive tendencies.

How many times would she lie to him? Go behind his back and put herself in danger because a dark impulse made her do it? How would he explain this to their son?

Stop. Breathe. Work the op and let everything else go.

She was safe for now. Alex wouldn't let her move. Erin would put her on her ass before she'd let Steph run out in the middle of a firefight. He trusted Erin and Alex to keep her where he wanted her.

He moved through the Ukrainian group, who seemed to have figured out that this had gone to hell and they better pick a side. The men at the back of the group were looking to their leader.

Fedor glanced his way and nodded toward Tucker. His voice was low as he spoke Brody's way. "Take him. He's in shock over something. I'm sorry about his pain, but I had to do everything I could to save my sister. I thought if I had the drive, I could avoid all bloodshed. Well, here at least. I would have gone after the fucker sooner or later."

"You're lucky I don't kill you here and now," Brody replied. "I'm only sparing you because of Anya."

"And your doctor might have something to say about it, too, no? I think we both have difficult females in our lives." Fedor moved in front of Tucker, blocking him from fire. "You need to move him out of here. De Vries is getting antsy and he's right about one thing. He's better armed than my men. I don't think he will go down without a fight."

And Taggart wouldn't let him get away.

"If you step back out that direction, I think you'll find a small tactical group led by a man who goes by the name of Mr. White," Big Tag explained. "Well, he has so many douchebag names we can't keep up with them, but feel free to call him whatever you like. He'll have the place surrounded by now and I think you'll find he's more than willing to provide you with an escort out of the US. He's got a couple of places where he likes to take his new friends."

So Ezra Fain had managed to get here in time for the party. Brody hadn't been sure the CIA operative would make it. When they'd realized they knew where Steph was being held, Taggart had called on Fain, making a deal to get backup. Fain and a team had been on a plane from DC and had only recently landed.

Fain would be more than pleased to get a man like de Vries in the hot seat, giving up secrets about how outside businesses were working against US interests and citizens abroad.

De Vries's group turned, realizing they were trapped.

"I don't believe you. You couldn't have had time to plan this," de Vries said.

Tag snorted. "I am a planner, asshole. And as I plan to be at my friend's birthday party soon, why don't you drop those guns and we'll take you in nice and easy."

Brody kept his sights on the mercenaries, fairly certain Fedor's men had no interest in a two-sided fight. He knelt down beside Tucker. He was the only one close enough to get a hand on the bloke. "Come on now, then. It's time to get you away from here."

Tucker moved, but not in the right direction. He paid zero attention to Brody, stepping toward the Belgian group. "What's my name?"

De Vries wasn't taking his eyes off the real threat. If he heard Tucker, he didn't let anyone know. "We can make a deal, Taggart."

"That time is over," Big Tag replied. "I'm no longer the man who controls your fate. Talk to the CIA, buddy."

Tucker looked over at Tag. "He knows my name. He might be the only person in the world who knows my name."

Taggart nodded. "And Mr. White will get that out of him. I promise you, Tucker."

"I know all the terrible things you've done, Razor. What kind of game are you playing?" de Vries asked. "Are you trying to hide from the authorities? What happened to the doctor you were working with? Now, Taggart, if you want a truly evil person, you should talk to Razor's lover, Dr. Hope McDonald. He's the one you should hand over to the Agency. He's the one who can show you all the terrible things they've done together."

"No. No. No." Tucker's hands went to his head as if he was hearing some terrible sound no one else could. An animalistic cry came out of his mouth, the sound jarring Brody to motion.

Oh, god. Brody felt sick to his stomach. Tucker had worked with McDonald? He was the kindest of all the men who'd had their lives destroyed. What had happened? Had McDonald turned on her lover? Or had he realized that time was up and taken the only way out that didn't include death or prison?

How would he handle it if he found out he'd been an evil son of a bitch in a life he didn't even remember?

Tucker buckled over, clutching at his head. It was part of the drug and the conditioning the doctor had given them. When they tried to think too hard, tried to remember, pain flared through their systems. He'd seen a couple of the Lost Boys throw up and shake for hours after the pain came.

De Vries looked at Tucker and seemed to realize this was the distraction he'd been praying for. He shouted something to his men that Brody didn't understand. What he did understand was the gunfire suddenly coming his way.

Brody leapt toward Tucker, who seemed utterly incapable of moving. He knocked the man over and felt his breath blow out of his body as he took a hit. Hurt like fuck, but he knew immediately that the bullet hadn't pierced the armor Tag insisted on everyone wearing. He was better equipped than the damn mercenaries who had managed to get their guns and ammo here in the States, but hadn't bothered with body armor.

Tag had forced anyone on the ground to dress in full-out tactical gear. Brody had dreaded the extra weight, but now it came in handy as the bullets started to fly.

He needed cover.

"Get him to the side." Fedor stepped in front of him, firing off a few shots as everyone seemed to scramble.

Brody got to his knees, getting a hand on Tucker's shirt. "Come on!"

Tucker's head came up, his eyes not quite focused. "Leave me."

"Not on your life." He didn't care what the lad had done before. Brody knew who he was now. Hell, they didn't know anything at all. De Vries could be lying through his teeth for all they knew. Now wasn't the time to figure things out. He needed to stash Tucker somewhere so he could get on to the work of the day—killing de Vries or making his life a living hell. One of the two.

"Move it," Fedor ordered. "I've already taken a hit. I'm getting my men out of here in a few minutes. I don't want trouble with Taggart."

So he would try to make sure Tucker didn't get them both killed. Brody looked up, glancing around the room. His best bet was ten feet to his left. There was what looked like a long row of almost ceiling-high crates.

He looked back and Taggart and O'Donnell had taken up positions, while the snipers seemed to be doing their jobs. Remy, Shane, and Declan were up in the rafters, using their skills to pick off de Vries's men one by one.

Brody got to his feet, twisting in order to lay down some cover fire of his own. His chest ached, his ribs tender after the bullet he took.

One, two, three shots and he sprinted toward the safety of the maze of boxes. He hauled Tucker along by his shirt, praying the damn thing was well made because he wasn't sure what he would do if it came apart in his hands.

All around him gunfire split the air. "Paradise City" became "Welcome to the Jungle" as Brody pulled Tucker deeper into the maze.

"Let me take him, mate." Alfi was suddenly at his side. His shirt sleeve was torn and blood soaked the material.

Damn it. "Why didn't you stay back?"

"Because I bloody well don't deserve to be safe when my best mate is out here near dying," Alfi shouted back. He pointed to the west side of the building. "De Vries managed to send a couple of men up the stairs. They're going up to take out the snipers and then you'll be a sitting duck."

Brody watched the black-clad mercenary sneaking up the stairs. The bad guy hugged the back wall, but dropped to one knee and brought up the AK-47 he was holding. It wasn't a sniper rifle, but it would do.

And it was pointed straight at him. Fuck.

Alfi stepped in front of him like a complete moron, since he wasn't wearing a damn vest.

Before he could shove Alfi away, a shot cracked through the air. The Belgian's head flew back, his body hitting the wall, and he went down.

Thank god for snipers.

"What the hell was that? Why would you do that?" Brody looked around, trying to see if anyone else had a line on them.

"I don't know," Alfi shouted back, frowning ferociously. "I guess I'm just stupid, but I know I'm not going to be the reason you die. I'll take Tucker, or you take him and I'll hold the line."

Tucker had somehow managed to make it to his feet. "He knows my name. I have to talk to him."

This was why the Lost Boys weren't allowed in the damn field. "You'll go with Alfi. I have to work my way back and make sure none of those fuckers gets close to where Steph is. Go with him. No excuses or I'll knock you out and he can carry you."

Taggart's voice came over his comm line. "Carter, we've got them all except de Vries. Can't see him and the comms are out with the boys above. I can't get info from them. It looks like he's in the maze, brother. On your side. Li's coming in after you. Don't shoot him."

Shit. His best bet was getting back out the same way Li was coming in. He couldn't engage de Vries as long as he had two civilians to protect. He couldn't be sure this close to the side of the building that the snipers would have a shot. "We're heading back out."

"I'll take him," Alfi said, hauling Tucker up with his good side.

Li moved around the corner. "Brody, I need you with me. De Vries slipped in here somewhere and we can't see him. I've got Erin on the other side and Theo and Case are taking the south end. I have no idea how the fucker got by us."

"Where's Steph?" If Erin wasn't with her, had she run?

"Alex got grazed," Li said shortly as he started to move past Brody. "The last time I checked, she was stopping the bleeding. It's not a big deal, but we brought Shane and Dec down to help wrap up the ones left alive for Ezra."

He nodded back at Alfi, who started to lead Tucker away, and then followed Li. "Where the hell is Ezra? I would have thought he would come in by now."

"No idea. Hope he didn't get stuck in traffic. Tag will have his arse." Li moved down the big aisle toward the far end of the building.

Brody touched the comm. "Alex, I need you to watch Steph for me. Don't let her out of your sight."

"She's fine," Li insisted.

"She's working on one of the Ukrainians." Alex's voice came over the comm. "We've got more than a few dead Belgians, but the Ukrainians came out of it with two GSWs. One's pretty serious, but Steph thinks she can stop the bleeding."

Steph was certain she could save the world, even if it killed her. "I need you to keep eyes on her."

Liam rounded the corner. "Shit. What the hell happened?"

Brody stopped, his body going cold as he heard a familiar voice. He couldn't see what Li was seeing.

"I thought he was hurt," Steph said, her voice shaking.

Shit and shit. He was going to kill them all.

"Let her go and I'll walk away," Li offered.

Oh, but that wasn't going to work. There was no way de Vries gave up his prize.

"I'm going to step out the back door and get into my car. I think I'll keep my nice shield for now," de Vries replied.

Brody took off running, his hand on his comm. "Keep him talking, Li. I'm going around."

Li wouldn't be able to reply over the line, but Brody was sure he'd heard.

"I'm on my way," Taggart said over the line. "Someone get outside in case he takes the doc out of the building."

Brody couldn't think of anything but getting to her. He ran down the way he'd come, sprinting past Alfi and Tucker. He hit the open floor, barely registering the fact that there were bodies on there. He caught a glimpse of Fedor and his men, all of them having given up their guns, while Case and Theo were ensuring the living Belgians were all zip tied and behaving.

Brody followed the blue line. They'd been in hiding for hours, going still and silent while the Ukrainians were occupied and staying in place. Perfectly silent and hidden for three hours before de Vries had shown up. While he'd waited, he'd found a map and studied that sucker. The blue line led to the loading dock at the back of the building. That was where de Vries would take her.

Brody rounded the last row. He could hear the sound of feet pounding behind him, but he doubted de Vries would hear it over the rock and roll. Another of Big Tag's little touches. That was the big boss. The things he did seemed arrogant, but they almost always served a purpose in the end.

Of course, he also had been trying to cover the sound of gunfire so the Agency didn't have to deal with the local cops.

It didn't matter why he'd thought of it. All that mattered was getting to Steph and saving her.

Again. For the last time.

"He's almost to the door." Li's voice came over the comm.

"Brody, you need to flank him," Taggart said.

And then he came into view. De Vries was dragging Steph along, her petite body held against his beefy one. Brody could see how his arm snaked around her waist right under her breasts, holding her so tight he couldn't see how she was breathing. Her feet were dangling and he could see the way she struggled against de Vries.

"Stop." Brody roared the command over the music that had covered his footsteps.

"Alex, cut the music," Taggart was saying behind him. "We're going to need to negotiate. And get Ezra on the goddamn line. He's late."

De Vries stopped as the music died and the whole building suddenly went quiet.

"Let the girl go." Brody tried to get a decent shot, but de Vries was holding her over his chest, protecting his neck with her head. He might be able to get a head shot, but if he was off even a few centimeters, he could kill the mother of his child.

"Somehow, I don't think this is going to happen, my friend. If you think for a second that I believe you're turning me over to the Agency, you're insane. Or if you are and they've got that psycho on the payroll, well, I'd rather die than be at Dr. Razor's tender mercies."

"He's not who you think he is," Brody said tightly. If de Vries would move a centimeter back…

"I know that man. I've seen what he can do," de Vries promised. "And I won't allow you to turn me over to him. Or his lover."

"Hope McDonald is dead," Taggart explained in a steady tone. "And the man you know as Razor isn't the same man you met before. I know it doesn't make sense, but I give you my word. I'm turning you over to the Agency. I won't say Mr. White won't hurt you a little, but he's not a psychopath. You'll be able to cut a deal with him. Let the doctor go and we'll sit down and talk."

"No one sits down and talks with that psycho." De Vries's eyes flicked between Brody and O'Donnell. "Now move away or I'll kill her. I swear I will do it. I'll take her down with me."

"Brody, please." Steph turned her face toward him, her eyes desperate.

Please what? Please let her go? Please save her? How could he ever know with her?

It didn't matter. He had to save her.

"Take the shot if you have it," Li growled.

De Vries turned and there it was. One shot. One second of opportunity before he lost it again.

Brody breathed out, seeing the place he wanted to hit—a small patch of skin above the mercenary's ear. The bullet would go to his brain, shutting down everything before de Vries could make another move.

He pulled the trigger.

Please. Please. Please.

De Vries's head jerked to the side and Steph was suddenly free. She was alive. De Vries was dead, but Steph was alive.

He had to force himself to stand there, to not immediately go to her or he would be on his knees.

One of them had to be strong.

"Damn it, Taggart," a familiar voice yelled. Ezra Fain strode in, a frown on his handsome face. "I told you I need them alive—that meant all of them. At least most. I've got four alive and one of them pissed his damn pants."

Tag pointed a finger his way. "Next time, don't freaking be late. I had to bluff and I hate bluffing. Now I have to go. I'm supposed to pick up the stupid cake. Why does Jake need a cake? He's getting pudgy around the middle."

"You are not going anywhere," Ezra began.

They began arguing, bickering like an old married couple, but Brody was numb. He turned and started to walk away.

"Brody?" Steph's voice made him stop.

It didn't make him turn around. "You should check on Alfi and Tucker. I think they're going to need you."

He walked away. It was time to go home.

Chapter Sixteen

"So you found the thumb drive?" Hours later, Avery stood in the big kitchen of Serena Dean-Miles's main house, making her famous grilled corn dip, across from where Steph sat with Nate in her arms. "And it was in Nate's diaper bag?"

"I love that," Serena said with a grin. "The whole time it was sandwiched between wipes and butt cream."

"It fell into one of the pouches. I never zip the inside pouches." Steph had been giving the women the rundown of how the mission had gone. It was good to have something to do rather than brood over Brody. "When Alfi told me he'd tossed it in the backseat of the Jeep, I remembered that the diaper bag had come open and I'd just stuffed everything back in."

Serena groaned. "I hate when that happens. I'll perfectly organize it all and Tristan will somehow get in that sucker and pull out everything. He's fascinated with Brianna's things. You'll see, Avery. You think you're out of the baby stage with Aidan, but toddlers require an enormous amount of stuff, too. Did you find the drive and pass it along to the Agency?"

She shook her head. "I told Li and he and Big Tag decided to figure out what was on it first."

"Ah, that's why they brought Adam up to the office," Serena said with a smile. "He was grumbling the whole time about how someone needs to figure out how to use a computer before they start the new business. I told him Hutch would take over for him but he's out of town this weekend."

"So what was it?" Avery asked, curiosity plain on her face. "I've been dying to know what that group was willing to kill so many people over."

"It was a video," she said, rocking Nate gently. "The journalist had smuggled it out of a diamond mine owned by one of the world's largest companies. Do you know what the Kimberley Process is?"

"No idea," Avery admitted.

Serena gasped, her eyes lighting up. "I do. I wrote this book about conflict diamonds. Well, it's mostly about a three way, but conflict diamonds were in there."

"That's right." Avery nodded. "I remember. The conflict diamonds were being smuggled out of the country disguised as bling on the backs of women's jeans."

Serena picked up a jar of paprika. "I thought it was a fun twist. Isn't the Kimberley Process a way the governments decide if a diamond is conflict free?"

She understood some of it. "Yes, all the legitimate diamond merchants of the world have an agreement that they will only purchase raw diamonds from mines that don't fund wars. It's worked quite well to get most conflict diamonds out of the public. But our poor journalist discovered that a merchant out of Antwerp had cut a deal with a terrorist group to purchase over twelve million dollars worth of raw diamonds. On paper, they'd come from a reputable mine, but Johann Kavner had the proof."

The terrorist group was known for slaughtering entire villages in central and eastern Africa if the populace refused to follow their narrow version of religious law. They'd also made headlines for stealing young girls to gift to their soldiers. It hadn't come as a surprise to Steph that they would trade in diamonds they had used slave labor to produce.

"So the company de Vries was working for panicked when they

figured it out," Serena surmised. "And they sent his group after Johann."

"Who tried to get away, but got caught a few miles from my clinic. They shot him, but Johann wouldn't give up the hiding place," Steph explained. "At some point he gave the thumb drive to Alfi. When they couldn't find it, they decided I had it since I was the one who treated Johann, and I ran. They took Anya and came after me. Luckily, I had friends and those friends had big guns and are paranoid about where their people are. I think if Tucker hadn't done what he did, I would be dead now."

"No, you wouldn't," Serena assured her. "Adam would have found you. He was tracking the van you were in. That's why he went in early this morning. He complained about that, too. He'd already tracked you down to south Dallas when they figured out they could use Tucker's tracking device. Another hour and he would have known where you were."

So she would have been saved no matter what. It had all been for nothing. And according to Fedor, he'd planned on killing de Vries himself.

It had been foolish to think she could save her son and her lover. "Well, that's good to know. It doesn't matter much now. Brody won't even talk to me."

Avery threw her a sympathetic glance. "Give him time. It was a rough day, and many men need time to switch from warrior mode to backyard barbecue party mode."

Numb. She felt so damn numb.

"Not me, my darlin'." Li kissed the top of his wife's forehead as he walked past her. He had a massive platter of all kinds of meat in his left hand. There were hamburgers and hot dogs and chicken breasts all ready to be cooked on the grill outside. Naturally, Jake required a carnivorous birthday party. "It was an excellent exercise, but I've already forgotten the whole first half of the day. That was work. Now it's time to play. I'm ready for beer and burgers, and hopefully not getting up at dawn's asshole to go to work."

Avery sent him a pointed look. "Well, I'm glad you're good, but some of our friends are having trouble. Have you forgotten you dropped Tucker off with Kai?"

"Is he going to be okay?" Steph practically leapt at the chance to worry about someone other than herself. She wasn't exactly sure what had happened, but Tucker had been quiet, almost haunted by what de Vries had said.

Of course, he hadn't been the only one who had stared blankly ahead during the ride home, as though the day had been far too much for him.

Brody hadn't looked at her during the hour it took for the CIA team to clean everything up, load up the dead and the living, and head off for wherever they intended to do the rest of their covert job. It had been made easier since Fedor owned the warehouse and had been more than willing to cooperate in exchange for not being renditioned to a foreign country and tortured for information he might or might not have. Ezra had left much of the cleanup to Fedor and his band of happy mobsters while the McKay-Taggart crew had bandaged up their minor injuries, gone back to the office for a debrief, and then all gotten ready for the birthday party.

Brody had done everything asked of him, but not once had he come over and requested to help her. He'd stayed across the building while she and Anya had dealt with the wounded.

When the time had come to walk away, she'd hugged Anya, and Brody had been there waiting for her. He'd loomed over her like he expected her to run at the first opportunity. When she'd reached for his hand, he'd switch to holding her elbow. It made her feel like a prisoner. He'd sat beside her during the debrief, not speaking a word or really looking at her. He'd looked through her, like she wasn't there at all.

She'd tried to talk to him afterward but he'd told her it had to wait. She'd been bundled into a car with Erin and Alex while Brody had gone with the other men. He was in the guesthouse, and she wasn't sure she would be welcome if she went down there.

Now she found herself in the midst of a happy party. It was surreal. She'd gone from a chaotic warzone to this perfect suburban paradise where kids were splashing in the pool, moms were putting together the last-minute details, and dads were sipping beers and watching over everything with indulgent smiles. Every time the door opened she could hear the sounds of party music and kids squealing in delight.

"Tucker will be fine." Li stepped toward the door that led out to the spectacular backyard. "I don't care what de Vries said. There's zero way Tucker had anything to do with Dr. McDonald. He was wrong or he was lying to try to sow chaos. Kai is going to make the lad see that everything is all right. And don't worry about Brody. My pretty lady here is correct. You gave him a huge scare and he's processing. Take him a beer, sit in his lap, and he'll come around. That is if you want him to come around."

"Of course I do." She wanted it more than anything. All she'd been able to think about when de Vries had her in the maze was getting back to Brody and Nate. "I love Brody. I always have."

She simply hadn't thought she deserved him. Maybe she still didn't, but maybe that didn't matter anymore. He'd made his choice. He'd gotten into bed with her and offered her something she'd never known before.

Perhaps when he came out for the party, she would have a chance to talk to him.

"Then you have to fight for him. He's been fighting for you for days. I think it's your turn now." Li kissed Avery again. "Wish me luck. I think this job is more dangerous than the one I did earlier. I'm going to have to dodge bloody bees. Serena's bushes seem to be home for a damn colony of them. I've avoided getting stung this long in my life, I'd like to keep it up."

He strode out the door.

"Sorry about the bees. They really are bad right now. Jake got stung mowing the yard. But you have to know that Liam's right," Serena said as she passed Avery the pepper. "You have to fight for Brody now. Men are actually quite fragile creatures. You running away the way you did hurt him. I saw him this morning when he realized you were gone. He was in shock."

"You not only hurt him," Avery added. "You scared him. You probably scare him every day. The same way you scare me."

"Scare you?" She rocked Nate, holding him close. Getting to

cuddle him had been the first time she'd felt good all day long. She'd hoped that when they were safe, the three of them would cuddle together, a family bonding moment. Brody had checked on Nate, but then he'd gone straight to the guesthouse. "How do I scare you?"

Avery sighed, exchanging glances with Serena, whom she seemed to have some silent language with. Serena picked up the bacon ranch cheese ball she'd been working on.

"I'll leave you two to talk, but Steph, you should know you're welcome to stay in the guesthouse as long as you need to."

She grimaced. With Brody seemingly unwilling to talk to her, she'd been ruminating for hours on what she would do in the next few days. "I think I have to consider going back to my clinic."

Serena stopped as though the idea shocked her, but she took a deep breath and seemed to let it go. "Well, just know you're always welcome. We'll eat pretty soon and the cake is coming out in an hour or so."

Serena opened the door, the sounds of the party breaking through the quiet contemplation of the kitchen. Steph could hear kids splashing in the shallow end of the pool. She caught a glimpse of Big Tag in a pair of board shorts soaking in the sun while his two girls and Aidan treated him like a jungle gym.

That was joy and happiness right there. Not a one of those kids thought twice about whether they were loved. They were surrounded by laughter and joy. By the family their parents had made for them.

Could she give that to Nate? She hadn't tried to make a family. Avery was the one who had to call even though Steph thought of her every day. Would she pass on her isolation to Nate? Would he grow up lonely and unsure of his place in the world?

Or could she change if she wanted to?

The door closed and the room went quiet again.

"You're seriously thinking about taking Nate back to Africa?" Avery asked. "You work around the clock most days. And how will he go to school?"

Shit. This was a serious talk. Avery had asked the question with a bit of annoyance entering her tone. She was never annoyed, and

Steph realized this might be a turning point. Had she always been waiting for this in the back of her head? Had she always wondered when Avery would dump her for being too difficult?

What would she do without Avery?

"I have to go back. I've made a life there." It wasn't much of one, but it was all she had.

"Have you? Or have you hidden out there?" Avery put the bowl to the side and gave Steph all her attention. "I think we need to discuss what I meant all those years ago. I told you you owed me a life."

"You told me I owed you two lives." She looked down at Nate, unwilling to meet Avery's eyes. He was so beautiful. He was the best thing she'd ever done and she had to wonder if he wouldn't be better off with his father now that Brody seemed to be done with her. How would they share custody if they were on two different continents? It wouldn't be like most separated couples. They couldn't carve up the week between them.

The idea of living like they were divorced made her ache. She hadn't even gotten the joys of being married.

Avery put a hand on her belly as she looked at Steph, intent plain in her stare. "Yes. Two lives. Not two walking deaths. Not a lifetime of aching martyrdom. Maybe in the beginning I did mean you should go out and give of yourself selflessly. I'm not such a Pollyanna that I didn't want you to hurt back then. You should feel it. But Steph, there's a time to feel guilt and a time to move past it and honor the lives that were lost by living. I'm changing our deal and yes, I get to do that. You owe me two lives. You owe me enough love and laughter and joy for two lives, and that means you have to change your mindset. You have to change it because you have to teach that baby how to live. And part of living is figuring out when to not give up."

Nate was staring up into her eyes. Such perfect love and trust. "I've been wondering if Nate wouldn't be better off in London."

Avery smiled. "Yes. Yes, I think you could be happy there. And don't think you can't find good work to do. You know you could still work for organizations that help Third World countries, but

325

Nate would have a stable life with family around him. And The Garden is a truly magical place. I can't imagine you going back to Africa as a single mom. What would you do if you had to deal with an outbreak?"

She'd always had a plan in place. She'd intended to send Nate to Avery and Liam if there was an outbreak. Perhaps in the back of her mind, she'd thought that was for the best, too. Steph held her baby close. Why was she eager to leave him? It broke her heart—even the thought of not being with him killed her.

She was punishing herself again and she was tired of it.

Maybe the best way to deal with it was to admit it. She would tell Avery what she'd been thinking, admit that she was right back in that place where she punished herself, and Avery would help her find a way out. She didn't want to leave her son and she didn't want to give up on Brody. The truth was she hadn't even tried with him yet. Not in an honest fashion. "I wasn't talking about staying in London with him, Avery. You're being far too optimistic. I was talking about giving him to Brody and letting him raise Nate."

"I think that might be for the best."

She gasped because that hadn't been Avery. She turned and Brody was behind her, a grim resolve on his face.

Avery's eyes had gone wide as she looked over at Brody. "She didn't mean that."

"Oh, I think she did." Brody set down the small bag he'd shown up with.

He'd packed? He was ready to go? Naturally he'd walked in when she'd said the one thing she couldn't defend.

"You have to understand," Avery began.

Brody cut her off. "I understand quite well and I think I should have this conversation with Steph, please. Could we have a moment?"

"It's okay, Avery." She slipped off the barstool. Nate had perked up at the sound of his father's voice. His tiny fist came out of the blanket she'd wrapped him in as though trying to reach out for him. How close they'd gotten in so few days, as though their souls had recognized each other at first glance.

"Steph, don't forget what I said. Please, this is your whole future." Avery picked up the potato salad and walked out back.

It was. Her future. Had she stopped thinking about it? The future, that was. When she'd been a kid, the future was all she could think about. She'd made plans. She'd been the only girl in her high school who'd carried around a massive day planner and eagerly bought the next year's as soon as it became available. She'd had five-year plans. Ten-year plans.

And then she'd had to get through each moment separately and with no surety that she would survive the next.

She was still there, still slogging through each moment as if the accident had happened yesterday. As if her pain and guilt was something she needed to hold on to because if she let it go for one second, she might find herself being happy.

"I'm sorry, Brody." She should have talked to him. After what she'd seen happen today, she realized how foolish she'd been to think they couldn't protect her.

If they were going to be a family, Brody had the right to know she would be honest with him, that she wouldn't make life or death decisions without him.

"I'm sorry, too."

He looked grim and she hated that she'd put that expression on his face. He wasn't grim. Most of the time he was laughing and happy. For all his height and muscle, he was a gentle soul.

"I should have talked to you." Maybe if she explained what had happened, he would try to understand. "I should have told you what was said that night."

"I'm sure they threatened you. Either Fedor himself or one of his men," he replied. "I'm sure they got you alone for a few minutes and told you all the terrible things they would do. Well, not do to you, of course. You wouldn't care about yourself at all. I'm sure they threatened Nate. I'm sure they gave you some song and dance about how they would come after your baby and they wouldn't stop."

So he did understand and he was still standing there looking at her with cold eyes. "Yes, he said he would kill Nate and you. He said he would take out everyone I loved."

He put a hand up. "Leave me out of this, Steph. Got nothing to do with me."

How could he think that? She had to tell him how she felt. She had to be brave for once, and that meant telling him the truth. "Of course it does, Brody. I love you. I couldn't stand the thought of someone killing you."

He sighed. "You have no idea how much I wanted to hear those words come out of your mouth at one point. For over a year, really. I dreamed about you saying those sweet words to me. I walked away because I was afraid of you. I also thought I wasn't good enough, but I'm over that. I could have been good for you if you had let me. I could have loved you, Steph."

Could have? Her chest constricted. "I said I was sorry. Can't you see I was afraid? I was afraid of losing you."

Weariness was stamped on his handsome face. "Yeah, I can understand that, but I've figured something out. Love takes bravery, and I don't know that either one of us is brave enough to do it. I was so damn scared when he had you. I knew I would die if you did, but now I wonder how often you'll put me in that position. How many times will I have to watch you sacrifice yourself for someone you don't even know because, at the end of the day, what you really want is to go out in a blaze of glory so you can make up for something that no one blames you for anymore."

"I'm working on that." She could feel the tears well in her eyes. "I am. I even promised Tucker I would see someone about it. I want to get better. I love you, Brody, and I love Nate. I want to be better for the two of you."

She watched him almost falter, saw the way his hand came out. He pulled it back before it touched her own.

"I'm glad to hear that, but I think we need time. I'm going to stay with Kai for a day or two until Tucker's ready to head home. I think I should take Nate with me if you're planning on going back to Africa. Alfi said he would go with you if you wanted to get the clinic back up and running. I think you'll have better funds, too, if the way Anya was yelling at her brother was any indication. You'll have to talk to Big Tag about it, but he cut a deal to keep the Ukrainians out of Ezra's hands. I think part of it was money for your work."

Once that would have meant everything to her, but now she couldn't care less. She'd been going back to Africa because she didn't know anything else. Wasn't it time to try? He was right. She needed to be brave. "I want to come with you."

He grimaced. "I don't know that's a good idea. If you want to stay here in the States, then we can work something out. Maybe I could see about transferring to the Dallas office. I want to be in my son's life."

He'd put the emphasis on the word son. Not her life. Nate's. She could see it play out in her head. They would carve up Nate's time and see each other in those brief moments of pick up or drop off. Eventually Brody would find someone not as broken as she was and he would start a life. She would have to watch it all and know it could have been hers if she'd been braver or stronger. If she hadn't screwed up her whole life.

How could she lose him now? How could she have just figured out what she truly wanted only to lose him? "I don't understand, Brody. You know I didn't ask you to come here. You did that yourself. You came here and you're the one who made me believe we could have something."

His face flushed but it was obvious he wasn't about to back down. "I was wrong. I thought we could have something too, but I was bloody well wrong. If we had something, you wouldn't have lied to me. You wouldn't have run away. Tell me something, Stephanie. Did you think you would see us again? Did you think you were going to die?"

Tears fell and Nate started to wriggle as though he could feel her anxiety. "Yes."

"And never once did it occur to you to take my hand and ask for help? How would you feel if I had a disease of some kind and didn't bother to ask you to help me because I thought if it kills me, then I probably deserved it? How would you feel? Would you feel loved? Would you feel like I was a partner to you?"

"It's not like that."

"But it is. It's exactly like that." Brody sounded wretchedly weary. "I would spend the rest of my life worried about you. And I would spend it knowing you didn't love me enough to live for me, enough to take a little time and see yourself the way I see you."

"It doesn't sound like you see me in a very good light right now."

He chuckled, a humorless sound. "That's the funny thing. I practically see you with a halo most of the time. But Steph, we can't work. I'm not the man who's going to fix this for you. That's another thing I've learned. I can't fix you. You can't fix me. But the minute I had the chance, I decided I had to fix myself. Do you think I didn't understand what Nate's birth meant? His birth gave me another shot at you and I've been a completely different person. That wasn't merely about Nathan. I knew when I found out about him that I got another shot at you. I wanted it bad, wanted you so badly. I've indulged you all this time. I haven't been thinking about the bloody present. In my mind we were already practically married and having a second kid. I always wanted us to have a future, but the first chance you got, you traded it in."

She hadn't. Had she? "Brody, I wasn't thinking in those terms. I wanted to save you."

"But you didn't care about saving *us*. There has to be an us in the equation." He scrubbed a hand over his head. "Look, we're not going to get this settled today and I need rest. Bloody chest hurts like a train hit it."

She stepped closer to him. He hadn't let her help him when they were in the field. "Can I see it?"

He put a hand up. "I'm fine. Anya looked at it when we were on-site. It's bruising, nothing more."

"But I could help."

"I'm not your patient, Steph. Tomorrow, why don't we sit down and we can talk about what to do with Nate. I'm not willing to only see him on holidays. In fact, I think if you're going back to the clinic, he should come home with me."

She shook her head. "I can't let my baby go."

"Why not? You left him with me last night and you never thought you would see him again."

Why was he being stubborn? "That was different."

"I don't see it that way."

The door flew open and Charlotte Taggart was standing there, her face flushed. She wore a bathing suit and it was clear she'd run from the pool. "Stephanie, I'm sorry, we need you outside."

"I can't right now." She needed to talk to Brody, had to make him see that she'd been wrong, but now she wanted to try again.

Charlotte looked back outside. "It has to wait. Please, it's Liam. Something's happened. We don't know what to do."

Brody didn't hesitate. There was no disappointment in his eyes, mere acceptance that this was her job and everything else had to wait. "Give me the baby, Steph."

Steph passed Nate to Brody and finally really looked at Charlotte. She was a pasty white. "What happened?"

She walked through the door and saw something terrible. Liam was on the ground with Avery at his side, trying to hold his hand. She could hear that someone was already on a cell, talking to 911. Steph ran across the lawn.

Avery looked up, tears running down her face. "I don't know what's wrong. One minute he was swatting at a bee and the next he collapsed. Please, Steph. Please. I don't think he can breathe."

She dropped to her knees. Liam O'Donnell's handsome face was red and swollen. His eyes were barely visible. There was no question in her mind what was happening. Severe anaphylactic shock. Liam was hyperallergic to bee stings. "Does he have an EpiPen?"

Avery shook her head. "No. I didn't know he was allergic to anything. Please, baby. Please hold on. The ambulance will be here soon."

His face was rapidly becoming a monstrous mask and Steph knew if it was this bad on the outside, that terrible swelling was happening inside, too. It was happening inside his throat, cutting off his air supply.

"No, they won't," Taggart said quietly. "Steph, there's a huge fire downtown. They're having to bring an ambulance in but traffic is blocked coming out of the city. They told me it would be a while."

"Does anyone have an EpiPen?" She tried to get her hands to stop shaking. This wasn't a random patient dying on the ground. This was Liam.

This was Avery's husband and she couldn't lose another.

"No, we don't have one." Adam shook his head. "I can try the neighbors."

It would be too late. His airway was closing. He couldn't breathe. This was the kind of freak accident that usually ended with the patient dying because there was nothing anyone could do.

Unless there was a trained surgeon who happened to be close by.

Unless that surgeon was used to working in the field where she had very little equipment.

Unless that surgeon had trained all her life to be cool and calm and to do what she'd promised that day when she'd stood in Avery's hospital room.

You owe me two lives.

Time seemed to stop and the truth of her life lay out in front of her. Now she could look back and see the path that had led her to this moment, to this man dying on the ground. Perhaps she'd always been on this path. Perhaps from the moment she'd been born this was where she'd been going.

If she hadn't been on the road that night, she would have been a plastic surgeon somewhere, happily fixing noses that didn't need fixing and making plenty of money. She wouldn't have been standing in Serena's kitchen pleading with Brody. She wouldn't have ever gone to Africa where she'd learned how to save a man without an operating room.

"I'm going to need a knife, something sharp with a smaller blade." She tilted Liam's head back. "Sterilize it please. I'm also going to need a plastic tube. Serena, get me one of Tristan's sippy cups. The biggest one you have."

Serena ran off.

She looked down at the man who'd become a big brother to her and the world shifted into place. Meaning. Kai had told her to find meaning in what had happened to her. This was her meaning. Yes, this was worth the pain. This was worth the years of guilt. She would do it all again so she could be here. Something lifted in that moment and she was lighter than she'd been before.

And she knew beyond a shadow of a doubt that she would win this battle.

"Liam, I'm going to perform a tracheotomy. I need you to understand one thing. I will not let you die. That doesn't happen today. Not on my watch."

"Here you go, luv." Brody passed her a knife. He must have given Nate to someone else because he was alone and seemed ready to help her any way he could. Like he had several times in Sierra Leone. "Ran it over a flame and doused it in vodka. Works in the field. How can I help you?"

She felt him kneel beside her, giving her strength. "Do what I tell you to. Let's begin."

Steph took a deep breath and did what she'd been born to do.

* * * *

Brody paced, unable to sit down. He was anxious, his hands shaking a bit now that the initial rush of adrenaline was gone, and he had to wonder how Steph was doing. He could still see her, see how frightened she'd been, and then something had happened. A calm, cool competence had taken over. She'd relaxed and started issuing orders like a general in the midst of battle.

She'd been the most beautiful thing he'd ever seen.

"What a crazy fucking day." Taggart passed out coffees before he slumped into the waiting room chair beside his wife. The entire room was filled with McKay-Taggart people. They milled around, comforting each other as they waited for news. "First we have to wage war in the middle of a downtown factory that smelled an awful lot like feet and then Li gets killed by a bee."

Charlotte slapped her husband's chest. "Don't even joke about that. He did not die."

He put an arm around his wife and hauled her close. "You're right, baby." He glanced up at Brody and whispered. "We're never letting Li live this down, but dude, your girl is a badass."

"I've seen a lot of stuff in my time," Case said with a shake of his head. "But that was some heroic shit. I have no idea how she did that. It was amazing."

Even the EMTs had been shocked at what she'd managed to do. She'd gotten in the ambulance with them, unwilling to let go of her patient for a moment.

Case's wife Mia had called a few of the women she knew from Sanctum in to help corral the kiddos while the rest of the group had hastily gotten into street clothes and come running to the hospital. He'd been thankful to leave Nate behind with trusted watchers because he needed a minute to breathe.

He'd been ready to walk away. He'd been angry, so scared that he wasn't sure he ever wanted to feel that way again.

But wasn't that the fucking point of life? To have something you love so much it killed you to think about losing it, someone who could enrage you one minute and bring you to your knees with gratitude the next. As he'd watched the ambulance drive away, he'd remembered why he'd fallen in love with her in the first place. The very spirit that caused her to feel the kind of guilt she did was the same one that made her heroic.

He'd said he couldn't fix her and he believed that, but maybe he hadn't tried hard enough to make her want to fix herself.

For now they all waited. Avery was in the back with Steph and Li. They knew he'd been alive when he'd gone into the ambulance, but had heard nothing since.

Taggart held his wife and kissed her head. "Baby, he's going to be okay, and now we know bees are like his kryptonite. Anytime he gets stung, I get to hit him with an EpiPen. That's a huge plus. Li O'Donnell does not get taken down by a flipping bee."

"Not while Doc Awesome is around, that's for sure." Theo held his wife's hand.

Erin looked up at Brody. "You weren't bad yourself, Carter.

You were quite the nurse."

He'd done everything Steph had asked him to from handing her the knife to wiping up blood so she could see properly. "It wasn't our first time to work together like that. I was at that clinic with her for months, you know. I would help her when she went into the more remote areas. Wasn't always an operating room, but she found a way to make it all work. She saved people I would have told you couldn't be saved."

"You were an amazing team," Erin replied. "And I can't thank you enough for that. I don't think any of us knows what we'd do without Liam in our lives."

Erin had been Liam's partner for a long time, since she'd been hired on at McKay-Taggart. Li and Avery had been Erin's support system when she'd thought she'd lost Theo and as she'd had their child on her own. As they would have been Steph's.

He'd forgotten how good they were together when they didn't let insecurities get between them. It had been natural to sit beside her and help her.

How could he leave her? But how could he stay when she showed no signs of changing?

"Brody, could I talk to you for a moment?"

He turned and Adam was there. He'd slipped on a T-shirt over his board shorts and looked surprisingly casual in a pair of flip-flops. "Sure. How can I help you?"

It would be nice to have a problem to work on, to get his mind off the fact that Steph was going to walk through those doors with news any minute and he wasn't sure what he would do with her. If things had taken a turn for the worse with Liam, how could he not pull her close and comfort her?

"I think this is a case of me helping you." Adam held up a mobile phone. "Serena told me you erased all of the doc's voice mails."

He had wondered if things would be different if he'd answered that first call. Hell, would they be different if he'd listened to the voice mail? He wasn't sure, but he knew he'd missed something precious. "Yeah, I deleted them. It's not something I'm proud of."

"You do understand that you only deleted them off your phone, right?" Adam asked. "You see, nothing is ever really gone. You still have the same account and the same number. Those messages were all stored in the cloud. I hacked into your personal cloud and pulled them back out again. I put them together in an audio file. I think you should listen."

"Why would you do that?" He wasn't sure he wanted to know. There wasn't anything he could do now.

"I think you should hear what she went through. It's not always easy, you know. Our wives won't tell us, but that motherhood thing doesn't happen overnight or the way it does in the movies where the mom looks down and all the pain goes away in a rush and never comes back because there's only room for love for your child. That's all bullshit. Stephanie went through this alone but you can hear a little of what she needed from you in these messages."

"Steph rarely needs anyone." That was the entire problem. She never reached out or asked for help. The only reason he knew about his child now was the fact that she'd finally found a problem she couldn't solve on her own. Even then, she hadn't come for him. She'd come to ask Liam for help.

"Oh, she needs you. I think she needs you more than she knows. Listen and tell me if you still think the same thing." Adam offered him the mobile. "Hell, listen because this is a piece of the story you don't know yet. Listen because you weren't there and you owe her."

"You had no right to listen to these." He looked at the mobile like it was a snake that could bite him, injecting him with noxious venom.

Adam shrugged. "And yet I did. Someone should. Someone should know what she needed, how she cried out, how she didn't stop hoping you would answer. Someone should know what she went through."

He placed the phone in Brody's hands, turned, and went back to sit with his wife, who threaded her fingers through his while Jake held her other hand.

They were a family. He was surrounded by them, happy couples who had found each other and managed to get through all the trials life gave them to make it to the point that they were more than the individuals they'd been before. For a moment today everything had fallen away and it had been clear to him that being a family with Stephanie Gibson was his natural state.

So why was he afraid that it would all fall apart?

It took bravery to love someone, really love someone. He'd told her he was worried neither of them was brave enough to do it right, but bravery was a choice. It was the conscious action a man took when he realized life was worth the pain, that no matter the cost, he had to try.

He touched the screen where Adam had queued the recording up and put the mobile to his ear.

"All right, so you're not answering and you were serious." She sounded deeply irritated, her voice flat. "Fine. I know I wasn't supposed to call you. I get it, but we have a problem, Brody. I don't know what went wrong. I am a damn doctor and still this is happening to me. Damn it. Okay, here it is. I know we were supposed to have our fun fling and walk away unscathed, but your sperm met my egg and they had different plans. I'm pregnant. Call me."

He felt his lips curl up. She sounded annoyed and he could almost see her frowning at him, her brows creasing. She was adorable when she was frustrated, though he tended to not tell her that because those words would take her from frustrated to mad.

"Okay, so it's been a week and you haven't called. I'm going to pretend something went wrong with your voice mail." Her tone was bland as though she was simply trying to get through this call with as little emotion as possible. And yet he knew that when her voice went monotone, she was usually roiling on the inside. "I'm going to handle this in a professional manner. Let me see how I can explain this to you without dragging a bunch of emotion into it. I know you don't like that so here goes. We are two human beings who engaged in a biological function that has produced a result. That result is rapidly forming a fetus in my uterus and I would like for you to contact me in order to discuss this situation like rational adults who both have a stake in the outcome. Thank you and I look forward to your call."

Yes, there was the anger he'd expected. He couldn't blame her for it, either. The recording switched to another voice mail.

He grimaced because Steph knew a whole lot of swear words and she wasn't holding back. He was relieved when that particular one ended and another began. Her tone was softer this time.

"I don't know why I'm calling you. You don't care. I do understand that, but I thought since it had been a while, you might be…I don't know…curious at least. I'm six months along. I thought about whether or not I should go through with this, but I couldn't see myself ending the pregnancy. I'm still not sure if I'll keep the baby. I would be a pretty crappy mom. I should talk to Avery about it, but I'm ashamed to call her. Anyway, I had a sonogram today. I went into Freetown and saw an actual OB. He's nice and seems knowledgeable. His equipment isn't top of the line, but it's better than anything I have." There was a pause on the line before she continued, her voice softer now. "I got to see him. Yeah, I said him. It's a boy. I thought you might like to know. I'll call again and let you know what I decide to do with him. I'm trying to make the best decision I can for his future. If I put him up for adoption, I might need you to sign some papers. Good-bye, Brody. I miss you."

He stopped, leaning against the wall, his heart aching at the dull sound of her voice. She'd considered ending the pregnancy? Of course she had. Steph looked at all options and he hadn't been there to weigh in. He'd been traipsing around Europe while she'd been alone and pregnant.

There was a click as the message changed again. This time she sounded guttural and in pain.

"Brody, I promised myself I wouldn't do this. God, it hurts. No one can tell you how damn much this hurts. I hate you. I fucking hate you for doing this to me. I wish you were the one trying to push a baby out of the tip of your dick. I hate you." There was a moment of heavy breathing. She'd called him while she'd been in labor? He knew why she'd done it. Against everything she'd said to him, she'd had hope. She'd tried. She'd reached out across the miles that separated them and she'd given him one last chance to be there with her.

Yes, she was saying she hated him, but he understood that. In that terrible pain, when she was alone, she'd needed him, wanted him there with her.

She groaned again. "Please call me back. I know you don't want to have anything to do with me, but I need you. I hate this. Oh, god. I miss you. I wish you were here to hold my hand because I think I'm going to pass out. I wish I had your strength." Another low groan. "I'm going to find Anya. It's time. I pray it's time because I don't know how much more of this I can take."

He didn't cry, hadn't cried in years, and yet he couldn't stop the way his eyes watered. She'd been alone and she'd needed him and he'd looked down at the name on the screen and turned his mobile off.

She'd tried. How could he not do everything he could to make it up to her? How could he even consider leaving her side?

There was a click and one last message. "Hello, Brody. This is the last time I'm going to call. I've decided to keep my son. I named him Nathan in case you're interested. He's..." She laughed over the line. "He's so big. He's big and he's beautiful and he's mine. I'm going to make this work, so don't worry about us. When he asks about you I'll only tell him that he was created in love because no matter what I said at the time, I loved you very much. Sometimes I think I loved you from the minute you walked into my clinic. Thank you for my son. I hope you have a good life ahead of you, Brody Carter. Good-bye."

It took everything he had not to hit his knees.

What had he done? He'd understood it in a logical sense, but now it truly struck him. He'd left her behind. He'd loved her and he'd let his fear rule. He'd done everything he accused her of and now he was threatening to do it again, though this time he'd said he'd take Nate. She needed someone to hold her hand and stand by her. Yes, she'd done some crazy stuff, but only because she didn't understand how valuable she was, how precious she was to him. He'd done a crap job of letting her know.

"Brody?"

He looked up, unashamed of the tears running down his face.

She was standing there, her shirt soaked in blood, and yet she was more radiant than he'd ever seen her. She was petite and fragile, and yet she'd never once wavered when the time had come.

If he could convince her to be that way in real life, could show her how strong she was, they could move mountains together.

"I just told everyone that Li is well on the road to recovery. He's not talking yet, but the doctors said my tracheotomy was perfectly done and he'll suffer no ill effects."

"Of course not. You're the most amazing doctor I've ever seen."

She moved closer, her hands coming up to touch his face. She wiped away the tears. "Brody, I'm sorry I hurt you and seeing you like this makes me want to curl up in a ball and cry, but I'm not going to do that. I'm well aware that I wrecked everything, but you should know that I'm not giving up on us. I will not. I'm going to move to London and there's nothing you can do about it."

Her shoulders were straight, her head held high. Something had happened to the woman he loved in those moments when she'd saved her friend's life. Something that had changed her, brushing away the insecurities that had marked her up until that moment. They would come back, the war far from over, but this battle had been won and it was a turning point. He could feel it. "All right. I can't stop you but why do you want to live in London?"

"Because you're there and I want to be close to you," she said.

"Because you think Nate needs a father?" He would convince her that he could be more. He would show her he was the man for her, that if she gave him a second chance he would be stalwart this time, the unwavering center of her universe. He would ground her, allowing her to fly because she'd been born to see how high she could go.

"Of course Nate needs a father, but I need you too. I need you more than you'll ever know. I understand that I screwed up and you need time. I'm going to give it to you. I'll find a flat somewhere close and when you're ready, you should know I'm going to be all over you, Mr. Carter. I won't pretend and try to steal one night from you. I'm going to be greedy. I want all the nights. I want all the days. I want everything you have to give."

The woman standing in front of him knew what she wanted and she wanted him. This woman wouldn't be turned away without a fight.

Not that he intended to give her one. "Yes."

"Hear me out, Brody. I understand that I can't take back..." She stopped. "Did you say yes?"

"He said yes," Adam called out before leaning over to Serena and Jake. "I think something's wrong with Doc's hearing because I could hear him from here."

Yeah, he'd forgotten they had an audience.

He tried to ignore them. "I said yes, Steph. Forgive me for ever saying anything else to you. I need you to understand that when it comes to being with you my answer is always going to be yes."

"But you were mad at me."

"And I will be in the future, but I love you and that beats everything else. You come first, before everyone else, before my own fears and insecurities," he pledged. "You and our son are everything to me. Come to London but you won't live anywhere but with me."

A gorgeous smile crossed her lips, lighting up her face. "Well, if you're in a mood to say yes, then I can fulfill my other promise. I promised Tucker I would ask you to marry me if we got out of that warehouse. Here we are. I figured something out. I figured out that it's all worth it, all the pain and doubt. It brought me here, to you. Brody Carter, will you marry me?"

He moved in before she could do something silly like go down on one knee. There was only one knee he wanted her over and that was his when they were playing. Which they would do for the rest of their lives. Play and love and laugh and hold on when the times got tough.

"Yes." He hauled her up into his arms, kissing her for all he was worth.

She threw her arms around him and he could feel her smiling.

"See," Taggart was saying, "weirdest day ever. Now we have to go to England for another damn wedding. Hey, Carter, do us all a favor and glom on to Nicky's wedding. It's a long fucking trip."

He ignored the hell out of Taggart—though it was a good idea—and got on to kissing his bride-to-be.

Chapter Seventeen

London, England
3 weeks later

"You look very much the gentleman," Nick Markovic said as he strode into the groom's room.

It was actually the locker room at The Garden, but it served its purpose for today. "Thanks. I was worried I looked a bit like an overstuffed penguin. And might I add, you're looking spiffy yourself."

Nick grinned and pulled the cork out of the god-only-knew-how-old bottle of Scotch that Damon had presented them with when they'd started dressing for the wedding.

The double wedding.

Nick was marrying the girl of his dreams, Hayley Dalton, and they'd been excited to share the day with close friends. Brody hadn't even brought it up. He'd been ready to elope since waiting even the three weeks they had seemed like too long. Nick and Hayley had convinced them that the more family and friends, the better.

"I was talking to Nathan," Nick said with a wink. "He's looking resplendent in his tux. You are only so-so, my friend."

He couldn't help but laugh. He did that a lot these days. He looked down at Nate, who did indeed look gentlemanly in the tiny tux they'd found for him. He was busy batting at the toys on his bouncy seat, completely ignoring all the male bonding going on around him. "That he does."

The Taggart brothers were sitting in the front of the locker room, jackets off until the moment they would be forced to put them on. Most of the crew had come over for the wedding and The Garden was filled with visitors. It had been a fun week to hang out with his friends and family. His mum had made the long trip along with his stepdad, and they'd even brought Alfi along.

He hadn't killed Alfi. Something about being happy made him more forgiving.

He just wished he could do something about Tucker.

Walt and Damon stepped into the circle. Damon brought over four crystal glasses.

"I'll take some of that," Walt said. "Now that I'm off pain meds from the gunshot wound, I can get back to my experiments with grain alcohol."

Walt had a very sheltered childhood.

Damon slapped him on the back. "It's a single malt, mate, and this is the best."

"Yes, well, where I came from it was merely something that destroyed brain cells," Walt shot back. "My parents believed in studying, not partying, which is precisely why I like it way better here."

They were an odd group. Damon Knight, practically a member of the gentry. He'd been born into English wealth and privilege. Nick Markovic, a former Russian spy. Walt, the genius who always seemed to find trouble.

And him. A rough-and-tumble bloke from the Outback who was about to marry the most brilliant woman he'd ever met.

Sometimes life took twists and turns that led a man to his future.

"Hey, the Americans are going to want a taste of that." Taggart led his brothers into the room.

"Don't leave the Irishman out." Li O'Donnell straightened his tie. "Never let it be said any Irishman walked down an aisle without a little fortification."

Taggart put a hand out, stopping Damon from passing the Scotch to Li. "Are we sure no bees were involved in the making of this Scotch?"

Li shot Big Tag the finger. "I'm never living it down. Give me that." He drained the glass in one shot before turning to Brody. "Heard Steph and Faith decided to team up."

It had turned out to be a match made in heaven. Steph had a stable clinic and Faith had a ton of contacts. Anya was running the place now and taking charge of the different doctors who came through, each doing their part to help. He and Steph would be back there in a few months, taking her turn as doctor.

The best of both worlds.

"The clinic is open for business," he said with a smile. "If by business you mean making absolutely no money at all."

"That's how charity works," Li said with a smile before he stepped back. "Now, I've got a girl to walk down the aisle. You better be there, Carter, or I'll find ya."

He wouldn't be anywhere else. "Hey, O'Donnell, since you're the one giving the bride away, does that mean I should call you Pops now?"

"Not on yer life." O'Donnell shuddered. "Though the wee one can certainly call me Uncle Li. You be good to her, Carter."

"I will." He shook Li's hand and the Irishman walked out to prepare for his part of the wedding.

"We will see you outside, brother." Taggart slapped him on the shoulder and then extended a hand to Nick. "I'm happy for both of you, and more than happy to have more lovely women in our family. Now I'm going to go help Charlie wrangle the girls because I overheard them planning to climb a couple of the trees in the garden."

The American crew left to find their places and he was alone with the men who had become his closest family. All except one.

"Owen didn't want to come back here?" He asked the question

of Nick. Owen had been Nick's partner for years before he'd become the last of Hope McDonald's experiments.

Nick gave him a tight smile. "He told me he wasn't feeling well. It's hard for him, these big gatherings. He doesn't know what to say and often finds himself in a conversation he doesn't understand because he's talking to someone who knew him from before. The others are all coming, but they don't have the same problems as Owen."

Owen knew his name, knew all the facts of his life before the drug had taken his memories. Sometimes not knowing seemed to be better.

It sure as hell had been for Tucker.

"Has Ezra found anything at all yet?" Brody asked. "I saw you talking to him earlier."

Ezra Fain had missed the poker game that served as both his and Nick's bachelor party, but he'd flown in for the wedding. He'd shown up and immediately gone into a private meeting with Damon and Big Tag.

"Two of the Belgians he talked to insist that Tucker is this Dr. Razor person." Damon poured himself another drink. "They said they'd worked for him on two occasions, though the person they were actually in contact with was none other than Dr. Hope McDonald. Ezra's been working on another case but he's going to try to figure out Tucker's real name. I seriously doubt it's Razor."

Nick shook his head. "It's hard to believe that kid was some kind of monster. He's the kindest of the bunch. Are you sure we're doing the right thing keeping this from the rest of them? If he was Hope McDonald's right-hand man, then he was likely the one who tortured them."

"But the drug seems to have destroyed that part of his personality," Walt explained. "So much of who we are is wrapped up in our memories, our past traumas, but there's also a chemical and biological component. Think of it like this—Tucker got an evilectomy. I know that sounds stupid, but that part of him, the part with evil impulses, seems to be completely gone. He's not the same man and I, for one, think that poisoning the others against him

346

would be cruel. Those men are the only family he has."

That was Walt in a nutshell. If Hope McDonald had been an evil genius, then Walt had taken all the good genes for himself. Brody put a hand on his shoulder. "So we keep telling him that we can't corroborate de Vries's story. Maybe after a while we can convince him it was all complete rubbish."

"But I have to look into it." Damon set the glass down. "I have to find out the truth. If we can find Tucker's identity, it might lead to the others. But for now, we stay silent. Walt is right. The man we know as Tucker isn't the same man de Vries described. And on that front, did you see that the stock was down for a certain firm out of Antwerp once Johann's piece ran in the papers? Remind me to thank Mia for that."

Mia Taggart was a journalist. She'd taken the thumb drive and found all of Johann's notes and pieced together the story the man would have written had he lived. She'd also written a piece on the journalist himself that was making Johann famous for his bravery and compassion.

And it was also making the world a bit safer since the terrorist group wouldn't be selling their diamonds so easily again.

Damon looked down at his watch. "Time's up, mates. You ready to do this?"

Brody looked at Nick. "I think we're both game."

"I've been waiting for this all my life," Nick agreed.

Brody picked up Nate. "You ready to get our girl, son?"

He followed Nick out, eager to be with his family.

* * * *

Later that night

Kayla Summers sighed and looked out at the dancing couples. The whole garden had been decked out with twinkle lights and flowers and candles. At the end of the wedding, confetti had been dropped from above making it look like it was raining flower petals.

It was so romantic it made her want to find a man and do what bridesmaids were supposed to do.

Damn it. She was all dressed up and ready to go. She was wearing heels and a push-up bra and she got nothing because everyone was either married or loony from mind-altering drugs.

Or Ezra Fain, who'd said he needed to talk to her earlier. It wasn't that the CIA agent wasn't superhot, it was just that he was someone she worked with and she was done sleeping with people she would have to see over and over again. Men were touchy things. When you slept with them for a while they got all needy and clingy.

Like the one who had his head in her lap, except she certainly hadn't slept with Tucker. And the truth was she didn't blame him for needing affection.

She was sitting on a bench near the tables where dinner had been served. It was odd to see The Garden used for such a normal function. Normally the beautiful indoor garden hosted play spaces where kink couples could get their freak on.

Except it really was normal since the truth was this ceremony had been about love and commitment and family, and the kink part was just something they did, too.

There's no such thing as normal, my darling girl. And if there was, wouldn't it be a boring thing to be?

Her dads. She'd been adopted by two men from California. They'd been the best parents she could have asked for. They'd always told her she was destined for great things. How would they feel if he knew her great things had been all about proving how much pain she could take? Her dads had a vision of her saving the country. They knew she'd worked for the Agency. They had no idea all the things she'd done, the terrible things that had been done to her.

"I think I should tell them." Tucker was curled up on the bench, his head in her lap. "Robert knows, but he said it was up to me whether or not I say anything. I should tell them."

"Tell them what? That some douchebag who had ties to terrorists figured out you were the weak link in the chain and tried to use you to get out of a rough situation?" She was toeing the line on this one. There was no way Tucker was the same man. Even if he was.

Kay knew that a person could change. She knew it better than anyone.

He turned so his face was staring up at her. "Do you really think so?"

So open and innocent. He was like a gorgeous manchild, and she felt a desperate need to protect him. "I know it."

He sighed, seeming to settle. "I hope so."

"What did Theo Taggart have to say about it? Or Robert?" After all, if anyone would know, it would be Theo or Robert. They had been held by Dr. McDonald, though she'd never heard either mention a second doctor.

"Theo said he's never seen me before," Tucker said. "Robert either, but who knows. There was a second site, one Big Tag doesn't think Theo and Robert ever saw. What if I ran that site? What if I'm the one who did this to Jax and Sasha and Dante and Owen?"

"I don't believe it for a second." He was too sweet. It was his nature. She couldn't see how simply erasing a person's memory would change something so fundamental. No one as sweet as Tucker could do those things to another human being.

He sighed. "I pray you're right. I don't want to have been some crazy monster doctor. I like being me. I know that sounds stupid since I don't know who me is, but I like it here. I like my brothers, and you're the best sister anyone could want."

Yep, that was what she got here. She was everyone's sister or aunt. Not that she was truly attracted to any of the Lost Boys, but damn, couldn't Damon hire a hottie who wasn't certifiable?

"I'm glad, buddy." She glanced up and saw Fain coming her way. He wasn't alone. Damon was with him, and that gorgeous hunk of American snark Ian Taggart. She totally understood why her twin sister had been all over that while she'd been in the field.

Of course, now he was married to a woman Kay respected. Mostly because Charlotte Taggart was a woman who truly got what the "sisterhood" meant, but also for her assassin skills. Kay appreciated any woman who could murder a man with a pair of Louboutins.

"I think I'm about to get pulled into an impromptu meeting, buddy," she said. "Why don't you go and find Teresa? She was looking for someone to dance with."

Tucker sat up quickly, straightening his shirt. "Really? Maybe they'll play a slow song and I'll be able to show her how good I am at rubbing myself on her. That's what Big Tag says dancing is all about."

Big Tag gave him a thumbs-up. "That's exactly what it's about. You go for it."

Tucker scurried off, seeming to forget his ennui at possibly being an evil motherfucker in a past life. Kayla stood, putting a hand on her hips. "You are going to get that poor boy slapped."

Tag shrugged. "It's all one big learning process for him. You got a minute?"

"Sure, what's up?"

"Fain would like to borrow you for a job," Damon explained.

She hoped she managed to keep her face perfectly bland because inside she was dying a little. If the Agency was asking, then it had to be something down and dirty. If the Agency was asking her, it probably had something to do with her prior MSS contacts. She'd worked for years as a double agent, trained to take her twin sister's place as a spy.

She'd lost her sister and sometimes she worried she'd almost lost her soul.

But still, if Damon wanted her to do something, she had to consider it. If her country needed her, she would have to go back into hell.

"What's the gig?" That was good. Very normal, as if she wasn't screaming on the inside.

Ezra looked down at her. "Do you know who Joshua Hunt is?"

She snorted a little. "Uhm, he's only the hottest actor in the world right now. He's starring in that new action movie—*The Quick and The Enraged.* I love that series."

What she wasn't about to admit was that she kind of had a supercrush on the man. He was tall, dark, and handsome. Right up her alley.

"I need you to go undercover as his bodyguard. I've already got the job lined up, but he doesn't know the name of the new guard yet. This job would require you to stay close to him and go to many of the functions he would attend." Ezra frowned as though thinking through how to say what he needed to.

He was hesitating and she didn't understand it. He wanted her to go undercover as the hottest man in Hollywood's bodyguard? The only thing that would have been better would have been to be asked to be his freaking fake fiancée, or anything that would get her in the man's bed.

Although bodyguard was pretty hot. She could likely still seduce him.

So she would have to go to a bunch of hoity-toity parties in one of the most glamorous places in the world. "What's the catch?"

Damon's jaw tightened. "Well, there is one small item of concern."

Taggart shook his head. "They're worried you're about to be offended. I think you're going to jump at the chance."

Now they really had her attention. "Like I said before, what's the catch?"

Ezra's shoulders squared as though he was readying himself for rejection. "He wants a bodyguard who will also serve as his sexual submissive and his in-public girlfriend."

Holy shit. She was getting the whole Fifty Shades. So, so many slutty thoughts went through her head. Beautiful, slutty thoughts.

It would be a montage of shopping and partying and sex with a movie star god.

Who might not be as good in bed as he looked, but she could work with that. She could whip him into shape.

Quietly, since she was the sub. But she'd found she could do amazing things from the bottom.

"Kayla, he's not trying to insult you," Damon began.

"She's not insulted. She's already planning on how she's going to top him from the bottom." Taggart did know her better than the rest.

"I absolutely am doing that. I already have ideas." She was also planning her wardrobe. She would need a bunch of designer wear.

Ezra seemed to relax. "Then you'll take the job?"

She smiled at the thought. "There's no business like show business, right? Hollywood, here I come."

Kayla, Joshua, and the entire McKay-Taggart gang will return in *Nobody Does It Better*.

Author's Note

I'm often asked by generous readers how they can help get the word out about a book they enjoyed. There are so many ways to help an author you like. Leave a review. If your e-reader allows you to lend a book to a friend, please share it. Go to Goodreads and connect with others. Recommend the books you love because stories are meant to be shared. Thank you so much for reading this book and for supporting all the authors you love!

Sign up for Lexi Blake's newsletter
and be entered to win a $25 gift certificate
to the bookseller of your choice.

Join us for news, fun, and exclusive content
including free short stories.

There's a new contest every month!

Go to www.LexiBlake.net to subscribe.

Nobody Does It Better
Masters and Mercenaries 15
By Lexi Blake
Now Available

A spy who specializes in seduction

Kayla Summers was an elite CIA double agent, working inside China's deadly MSS. Now, she works for McKay-Taggart London, but the Agency isn't quite done with her. Spy master Ezra Fain needs her help on a mission that would send her into Hollywood's glamorous and dangerous party scene. Intrigued by the mission and the movie star hunk she will be shadowing, she eagerly agrees. When she finds herself in his bed, she realizes she's not only risking her life, but her heart.

A leading man who doesn't do romance

Joshua Hunt is a legend of the silver screen. As Hollywood's highest paid actor, he's the man everyone wants to be, or be with, but something is missing. After being betrayed more than once, the only romance Josh believes in anymore is on the pages of his scripts. He keeps his relationships transactional, and that's how he likes it, until he meets his new bodyguard. She was supposed to keep him safe, and satisfied when necessary, but now he's realizing he may never be able to get enough of her.

An ending neither could have expected

Protecting Joshua started off as a mission, until it suddenly felt like her calling. When the true reason the CIA wanted her for this assignment is revealed, Kayla will have to choose between serving her country or saving the love of her life.

At Your Service
Masters and Mercenaries~Topped Book 4
By Lexi Blake
Now Available

Juliana O'Neil's promising future was burned away in the heat of battle. She had been an officer with a bright future in the military, but now she is struggling to survive. Her husband gone and her career in shambles, she finds a job at Top as a hostess and tries to put together the pieces of her life. The last thing she needs is any kind of male attention, but she can't help but be amused at her neighbor and coworker's lothario antics. Not that she would have anything to do with him, at least not for more than one night.

Javier Leones doesn't understand monogamy. No woman could ever be enough for his endless libido, but he has to admit Juliana has his attention. For reasons he doesn't fully understand, he can't seem to get the gorgeous redhead with the sad eyes out of his head. After one scorching night together, he realizes he'll never be able to get her out of his system. But with his reputation, he fears she'll never see him as more than a one-night stand.

When their passions collide, these new lovers will be forced to confront Juliana's past and come to terms with Javier's present. Will they find their way or will this reservation be canceled at the last minute?

Smoke and Sin
The Perfect Gentlemen, Book 4
By Shayla Black and Lexi Blake
Now Available

More than a decade ago, Roman Calder had a scorching affair with the sister of one of his best friends. Augustine Spencer drove him so crazy he thought of nothing but her. The only thing they did more often than heat the sheets was fight. Unprepared for the intensity of their relationship, Roman broke things off and concentrated on things that made sense to him: his career and putting his best friend, Zack Hayes, in the White House.

Gus Spencer is known to Washington insiders as the president's secret weapon. Gorgeous and brilliant, Gus runs the press pool with the determination of a shark. No one dares to cross her, not when she's known for having a spine of steel...but long ago one man melted her down. Despite the fact that she'll never forgive Roman for breaking her heart, now that they work together she can't get him off her mind.

When a dangerous investigation leads both Roman and Gus to London, the heat between them becomes unbearable. As they begin to unravel an international conspiracy, they find themselves falling all over again. But when a killer threatens their world, can they fight to stay together or will the sins of their past keep them forever apart?

Thieves

A new urban fantasy series by Lexi Blake

"Author Lexi Blake has created a supernatural world filled with surprises and a book that I couldn't put down once I started reading it."
Maven, The Talent Cave Reviews

"I truly love that Lexi took vampires and made them her own."
KC Lu, Guilty Pleasures Book Reviews

Stealing mystical and arcane artifacts is a dangerous business, especially for a human, but Zoey Wharton is an exceptional thief. The trick to staying alive is having friends in all the wrong places. With a vampire, a werewolf, and a witch on the payroll, Zoey takes the sorts of jobs no one else can perform—tracking down ancient artifacts filled with unthinkable magic power, while trying to stay one step ahead of monsters, demons, angels, and a Vampire Council with her in their crosshairs.

If only her love life could be as simple. Zoey and Daniel Donovan were childhood sweethearts until a violent car crash took his life. When Daniel returned from the grave as a vampire, his only interest in Zoey was in keeping her safely apart from the secrets of his dark world. Five years later, Zoey encounters Devinshea Quinn, an earthbound Faery prince who sweeps her off her feet. He could show her everything the supernatural world has to offer, but Daniel is still in her heart.

As their adventures in acquisition continue, Zoey will have to find a way to bring together the two men she loves or else none of them may survive the forces that have aligned against her.

Now Available:

Steal the Light – Free for a limited time!
Steal the Day
Steal the Moon
Steal the Sun
Steal the Night
Ripper
Addict
Sleeper
Outcast

We Own Tonight
By: Corinne Michaels
Now Available

From New York Times Bestseller, Corinne Michaels, comes a sexy new STANDALONE romance novel.

I'm not a one-night stand kind of woman. I'm especially not the woman who has a few drinks at a concert and ends up in bed with my childhood celebrity crush, Eli Walsh.

However, that's exactly where I find myself.

What's a girl to do after a drunken mistake? Run. I grab my clothes and get away from the powerful, irresistible, and best-sex-of-my-life superstar as fast as I can. His gorgeous green eyes, rock-hard body, and cocky smile have no place in my world. My life is complicated enough.

Someone forgot to tell him that.

Eli is relentless. Pushing his way into my heart, wearing me down, proving he's nothing like I assumed, and everything I need. But when my world shatters to pieces, he holds the broken bits together. Unwillingly, I fall desperately in love with him.

He made me think we'd have forever . . . I should've listened when he said we could only own tonight.

* * * *

Chapter One

Heather

"Damn it, Heather. We're always late because of you!" Nicole yells from outside the bathroom. She's been my best friend since the sixth grade. You'd think by now she'd know to pad things by twenty minutes if she wants a snowball's chance in hell of getting anywhere on time.

"The peril," I taunt her as I finish putting my hair up.

"You drive me nuts."

"Such is life."

I hear her mutter something under her breath as she walks away. I don't know why she gets so upset. We have plenty of time. With the way Nicole drives, her lead foot will have us at the concert fifteen minutes before the opening act.

Of course, I'm taking my sweet ass time getting ready. I have zero desire to be forced to put on makeup or any version of pants.

Nicole's idea of girls' night out and mine are totally different. I could stay home, drink a martini, and be happy. My best friend wants to paint the town red. I'm too old for that shit. I end up smelling like a garbage can and feeling like I ate a jar of cotton balls. I'd rather be comfy in pajamas than wear these jeans that I had to lie on the bed to shimmy into. I can only imagine what I looked like while I was sucking it in and bending backward to get the damn button closed. Then I did about fifteen lunges to "stretch" the pants, all the while praying I didn't bust a seam. Nothing like a workout just to get dressed.

I make a mental note to call my trainer friend at the boxing ring.

She knocks again. "I'm leaving you."

No, you're not.

I open the door a smidge. "I have the tickets in here. So, you know what? Go ahead." I stick my tongue out and then quickly close the door and lock it. If they hadn't already left me twice before, I wouldn't have to go to such lengths. I learned quickly that I always had to have the upper hand with my three best friends. Then again, if

I had let her leave me, I could be watching Netflix and shoveling popcorn into my mouth.

Nicole may not have figured out to pad time, but she has learned I have a spiteful side, so she lets me finish without another interruption. I could stay in here longer just to piss her off, but that would mean more time staring at the pink tiles on the wall that I loathe.

My house isn't bad, but it isn't great, either. When my parents passed away, it was passed down to me. It's old and probably falling apart more than I'd like to admit. Yet, I can't get rid of it. It's the only thing of them I have, and it's the only place I can afford.

The mortgage is paid off, which allows me to put what little money I have left over after my monthly bills to go toward my sister's medical care.

Once I'm happy with my appearance, I head out with a shit-eating grin.

She looks at her watch as I emerge and shakes her head. "I swear."

The best way to keep Nicole from blowing up is with diversion. "You shouldn't swear, it's unbecoming of you. Are we picking up Danni and Kristin?"

"No, and I'm grateful we aren't, because we would miss the opening band."

She and I are the two most sarcastic and the biggest assholes out of the group. When we start to bicker, it gets bad—quick. Without our two mediators, it's best not to engage.

"Are you sure?" I ask ignoring the jab.

"Yes, I'm sure. They're meeting us there."

Nicole and I walk out and get in her car. I wish she'd buy a normal size vehicle. I'm five-foot-five, and my knees mash my boobs because of how squished I am. Between my already tight jeans and this sardine can, I'm going to bust a gut.

"Please," I say dramatically, "tell me they're not bringing their husbands."

She laughs. "Dickhead One and Jackhole Two aren't coming. They're going for a boys' night." She sticks her finger in her mouth and makes a gagging sound.

Thank God for small miracles. Their husbands are the worst, especially Danielle's.

"Maybe the two loser husbands will fall madly in love with each other," I muse while I shift to get comfortable.

Nicole smirks as she watches me. "And figure out they were never meant to be married to such amazing women like them."

"And then we'll finally build that compound where the four of us can live."

"No. We're going to need penises. There's no way I'm living with you people without having someone to bang. You three will drive me so far up the wall that I'll need the release. Daily."

"You're ridiculous."

"You're damn near celibate."

Here we go again. "Shut your face." She whips out of my driveway so fast that I almost smack my head on the window. "Nic!" I yell as she takes another turn way too fast in this damn death trap. "Jesus! Slow down!"

"Stop being dramatic. I'm with you, and you have a badge. No one is going to ticket me."

"I don't care if you get pulled over." I right myself and grab the edge of the seat. "I care about dying."

"You're going to die from lack of sex if anything." She rolls her eyes and cues the '90s station. "Listen to Four Blocks Down, and get ready to watch the boys shake their delectable asses on stage. After that, you can remove the stick up your ass, maybe then you won't be so miserable."

"I'm not miserable." I slap her arm.

"Okay." She shrugs and ignores me, which is her typical way of blowing me off.

Am I miserable? No. I'm happy . . . for the most part.

I have a great job that keeps me fulfilled. Being a female police officer isn't easy, but I love it.

The only real downside to my job is that I come face to face with my ex-husband every day. Luckily, things didn't end *that* badly. But I'd be full of crap if I didn't admit how much it bothers me. Things with Matt are—weird. Sometimes people just don't work or you realize the person you married isn't what you thought. I wish I could transfer to another town, but my sister Stephanie and the twelve years invested in my pension keep me here.

Nicole belts out another round of lyrics. "Sing it with me, Heather!"

I don't want to, but I'm taken back in time when the four of us had bangs that were so high they could cause whiplash, wore colors that no one should ever wear, and drooled over Four Blocks Down without a smidgen of shame.

Smashed in the tiny death trap posing as a vehicle, I let go a little.

We both sing along, belting out the lyrics of our first crushes. "I wish I still had my Eli pillow case," I grin.

"I had a Randy towel. I would like to wrap myself up with him again." Nicole sighs.

I swear this girl needs sex more than anyone I know. "Does your vibrator ever get a break?"

She looks over at me with her usual you're-an-idiot face. "You're going to realize very soon, my love, if you don't use it . . . you lose it."

"And you're going to overuse it," I say. She's the only one of us who never married. Nicole lives in downtown Tampa. She has to schlep it all the way out to Carrollwood to pick me up, but she knows if she didn't, I wouldn't go.

Sometimes, I envy her life. She has everything she dreamed of. Opening Dupree Designs and then landing her contract with one of the wealthiest developers in the city was pure luck. She slept with him, got a few more jobs, and before she knew it—she was on top.

Then she dumped him.

We park the car at the arena, and Nicole shifts in her seat. "Listen, I know you're hell bent on being the responsible one of us, but tonight," she grabs my hands, "I beg you to let loose. You *need* a break."

I glare at her. "I do let loose."

"Your hair is in a bun," she raises her brow. "You're the

definition of tight."

I touch my hair, hating that she has a point. But this is me. I like to make good choices. Other than marrying Matt, which wasn't *bad* per se . . . just hasty. Never mind that he was an asshole. And he sucked in bed.

Okay, so maybe it was a bad choice.

Moving on. "I'm not uptight, Nic."

"I didn't say uptight. But let your hair down. It'll make Danni jealous since she can't get her hair your color blonde no matter how much money she spends. Maybe one day she'll get over herself and stop trying." Nicole and Danielle have a love/hate relationship. This week it seems to be more on the hate side. I wish they'd get over this already and talk it out, but they both claim there's no issues.

From what I can gather, Nicole slept with Danielle's ex three days before she got married. I don't know if it's true or not, but I wouldn't be surprised since it is Nic we're talking about. When I heard the back story, I distanced myself from the entire thing. No way was I getting in the middle of it, but Nicole typically has something snippy to say about her and vice versa.

Feuds aside, Nicole is right. I don't ever go out. If I'm not being a couch potato, I'm with my sister.

I pull my hair out of the bun, allowing my blonde locks to fall around me. Thanks to the twist, it almost has curls. Nicole grabs her bag from the backseat and tosses her makeup pouch onto my lap. "Put some of that on. You know, look hot. Not like a frumpy divorcée."

"I often question why I didn't drop you after high school." I grab some eyeliner and darken my brown eyes. I add a little blush and lip gloss. "Better?"

"Much."

We head into the concert, and I can't stop giggling to myself. Everyone is around our age—all here to see a freaking boy band. The group we all lusted over as teens is now fully grown, but here we are, ready to swoon and scream their songs.

I can't remember how many dreams I had about Eli Walsh or how many notebooks I filled with Mrs. Heather Walsh signatures.

I'm sure I'm not alone, either. There are probably a few hundred middle-aged women here tonight who had done the same thing.

Some more scantily clad than others.

"What the hell is she wearing?"

Nicole glances over and makes a disgusted face. "Dear, Lord. Someone needs to tell her that a muffin top and a mini skirt don't mix."

I snort.

"I feel like this is our version of a high school reunion," I cogitate while scanning the crowd for Danni and Kristin. I know we're not spring chickens, but when did we get as old as some of the people standing in line? Sheesh.

"Heather!" Kristin waves as they rush toward us.

Even though we see each other at least every three months, I miss them. We made a promise when we graduated high school we'd have a quarterly date, and so far, we've all made a point of sticking to it. It helps that we all stayed in the greater Tampa area, but I think no matter the distance, we'd always be there for each other.

Some friendships are unbreakable—even if someone sleeps with someone else's ex.

"I've missed you," I say as she wraps her arms around me.

She plants a kiss on my cheek. "I missed you more."

We all stand here, hugging it out. We're dorks, but I couldn't care less. Other than my sister, they're the only family I have.

"How's Steph feeling?" Danielle asks.

"She's doing good, I think. I'm waiting for her to call me." It's so sweet how Danielle always asks about Stephanie.

"I'm glad she's doing okay." She smiles.

"Yeah, she should've called though. I should probably give her a call . . ."

Danni grabs my hand, stopping me from going for my phone. "I'm sure her nurse would let you know if there were something wrong."

She's right, but the worrier in me can't help myself. I've spent what feels like my entire life making decisions around Stephanie. I

366

don't take any chances when it comes to her.

"I'm just going to check," I explain as I grab my phone from my bra.

Danielle laughs. "I should've known better than to try to stop you."

There are no missed calls or texts.

Breathe. I'm sure she's fine, don't overreact.

I send a quick text because I'll never let it go.

Me: Hey, you okay? I haven't heard from you today.

She answers right back.

Stephanie: Yes, Mother.

Brat.

Me: Have you had any more tremors?

My sister suffers from Huntington's disease. She was diagnosed at nineteen, and it took her independence before she even had time to enjoy it. I tried to care for her. I did everything I could to keep her with me, but when she started suffering from relapsing paralysis and struggling to speak, we knew it was beyond my capability.

Watching your twenty-six-year-old sister battle with early onset dementia is devastating. The last few weeks have been good, though. She's been cognitive, alert, and even happy. Her symptoms are sometimes so mild that I forget how sick she is, but then the disease rears its ugly face again and there's no forgetting.

Stephanie: Nope. And aren't you out with the girls? Go have some fun, Heather. Tell them I said hi!

"Is Steph okay?" Nicole asks when she sees me typing away.

"She's fine. I mean, you know . . ." My mood drops immediately as I think about how she'll never experience this.

Danielle touches my arm, and I force myself to smile. "She says hi."

"Give her our love," Kristin replies. I type out their message and tell her I love her before tucking my phone away again.

"Okay!" Nicole exclaims. "Let's go see these amazing seats that our super-fan Kristin scored us."

Kristin gives Nic the stink eye, which would be way more effective if she weren't in their fan club. Yup, my thirty-eight-year-old best friend is in a fan club for Four Blocks Down. I'm positive she regretted telling us this piece of information, but it landed us front row seats, so we haven't been too hard on her . . . yet.

"You can sit in the nose bleeds if you want."

Nicole wraps her arm around her shoulder. "You love me too much to deprive me of Randy." She lets out a dreamy sigh.

I laugh. "As if you're ever going to get that close to him. And he's married!"

I try to put Stephanie in the back of my mind. My sister's illness is ripping me apart. I wish I could help her, but I can't control any of it. It makes me feel helpless all the time.

Stephanie grew up listening to me blare the music and dance around like a loon, and instead, she's stuck in a damn assisted living facility while I'm out. It isn't fair. None of this is fair. She should be here with me.

"Hey," Danni nudges me. "You look beautiful."

I give her a small smile. "Thanks." I'm no longer feeling carefree. I can't stop thinking about how much I wish I could be doing this with her.

"I'm sorry." Her smile falls slightly.

"For what?"

She shrugs. "I made reality come crashing into our big fun night of no worries."

"Stop! Don't feel that way." I wrap my arm around her shoulder. "My reality never leaves me. My sister is dying. It's just the way it is."

Danielle's smile falls completely now. "I'm so, so sorry, Heather."

I know she didn't mean to bring me down. I wish I could be

more like Nicole. No responsibilities, sex with random strangers, nothing to worry about . . . but that isn't how my life goes.

Nope. Mine is a series of tragedies. While my friends were partying in college, I was working full time. My nights and weekends weren't filled with formals or trips to the beach, they were consumed by doing homework with Steph. I'm not bitter. I'm actually grateful in some ways. It forced me to cherish life and the people in it. Every day I have with Stephanie is a gift.

I shake my head. "You have nothing to apologize for. Let's act like idiots and pretend there are no problems in the world."

"You want to party like it's 1999?"

"Yeah, just like that. If only we had our Four Blocks Down dolls."

"They are collectable memorabilia," Kristin corrects before blushing scarlet and mumbling about needing to go find our seats. Nicole, Danielle, and I laugh hysterically as we follow her inside.

I wave to two of the guys in my squad, who are apparently working overtime detail as security as we pass them. Shit. I didn't even think anyone from my squad would be here. Usually, it's the other district that handles the MidFlorida Amphitheater. They look thrilled to be here—not. I make a note to behave so my entire department doesn't find out that I came to see my favorite boy band. However, knowing them, they've already texted everyone. I swear, cops are worse than teenage girls with their gossip.

I'll never live this down.

Music plays from the two opening acts. I sing along because . . . their songs were my jams when I was a teen. I would blare their screw men anthems through my speakers, windows down, singing off key, and belting every note because they were my idols. I owe many of my breakups to them telling me that I didn't need to take it.

"Ah!" Danielle squeals after the second band finishes. "FBD is next! I had the biggest crush on—"

"Shaun," Nicole cuts her off. "We remember you licking his poster."

"Oh my God!" I giggle. "I remember that. She straight made out with it." I guzzle the rest of my beer and shake my hair around.

"I wanted him to be my first kiss," Danielle explains.

We all did. Hell, I may have had multiple fantasies with Eli, but I wouldn't have kicked any of them out of my bed. They were everything when we were younger. I think somewhere in my mind we're all frozen in time.

"Want another beer?" Kristin yells.

I've had three already. I'm halfway to drunk. I shake my head no.

"Yes, she does," Nicole answers for me. I look at her with my mouth open. "I'm driving. You're having fun." She turns back to Kristin. "She'll be drinking all night."

"Oh," Danni laughs, "this is going to be epic."

"Shut up, I'm a good drunk."

In my mind.

"You're good for a laugh," Danni tacks on.

The lights go out, and the mood shifts. All of us start to scream and hold hands. This is Eli and Randy's hometown, so it's extra special. Their homecoming concerts are always louder and longer.

"Are you ready, Tampa?" PJ's voice booms.

We all yell louder.

"We said," Shaun's voice comes through this time, "are you ready?"

I bounce with Nicole, unable to control myself. I allow the energy of the room to fill me. I'm probably the loudest of the four of us. I don't give a shit, either. "Hell yeah!"

Kristin looks at me with a huge grin. So unlike me.

"That's it, Tampa!" Randy's face flashes on the screen on the side of the stage. "The Walsh brothers are home. And we want to hear you!"

Eli's face. I sigh. "Did you miss us?"

"Fuck yeah I did," I scream.

"Good." The screen displays both Eli and Randy. "We missed you, too. And you're about to see a whole lot of us. FBD is back, and we're ready to blow your minds."

The arena goes black.

And slowly, I see something rise out of the stage.

I stand mesmerized.

The light shines in my eyes, blinding me, but when I can see again, I would swear that Eli Walsh is staring right at me.

Emerald-green eyes pierce through me. His dark brown hair is cut short on the sides and the top falls errantly around his forehead. I take in every ounce of his perfect body. The way his arms pull against the fabric of his shirt, the pants that hug his perfect ass, and the span of his broad shoulders, makes me want to climb him like a tree. Then, with our gaze connected, he winks and throws a wicked grin my way.

Holy shit.

I stand there and gaze back at him like a fish with my eyes wide and mouth open. He looks away, but it happened. Eli Walsh smiled and winked at me. I just died.

Learn More: http://corinnemichaels.com/we-own-tonight/

About Lexi Blake

Lexi Blake lives in North Texas with her husband, three kids, and the laziest rescue dog in the world. She began writing at a young age, concentrating on plays and journalism. It wasn't until she started writing romance that she found success. She likes to find humor in the strangest places. Lexi believes in happy endings no matter how odd the couple, threesome or foursome may seem. She also writes contemporary Western ménage as Sophie Oak.

Connect with Lexi online:

Facebook: Lexi Blake
Twitter: authorlexiblake
Website: www.LexiBlake.net

Sign up for Lexi's free newsletter at www.LexiBlake.net.